# Riptide

*Drifters, Book Four*

SUSAN RODGERS

First Edition—December 2014



Cover design by Alanna Munro. All rights reserved.
Edited by Kathy Gillis and Stephen Reaman.
Book design and formatting by Valerie Bellamy, Dog-ear Book Design.

ISBN: 978-0-9869502-8-5

For all of you
who also
now believe
in hope.

# Contents

A riptide is a strong current, especially flowing outwards from the shore, which presents a hazard to swimmers and boaters. Also known as a rip current.

# Prologue

"Trudy, I need a favor."

*Huh.*

Frank wasn't the kind of guy to beat around the bush. He always liked to get right to the point.

Trudy dropped into a comfortable old wooden Windsor schoolteacher's chair inherited from her father. She leaned back against the sturdy wood and settled two black high-heeled shoes on a boxy antique maple desk. Popping a pink peppermint into her mouth, she prepared herself. Last time she heard from Frank was after their break-up when he called to ask her to ship his drum mics out to Vancouver, along with a pair of leather hiking boots he had left behind at their Charlottetown, Prince Edward Island home. Trudy wasn't much in the mood to do him any niceties. She stiffened as her defenses ballooned to high alert.

"Speak," she said drily, ready to punch the *end* button on her iPhone at any moment.

"Put it this way," came the serious voice from the other side of the country. "Should you choose to help out, your life will suddenly become very interesting."

Rubbing a temple to help keep her temper in check, Trudy hesitated. Was her ex insinuating that her life wasn't interesting? If nothing else, she was at least curious. Hearing from Frank out of the blue like this, on a Monday afternoon in midsummer, was a complete surprise. The drum mics were shipped out last fall. The spring prior, he had vacated their modern split-level home. Trudy had long since deleted his friendship from her life. All it took was a sturdy pounce of the mouse on her Facebook page. So what if her finger paused for about twenty seconds before she actually clicked?

Now, she employed a tactic she often used with her more belligerent or traumatized patients, the ones who were in such pain they couldn't find the words to express themselves. She sat silent and waited for Frank to fill in the blanks. It didn't take long.

True to his nature, Frank got right to the point. "Trudy, I've been asked by some friends to recommend a therapist in Prince Edward Island. There's a high profile young couple heading your way for the remainder of the summer and into the fall who need some PTSD counseling. They plan to keep their visit to the island on the down low but they need some guidance and direction to help them find tools to navigate their way through anxiety and triggers. Are you in?"

"Whoa Frank, slow down. First of all, you know I'm not seeing a lot of patients anymore." Trudy was working on a book, in fact. She was a good therapist, but after twenty-five years of counseling some of the Canadian east coast province's more extreme cases of anorexia, bulimia, trauma survivors and cutters, she needed some time to heal herself. Some distance. Especially after...well, especially after her nasty divorce from Frank. The sudden breakup had thrown her for a loop, coming out of left field the way it did. "Second, what do you mean by high profile? I'm not sure I want to give up my all too brief P.E.I. summer to a couple of bickering celebrities with huge egos."

"Trudy," he sighed in that exasperated way of his, as if she were a child and he the all-knowing parent. "They're not bickering, just troubled. They've had a rough few years. In fact, I don't think I've ever seen a couple more in love. It's inspiring. But—they're hurting. Some quiet time on P.E.I. will do tremendous good on its own, but they need a little guidance to help them navigate the roadblocks, to develop a plan to manage the hard memories. You'll love them."

"Humph. Why me?"

"Because I trust you, Trudy. Because my friends trust me to find the right person, someone honest and truthful and caring and compassionate, who has a success record with deeply troubled individuals. Most importantly, someone who is discreet, who won't be cowed by fame."

Intrigued, Trudy pondered Frank's offer as she tossed the peppermint around on her tongue. It might be nice to have a little diversion from the research and writing of her book about patients who cut themselves in order to find a pain they can feel instead of a haunting psychological torment. Might be nice to see actual people occasionally during the week instead of just her dozy tabby cat, Oliver. Might be nice to break up the day with more than just a daily run or a trip to the local coffee shop.

"So who is this young couple, Frank?" Trudy crunched purposefully in his ear as she chomped the last bit of the sugary peppermint. If her ex was annoyed, he managed to refrain from commenting on it, or chiding her, as she half-expected.

"Are you sitting down?"

"Uh…yes?" Sheesh. This was Canada. He was talking about people from Vancouver. How famous could you get? Maybe the potential clients were a hockey player and his wife? A Vancouver Canuck?

"Remember the exclusive Shawna Coupland interview that aired last week? The one everybody was talking about on Facebook, that was all over the news? Second highest forwarded tweet ever, following Ellen Degeneres' group selfie from the Oscars? The American newscasts were all over it."

Sarcasm edged Trudy's voice. "Yes, I'm so into pop culture, Frank. There was no television in the house for you to steal last year, remember?"

He cringed at the bitterness still edging his ex-wife's voice. But Frank didn't need to be reminded of Trudy's lack of interest in pop culture or celebrity. He was well aware. That was one reason why, out of all the contemporaries he left behind in Charlottetown, the small province's capital of 35000 people, he knew instantly that Trudy was the best choice to help this young couple. She didn't give a hoot about television or pop music. She rarely went to the movies, in fact mostly all she seemed interested in were her plants and flowers and, of course, tawny-striped Oliver who kept her company during the day while he dreamt the hours away on a wicker chair. Trudy's office alone was a veritable jungle hideout. The woman was pretty much a recluse. Frank wasn't. He believed in living his life to the fullest, in sucking the marrow out of life.

Lack of interest in pop culture aside, he knew that Trudy did listen to the radio on occasion. She usually tuned into CBC, the Canadian public broadcaster, for the occasional insight into local, national and world news.

As she rearranged her feet on the desk, startling Oliver out of his mousey visions, Trudy scrunched her eyebrows together and pondered who her new clients might be. She recalled some rumblings on the news one day about a couple of actors involved in a stabbing incident…something related to a stalking. Awareness crept up on her slowly, and then the proverbial light bulb switched on. Frank was talking about that woman, the singer and film star—she had a Prince Edward Island connection. What was her name?

Frank provided further illumination. "Trudy, you've got to promise absolute discretion. My friend, the one who is pals with the big film and record producer here, Charles Keating, asked me to find someone this couple can trust implicitly. But I'm warning you, this is not going to be an easy gig. This girl has been hurting for a very long time, in silence, as many do. She's not only finally admitted most of her troubles to her friends, but she's also gone public to the world. Which one would think is a good sign but, as you and I both know, recovering from child sexual abuse and then serious tragedy has left her deeply scarred. She is a gem to the world. Her music heals and comforts millions. She deserves a chance at a productive safe life."

"It's that singer, Jessie something or other."

Frank paused. "Yes. And her fiancé, Josh Sawyer. He's an actor in that popular Canadian western, *Drifters*. So was she, for the first few seasons. That's where they met."

"I thought they met in a cluster of garbage bins."

Surprising her, Frank laughed. "Why Trudy, you scoundrel. Have you been reading *People* magazine? Is it stuffed under your mattress with your life savings?"

Bristling, Trudy ignored the barb and responded sharply, "There was a write-up in the paper about them. They just got together again after a long absence or something."

A heavy sigh on the other end made Trudy regret the bitter edge that suffused her voice. She almost caved and pretended she cared a hoot for Frank's feelings when the sincerity of his words reminded her that he was indeed a man who cared honestly for others. Most of the time.

"Yes. Like I said Trudy, this is not bound to be a piece of cake for you."

"In other words," she said quietly, "be cautious." She filled in his thoughts for him. Echoing his lower voice, imitating him, she teased, "You're bound to start to care about these people. Maybe get a little too wrapped up in their lives."

She knew she did that. She got too caught up in her patients' lives time and again, to her detriment. Hence, time off to write the book. Hence…the excruciating divorce. Hence, life alone with living things that can't hurt you, like calming plants and a bossy cat.

"You're the best bet to help these people, Trudes. They need you."

After all this time, Frank still had the capacity to stir her heart into motion. That gentle way he had of saying the old nickname, like warm honey sliding across his lips…she closed her eyes, eased her feet off the desk, and leaned into her palm, her elbow resting on the old teacher's desk that reminded Trudy of her father.

"What if I can't, Frank? What if I can't help them? Will the world blame me for it?" She was only half-joking.

"No, Trudy," he said definitively as if this was something he had considered long and hard on the lengthy commute to his shiny new downtown Vancouver clinic that morning. "No one will blame you. But the world will be a darker place without this girl's music. Without her films. That I can guarantee."

Trudy softened. Frank was a man who appreciated music on a level she would never understand. Trudy was a scientist, someone who liked to solve problems and puzzles. She was mathematical, objective, smart. Frank, like her, was a man who lived to solve people problems, as he called his work, but, unlike her, he was a dreamer who lived a full life. He played drums for a number of bands, in different styles—rock, jazz, blues, even country on occasion. He was a man who *felt* life on a different level than many. He appreciated art, visually, on canvas and in film, in lyrics and melody. He was a Jessie Wheeler fan. He wanted the girl to survive, and thrive, so that her music would continue to float in and around his soul, buoying it, lifting it.

"Okay," Trudy said flatly, opening her eyes and fingering a decades old crack in the aged varnish of the desk between her neatly stacked metal meshed *in* and *out* baskets. She traced the length of the crack—nearly six inches. How far and how deep would this singer's wounds go? Well. There was only one way to find out.

"Frank?" she asked. "How soon until they arrive?"

Ten feet away, Oliver stood on the wicker chair's pink floral cushion and stretched first one paw and then the other, yawning at the same time, eyeing Trudy as if he sensed that his seat would soon be taken over by a human with all too real hurts. His paws landed with a gentle thud on a sunny spot on the wide pine floor before he looked up at his roommate expectantly. As Trudy frowned and hit the *end* button on her cell, then settled backwards into the chair once more as she pondered this strange twist to the rest of her sanguine summer plans, she told herself that she was glad her twelve pound cat was her only responsibility. She was glad that Frank was living across the country in some high-rise condo eating take-out sushi rolls and succulent Pad Thai instead of also staring at her with expectations of a five o'clock supper. As organized and detailed as Trudy generally was, tonight, almost in defiance of Frank, she would settle for light fare, just marmalade toast and tea.

She flipped open her laptop and hauled her middle-aged body up to a standing position while she waited for the computer to warm up. Oliver needed to be fed before she immersed herself in research. Jessie Wheeler and her beau Josh Sawyer would be in her office in a few days. Trudy had work to do. The laptop would burn the midnight oil tonight. Frank had promised to email links to news articles and even some of Jessie's videos on YouTube. The link that would captivate Trudy the most—which enthralled the world before her—was the candid interview with Shawna Coupland. The tale it told was harrowing, honest, real. Shocking. Surprising.

At three a.m. Trudy finally yielded to a succession of yawns, pulled a pink cotton nightgown over her head and collapsed onto the right side of her lonely queen-sized bed. She grabbed Frank's old pillow and held it to her chest, as she always did in order to encourage a restful slumber, but in her dreams a silhouetted man in gray holding a dagger above his head haunted her. The accompanying sounds were the cries of a young girl whose father was ruthlessly torn away from her on her twelfth birthday.

Waking wearily at five, the sun streaming heartlessly into the space between the bottom of the blind and the window ledge, summer songbirds chirping brightly in the maple tree outside, Trudy gave up the battle, rose, and dropped an English Breakfast tea pod into the Keurig. Leaning against the granite countertop as the brew master did its thing, she wrapped the tie on her terry cloth robe tighter around her waist.

Trudy's famous clients had yet to arrive, and already they had her on the run.

# Chapter One

Jessie focused on the window and relaxed her eyes until her vision blurred as if she were wearing a pair of old foggy contact lenses. The raindrops slipping and sliding their watery trails down the pane were more enticing than the stilted dialogue happening around her. Just before the sun ducked behind a slate cloud, it left its mark on the window. Miniature rainbows were visible in the droplets, reminding the singer of her father, impressing his presence into the small room and imbuing him within her struggling spirit. The brief rainshower seemed appropriate that day. Inside, the small office was filled to capacity with greenery—plants and flowers that Jessie's limited gardening knowledge could not begin to identify, although she recognized various ferns and was buoyed by colorful blooms of yellow and peach and rose and white. She was in a jungle, ensconced by a verdant life force. Only the wooden birdhouses with their distressed paint jobs, as well as trickling water fountains and haphazardly placed round ceramic stones—imprinted with inane imprinted words like *hope* and *faith*—pointed out that the jungle was far away and this environment was an imposter. Like Jessie. She was someone who was trying to find her place in a world that had stolen too much joy.

The softly trembling rain and the hopeful, teeny rays of the sun were beyond the window, trying to get in. Absently she wondered how all this lush greenery could possibly survive with the rain and sun on the outside.

"Jessie?"

Against her better judgment, Jessie pondered turning back to the fifty-something woman seated comfortably in the wicker chair across from her.

Trudy was watching Jessie from behind small indigo-framed reading glasses perched atop her perky turned up nose. Her lips were painted on, a deep burgundy gloss highlighting her diminutive smile. Gray streaks ran from the bangs of her black hair through the ponytail clasp—some kind of Celtic knot style pewter barrette that kept her hair under control—and her cotton blouse with the green and pink flower print was just a little damp under the armpits.

*How apropos,* Jessie thought, forcing her gaze away from the prisms on the streaked window to meet the eyes of the woman with the bright yellow sunflower notebook on her lap.

"Sorry," she said wryly, sinking down into the relative safety of her own wicker chair. Next to her, she could hear Josh settling further into his as well. A small grunt from his corner of the overbearing jungle instantly communicated his opinion of Jessie's cavalier attitude towards their meeting. She avoided his eyes altogether and, instead, forced herself to focus on Trudy's kind eyes. Jessie was sorry that they were green with a hint of gold reflected from the floor lamp. She hadn't expected her and Josh's therapist's eyes to be the same color as Deuce McCall's. Jessie wondered why that hadn't been considered when Charles and Dee's friend from Vancouver had found and recommended this obviously compassionate, sensitive woman to start her and Josh on a path of *detoxing* and *healing* from a shared past of terror and pain and lies and loss. How was she supposed to even start walking down this road again, reliving Sandy's death and Josh's survival and forced sex and confinement, and on top of that desperately missing Jacob and his music, when the woman who was hired to help them was pondering her with eyes that mirrored those of her aggressor?

*She's kind,* Jessie whispered inwardly, trying to convince herself. *Her eyes are lit from within. Deuce's were dark, sinister—most of the time.* It was a mantra she felt she had to use to get through this first meeting. She tucked one knee carefully over the other, crossed her hands in her lap, and tried to present herself as a lady. Frowning, she waited for Trudy to speak again.

"Jessie, Josh was asking whether you want to go first."

Clearing her throat with a small rumble, Jessie shifted again. *Go first*? Oh, yeah, the initial intake interview Trudy mentioned when they first wandered into the wilderness office twenty minutes ago. They would have to meet separately before officially starting therapy so the counselor could see exactly where they were at in their healing game. With a sense of impending dread, Jessie nodded and mumbled, "Sure. Okay."

Trudy closed her notebook and smiled at Jessie. Clearly, there was fear in the girl's eyes, but it didn't frighten Trudy away. She had researched in depth the horrific story that brought these two actors to her Charlottetown office this day. Everyone seemed to know their story, it seemed. Jessie went public with it a few weeks ago, in the tumultuous heat of the summer. Questioned sympathetically on camera by the famous no-nonsense celebrity interviewer Shawna Coupland in New York City, Jessie told the world what happened to her as a teen runaway in Charleston—the tragic killing of her young boyfriend Sandy and the death of their friend Rachel, and the ensuing madness when her stalker and tormenter reappeared in her life just after she got engaged to the man she loved, actor Josh Sawyer. It was a story that could have been written by Hollywood's best screenwriter, yet sadly it was true, almost resulting in Josh's own demise. As it stood today, Jessie's fiancé carried a long scar that wrapped around his side from his back to his stomach, a potent reminder of a shared torment. He also had to live without a spleen as a result of the stabbing, which was possible, but came with its own set of reminders and rules and agonies. Yes, they suffered greatly over a past that threatened their future, but the couple was here in Trudy's office, in lush Prince Edward Island, a gorgeous engagement ring on Jessie's finger and a promise to set work commitments aside. They needed to focus on survival now, by facing Jessie's sexual abuse as a child and adult, by facing a trauma that almost killed Josh, by facing the myriad hurts and lies woven in between like a sticky spider's web, where they stared at each other afraid to speak the truth for fear that the enemy would win.

Standing, Trudy reached out a hand and shook Josh's as he faced her. She sensed that he was embarrassed and apologetic about Jessie's behavior. But, regardless of the fact that Jessie was an International star—as was he, now, albeit only in the acting world, whereas Jessie had also cemented a reputation as one of the world's most beloved singer songwriters—Trudy had seen the signs and heard the symptoms before, all too many times, in fact. Sadly, one in three girls were affected in some way by child sexual abuse. Many went down the road of fear and silence and then on a regime of anti-depressants that messed their heads and bodies up even more. Jessie had travelled a similar dark path, substituting the anti-depressants for excessive consumption of Jim Beam and smoking of weed. Add to her experience of child molestation by a stepfather and then the ever-present fear of a stalker, her fame and the loss of her teen boyfriend, and Trudy was surprised that Jessie hadn't sunk even further into self-medicating, with harder drugs, perhaps, or sexual promiscuity. What she had yet to understand was that Jessie had a safer drug—music—that healed a lot of ills or, at the very least, kept them at bay.

Still two steps behind, it took Jessie a few moments to collect her thoughts before she rose and accepted Trudy's hand. With sweaty nervous palms she smoothed her mid-thigh length sundress with the large orange print—a flower of some type she didn't recognize, imprinted on a white background—and then she stepped forward with one dusty brown boot and leaned into Trudy's space.

"Thank you," she said quietly, meeting the woman's eyes only for a flicker of a second. Counseling. She had to do it. She promised Charles and Dee she would spend the remainder of her summer as a dragon-slayer, fighting the winged beasts with the infernal blistering fire-breath that still woke her in the dead of night, and the triggers that set her off at unexpected moments, spiraling her back to Deuce's grasp and the horrid thwunk of the dagger. The dagger—seven times now, it taunted her in sleep. Six times the shuddering thrusts plunged heartlessly, unrepentant, into Sandy's chest and belly, and then one more asserted itself in Josh's side, tearing his spleen apart and disintegrating parts of Jessie's mind along with it. Yes, she was in need of counseling, especially if she had any hope of building a future with Josh, her rock, the man she loved, the man who stood shyly beside her now in this weird damp jungle, shifting his weight uncomfortably from side to side, the cuffs of his blue vintage long sleeved shirt falling loosely over his knuckles despite the fact that Jessie had tenderly folded them back for him earlier in the day. He looked at her now, silently asking what they should do next, his thumbs now tucked into the pockets of his faded jeans, his brown eyes questioning, the sorrow and fear of the last few years still visible in their depths.

Jessie grasped his hand then, pulling it gently out of the pocket where it was partially hidden from view underneath the loose tail of the cotton shirt, and her own soft baby blues urged him to follow where she led.

"Thanks again, Trudy," Josh mumbled as he and Jessie left the office together.

Trudy followed them to the door with one last hopeful piece of wisdom.

"I can't make any promises to the two of you. This is work you have to do yourselves, and it's a long road, this healing thing. What happened to you both is a part of your history now. It's who you are, a fabric of your being. But what I can do is help you manage. Find the tools to help you move on."

Finally, Jessie turned back to her and met the counselor's eyes. They weren't quite as green here in the hallway, underneath a different light source, one that was a little more on the yellow side of the color temperature scale. She let her shoulders relax a little with undisguised relief, and she sighed. Still, she didn't smile.

Trudy added fervently, "Jessie. You can do this, honey. But you have to help us—Josh and I—help you. This isn't a one-sided thing. I won't lie to you. It's going to suck. But it's time. You deserve the chance to live the way you want to."

At that, Jessie finally let her guard down and the corners of her lips turned up, just a little. Trudy—and Josh, who knew Jessie better than anyone—took it. It was a tiny nugget, but it was something.

"Ah," Jessie said. "A little farm, maybe? With chickens?" She peeked up at Josh, then, the first time she met his eyes since their arrival at Trudy's office, which was accessed through a side door in the therapist's generous suburban home.

Josh wasn't up to smiling back just yet, after the hard objectives Trudy laid out for them. The woman didn't believe in candy-coating the situation, that was certain. Instead she had laid out the stats. For instance, how many relationships survived counseling for survivors of severe trauma. Not many. Yeesh. Josh and Jessie hadn't even started therapy, and the odds were already stacked against them. Humbling. Hell, they had barely even started their relationship again. Only last month had they decided to try again. Now they were hiding in Prince Edward Island for the last dwindling weeks of summer. Nestled into one of the pretty pastoral landscape's famous old farmhouses, a cedar-shingled Lucy Maud Montgomery Victorian on the north side of the island where Jessie stayed a few summers prior, they were rocked to sleep by incessant waves tumbling against a sandy shore, encouraged by the timeless message of endlessness and infinity, and the soothing rhythms of a pale and hopeful moon.

As Trudy's screen door nudged closed behind them, Josh and Jessie weren't aware of their new therapist's gaze on their backs. Instead, the hard facts of her message taunted them, like dozens of miniscule insects prickling the skin as they try to burrow inside. Both were initially quiet in their leased black Mercedes SUV. Josh laid a big hand comfortably over Jessie's on her lap as he steered the car around a few quiet corners and out of the pretty subdivision where people lived normal lives as teachers, lawyers, doctors, police and firemen. On the North River Road, heading back to Route Two and their quaint Victorian by the beach, he finally broke the silence. Above, the sun valiantly emerged as the raindrops ceased. A faint rainbow colored the sky with promise.

"Need anything else in town?" Josh glanced sideways at Jessie, who was pale and silent, her right elbow on the door rest, her nervous hand rifling through auburn curls. She didn't respond. There was no sign that she heard him. "Jessie?"

"Hmmm?" She turned to look at him and he could see the grief in her eyes. Fear, maybe.

"Jessie," he said, finally acknowledging to himself that just being together was not going to be enough to erase the past. "We can do this. We're survivors, you and me."

She leaned her head sideways against the window and watched him navigate the calm two-lane highway. Jessie studied every nuance of her man. One strong hand rested on the steering wheel, a black boot pushed the gas pedal, and that elusive lock of chestnut hair that refused to be tamed fell just over his ear and onto a chiseled cheekbone. She let her eyes drift to the sorrowful chocolate eyes that caught her heart in the first place, captivating her with their boundless access to Josh's soul.

Jessie eased her fingers away from their tremulous fidgeting and sandwiched his hand between hers. "Josh," she started. "What if I change my mind? What if I don't really want to do this? I mean...we've come this far. We're doing okay."

He exhaled slowly and then looked back over at her, imploring her not to give up. He raised his eyebrows quizzically. "Are we? Doing okay?"

She looked away, watching the neat farmhouses and bungalows glide by, their pretty flower gardens and perfectly manicured lawns sparkling in the sun after the summer rain. Some had swing sets and slides in their yards, and dogs barking playfully as they frolicked with tricycle riding children who were wearing colorful sunhats. Always, a parent was standing guard over their offspring as they picked vegetables for dinner or mowed their already tidy lawns.

Josh squeezed her hand. "Jess. You don't sleep. You barely eat. You think because you told the world what happened to you—to us—that it erases things? Makes it go away? You still have nightmares almost every night. You still hide inside yourself when you see something that triggers the memories, or when you smell something, even. It's time we learn how to deal with this, before..."

He stopped suddenly.

Jessie turned back to him, a sad child diminished in the seat next to him. "Before what, Josh? Before we have this wedding and make it harder to leave each other if things go bad?"

"Aw, Jess. No." He waved a hand towards a yard where a dad was driving a child around on a ride-on mower. "I was going to say before we have kids. That's all."

She watched him again, her eyes searching for truths. He was right. As much as they loved each other, clearly their lives together were still challenged. All was not roses in the Sawyer—Wheeler camp. How could it be? Jessie and Josh were war victims, of a sort, suffering post traumatic stress disorder on North American soil. They were still hurting, and there was much that was not yet unearthed about McCall, about what damage he did to Jessie physically.

Josh's imagination played dirty tricks on him in the depths of night while he held her after midnight anxiety attacks, both of them trembling as he tried to console her with soft murmurs of hope. If it was bad enough that she couldn't seem to calm, and words failed him, he quietly breathed the prayers they were rote taught as children.

"Hey," he said, detecting Jessie's escalating bitterness and dread. She was biting her bottom lip, staring at him as if he were about to disappear at any moment. She did that a lot, these days. It reminded Josh of that last month or so before she made the choice to extricate herself from his life a few years ago. He knew now that when he caught her watching him like that, she was trying to memorize his every feature—the way he moved, the way he spoke, the way he brushed that annoying piece of hair away from his eyes. It frightened him, Jessie studying him this way. "Jessie, I'm not going anywhere. And neither are you. We're in this together. We've earned each other. We paid our dues. I love you, girl." He raised his right hand and let the backs of his fingers brush her cheek. She grabbed his hand between both of hers again and held it firm against her skin.

"Okay," she whispered.

"Okay?" he echoed, glancing away from her to focus on their turn off Route Two onto the road that would take them to South Rustico, back to a safe place where she could continue to hide.

"Yeah," she said. "I'll try."

And, although Josh knew she would, he was still afraid. This was a beautiful place, Prince Edward Island, with its regal red sandstone cliffs and white sand beaches, and homey farmland fields of golden canola, soybeans and leafy green potato plants that stretched for miles and miles. But with this counseling there would be secrets unearthed between he and his girl that would rock what little foundation they seemed to have these days, and Josh wasn't really sure how well either of them could weather a storm that might bring them to their knees. All he knew for certain was that they may have survived the menace that had been Deuce McCall, but Jessie's stalker was far from dead. He was with them every moment of every day, mocking their dreams and haunting their lives, as real as he had ever been. He had stolen the beauty of innocent true love and all it contained. He robbed Josh and Jessie of irreplaceable time, and replaced it with fear. He stole moments they would never get back, and wrenched a purity from their love and togetherness that could never again be theirs. Their relationship would always bear the burden of Deuce McCall and what he had done—to her, to their friends and family, to them. To Jacob.

That was another thing. Josh knew, although it was clear he and Jessie loved each other deeply—had missed each other in a way that tormented them for much too long—that Jessie still missed Jacob, too. The musician was her island to float on during a time when Josh was not a part of her life, when she needed someone to hold on to in order to banish the demons that haunted her, to keep her sane. Jacob fulfilled that role well—he and Jessie were close. They had been lovers. And she missed him, her friend in music and its shared intimacies. He was back in Vancouver now, working on his second love—music—with Charles Keating. Jessie was taking a break from the entertainment biz, and Charles was filling that inimitable gap with Jacob Ryan. Jacob had saved Josh's life with two well-placed bullets. But there was no room in Jessie's life for both of her loves.

She chose Josh. But that didn't mean she didn't mourn the loss of Jacob.

Josh turned into their lane, which was essentially just two parallel narrow, rugged, dusty dried-up trails with tufts of green and squished old dry grass growing between them on a slightly higher patch of ground. He marveled at the red dirt *this* island seemed to float on, with its rare and beautiful copper oxide soil, and wondered at its hardy nature to grow potatoes and corn and broccoli and wheat, and families who seemed a little more relaxed and at peace than back in hustling Vancouver.

As they trundled down the lane, he felt his breathing slow and settle as, on one side, his eyes wandered over a potato field edged with plum tufts of sweet clover that tickled his nostrils. Vibrant golden-hued devil's paintbrush also nestled there, amongst stalks of pale green timothy, and bleached dried grass teased the car's occupants with its promise of more hot summer days ahead. Josh glanced over Jessie's head to the right. Low plants he thought might be soybeans, according to the old Newfoundlander at the country store earlier that day where they bought gas, were bordered by more wildflowers, the prettiest of which he thought were maybe perfect tiny forget-me-nots. There was some wild mustard in there, too. No ubiquitous Vancouver cherry blossoms, but P.E.I. in summer had its own cozy charms, gifts that nature blessed the lucky locals with each day.

As he halted the SUV in front of their temporary sanctuary, he flipped off the ignition and leaned back in the seat, playing a little with the keys as he turned his face towards Jessie, who he saw with a little burst of affection was smiling up at their quaint weathered house. She visibly relaxed when they were here in their island home, with its corny nautical beach themed lighthouses and seashells. Outside, wooden slatted lobster traps and sandstone rocks decorated the vibrant country flower garden.

Twisting around, trying in some small way to give him hope that she could barely allow herself to feel, Jessie appealed to her man's seemingly endless patience.

"Josh," she said, taking his hand in hers again, the keys jingling just a little, like a bell, Jessie thought, twinkly and true, another angel getting its wings. *Not Deuce,* she considered, wincing at the stark and sudden intrusion to her thoughts. He was always there, slithering around her mind, haunting her. She pushed the aberrant notion away but not before Josh saw it skid across her sun-kist cheeks. As his eyes narrowed, Jessie completed her original thought with an intensity in her blue eyes that Josh saw a lot these days, which frightened him.

"Babe," she finished intently, "I love you, too."

They stayed that way for a few moments and Josh felt tears prick his eyelids before he leaned forward and placed a hand behind Jessie's head and drew her towards him. He leaned his forehead against hers just for a second before he lowered his eyes and peered deeply into hers. Then he closed his eyes and kissed her softly, lingering, just being present in the moment with the woman he loved with all his heart, who he was planning a wedding with—with whom he wanted to have children.

Then his belly growled and his fiancée laughed, a sound that warmed Josh's heart immensely. *Small joys,* he thought. They all meant so much more now.

"C'mon girl," he said, chuckling. "Feed me or I become a bear." He opened the driver's side door and stepped out into the warm sunshine, noting that the rainbow that had formed across the way, west of them, towards Cavendish National Park where hordes of tourists flocked every summer to forget their troubles and bronze their bodies on the beach, had intensified. Its pinks and purples were darker now, more deeply saturated. He pointed it out to Jessie just before she stepped up the wooden risers to the front door of the century old home.

"See?" he said. "A rainbow. Everything is going to be okay, little one."

Josh placed his arm protectively around Jessie's waist and they waltzed slowly up the stairs and into the charming farmhouse. He didn't see a cloud pass over Jessie's face when she'd spotted the rainbow's darkest colored bow. She tried not to look for it, but there he was—McCall—even in the most beautiful of God's promises. She once wrote a song about the different loves in a rainbow. She had thought long and hard about every kind of love, including unreciprocated love, such as what McCall felt for her.

He was omniscient, he was everywhere, he was dead but he still tormented her. Would she ever get past what he had done, the moments he stole from her and Josh? She didn't know. But Jessie owed it to Josh, to Charles and Dee, to Stephen and Charlie and their other friends, to at least try. Hell, she owed it to herself to try.

She deserved happiness. She deserved this man she loved more than life itself.

It was time to make dinner, but she pulled Josh towards her and kissed him tenderly first. They detoured upstairs to the bedroom and suddenly the world seemed to right itself again. Jessie pushed all thought of McCall out of her mind and loved her man the best way she knew how. He held her tight and together they prayed that moments like these would now become a part of their every day, and that they would last forever.

# Chapter Two

Pepper steaks sizzling on the barbecue added a homey aroma to the beachfront homestead. The smells of summer worked their own healing magic. Tantalizing steaks on the grill cozied next to seared mushrooms, red peppers and onions marinated in soy, ginger and olive oil, speared with double bamboo shish kebab skewers to make them easier to turn, held their own restorative spell. Josh handled the grilling while Jessie tossed a spinach salad and dropped a cup of basmati in the rice cooker. They ate on the back deck, sitting in large Shaker rockers with their feet up on the rail, plates in one hand and forks in the other. It was a little tricky when it came time to slice the steaks, but they managed by resting the plates on their laps.

The sparkling ocean, its wavelets catching the evening sun so that it seemed diamonds were floating on the crests, relayed a greeting of hope, peace and contentment. When they had finished eating, they set the plates on the deck by Jessie's chair and she got up and lowered herself onto Josh's lap. Together they watched the sun go down in the west towards the tiny hamlets of North Rustico and Cavendish. The sky settled into sleep with its promise of pinks and oranges and even a little purple tonight, ribbons of color that drenched the beach, the sandstone cliffs, the sky; a breathtaking universal message from the Gods that life goes on despite the heartaches it can ruthlessly deliver. Little white birds—snipes, perhaps—strutted speedily to and fro, playing with the tide, teasing and daring it, their tiny feet running so fast their miniature bodies could have been mounted on wheels. When Jessie walked the beach earlier that day she thought she could see them smiling. Who wouldn't, frolicking in the waves in such a pristine, beautiful place?

Now, she snuggled closer into her man's chest and he wrapped his arms around her and buried his face in her hair. Jessie heard him sigh and felt his body relax. This was paradise. A dream. She could care less if she ever sang in public again, or made another film. She planned a future with this man—marriage, children, and maybe someday grandchildren. Praying the universe agreed with her, Jessie laid a hand on Josh's cheek and turned his face down to meet hers.

"Hey, you," she commanded drowsily, her words slurred with the need for sleep. "Can we stay here forever?"

The corner of one of Josh's lips turned up. Jessie recognized his teasing mode the instant his eyes lit up. "You might get hungry," he said. "Or what if you have to pee? You're not peeing on me. Just sayin'."

Swatting him lightly, Jessie laughed. "I mean on this island. Dork. Not just on the deck." She looked back out to the chilly Gulf of St. Lawrence, the semi-enclosed sea which, east, would carry a boat into the roiling Atlantic Ocean. A white lobster boat was churning its way through the peaceful salt-water oasis, its motor chugging through the low waves, the bow bouncing lightly up and down. Jessie could see a number of people on the open back deck, laughter embracing the distance between them and the tranquil couple watching as they reclined on their own nearby deck. *There's nothing like summer in P.E.I.* Jessie thought as, through her hazy mind, vague memories flitted around. Another fishing boat, another time; her dad's guitar and pleasing singsong voice serenading a long ago boatload of jovial friends, the sea-winds carrying his essence to distant shores far and wide.

Josh brushed his lips across her forehead. "Okay," he said contentedly. "Twist my arm." She cuddled in closer, slipping a hand underneath the sleeve of the blue T-shirt he'd thrown on after their post-lovemaking shower before dinner.

As far as Josh was concerned, this was heaven. So much lost time…now they were together, finally, alone with only one obligation—to do a little counseling to help prepare for the future. He whispered into her hair. "I love you, Jessie. So much. I need you. Please don't ever go away again."

A fluffy cotton ball forced its way into Jessie's throat. Her voice was low and raspy when she answered him. "You'll have to take me out on one of those fishing boats and push me overboard if you want to get rid of me, Sawyer. I'm not going anywhere. Ever again."

"Feed you to the sharks, you mean? Shark bait?"

"Dork. There are no sharks here." She wrinkled her brow. "I don't think. Maybe way off the coast."

"Good thing. You'd probably poison them." He fingered her hair. "All that hair product. Toxic. I'll never understand why women use so many chemicals in their hair." He was teasing her again. She could hear the smile in his whisper, feel his happy breath on her neck.

"Josh!" she protested, humbled. "My hair would be one big frizzball if I didn't put something in it, here or in Vancouver! The humidity is nasty. You wouldn't want anything to do with me."

"We'll just cut it. Make it short." He mimicked using scissors.

"Like heck," she retorted, but she felt a wave of anxiety pass over her then. Things were different with Josh now. They were starting anew after what seemed a lifetime of terror. There were things about herself that she was afraid to let him see…choices she had made, things Deuce had done or made her do…she felt like she had a B side now, like those old 33 rpm vinyl records, a less than perfect Jessie Wheeler hiding somewhere inside that most of the world now knew about. It changed how she felt about herself, leaking out all that toxin for public consumption. That and the plain truth that she and Josh now had a far less than perfect history—well, suddenly life was not so beautiful anymore. She knew Josh still harbored resentments. She knew he was curious about Deuce, and the southerner's hold over her. Yet these were things Jessie feared raising. Couldn't they just let them pass? Pretend the bad things hadn't happened? Let them slide into the abyss of lost dreams or under the proverbial rug? Addressing the bad things that had seeped into their lives like a growing bloodstain would only serve to add hurts on top of hurts. Salt in open wounds. Jessie shivered, wondering how they would endure facing the entire truth head on.

"Hey, little one," Josh whispered as he wrapped an arm tighter around Jessie's shoulders. "I think it's time to vacate the deck and light a fire. You're right about the east coast. The Gulf really cools off at night, eh?"

"I'm okay," she said. "Just a little while longer." Jessie turned her body around so that her back was against Josh's chest, and she pulled his arms around her belly. Feet up on the rail of the deck, she fingered his forearms and tried to relax. The fishing boat turned the corner towards safe port on its path down the channel between red buoys to mark starboard on the right, and green to mark port on the left. If it slipped outside its manmade narrow channel, it would likely ground itself on a shallow sandbar. The partying folks aboard might run out of beers before they could get a tow or wait for the wind and tide to set them free.

Jessie watched the boat disappear, wondering how long before—if ever—she would feel like she herself reached a perfectly safe harbor. Yet sitting here like this in Josh's arms, she felt close. There were still secrets that would have to be unearthed, though. Their own channel was narrow, precarious, and a strong wind could blow them outside the safe parameters that marked the path towards home. She felt she knew her man well, and she trusted him. But she wished she could just remain forever the Jessie he had known and loved back during *Drifters* season two, the private girl who kept the nasty stuff hidden away. She felt like showing him the real Jessie would frighten him away. She didn't have a good feeling about the counseling. Trudy seemed kind enough, and also firm enough to demand they co-operate. But regardless of the woman's track record helping damaged souls, she was only human.

Jessie resolved to skate through counseling on a thin layer, an outside one where any 'looking in' could be done on a peripheral level. *This* feeling was too good. She loved this man, and adding too much grease to the fire would only stir things up and threaten this all-too-tenuous thing called love. She was an actor. She would find a way to fool Trudy and just get by, participating enough to convince Dee that therapy helped her sort some shit out. The other bad stuff? She'd just lay it to rest.

She lifted Josh's fingers and kissed them softly as the consoling *rrrrrr* of the fishing boat faded and disappeared. In the west the tangerine-pink sun sank lower on the horizon and slipped beneath the restless waves, another perfect summer day gone to glory in the pastoral oasis of Prince Edward Island. It was breathtaking, and both Jessie and Josh were humbled at the universe and the things they didn't understand, like birth and death and nature and beauty and a pink and purple sky and miniature white birds trying to outrun tiny wavelets.

There were times in the past when circumstances tore them apart. Now, with his arms around her belly and hers caressing him overtop, it seemed life finally held them sacred in its fragile grasp. *Each* and *every* moment counted. Silently, they vowed to hang on to each other forever, come hell or high water. Life was too short to let the good things slip away, to take moments like this divine sun-kist evening for granted.

"Josh?" Jessie asked gently, afraid to disturb his own sweet and troubled thoughts.

He sighed again before he answered. He, too, understood the significance of perfection imbued with pain. "Yeah, kiddo?"

"What do you think about cutting back? On work, I mean. Not just this summer, but forever. I just want to be with you. We've lost so much time…"

"You'll get sick of me after a while." But he felt the same, although he'd had an offer for a film this summer that he, in some ways, regretted turning down. His career had just started to escalate, and it was a ride he wanted to take. Now to balance that with this woman here…well, somehow they would make it work.

"Never. I'll never get sick of you."

"We'll work it out," he said, his voice a little groggy from the intoxicating salty sea breeze cocktail mixed with the usual jet lag malaise.

"Are you mad about giving up the film?"

"Nah. There will be others. What's left of this summer is about you and me."

"Damn straight there will be others. You're a rocket, Josh Sawyer! Onwards and upwards. But…let's make sure we try to work our careers out so that we don't have to be apart much, okay? Moments like these are…well…" The cotton ball had returned and Jessie couldn't finish her sentence. The thing about perfection was that it had the power to remind you of its absence. And they had suffered many absences, these two.

Josh thought about the film he had asked his sister-in-law manager Hilary to turn down on his behalf. It really was a fantastic role, and he would be the hero this time, not the villain, as he had often been cast in the few years following *Drifters'* second season...the time when the world thought he had beat his girl and put her in the hospital. Now the better roles were coming in. And Josh wanted them. But—he wanted Jessie more.

"Don't you worry," he told her as he snuggled his lips in closer to her neck. "We're in this together, Jess. We'll be one of those couples that does everything together. We'll communicate and plan and let the bad stuff slide off. We'll get married, we'll start a family..."

She smiled. Maybe everything would be okay, once and for all. Hell, it was about time.

He went on, the last vestiges of pink sky hopeful reflections in his eyes, "We're in this together, you and me. When we're ninety we can sit here in this chair and recall all the good times while our grandkids and great grandkids do the dishes."

Dreaming. It was half the fun of being in a new relationship. Jessie relaxed further into him and resolved to let the bad times go. They were in the past. They were done, kaput. Trudy would let them chat and give her a few tools to help her with anxiety, and life would march on with zest and gusto. It would be ideal, as perfect as the sunset and the footprints left by the little white birds—sandpipers or snipes, she resolved to find out—that frolicked on the beach.

For the first part of that night as Jessie slept, the nightmares let her be. Rare happy dreams were one cure to keeping Deuce McCall at bay. When the sun streamed in at five a.m. and nudged Josh awake, he reveled at the robust pink blush in Jessie's cheeks, and he lay awake for a while, afraid to move for fear of waking her, because he knew as well as she the grace in their oneness, and that even the slightest bump could send them back down a dark road. But he was determined to win, this time. Josh was dead set on keeping Jessie by his side forever. He would do whatever it took to keep her happy, to help her get past the demons and triggers that haunted her almost daily.

Finally, his bladder protested and he had no choice but to slip away. He was only gone for a few moments, but when his movement jarred Jessie and she awoke to glide her hand over the sheets to reveal an emptiness, her eyelids fluttered open and she felt the familiar fear and alarm return.

Josh returned to find her eyes vacant and staring. She wasn't yet fully awake, and her panic was palpable. He slid into bed beside her and did as he always did, kissed her forehead and that sweet place at the corners of her eyes, and he whispered her name and held her close until her breathing was once again even and controlled. It saddened him, and he lay awake for a while thinking of Trudy and praying their new therapist could end this girl's terror once and for all. He let his hand drift through Jessie's hair and thanked God for letting him be the one to hold her. Josh never loved anyone more than Jessie, and he never would. That was a fact. They had already survived a terrible storm and now all that remained was to get through a little rain.

He closed his eyes, and had just fallen asleep again when Jessie's body shook and, in the depths of her sleep, Deuce once again slipped his dagger into Josh's side. Only Deuce's face turned to Jacob's, and Jacob stood over Josh's body with blood dripping from the dagger, his face grief-stricken with tears.

When Josh carefully prodded Jessie awake, she was genuinely relieved he was holding her, and that he was alive and well, but she was chagrined and embarrassed again that Jacob's tears were her own. How long would Josh put up with this? Forever? Not likely. Last night's perfection had slipped away with the sunset. The soft, hesitant new sunrise, the incessant waves turning over onto themselves outside their window, the beleaguered cry of the mourning doves and the answering call of the blue jays…all were present at the start of this new day, but they were just a smokescreen. No beauty could completely bury a past as tumultuous and horrendous as Jessie's. No song, no stardom, no Oscars, no Josh…had the power to set her free. She was a prisoner, and psychotic misguided lovesick Deuce McCall was still her puppeteer.

# Chapter Three

One thing about the continuous flow of nightmares that marched through Jessie's life as real as soldiers on patrol—they left both her and Josh constantly fatigued. Both were tired as usual that day, but maybe they would find time for a nap later, with maybe a little loving beforehand. The day was fairly open with the exception of Jessie's first counseling session, her initial solo interview, scheduled for three p.m. So after a comforting Josh-style breakfast of eggs and bacon, with french vanilla granola and strawberry yogurt on the side, the couple dressed in beach gear, spread sunscreen on each other's backs, and dragged their kayaks down the beach for a leisurely morning paddle.

Any physical activity in the first months after Josh's attack from McCall and the subsequent spleen removal surgery was cautious and abbreviated. Each morning, he studied the incision for signs of infection. A hotness, swelling or redness around the incision itself would raise a red flag, as would a fever or sudden fatigue and loss of energy. These days Jessie, too, forced herself to run her fingers around the scar, to stare at it and will it to remain a healthy pink. At first she recoiled when she touched it, but as time went on she sent it healing energy instead, as if her love for Josh could negate the bad spirits that had once stolen Sandy, a boy she loved, and that almost destroyed Josh as well.

The type of surgery Josh endured—open, as opposed to a simpler laparotomy, because of the level of damage—was more invasive and thus more susceptible to ongoing problems. The spleen is responsible for fighting off bad bacteria. Without it, Josh was more prone than most to serious illnesses such as pneumonia or meningitis. This added to Jessie's worries and anxiety. Not only did she feel responsible, but also she was still worried about losing him. Stats showed that, in the first two years after a splenectomy, if a serious infection occurred, fifty per cent of the patients would not survive.

In today's kayaking expedition, Jessie took the lead. She paddled slowly and stuck to the calmer shoreline, certain that Josh would follow. He was a man who liked adventure, the rowdier the better—motocross, horses, feeling the wind rifling through his hair while cruising down the highway on his Harley. Calm paddling wasn't usually on his radar, although he seemed to have mellowed after his brush with death.

Jessie cruised along and soaked up the tranquility of the boundless shoreline. P.E.I.'s homey red sandstone cliffs rose splendidly up and away from inviting sandy beaches dotted with falling tree branches and yellow and red kayaks pulled up on shore to rest. Wooden steps that seemed rickety from a distance but were probably perfectly safe led up the cliff face to simple trails through coniferous trees above, to beguiling woodsy cottages that offered escape and shelter for island couples and families, and CFA's—Come From Away-ers, like Josh and Jessie.

These homes were a mystery to Jessie. Mostly hidden from view by trees, each had their own set of the wooden steps. Even by squinting and peering closely at the top, often only a glimpse could be seen of the cottages beyond. This left the people and their dwellings to the imagination. Sometimes Jessie caught a snippet of color moving through the woods here or there. Imagining it as a child's sundress, she could sometimes hear an accompanying echo of laughter and joy, maybe from around a campfire pit, or from swings. Or maybe from a child tossing a Frisbee for a golden retriever named Buddy or Max.

As he glided seamlessly along the surface, Josh's preference was to study the mysteries under the water. Sea grass, marshland, mussels and starfish… an intricate pattern lay on the murky bottom of the Prince Edward Island bay, testament to life's infinity and tenacity. Sometimes Josh could spot crabs down below, their ragged claws scuttling in the current, perhaps wondering why a sudden shadow was gliding noiselessly above. Always, Josh kept an eye out for Jessie. Sometimes the water got a little rougher here and there, or the wind came up. Although they wore life jackets, he knew she was not a strong swimmer. His mother had made sure he and his brother Zach and sister Kayla went through a learn-to-swim program. Jessie told him she took lessons for a few years, and could swim at least, but Josh knew that by twelve her childhood had suddenly come to a crashing halt. There were no more lessons for her then, or puppy dogs or Frisbee games or figure skating or gymnastics. Just music, something she could hide behind at her leisure, endlessly.

Today the wind and water were benign, warm and refreshing. After their paddle, Josh and Jessie pulled the kayaks a safe distance back up the beach towards the red cliff leading to their summer home, and they collapsed on the warm sand to soak up the sun. After a short doze with Josh by her side, his hand resting on her hip, Jessie sat up and began scooping handfuls of sand into a big pile. Amused, Josh watched her, and then eventually he joined her, grinning at her industriousness and wondering what the world would think of one of their favorite entertainers perched on her knees, hair in a messy ponytail, playing like a child on the beach. That was one of the things he loved about Jessie—her childlike nature. The smiley-faced Chucks, the tendency to curl ringlets in her hair—every day Josh saw evidence of Jessie's thwarted childhood. It lent her an innocence that he coveted. Juxtaposed with a tragic past, it made her a rare and special woman. He knew she still had a naiveté along with many complicated layers of loss and pain, and this moment in the sun, her fingers digging and building, a frown of concentration etching the serious face, he could not have cherished her more.

He reached forward and carefully moved a tuft of hair behind Jessie's ear. It was hiding her eye from view, and he wanted to see all of her as he wondered at what she was building as she layered fistfuls of sand on top of each other. Josh needed to see a sparkle in her eye to replace the early morning's tears.

Not looking up, Jessie spoke as her hands worked from the top of the now two foot high pile. "My dad had this friend from Summerside. He was a visual artist, and he taught me to make sandcastles from the top down."

She seemed to be forming something. A turret, maybe? Grabbing a nearby half clamshell from the beach, Jessie used it to slice the sand downwards an inch or two on four sides, then to shave the top on an angle. The turret crumbled a little, so she took the clamshell to the wavelets just below her and Josh, filled it with seawater, and sprinkled it on the sand she was carving to create a more suitable surface.

She continued. "I used to make sandcastles out of upside down buckets. But this way, from the top down you can carve and form and add rocks and shells, and a moat around the whole castle. You can even make stairs, see?"

And the hands that played guitar so sweetly deftly formed miniature stairs with the clamshell as their guiding tool. Jessie's face was a healthy pink, her hair delicately windswept, and her skin newly suntanned. She smiled girlishly up at Josh, who admired his fiancée's blossoming sea-breezed appearance and who silently, for the thousandth time that day alone, counted his blessings before leaning forward and tackling a diminutive staircase of his own.

He took the opportunity to hesitantly ask a question that had been on his mind but which he was loath to ask until the right moment presented itself.

"So, speaking of your dad, I was wondering since we were here whether you would like to visit his grave, Jessie."

The clamshell sank to Jessie's side. She plunked back on her heels and regarded Josh. In Charleston she had introduced him to Rachel and Sandy, or at least to their grave markers. Now it was time for him to meet her father, and...Jessie left the thought unfinished. Her gaze drifted sideways and flitted out to the bay, where a powerboat was easing into a slow moving rhythm with the waves. Behind it, a red and yellow striped sail with two dangling legs beneath it rose against the skyline—a parasailer, joyously afloat on the wind, like the white and gray seagulls that frolicked around the beach each day.

Tentative, Josh spoke again. "We've been here a few days, Jessie. I think it's also time I meet your momma."

Then Jessie was studying her castle, dreams of princesses and unknown happily-ever-afters rapidly diminishing in the escalating heat of an August day. "I suppose," she replied quietly. "Maybe just a quick visit or something. Keep it simple. She doesn't know me, anyway."

She met his eyes, then. Her own were two pearls whose essence and light seemed to come and go like the changing tides, only quicker and more fleeting. Josh's belly ached to see her this way. Oh what he would give to let Jessie live in the light *all of the time.*

Spying the lightning fast flicker of pain that flashed though Josh's eyes, Jessie, in the interest of not ruining their enchanting beach bum morning in this sacred place, threw him a bone.

"You know that the spot where my dad's car went off the road is not all that far from here, eh? It's also..." She licked her dry lips, hesitating. "It's also just down the road from where I moved my mother, actually. It's because the seniors' home overlooks the river. He died in it, but he paddled his canoe there a lot. So the way I see it my dad *lived* there a lot more than he *died* there." She wrinkled her nose at him and crooked her head to one side. "Does that make sense?"

"Yeah." Josh chuckled at her expression that, to him, was kind of a cross between cute and sexy. He made a mental note to take more beach holidays with his girl in the future. Settling into a more comfortable position, he began to carve delicately away at the pile of sand.

Jessie wholly approved of how the hot sun caressed her man's body as he moved. He was laying on his side now, his head resting on one sandy hand, the elbow crooked on the beach. With the other hand gripping his own shell, he whittled a tiny bridge out of their sandcastle.

Later, they left the castle to its own devices, including a tide that would sweep it away when it reclaimed the beach in late afternoon, and they sauntered off inside to shower and snack on some farmer's market hummus and veggies their landlady had stocked in the fridge.

After lunch, Jessie dangled the keys in front of his face.

"Feel like a drive?" she asked, and from the nervous look in her eye Josh knew that the more serious part of their visit to the island was upon them. Later, most afternoons would play out that way. After a morning of relaxation and boating, sunning, reading, and other summertime pursuits, the afternoons would be devoted to counseling, songwriting, script reading, or—in this case—visiting Jessie's mother in the private nursing home.

A two lane rural country road bordered by waning purple and pink lupins, their long flowering robust spikes poisonous to livestock but admired by tourists who cherished their image on everything from pottery mugs to T-shirts, led to the seniors' lodge. A few gentle rolling hills through verdant farmland, and scattered Victorian farmhouses interspersed with the occasional modern bungalow, all with perfectly trimmed lawns and most with thriving vegetable gardens, made the short trip pleasant, the landscape effective in reducing the stress the afternoon was sure to unleash.

Josh pulled the SUV up a slightly sloping paved driveway and parked in a designated visitor's area in front of the home, which was a modest rambling periwinkle blue and white clapboard rancher with an extra wing added on to accommodate its residents. A yellow butterfly greeted Jessie, escorting her as she walked up the wheelchair ramp towards a set of glass doors. The pungent sweet fragrance of lily-of-the-valley lingered in the air, eliciting a twinge of heartache and remembrance. The white flowering plants brought to mind the pale innocence of childhood summers and a one and a half story century home near the other shore of the island, in Bedeque, where the summer salutes of proud tiger lilies and graceful petunias welcomed Jessie's small family back home after leisurely summer daytrips.

Inside, Josh protectively placed one big hand high on Jessie's back as she inquired about her mother. His other hand clutched the Gibson guitar case. The staff was on the lookout for Jessie. Apprised of her arrival, they were thrilled when she showed up with Josh by her side. They were islanders, though, known for their friendliness and hospitality, and so it was business as usual at the seniors' home once everyone said or waved their hellos to the famous couple.

Jessie was relieved to find her mother out on the back deck, since it was such a gorgeous summer day on the island—too nice to be stuck indoors. Belted into a wheelchair, the older woman was gazing over the landscape as if admiring its beauty, but Jessie wondered how much she was actually able to compute. Her expression was childlike, innocent. Emily Wheeler's salt and pepper gray hair was pulled back into a loose bun, and her hands were folded into her lap atop a light cotton coverlet that fluttered gently in the soft breeze like the sheets and towels Josh and Jessie spied hanging from clotheslines during their brief drive.

Bending down in front of the wheelchair and taking her mother's hand, the mother who Jessie willingly and gladly abandoned at age fourteen, she tried to make eye contact, but succeeded only in catching the older woman's attention for a brief moment, with no sign of awareness or recognition.

"Hi Momma," Jessie attempted, a confusing mixture of emotions flooding her mind and heart, drowning her in their overwhelming capacity to still affect her after all this time. She felt Josh's comforting presence behind her as he took a seat on a nearby wooden picnic table, its bright yellow paint flaking at the edges, testament to a steady onslaught of Atlantic salt air. He leaned forward and grasped Emily's hand, surprising Jessie because his warm touch stirred something in her mother. Emily's eyes flickered and she tilted her head towards him. Maybe it was the strength in the male hand, a reminder of her beloved long-lost David. Or maybe it was Josh's own energy and power—a deep capacity to love and be loved in return.

"Hello, Mrs. Wheeler," he was saying as Jessie recovered her senses. "My name is Josh. I happen to be in love with your daughter."

A smile tickled Jessie's lips as a pink flush bloomed over her cheeks. She trained her gaze on her toes. How she loved to hear him say that! She laid a hand over his on her mother's lap. "Momma," she said, a wide grin now crossing her face, "I'd like you to meet Josh Sawyer. This is the man I am going to marry. He's going to be your son-in-law."

Emily's glance danced from one to the other, then, and her eyebrows narrowed as if she was trying to make sense of the two of them. She didn't utter a sound but her hesitant eyes said everything for her. Then it all seemed too much to handle and she gazed back out to the Southwest River, which flowed incessantly along at the bottom of the sloping knoll behind the seniors' lodge, beyond the black and white dairy cows spotting the hill, grazing on their feast of luscious summer grass.

Sitting back on the picnic table beside Josh, his hand in hers, Jessie pondered her mother. She had lost weight since Jessie last laid eyes on her. Her cheeks were thin and her skin was pale and sickly. The once proud shoulders were hunched over. Still, it was easy to tell the woman had been tall and vibrant once upon a time, in better days. Squeezing Josh's fingers, Jessie prayed that their own history together would result in children and grandchildren, and that they would somehow get to end their days after years and years of togetherness and happiness, that neither would be stolen from the other too soon. She was afraid she might someday slide into oblivion like her mother. Maybe it was a family trait. She sighed, and fixed her glance on a grazing Holstein cow in the distance as the warm breeze buffeted the hem of her short sundress, lifting it as if a playful spirit was trying to engage her attention.

"Hi Dad," she whispered, feeling his calm presence around them in the P.E.I. sunshine.

Josh lifted an arm and placed it contentedly around Jessie's shoulders. "Want your guitar, little girl?" It sat by the picnic table, ready and waiting to entertain the nursing home residents and staff. At Jessie's nod, Josh bent down and turned the case around for better access. He snapped up the clips, lifted the lid, and carefully removed the treasured instrument.

"Oh!" came a muffled sound from between Emily Wheeler's lips. Whether she recognized the Gibson as her husband's was debatable, but there was no question she understood the guitar and its power. She clapped her hands, delighted.

As Jessie tuned, the staff wheeled a few other residents onto the large deck and positioned them so they could enjoy the entertainment. The more mobile patients perched on picnic tables and in deep-set yellow, blue and lime green Adirondack chairs. For the next half hour Jessie played tunes that her father had often entertained the little Wheeler family with—some were his own compositions, but most were familiar songs that many east coast musicians played back in the seventies and eighties, folk tunes like *Sonny's Dream*, and a few pop songs. At the end she asked for requests from the thrilled audience gathered around her, and when one old gentleman asked her to play a song from his youth—a popular wartime tune, *I'll Be Seeing You*—she did her best.

When she finally packed the Gibson away, many residents were left with teary-eyed memories of their own. Emily Wheeler did not recognize her daughter, but her cheeks were wet. She certainly recognized music. Her husband's favorite tunes? Maybe.

A small smile played on Emily's lips as she stared out over the sparkling river and, watching her, Jessie wondered where her mother let her mind take her, on what fantastical journeys...to the past? To the future, unknown but perhaps freeing, promising, if one allowed him or herself to believe in some magical place akin to Heaven, where one could listen to beautiful music all day and frolic in the arms of a loved one?

One thing for certain, Jessie would come back here again and again this summer, guitar in hand. For her, big shows and audiences of thousands were exhilarating and had their own rewards, but they were big machines. This—sitting outside on a deck accompanied by chirping songbirds, overlooking a cheerful beguiling river her father once loved, playing old tunes for people who rarely had the chance to hear them—was divine.

As she and Josh were saying their good-byes to the nursing staff, leaving her mother with a light brush of lips across a sallow cheek and a gentle tuck of the coverlet around her thin legs, Jessie noticed one old man leaning against the reception counter, his gray eyes fixed on them. Something about him seemed familiar, although his unwavering stare unnerved her. He wasn't tall, but he wore a mop of gray hair like Einstein, unruly as if he either didn't care to comb it out or cut it, or as if it was his statement to the world—*I am me, I have my own opinions, let me be.* His stance radiated the same message. One elbow rested on the counter and his feet were crossed at the ankles. His head was raised high, proudly, a frown reverberating through his countenance.

He called out to Jessie when she caught his eye again just before leaving through the double glass doors. "Mizz Wheeler. Nice job on your dad's old repertoire. Only you played a few out of order." His voice was high, as if he was a little nervous to speak to her. As he watched the shock impact of his statement register the way he hoped it would, his gravelly voice strengthened. "I been wonderin' why you come back here, girl."

Josh sensed Jessie tense beside him, and he glanced over in time to see her eyes flicker with recognition. "You knew him, my dad. You were at the bar a lot. Most times, I think."

"I'm disappointed, Jessie. I thought you would know me right off the bat. I gave you virgin Singapore Slings and let you sit at the bar and watch your dad entertain the masses. Not quite the way *you* do these days, but he had his own fan base, that's for sure."

"George," the name slid out simply. "You owned the bar on the highway near Summerside. You used to tap me on the shoulder and send me downstairs. Something about the liquor inspector coming, I think." She remembered the way his fingers stank of cigarette smoke as they touched her, the brashy-yellow nicotine announcing the man's addiction, how she used to duck sideways to avoid being stung with the smoking coal-red tips he waved about as if they were extensions of his fingers.

He shrugged his shoulders. "Not just that. There were things I didn't think a kid should see." The gray eyes softened, emitting a sad light like a lighthouse beacon hidden beneath the fog. "I wondered if you came back to find out what happened to your dad. Or are you here just to hide for a while after that nasty business out west?" He said it in a way that left no room to the imagination. Was Jessie here of her own accord or did she actually truly care about her family?

Hesitating as she considered George's blunt query, Jessie stepped closer to him, her pink toenails little guiding lights of color on the institutional beige ceramic floor. Her fingers curled into loose fists, nerves from this visit to her past starting to get the best of her.

Her voice was low, calculated. "What do you mean, am I here to find out what happened to my dad? I know what happened to my dad. A tourist on the wrong side of the road couldn't wait to pass a farm tractor or a slow moving car, wasn't it? Scared him into the river. He had no choice, it was either that or a fiery collision that would kill more people."

George hesitated too, and carefully regarded Josh, who was standing back but telegraphing a hard-edged look of warning.

All Josh knew was that when Jessie's knuckles turned white, they were entering a danger zone. She was already anxious about this visit to a mother she felt had abandoned her when she was twelve. There was no room in her already hurting mind and heart for rumors and innuendo about her father's untimely demise.

But George steeled himself for battle. The old man knew something untoward had happened that day so long ago, in fact he dearly loved Jessie's mother and father, and cursed the futility of trying to make bad things right. Just look at Jessie's mother, out there hiding in another dimension practically, her mind eroded and destroyed to the point of no return. Remembering a passionate little girl whose love for her father was immense, and a father who adored every move his little girl made, and the mother who created the child, George's own heart ached. Why was love so brief sometimes? Those who had it often didn't cherish it, nurture it, let it blossom and grow. Instead they suffocated it, took it for granted, yelled when they should have been loving. Turned their backs and went to sleep instead of choosing to make love. It was over all too soon for some folks, for Emily and David Wheeler, who had taken great risks to be together in the first place. But that story was for another time. Today, George just wanted to plant a seed. Because Jessie deserved to know how and why David died, taking his music and family to the muddy bottom of the Southwest River with him, drowning them as the great blue herons flapped their expansive wings overhead and cried out in dismay at the loss of so much love and passion.

"It wasn't entirely an accident, Jessie. Your father's death was supposed to be a warning."

"Damnit, mister! Is this really necessary?" Josh was at Jessie's side in a second. Didn't Jessie have enough on her plate? Josh grabbed her hand. "Come on, Jess. He's just trying to get to you."

She shrugged him off. "Tell me why you think that, George."

Josh recognized the cool detached manner in which she spoke. He closed his eyes. *Enough, already,* he demanded of the universe. *Enough.*

George shifted around so that he was leaning against the counter with his back to it, both elbows resting on it. He was trembling, and Jessie wondered whether that was from the gravity of his words, or from some seniors' disease. He had to be in his late eighties, judging from the crinkles in his skin and the creamy translucent pallor to his face and hands. His eyes were aged, too. Cataracts had cleansed them of their purity, yet underneath the white foggy clouds they seemed crisp and focused, albeit guarded and sad. The man's mind was sharp as a pin.

"Mizz Wheeler," he said, a hint of defiance coloring his tone. "I am sorry to be the bearer of bad news after all this time. I loved your father. He was a kind man with a fine sense of humor and a mind of his own. He was a man deeply in love with a beautiful woman and with a sweet little girl who deserved a lifetime of innocence and happily-ever-afters. But he was an artist. He was not smart when it came to money, either in earning it or knowing how to manage it when he had it. He got his family into a hole he couldn't dig his way out of, and so he borrowed money. All those guitars, you know the type. But he couldn't pay it back. And finally someone decided he needed a little nudge."

Jessie's fingers were now completely white, not just the knuckles, which she had tightened into closed little balls. *Music,* she was thinking. *Like sex. Polarized opposites of the same thing—good and bad.*

Behind her, Josh groaned.

Her next words were spoken crisply, their edges terse and succinct. "How do you know this?"

"This is a small island. I ran a bar. People drink. Their lips get loose. They talk." George shrugged, as if she should already know this. He considered how Jessie was taking this news, and was sorry to see that her eyes were tearing up. "I'm sorry, honey," he said quietly, "to be the bearer of such news. But it's been a long time, and you're here now, and your father deserves the truth. So does your mother."

Her breath caught at that. "She knew?"

George's eyes narrowed. "She *knows.*"

"Oh, for Pete's sake," came Josh's low aggravated voice behind Jessie. "He's playing you, Jess."

"What do you think," George said directly to Josh this time, "that Emily isn't aware of things around her? Of course she is. She's never been officially diagnosed with Alzheimer's, she's just tuned herself out. And why not? What's so great about this world that anyone would want to stay in it alone? Husband gone, and daughter deserted her?"

Josh stepped forward. "That's enough." He clenched his own fists, but what was he going to do, get in a fistfight with a man who must be pushing ninety?

"You don't know what you're talking about," Jessie said staunchly, her face pale beneath the new tan. "Why I left her."

George raised his eyebrows. "Bullshit," he spat. "I watched that Shawna Coupland interview. The whole world knows. And let me just say it wasn't much of a surprise. Your Momma's sugar daddy always got what he wanted. Sick bastard." He tottered forward then, his footsteps unbalanced and stuttery. It was strange—this man was old, aged, practically crippled, yet he held a lot of power, it seemed.

"Look Jessie," he said, his energy failing and the strength he had somehow called upon now diminishing. His already gravelly voice was suddenly trembly, wavering. "I really am sorry to have upset you. But your father deserves to rest in peace. And I know that you have ghosts of your own to defeat while you're here. This island is supposed to be a place of healing. But you need the truth for that, you need to dredge up all the sludge and chuck it away so you can let the healing really come. For you, for your dad, and for your mom. For your family, Jessie. For what it used to be."

He took hold of her arms then and, as his hands slipped down Jessie's forearms to her hands, which he gripped with icy fingers, she felt a strength there, and Jessie remembered a man who had kind eyes, whose whole body radiated joy when her father was around, who loved the music as much as anyone, and who was always kind to her and her mother. He seemed to be imploring her now to find the truth and, somehow, she heard some inner voice saying *listen.*

"Okay," she murmured, hardly believing herself. "Where do I start?"

"You start," he said, his grizzled face softening, "at the beginning. I will have my son bring in a white banker's box from home. Come back soon."

Unable to help herself, Jessie wrapped her arms around the old man's bony shoulders before she turned to leave. Facing Josh, she was saddened by the disbelief and disapproval etched on his face, but she knew that he had a plate full of concerns for her anxiety this summer. She pushed by him, grabbing the Gibson from his hand as if the guitar were her father himself, hers alone to cherish and care for. As if it didn't belong in Josh's hands all of a sudden because he was distanced from this new—old—drama.

Josh fired a look of reproof across the room to George, but it was replaced with surprise when the old man said, "Don't let it go, young man. Love. It's a rare Orchid. And men have died trying to find those."

Outside, Josh found Jessie standing by the SUV, the guitar clasped tightly in her fingers and the salty island breeze lifting and fluttering her skirt, but she didn't seem to notice. The yellow butterfly was back but it, too, escaped her gaze. Instead, she turned to Josh.

"Want to go get ice cream?"

He frowned. They had planned to go sit on the hill her father's car had careened down all those years ago. But now—of course, that was too much. Ice cream seemed to be an island tradition, from what he had discerned during their flight to the east coast province. Ice cream...it would be a safe pursuit. And then—and then, Josh would drive Jessie to Charlottetown, to the jungle-like atmosphere with the trickling water fountains where Trudy would interview Jessie alone for the first time. Sarcastically, Josh doubted the therapist would get too far today. Jessie was already detached, her reserves seemingly already depleted for the day. Maybe coming to P.E.I. was not such a good idea after all. So much for the healing place.

He took the guitar from her and placed it in the back seat, the safest part of the car. She treated that guitar like her dad himself—it was sacred. Josh's eyes fell onto the partially destroyed happy face sticker that taunted him from the neck of the case. That sticker alone was almost entirely responsible for Jessie's return to Vancouver, to their friends, to him. He was humbled. Maybe her dad was still around, somehow, in some weird untouchable dimension. Maybe he still had a hand in her life.

They drove east through gently rolling farmland to the quaint town of Kensington where the Frosty Treat dairy bar, popular with the locals, was literally humming on this hot day. They were greeted by a buzzing parking lot filled almost to capacity with extended families and sprightly teenage couples. On the outdoor deck waiting to order was more than one longhaired girl with thin bikini straps peeking out from underneath either a sundress or tank top. Hanging on their jock boyfriends' arms, the girls were all texting on their smartphones with one eye while impatiently staring down the line-up with the other.

The well-liked spot was less than fifteen minutes from one of the island's best beaches, Cabot Park, and Jessie felt a spasm seize her belly as she remembered coming here years ago with her mom and dad. If they didn't stop at the Frosty Treat on their way to the beach, well, they darn well always did on the way back home.

The dairy bar itself split the parking lot. On one side was a new spot Jessie didn't remember from her childhood but which she recalled from her last trip to P.E.I. a few years ago. It was a garage shaped wooden building painted the identical vivacious summer yellow of the ice cream bar. It sold cottons and trinkets from around the world, judging by the outdoor display of dark handmade drums designed with exotic woods, flamboyant women's tops blowing in the breeze, and flimsy straw hats. The parking lot on the other side of the low snack bar was lined with clay statues of Buddha, some just slightly tipping in shifting earth perches. They were nestled on soft green grass bordered by a variety of well tended calming flowers, including welcoming forget-me-nots planted by the wheelchair ramp, fluttering merrily in their verdant earthy bed on this perfect summer day.

On top of the small wooden building sat an old sign, maybe original to the place when it was built in 1973, according to the older style of lettering on the sign itself. It promised tasty burgers, fish and chips, and fresh fried clams fried up in the mecca below. The smiling, frozen painted face elicited a shiver that travelled unwarranted up and down Jessie's arms and legs. The old-fashioned graphic reminded Jessie of Peeling Benny and his vacant dairy bar in Vancouver, once a place of burgeoning love and refuge but now just another reminder of the torment of Deuce McCall, for inside Benny's abandoned building was where Josh was kept during the long night and day after being chloroformed and forced into McCall's sinister presence.

Silent during the drive, Jessie emitted a slow *pffffttt* through closed lips when she assessed the bustling crowd and the old sign, as Josh pulled into the far end of the Buddha populated side of the lot beside the perky P.E.I. hotspot. Initially Jessie shrank into her seat, but then she found some resolve and energy and hoisted herself cautiously out of the car. Nervously eyeing the beige Camry next to them, whose teen driver's wide eyes were curiously staring at her from behind noisy gulps of a large milkshake, Jessie yanked a baseball cap down over her head. She broke eye contact with the girl and padded quietly just behind Josh, two fingers of her left hand in his back pocket, to the row of windows lining the outdoor counter, where colorful hand printed signs tempted kids of all ages with succulent sundae and milkshake flavors like hot fudge, marshmallow, strawberry, pineapple, and even coffee. The place was crazy busy and, after an uncomfortable ten minutes in line—whereby Jessie grasped Josh's hand, leaned into him and nervously fixed her eyes on the menus so as to avoid stares, whispers and shy smiles—the middle-aged server didn't even pause when he spoke to them. Either he did not expect to see celebrities at the dairy bar, or he simply didn't watch movies and television.

The guy folded hairy elbows on the counter and leaned towards them, his red baseball cap with the cartoony ultra-happy Frosty Treat spokesman on it, front and center, almost mirroring Jessie's, a blue cap that proclaimed her desire to fit in. Hers featured a local Junior hockey team, the Summerside Western Capitals. She and Josh had each bought one at the Charlottetown airport upon arrival in their island sanctuary, meant for days just like this one, where hiding was not necessarily an option if one wanted ice cream but where a baseball cap could at least deter a few stares. Josh had his pulled down over his somber brown eyes, too.

"What would you like, Princess?"

And at that, the final nail was driven in Jessie's coffin for the day, for Princess was what Deuce McCall called her. Instantly she turned away, defeated, so after a moment wondering *what the hell,* Josh stepped up to the counter.

"Uh, hot fudge shake for me, and uh…" He glanced at Jessie's back as she steered her way through curious stares back to their vehicle. Turning back to the server, he shrugged and mumbled, "One of those cones with chocolate on one side and vanilla on the other."

The intense server didn't blink or seemingly take a breath. "Regular or small?"

"Yeah, uh regular cone I guess, oh and can you coat it in chocolate like that one?" He pointed towards a small boy whose mother had lifted him onto the counter next to where Josh was ordering. There were three line-ups in use at the busy spot that day and, as the young mom was paying, the little boy was trying to get control of the thin coating of chocolate that covered his ice cream. Josh couldn't help but grin, and he wished Jessie was there to smile along with him, as a big patch of chocolate slid off the cone and onto the ground far below the boy's dangling toes, much to the child's dismay. Josh winked when the little guy was quicker the second time a piece broke free off the melting cone, and chubby fingers caught it and popped it into his mouth. They shared a secret then, and the wide grin with which the child rewarded Josh's attention warmed his heart.

From Josh's window, an impatient voice cut into sudden thoughts of future children of his own. "Sir? The milkshake—what size, please?"

"Yeah, large, thanks man."

Would he and Jessie have kids? Undoubtedly. But even without the haunting fear that accompanied raising children with a woman as troubled as Jessie, there was still the nagging worry of immersing the kids in a glass-walled celebrity lifestyle. Tossing that negative thought aside, Josh thought of Charlie and Jane, and Steve and Sophie, and he assured himself that together they would all figure out how to make it work. *Besides,* he thought, *we can always hide away here on Jessie's little island.*

He waved good-bye at his new young friend as the child's mother lifted the boy down off the counter.

Then, as her vision cleared, the young woman made eye contact with Josh and she jumped, surprised to see the famous guy at her dairy bar in small town P.E.I.

He smiled tentatively at her.

"Hello," he said simply, at the same time extending a hand to accept his milkshake from the server, who hustled off to make Jessie's cone.

The woman shook her head slightly, and focused on Josh. "Really?" she asked in disbelief, wiping a loose strand of hair away from where it partially covered one vibrant green eye. "Seriously?"

He shrugged but felt his cheeks color slightly. Then Josh attempted to bring some normalcy to the moment. "You might want to get some extra napkins." He nodded towards the little fella at the young mom's side, the little guy's mouth generously afloat with melting ice cream.

She laughed whole-heartedly and reached forward to take Josh's hand. "Just so I can say I actually touched you," she said, her voice warm and mellow on this hot day as she regained her equilibrium.

Josh squeezed her fingers slightly, then leaned forward and gave the woman a gentle hug and let her brush her lips against his cheek. "Take care of that little guy. He's awesome."

"I will," she said, happy but outwardly calm in the presence of this Canadian celebrity. She paused before leaving, and studied him. "So much cuter in real life," she said idly, as if she were puzzled at that realization. "Bye, Josh Sawyer. Take care of that girl of yours." Then, as she suddenly realized that he likely wasn't alone that day, she strained past him to see if Jessie Wheeler was nearby.

He saddened as he realized who she was looking for.

"She went back to the car."

"Hmm. I suppose I get that."

"Too many people, I think."

He reached forward and accepted the chocolate dipped cone from the server, then thrust a ten-dollar bill at the guy, who stepped to the side and punched in some numbers at the cash register.

"Yeah," the mom said in understanding, inching slightly closer to Josh to allow the person behind her in line to order at the middle window she'd just vacated. "Look," she added thoughtfully as she started to turn to go. She sensed the weariness washing over Josh like a mud splatter on a car window during a rainy day drive. "Everyone deserves a chance at happiness, Mr. Sawyer. Sometimes we just have to remind ourselves what that—happiness—looks like." She glanced down at her son, who was frowning miserably at the mess of chocolate melting in the hand where the hardened dip from the cone landed.

"I hear you." Josh grinned as he was handed his change and a bunch of napkins from the server. He thrust the napkins forward into the young mom's hands. "You need these more than me. We've got some in the car."

"Thanks." She smiled genuinely, the envy of every woman at the Frosty Treat that day. Josh grabbed his baseball cap from his head and placed it backwards on the little guy's curly locks. "See you," he said, and then turned away from the captivating green eyes of the wise and patient mother.

As he sauntered towards the far end of the parking lot, contemplating whether or not to lick Jessie's chocolate dipped cone to keep it from melting over his hand, he was surprised and even somewhat miffed at himself. For one, when the woman hugged him, something had jarred within. She was genuine and obviously a good mom to her kid, as evidenced by the fact that she didn't freak out over the mess the child was making. Josh couldn't help but ponder the fact that she was also likely living a normal life away from prying eyes and stares and whispers; away from a sinister and hostile experience like the one that left deep scars within he and Jessie's psyches. Despite his and Jessie's deep love for each other, a wave of loneliness washed over Josh as he was reminded of the sadness that permeated their lives.

He had to knock on Jessie's car window to get her to open it for him. She jumped, and instantly he was sorry for startling her, but it brought her back to the present, at least. She depressed the button for the window and, as it lowered, took the quickly drooping cone out of her man's strong grip.

She had been sitting in the car like a child, with both feet on the ground, her hands in her lap, and her shoulders slumped. Josh was almost surprised that she even accepted the ice cream, because she seemed so far away. He could feel the eyes of everyone behind them on his back, watching the simple interaction of handing an ice cream cone to his famous fiancée, and it bothered him. Bristling, Josh met Jessie's eyes and wondered whether she had seen the brief interaction with the green-eyed woman and her young son. As he walked around the SUV towards the driver's side, Josh couldn't help but glance back towards the busy dairy bar. He saw the woman leaning against an old red Honda Civic, watching him. Her son, perched on the hood of the car next to her, waved to him. Josh waved back, somewhat relieved for the mom that the kid had made it to the cone part of his messy ice cream so it was at least somewhat under control.

Climbing into the car and slamming the door behind him, Josh noticed that Jessie's eyes were trained on the boy's mom. She turned to face him then, and leaned back against the seat, but she didn't speak. Her diaphanous eyes said all she needed to say, and she wrapped her left arm around her belly as if to keep it from aching.

Josh leaned sideways against his seat, too, and sucked on the milkshake, watching her, wondering what the hell had come over her at the counter. He pushed thoughts of the young mom, her child, and their hopefully unscarred lives to the back of his mind.

He leaned forward and let his fingers get lost in Jessie's hair. Pulling her towards him, he licked her lips and grinned when he felt her smile under his soft caress.

"Yum, chocolate," he teased, and was happy when Jessie's left arm gently slipped around his neck. They kissed until her ice cream started to drip more profusely and she had no recourse but to let him go.

Much to the disappointment of the Frosty Treat's other patrons that day, Josh turned on the ignition and pointed the car towards Charlottetown, a half hour drive away. Behind him, excited chatter escalated and made its way onto Facebook and Twitter. Josh didn't look back and, instead, flipped on the radio. There didn't seem to be much chance that there would be conversation on this trip.

The SUV glided along Route Two, one of the island's main arteries, its occupants lost in thought, miles apart. But after he slurped the last bit of his shake, twisting and tipping it in his fingers to get the right angle to suck up the last bit, Josh dropped the empty container into a cup holder, wiped the condensation from the cup on his jeans and then grasped Jessie's fingers in his own. He lifted her fingers and kissed them.

He knew that love was rare, and he intended to hang on. For one day he, too, like George, would be pushing ninety. And when that day came, he fully intended to have his woman by his side after a lifetime of happiness and whatever else life brought them. Together they would prevail. But for now, on this weird day, he realized one thing for certain. They would have to take this one day at a time, one simple baby step at a time. Hell, one *breath* at a time. And maybe someday they could bring their own children to the Frosty Treat where they would have to grab a handful of extra napkins to help guide them through such pitfalls of life as facing a melting ice cream cone on a really hot day.

"All right, little one," he said affectionately, allowing himself to relax. "We're in this together, you and me. We'll get that white box from the old man, and I'll go through it with you."

At that, Jessie looked over at him—her man, her rock, her guiding light. She crunched her own cone, popped the last bit between her lips, and tried not to smile as Josh used his thumb to wipe a dribble from the corner of her lips.

"Thanks, Josh," she whispered, and he knew she wasn't talking about the ice cream dribble.

"You're very, very welcome," he said gladly.

And he was grateful for that moment, for that's what life is made up of—moments, one at a time, all strung together like the strings on a guitar that, when played together, make the most beautiful music.

All too soon they arrived at Trudy's place, and Josh had to let Jessie go, if just for the littlest of whiles, so she could deal with her own demons, so that maybe someday they could grasp fully their own elusive happiness, and run with it, and never let it go.

# Chapter Four

"How's your day going?"

Trudy sat across from Jessie in the little jungle sanctuary, soothed by trickling water from more than one tiny fountain. The singer was already frowning, staring at anything but her therapist. Josh had made eye contact with Trudy when he escorted Jessie inside, one arm placed gently around her waist as he guided her through the side door of the two-story home. His brown eyes were intense, aware, and he maintained eye contact for longer than usual. Clearly he was telling Trudy that Jessie was having a bad day. Nodding at him, Trudy tried to communicate back that they would be fine together, that he shouldn't worry. But how do you really convince someone not to be concerned when they are faced with the harsh reality of post-traumatic stress on a daily basis?

Jessie shrugged, and dug her fingernails into the back of her left hand. She focused her glance on the cat, Oliver, who was intent on giving himself a bath as he sunned contentedly on the chair where Josh would be sitting if he was part of this session. "It's okay. I'm getting by."

"Jessie…" Trudy watched as the nervous movement paused while the girl listened. She could see bright pink half moons forming on the back of Jessie's left hand. "When I met with you and Josh yesterday, you filled me in on what's been happening. He expressed concern over the recurring nightmares, and the triggers that are, let's face it, probably everywhere. How do you feel about his concern?"

It was a few minutes before Jessie spoke. She still hadn't made eye contact. "I think things are getting better. I just need some time."

"Tell me…" Trudy settled more comfortably back into her chair. "Are you here because you want to be here? Or were you coerced into coming?"

Startled, Jessie finally looked up. Trudy was struck by the color of her eyes—a light pearl blue. There was a kindness there, but also an underlying fear. This was a look Trudy saw far too often in the women who sat in the wicker chair over the years.

"How do you mean?" Jessie asked, digging more nails into her left hand and tossing her hair.

"Is this your choice? To get help?"

Sinking deeper into her own chair, Jessie swallowed. She watched as Oliver repeatedly licked a paw and wiped it over his face. *How did he learn to do that,* she wondered. The cat seemed so content, lying there ignoring the heavy weight that filled the air in the small room.

"No, actually," Jessie responded truthfully. She ran a hand through her windswept hair. "I am not thrilled about bringing this all up again. I kind of just want to let it go. It's over."

"I have to tell you…that will make this all a little harder…if it's not your choice. We will find it a little more challenging to do the work we have to do."

Jessie nodded. "I get that. But I just want all of this to be over."

"You know, Jessie, for someone who wants the bad stuff to disappear, I'm a little surprised that you did the interview with Shawna Coupland. Can I ask why?"

"Did you see it?"

"Yep."

"Then it should be obvious," she said abruptly. "I did it to set Josh free. To let the world know the truth about what happened. That he didn't hurt me."

"So the world would accept him."

Jessie blinked. *Hell, yeah.* "Yes."

"That must have been tough, to go public like that."

"Yeah. Sucked." Again, the fingernails digging into the palm. Trudy looked for other clues—was Jessie a cutter? The girl was wearing a sundress with a brightly embroidered short denim jacket over top—long sleeves on a super hot day. Filing a mental note, Trudy would ask Josh whether there were parallel ladders of scars, on her arms, breasts, the common areas where cutters left their pain.

"You really love him."

"Yeah." Looking down at her hands, Jessie saw the pink cuts she was digging into her hand. As the realization of what she was doing dawned on her, she repositioned the fingertips of her right hand so she could rub the marks instead.

"Things are good between you?"

"Yeah. If you can get past the fact that I almost got him killed, yeah."

"He's doing okay now."

"Well, I'm keeping a close eye on him. Without the spleen…" Her voice trailed off and Trudy could see layers upon layers of worry burdening this young woman.

"What's he up against?"

Again, Jessie tuned out for a few minutes before responding. She fixed her gaze on the window this time.

"Jessie?"

Looking back at Trudy, Jessie seemed surprised to see her there. She circled her eyes around the room as the truth dawned on her that she was sitting in the office of a woman she didn't know, discussing things she wanted to keep solidly buried, like a loathsome treasure underneath the sand castle she and Josh built that morning. She adjusted her position, crossing one ankle over the other and smoothing out her short sundress so that it almost reached her tanned knees.

"What?" she asked.

Trudy was gentle, careful. "I was just wondering what you think Josh is up against, living life without a spleen."

"Oh. Well…the spleen is what helps the body protect itself from infection. So we have to be vigilant. Watch him for fevers, any signs of pneumonia, illness…get him to regular check-ups." Again, she swallowed nervously, and shifted her ankles around. But at least she was looking at Trudy now.

"That frightens you."

"Well, yes. Especially in the first two years." Jessie watched Trudy take this in. There was something trustworthy about this woman. Something about having a cat sharing the space with them. Oliver seemed comfortable there. He looked up at Jessie as if he was sending her a message, telling her with his big eyes that it was okay to share her fears here in this lush refuge.

"The thing is. I feel like...like I've hurt him enough. You know? And now we have to live with this time bomb."

"A lot of people live long lives with no spleen. He's strong."

Jessie cocked her head, testing Trudy. "Can you guarantee me that he will be okay?"

"No. But I can't guarantee that on my morning run I don't get hit by a car, either." She leaned forward. "Jessie, each day is a gift. And sometimes each day is one breath at a time, at least until we have the tools to handle our fears, to triumph over them. If you let me, I can help you find the strength to overcome your pain, the fears that have been holding you hostage, so that you can enjoy life a little more. But it's a long process."

"I'm only here for a few months." *Let's just get this over with.*

"Then I'll set you up with my friend back in Vancouver. And maybe we can still chat sometimes, if you want to. But for now, let's just get to know each other, okay?"

"Fine." This day was already too much for Jessie. She would do anything to just get through it at this point.

"All right then. This is how it's going to go. We're going to meet alone a few times, and with Josh a few times. I'll also be meeting with him alone. I promise not to share anything between you. That will be up to the two of you, if you choose. My role is to facilitate some healing, find some tools, maybe unbury some truths. How does this feel to you?"

Nodding, Jessie said, "Fine."

"Questions? How does this make you feel?"

"The truth?"

"Yep."

"Scared."

"Can you tell me why?"

"Because I don't really feel up to a treasure hunt that's going to uncover shit about my past. Like I said earlier. I don't really want to go back there."

"It makes you feel..."

"Vulnerable. Self-conscious, I guess. Embarrassed."

"Jessie, there's an upside to this, to you sharing your feelings in a way that might feel risky. Besides feeling the bad stuff, therapy could also make you feel some 'safe' feelings. These safer feelings may be new to you. They'll help you get past the bad."

Regarding Trudy carefully, Jessie sighed. "Look, no promises. Okay?"

Taking that as an attempt at trying, Trudy nodded. "You got it. One day at a time." She smiled warmly at the girl whose music touched the world, then crossed her legs at the knee and grabbed her sunflower notebook from a nearby table, where it perched precariously on the edge underneath an exquisite orchid.

Jessie thought Dee would like this woman, a kindred spirit, another lover of flowers and plants, living things that she nurtured until they blossomed.

"So," Trudy said with a wink. "Tell me about this man of yours. What was it about him that stole your heart in the first place?"

And at that, she earned her first genuine smile from her client.

Eyeing the floor so Trudy couldn't see her face, a hint of pleasure coloring her voice, Jessie joked, "His butt." She was picturing her man in his Drifters outfit, suspenders hanging enticingly down over his sexy hips as he trained with the television show's horse wrangler. She added, grinning, "And his forearms." To illustrate her point, she held up an arm and wrapped her other hand around it. "Luv his forearms. Strong. Sexy."

Rolling her eyes, Trudy leaned back and laughed openly. "Ah, I should have known."

Jessie's tongue-in-cheek admission launched a simple conversation that opened a few doors and began to build the first bridge between therapist and patient, a bond that over time would hopefully build a helpful and confident trust. Trudy had to build a powerful connection between security and kindness in order to replace Jessie's original fusion of pain and attachment. Josh was the common ground here. Jessie's deep love for him was obvious. On some level she was healing and had proven that she was now able to form deep alliances, but Trudy knew that the people Jessie were connected to were also the ones she knew she had badly hurt, both by exiting her life for a year and a half, as well as through choosing not to include them in her own torment with her stalker. And then there was the near tragic loss of Josh, the man she loved, and…another man as well.

"Jessie, tell me about Jacob. Who is he and what does he mean to you?"

"Oh boy." The curve ball threw Jessie, and she focused on the window again, playing with her eyes to try to make a spot disappear.

*One step forward, two steps back,* thought Trudy expectantly. She waited. Therapy would only work if she knew the singer's past, and what she and Jessie were up against.

Eventually Jessie came around again, but only after Trudy once again employed her break-from-hypnosis technique of calling Jessie's name.

"Jacob. Wow, you really know how to get a girl feeling shitty about herself, don't you? Can I go now?" Jessie pulled out her iPhone and checked the time. She held it in front of Trudy. "My hour's almost up. Josh is probably asleep in the car, waiting for me."

"I sensed I hit a nerve, Jessie. I'm sensing you relived a little of the old pain, there."

Jessie scowled and shot her a look that flickered with anger. "Jacob's in the past. Let's leave him there."

"Another time, then. When you're ready."

"Fine," Jessie grumbled. She stood. "I'm going, okay?"

Trudy nodded and stood as well. Oliver stretched as if to say *So long.* Reaching out her hand, the therapist took Jessie's and gave it a squeeze. She knew that this was a woman who was often catered to, who generally called her own shots, especially when she was uncomfortable. Trudy would need to work with that knowledge, and try not to put her patient on the defensive. "This is a good thing, Jessie. Give it a chance."

Somber, Jessie shrugged. "I don't know. I'll see you."

As they parted, Trudy gave Oliver a scratch behind the ears. The cat turned a somersault. He was easy to communicate with. He was very clear about wanting a belly scratch. Outside the window, Trudy watched as Jessie whipped open the door to the SUV and climbed in alongside Josh, who stretched and yawned before leaning in for a kiss. The lovers held each other for an extended moment, their foreheads touching.

Yeah. Jessie Wheeler would be just fine, all right. She was no longer alone in the world. She had another lonely soul to help her through. All would be well.

As the SUV pulled out of the parking lot, Trudy saw Jessie shrink lower into her seat. The singer did not look back.

# Chapter Five

The next day, another bright sunny August morning beckoned Josh and Jessie out of doors and into a fragrant world filled with butterflies and chirping robins and chickadees. And…farm tractors. They were trundling sluggishly in the car behind a wagon filled to the hilt with huge round bales of hay destined to keep some farmer's livestock fed for the upcoming winter. Josh was having a laugh over it—this was not a sight you would see on the streets of busy metropolitan Vancouver—but Jessie grumbled. Yesterday's session with Trudy had left her tense, and later today would be Josh's turn. Oh, if she could be a fly on the wall…

She was also lost in thought over the mysterious box she would soon claim from George at the nursing home at the top of the pretty hill in Clinton. George's comments that Jessie's father had been the victim of a crime terrified her. But they would wait a bit before going back to see Emily and to claim the box which, in all likelihood, had not even made its way there yet. But it was killing Jessie not to know what was in it—*if anything,* Josh had said last night.

They had been sitting on the deck again, this time side by side and hand in hand, their chairs pushed close together. He had asked about the therapy, but she wasn't talking. She just said it was *fine.*

"Your momma looks like you," he said, lifting her hand for a kiss.

"I look like her, you mean," Jessie responded quietly. "Got my dad's eyes, though."

With a wink and a grin he said, "Good thing. I like those eyes."

A sleepy orange setting sun dipped into the water as a pale white moonlight slowly slipped into its place, almost unnoticed. In the bay, two black cormorants frolicked and played, and Jessie wondered how they managed to hook up in the first place. If their dating ritual was anything like humans, then she pitied them. As wonderful as falling in love was, sometimes it really hurt to get there. But then when you were there…she peeked sideways at Josh, who was sitting by her with his feet on the rail and a happy grin lighting up his chiseled cheeks. She brushed her favorite piece of his hair aside so that she could see him better.

He smiled. Her touch was like a feather, light and delicate, but her hold on him was immense.

"So what about that box?" he asked her.

"Mystery to me," she said. "I'm not sure what to expect. George is a good man, though. Sharp as a tack, too, all these years later." She told Josh about the days at the club outside Summerside where her dad played while she and her mom sat on stools at the bar and cheered him on. She ended with a reflective, "Good times."

"I want to be with you when you open that box, okay Jess?" He was still staring out at the ocean, the horizon a sharp blue line edged with a mystic violet-pink and gold.

"You will be," she replied, but inside a little voice was jumping up and down screaming *are you sure about that, mister?* It was still new, being in this relationship with him. Yeah, she loved Josh, but she was still in self-preservation mode, and would be, for a while yet. She wasn't ready for Josh to see the rest of her fears, her worries, and her past. Vulnerable, that was the word she'd used earlier that day in Trudy's jungle.

"There might not be anything in it," Josh remarked carefully, regarding Jessie with a mixture of concern and realism. "Or you might not like what's in it."

"I can handle it," she said as she raised her chin stubbornly.

"Yes, I'm sure you can, Jess. But I'm there with you, okay? No more of this lone ranger shit. No more going rogue."

It irked her to hear him speak that way. Between Josh and Trudy…yeesh. And in the back of her mind, Deirdre and Charles Keating, too. Everybody was asking Jessie to suddenly be someone she was not. After so many years of being alone, of keeping everyone at arm's length, it was not easy having to share so much of herself.

Sensing the sudden spike in her blood pressure, Josh backed off. He knew it would take some time. Jessie pulled her hand away and ran a finger over her bottom and then top lips. She gripped her hands together in her lap while he watched her, curious. There were still things to learn about this new Jessie, the damaged one who ran away when things got tough.

On the deck rail, Josh's iPhone started to play the Red Hot Chili Peppers' tune *Under the Bridge* that singer Anthony Kiedis wrote about shooting up alone in L.A. It was Josh's reminder of the old days when what he called the *Black Death* ran his life. It was his reminder not to go back to those dark days. He grabbed the phone before its vibrations tumbled it off into the grass or smashed it on the deck at his feet.

"Yo!" he hollered, a wide grin lighting up his face after he spied the caller I.D. He glanced at Jessie, whose palpable annoyance disappeared after he mouthed *Steve.*

Jessie leaned in so she could hear.

"Got news," came Steve's voice from across the country.

"You got the part!" exclaimed Josh, a blaze of jealousy rolling through his belly, but he pushed it away.

"Damn straight! It starts in three weeks. In L.A."

Frowning, Jessie couldn't hide her mixed feelings. She leaned back and started chewing on a fingernail, a habit she rarely resorted to. In front of her, the magical picture show that entertained centuries of people before the technological revolution—the sunset—was ending. A blue-black darkness was settling over them, although the patio lights were warm and cozy despite their constant attraction of fuzzy miller moths and pesky mosquitos. Steve getting a part in L.A.—on a series, no less, which meant at the minimum likely six months of shooting—would result in a household move. He was a good friend to her and Josh. She didn't relish more changes, although she was happy for him.

"Is Sophie going with you?" Josh was asking. Jessie could hear the mixed emotion in his voice, as well.

"Hell, yeah! Her writing's working for her these days. With my paycheck she can let go of the day job and work from home. In fact…get your tux out. We're tying the knot at Christmas."

"Crazy bastard," Josh teased, laughing and reaching once again for Jessie's hand. At this early juncture in their reunion he and Jessie had yet to set a wedding date. Jessie was trying to smile at him but she had tucked a foot up onto the Adirondack chair and was scrunching up into herself so that she looked small and afraid. He noticed, and softened. "Congrats, Steve. That rocks. Hey," he said into the phone. "Why don't you tell Jessie?"

He handed her the phone and watched as she expressed happiness for their friends. Seemed life was still too unknown for her and Josh at this point—they'd lost so much time. Things were so different. Yet…she was trying to lighten up, for Steve's sake. Josh laid a hand on her thigh and rubbed gently.

"Steve, what are Josh and I supposed to do without you guys? You can't go to L.A.! You're killing me."

"Hey, little girl," Steve said kindly, and she could practically see the grin on the end of its thin red thread across the country, the one that unified the old friends and would continue to do so until eternity, and then some. "You and Josh will come visit, we'll visit, and some day we'll all work together again."

"Yeah," she said. Then she rallied. "I really am happy for you, Steve. It's all coming together for you guys now."

"For you guys too, eh?" Jessie could hear the question in his voice. Everybody would be wondering how she and Josh were doing in this early stage of hope and renewal.

"It's good," she said, but she didn't look at Josh and, sitting beside her in the increasing blue twilight, Josh felt his heart hurt. "Started counseling. It sucks. I hate it."

They talked for a bit and then Steve put Sophie on the line. Jessie brightened up when they started discussing dresses. She thought about sharing ideas about her own upcoming nuptials but this was Sophie's day—there would be time for her and Josh later. They chatted for a bit about their friends—Maggie, Sue-Lyn and Carter, and Charlie and Jane, who were preparing for a new baby to enter their lives. They discussed life in Vancouver and some general entertainment biz gossip. Just as the girls were about to sign off, Steve came back on the phone.

"Hey," Jessie said, missing him and the comforting loving friendship that reverberated throughout his voice. "I'll put Josh back on the line."

"Hey wait," he called to her, hoping he would catch her before she passed the phone back over. "One more bit of news."

"Spill it, Stevie."

"Up for a visit?" In Vancouver, he was winking at Sophie, who was grinning effusively.

Jessie sat up straight and fast. "Yes!" she squealed. "When?!"

By turns startled and then curious, Josh stared at her.

When she hung up, the old Jessie was back. She jumped into Josh's lap and hugged him tight. "They're coming to the island! They'll be here in a week! I can't wait!" Happily, she snuggled into his neck.

It would be good to see Sophie and Steve. They would go kayaking, build more sandcastles, maybe even do some wedding shopping. Things would feel a little more *normal* for a while. Maybe they would have a bonfire on the beach, go out to dinner, to brunch. Maybe Jessie would set counseling aside while they were here, because who wants to go through that shit while your friends are visiting?

After a while, Josh stood and pulled Jessie up with him. "C'mon little one," he whispered into her neck as she yawned and stretched. "Time for bed."

As they puttered around the deck ensuring the barbecue was off and that everything was secure in case a big island wind came up, he asked her if she had any more thoughts about their own wedding.

"Soon," was all she said, but she was smiling, and Josh felt himself relax a little. Frankly, he would marry her tomorrow if he could arrange it, the heck with fancy dresses and tuxes and even friends and family. He just wanted her. Jessie looked up at him as she grabbed a handful of shells from where she'd dropped them after an earlier beach walk, and laid them out one by one on the rail, lined up like soldiers. "Josh," she said, half serious, "you might decide you don't want me any more after all this therapy bullshit."

The fire in her eyes faded a little.

*Jesus, is she serious?* Josh was shocked that the thought would even cross Jessie's mind.

"Let me show you how much I want you, Jessie," he said, tenderly scooping her up in his arms. "Come with me." She shrieked with delight as he carried her up the stairs to their bedroom, where the perpetual whhhfff-ttsss of the ceaseless ocean waves coming home cradled them and rocked them to sleep after they shared some sweet touching and loving. As she drifted off, Jessie murmured his name one last time that day.

"Josh."

"Yeah?" He slipped a hand onto her thigh and rested it there.

"I do love you. We'll set a date soon, okay?"

"Okay. I love you back. Get some sleep."

She tucked their light summer quilt up around his hips and brushed a hand through his hair, letting the backs of her fingers rest on his cheek. They peered into each other's eyes until a heavy fatigue won the battle. They were so tired from the expansive day that they slept without moving until dawn encroached upon them, bringing with it yet another searing nightmare.

Now, this day, as they cruised slowly along behind the farm tractor and its load of hay, they were both in good moods despite the omnipresent nightmare induced fatigue that haunted them with dark shadows of the past, hovering and taunting. They were on their way to the hill where Jessie's father's car had turned and rolled over and over until it landed upside down in the river below. This summer marked twenty years since his passing, and it was time to share him with Josh. Eventually they found the spot. It was marked by a faded old truck half buried by decayed straw and manure in a nearby farmyard that once enjoyed the company of Holsteins, horses, and a motley selection of orange and gray-striped farm cats. Now the farm was as vacant as the truck, whose cab was empty and lifeless, its windows long since shattered and gone, the bed of the truck behind it now disappearing into the earth.

The hill that David Wheeler last saw as he careened over and over, wondering frantically where this journey would end, was spotted with wildflowers—forget-me-nots, mostly. To Jessie, their little blue and white flowers and yellow center were a message from beyond; from a universe or dimension most people on earth have yet to understand. Dense lush grass welcomed them as well, the tips starting to crisp and brown in the heat as Jessie and Josh walked hand in hand down to the water's edge. Two blue herons protested—or perhaps welcomed them, only the great birds knew—as they spread their mighty wings and vacated partially hidden branches in great Maples bordering the river's edge. Skimming the water was swamp grass and stale, barely moving surface dirt peppered by the occasional sprightly water bug gliding across the surface, long legs and tiny body spiderlike, its purpose as mysterious and necessary as the algae and shellfish living their unhurried lives below. A musty damp heat tickled their noses, and somewhere nearby a juniper bush was in flower, its sweet perfumed fragrance a perfect complement to the comforting chirping birdsong of tiny-bodied winged beings.

Vaguely Jessie wondered how much damage besides the obvious was done to the watershed environment the day her father died. You can't launch a car with all its oil and gas and various lubed up parts into such a pristine life force and not create devastating havoc amongst the flowing water grasses and sedate marine creatures. Yet here today there seemed no evidence of the horror of that terrible day, the trauma that spiraled Jessie and her mother downward into solitary lives and difficult choices and, if you asked Trudy, dissociative behaviors.

Narrowing her eyes and focusing her stare towards the sunlit sandy bottom, Jessie could see that the water in this part of the Southwest River was only about four feet deep. Deep enough to drown her father, apparently, as disoriented as he would have been on that dark day after his fateful tumble down the pretty hill. Jessie wondered if he'd thought of her as he struggled for a pocket of air, or to release a stuck seatbelt. For certain he thought of her now, she felt. Songs maybe came from him still...they seemed channeled from somewhere, at least.

Josh broke into her serious reverie. "Hey, Jessie," he said. "This is a beautiful place. This hill. The river." He pulled her towards him and wrapped both arms lovingly around her neck.

Above them the herons flew in wide circles, followed by some frisky blue jays. Everywhere in nature there were twosomes. It was inspiring, another message from beyond. Closing her eyes, Jessie agreed with Josh. She breathed him in and cherished the moment. He was everything to her, as David had been to her mother. She let go of a little more of the torment that haunted her from the day her mother withdrew from society, from her, from *protecting* her when she was twelve from a man who terrified and still haunted her. Yes, if Jessie lost Josh permanently she, too, would lose her mind just as quickly, no doubt. Recognizing this reaffirmed her belief that the choices she had made in the last few years were the right ones. Her mother had not shielded her when she needed protection, but Jessie had made decisions intended to keep Josh safe. In the end, was she successful? On some level, at least. Entirely? No, as evidenced from the scar he would wear on his side forever. But he was here, with her now, and she was grateful.

They waded through the stagnant August heat back up the hill a ways, in bare feet, clinging to their flip flops with one hand and each other's fingertips with the other. They turned and sat and watched the river while tourists hauling campers sped behind them on their way from the Confederation Bridge to the Cavendish tourist district and its many campgrounds, shops, restaurants, and family activities, oblivious to the fact that two well known actors were reclining below them, nestled amongst wildflowers and serenaded by nature.

After a time Josh pulled Jessie to her feet and led her back to their car, which they'd left parked alongside the road on the sandy shoulder.

"Do you want to come to Charlottetown with me, Jess? Or do you want to just go home and soak up some sun?"

She frowned and pulled her dress away from her glistening skin. "I'm melting," she complained. "Drop me off at the house and I'll just go for a swim or something."

Wishing he could soak and sunbathe with her, Josh accepted the fact that he had committed to therapy. Still, he was lamenting the film opportunity still being offered to him that Hilary felt obliged to tell him about in an email yesterday. The producers had upped their offer and were awaiting a response. Josh hadn't had the heart to turn it down flat. Something in his gut had him write a brief note back to Hilary—*give me a few days.* Now though, at the sight of Jessie sitting reflectively next to him in the SUV with wispy wet tendrils of sweat soaked hair clinging to her forehead, he told himself where his priorities lay and he pushed the film offer aside.

The SUV teetered a little on its way down the long driveway to the farmhouse, its tires balancing on a dried trail of sun-hardened red clay. Josh swung the car in front of the verandah and jumped out, leaving the vehicle running as he whipped open the passenger door and hoisted Jessie to the ground. He stood in front of her and wiped the sweaty locks away from her forehead.

"I'll see you in a few hours. Don't go out too deep. You know what they say about riptides around here on the north shore."

"Yeah, yeah, I know, and if I get caught in one, swim sideways until I am out of it."

"And wear sunscreen. Re-apply every twenty minutes. Roll over occasionally."

Running both hands through his layered hair as she faced him, Jessie chided him. "And don't talk to strangers, and look both sides when crossing the street." She kissed him and asked the universe to freeze the tender moment in her memory because within the hour he would be sitting in Trudy's jungle office being asked to recall some really bad times that Jessie wished he could just let go of once and for all. And as sweaty and unkempt as she felt right now under the blazing sun, the thought of what Josh would learn about her and feel about her in the next few months completely unhinged her, making her physically sick with worry.

He let her go with one last big squeeze and a fond, "I am so in love with you, Jessie Wheeler."

In her opinion the statement felt bittersweet as she leaned against the doorframe of the house, the flimsy wooden framed screen door in one hand, one foot on the inside and the other firmly planted on the verandah. Gazing after the SUV as it puttered back down the quaint country lane, she heard the Chili Peppers blaring from the speakers and saw a strong forearm jut out from the open window to wave goodbye. Silently, she wished her man well.

A short time later, while Jessie was soaking in the refreshing Gulf, contemplating the inherent messages nestled in the shapes of the clouds spotting the blue sky above, Josh was asking Trudy for a miracle.

He sat uncomfortably amongst her ferns and orchids, a thin line of sweat dripping down his own cheek, praying for air conditioning but knowing that, in this steamy tropical world his therapist had created, it was unlikely the house was equipped with such an amenity. He asked just how much he was allowed to know about Jessie's stalker and her experience with him.

Trudy regarded him carefully, her head back and knees crossed, the sunflower notebook almost sliding off her lap. The question caught her off guard.

"Why do you want to know?" she queried him, thoughtfully. It wasn't unusual for a spouse or partner to feel a need to know the intricate details of a violent sexual assault. But often it was a couple's undoing.

Josh was having a hard time sitting still. Between the oppressive heat and the battle with his conscience over what he felt he should and should not know about Jessie's past struggles, he was antsy and off balance. And he couldn't get the image of Jessie alone at their beach out of his mind. Too many locals had warned them about riptides, and she just seemed so distant and inattentive these days…

"The not knowing is driving me crazy," he responded with a firmness he hoped would allow Trudy to see past his dilemma. He knew this admission would hurt Jessie. He knew she would put another barrier between them—self-preservation. But he also felt that they, as a couple planning a future together, had to clear all of the dragons out of their collective caves. "Trudy, the thing is…I lie awake and watch her sleep sometimes and she seems so peaceful—like a child. And my imagination takes over and I see some big man forcing himself on her as a little girl…and then this Deuce McCall…what he did to her is inexcusable. Disgusting, twisted…my imagination goes overboard and I feel like if I knew the truth then I could stop inventing things that he may have done or not done to her. Jessie is my life. Even when she wasn't physically a part of it, she was still everything to me. Sometimes I thought I could feel her pain even when I had no idea where she was or what she was doing. She would just pop into my head and I felt like I could feel her crying out for help, begging for mercy. It damn near killed me. I thought…I thought I was going crazy. Now, I just want to know, once and for all. How bad was it, and is she really going to be okay? Are we going to be okay?"

He stopped shifting in his seat then, and Trudy uncrossed her legs and spoke candidly, pushing the reading glasses further up her nose.

"Josh, there is no question in my mind that you love Jessie deeply. But you might want to consider that there are some things about her that will take a great deal of patience to uncover, to adjust to, to accept. She's not your typical child sexual abuse survivor, she has other traumas to get past as well, mostly as a result of who she has become in the eyes of her fans, of the people who appreciate her music, her acting. Actually," she grabbed the notebook as it started to slip off her knees, "let me rephrase that. In some ways she is very typical. She's distant, aloof, and dissociative. She thinks, like many of these women do, that the past is the past and that she has it all under control. But she suffers the nightmares, the triggers, panic attacks. Depression. Same as many others. And she has to face a world that now knows what she's been through, what the two of you have been through. It's a whole new level of pressure. Why else are the two of you hiding out here, on our small island?"

Josh nodded glumly, and looked down at his hands. He rubbed them over his jeans to dry them off a little. Between his nerves and the hot day, and Trudy's stubborn insistence on installing a jungle in her home…ahhh. He was just feeling cranky, uptight.

Trudy continued, her voice gently encouraging over the diminutive nearby tumbling waterfalls. She leaned forward so as to express her point more firmly. "Honey," she started, "you'll be opening a Pandora's box by asking her to reveal more than what she's already felt safe to tell you. And frankly, I don't know if she'll open up more at all. She's been hiding inside herself for so long that I'm actually amazed she's managed to establish the deep friendships she has. You included. And that's saying a lot, Josh. Many of these deeply traumatized women have a very difficult time adjusting to any kind of normalcy when it comes to relationships. This is saying a lot for you, for all of your group of friends, that she's let any of you in on any level."

She sat back as Josh took this in. He looked up at her defensively. "She's stronger than you think."

"Yes, Josh, but Jessie has already revealed that she has a breaking point. That when the world comes in too close she sees no choice but to disappear. To reinvent herself. I'm afraid that at this early stage in her therapy—and yours too, don't forget—that pushing her too hard too fast might not garner the results you want."

"Not want," he said in a small voice. "Need. I need to know, Trudy. I need to know so that I can let it go. I keep looking at her…and wondering…it's killing me."

"You do realize that you can't just find out more of this darkness and expect that it's the light you will need to make it go away. By virtue of knowing, the bad stuff will not just disappear. It will climb inside you and haunt you in a completely different way. It'll get inside your bones." She needed to be completely certain that Josh could handle this direction he wanted to go in. He would have to be strong enough for both himself and Jessie. For there could be no doubt that opening this can of worms would be the darkest hole they had been in yet, as a couple.

"I know," he said quietly. "I've thought a lot about this. And I have to admit, I don't know where this is going to end up, but I do know one thing. We've got to let it go, somehow. We've got to set it free so we can move on. I want the old Jessie back."

Trudy paused then and studied him. Josh was a man who she knew had fought his own tough battles long before Jessie and her own version of light and then dark entered his life. He was a survivor. He sat before her today, struggling to stay calm and collected—as most people did when they came to see her for therapy—when in fact he was tormented and in pain. One of the hardest things a person could be asked to do in this life was to watch a loved one suffer, and he did this every day, setting his own needs aside for Jessie. The lack of a good night's sleep was showing—dark circles etched themselves wearily over the tiny wrinkles underneath his eyes. He was edgy, anxious. His liquid brown eyes were intense, sad. He constantly moved his hands up to his face to absently run them through his hair, he wiped them on his lap, he leaned on one elbow and agitatedly brushed his lips with his fingers. He fidgeted. Like many of Trudy's patients, he had a quiet desperation about him. His body language was screaming *I love this woman, please please help us.* But he was also crying *I pray it's not too late.*

Trudy tried another tack. "Josh," she started. "You've been back with Jessie for a short time now. Tell me about her and this 'second time around' relationship. Obviously she's been through hell. *Is* she still the same old Jessie?"

That startled him. He stopped moving altogether and froze. He blinked at Trudy a few times before finally sighing and sitting up straighter in his wicker chair. The fidgeting ceased.

"Ouch," he said. "That hurts."

"Why?" she asked softly, gently prodding.

"Well, because," he answered, his words edged with annoyance. "Of course she's not." His eyes flickered, his own inner struggle climbing its way to the surface, beseeching Trudy. *Please help me understand. Please help me get through this. Please help me get my old girl back.*

"How so?"

His voice was a whisper. "She's so distant. Like she's only half there. An outline."

Trudy waited.

"She's often somewhere else…in her head." He waved an arm as if to give more depth to his thoughts.

"Where do you think her mind is?"

"Writing songs? I don't know."

"What about…" Trudy waited for Josh to finish the sentence, which he did, quickly. His mind was already there.

"McCall? Maybe. I think I can tell when she is thinking about him. Her eyes cloud over and she wraps her arms around herself."

"And?"

"Well, I think she thinks about Jacob too, actually." It hurt to say his name. In some ways Jacob was a hell of a lot more of a threat than Deuce the fuck McCall. Josh swallowed painfully and struggled to remain in control. *Jesus, this is hard.*

"She misses him."

"Hell, yeah. I mean, she doesn't say it out loud but it's obvious. She plinks away at the guitar and she gets this faraway look in her eyes…they played a lot of music together. They wrote songs together."

"And that's something you don't have with her."

"She's more than just music."

"But it's a big part of her."

"The biggest…actually…" There it was, a truth Josh had long known but never wanted to admit. But something about Trudy's encouraging demeanor, and maybe these fucking plants and the trickling water made the place feel safe. So he let go of one of the truths that haunted him while he lay awake and watched Jessie try to sleep.

"She's with you. That's a choice she made."

"Yes, but..."

Again, Trudy exercised her right to wait. These things took time.

Josh shifted again as he fought for the words. He stared at the floor for a second but Trudy knew he was seeing far beyond the dust balls floating on the hot stiff air towards her hardwood.

"Look, I know she loves me, but she's definitely not the same old Jessie. But the thing is, I'm not the same old Josh, either. We've both been sucked dry from all this Deuce McCall bullshit and although I know we're damn lucky to still be here on this earth, together, in whatever way, shape or form we can be considered together these days, well all I can say is that we've both been changed by all of this. For one thing, yes she misses Jacob but guess what, I was in another relationship too, one that felt a hell of a lot more normal than being with someone who wakes up screaming, and who is pulling away from everyone around her. She doesn't want to do film anymore, at least not now, and she doesn't want to perform, either. Or record. She hasn't set a wedding date, she wanders the house and gazes in all the rooms and then when I speak to her it's as if I've woken her up. And the thing is, I've got this...I've got this..." He hesitated then, and bit his knuckles as if he knew he'd gone too far and said too much.

"What, Josh?" Trudy probed cautiously.

"I've got this...offer...to do a film...in the States. Virginia, actually, and I kind of want to do it. I keep telling myself it's wrong to want it, and in my heart I know I need to be here with Jessie, but sometimes it's so fucking hard...to be with her...you know?"

He closed his eyes then and Trudy's own heart ached for this young couple that, like many she had seen before them, were so deeply buried in dark clouds you wondered if they would ever again see the sun. With a twinge she thought of her own dead and buried relationship with Frank, and she wondered how any relationship that was originally founded on joy and love and trust ever managed to survive this thing called life.

"All right," she said. "We've got some work to do here, Josh, and I think you know as well as I do that it's not going to be easy." She paused and pulled off the reading glasses. She shoved them on top of her head where they took on a new role as a hair accessory, and then she regarded Josh carefully, contemplating how far she should encourage him on this first real day getting to know him. "Let me ask you one more question. The woman you were seeing, is it Michelle?"

He nodded, his defenses instantly mounting. "Yeah."

"Are you in touch with her at all?"

This time he shook his head. "No. That would be suicide, in more ways than one."

Trudy raised her eyebrows. "Oh?"

"It's too soon. I had a future planned with her...we were living together. We were going to get married. We were planning a family."

Trudy paused. "Aren't those the same things you are planning with Jessie?"

Josh bit his lip. He actually felt tears threatening, which surprised him. Again, his voice was low, concentrated, husky. "Yeah," he said. "But why does it feel so fucking much harder?"

Trudy swallowed her own pain then, for she could not counsel couples and walk abused women through therapy without feeling their great hurts too. She wrapped her fingers around the sunflower notebook, which she had not written one word in—she really only used it to have something tangible to hold on to—and she squeezed tight. Then she looked up and answered her client as honestly as she could. "Because," she said, "the great loves are the hardest, Josh. They run the deepest on both ends of the spectrum. The highs are higher and the lows are lower. You are challenged with finding the highs again, or the mediums, even. Somewhere in that hurt scared woman you love is the same Jessie who pulled you out of garbage and believed in you. We just have to find her again. And then—trust me, because I can see it in your eyes, and hers—things will become easier. And richer, and truer, and you will cherish every moment you have together because of the hell you've both endured. You will live life on a deeper plane, my friend. One that is all the richer for having known what you've lost."

Josh paused and chewed a fingernail before responding. "Why do I feel like you've been there?"

Smiling, Trudy rose, effectively ending their session. She reached out and took Josh's hand in hers and held it for just a moment. "Maybe I have," she said, and left it at that. She couldn't tell him that her own Camelot had faded into the past, that her own magical days of love and joy were now just bittersweet memories.

"You'll be fine," she encouraged with a whisper, although she had no idea where that thought came from, just that it entered her head on a whim.

On the drive back to South Rustico, the Chili Peppers at a much lower volume than during the drive into Charlottetown, Josh was reflective and cautious in his thinking. In closing, Trudy had asked him to bring Jessie in tomorrow. They would ask her about sharing some of the more intimate details of her experiences with Deuce. *In that safe environment,* he thought, *maybe she will talk.* Although in truth, Josh had his doubts. When he was alone, without Jessie by his side, he had a lot of doubts, in fact. He loved her deeply, but he had to admit that maybe, sometimes, love was not enough.

# Chapter Six

The next day, Jessie walked out of Trudy's office. She stormed out, in fact.

Josh found her waiting by the SUV, pure and utter disgust peppering her suntanned cheeks and spotting her pearl-blue eyes with unshed tears. She had her arms crossed as she leaned against the driver's side door, fiercely trying to find the words.

"How dare you?" she growled as Josh drew nearer, the keys jangling from his right hand.

He stopped five feet away, cocked his head to the side and scratched his head.

Jessie's heart was pounding. Eyes sweeping over him, her heart leapt. He was still the Josh she loved deeply, and the way he stood there in a white V-neck T-shirt and faded jeans, with one ankle turned over on its side, a look of consternation on his face, was more than she could handle. She wanted to go to him, pull on the T-shirt so that he would draw closer, nuzzle in his chest and have him wrap his strong arms around her. She wanted him to whisper that he was sorry, that it was a stupid idea, that it would be creating demons out of some smoky mist that she hoped had passed them by on its dark journey to the underworld.

"Jessie, I just want to understand, that's all," he said, unmoving.

"Understand what?" she cried. "Why can't you just let it go?"

"I want to know what that freak did to you! God Jessie, sometimes I touch you and you pull away! Did you know that? Are you even aware of that? I need to know if there are triggers there, in *our* lovemaking, when *we* make love, that remind you of him! Are there areas I need to be avoiding when I touch you?"

She turned away from him and toed the ground with her flip-flop.

"Don't do that!" He raised his voice, which was something Josh rarely did with her. But this behavior—her avoidance—really pissed him off and pulled his own short fuse, which was exacerbated by severe sleep deprivation.

Jessie stamped around the SUV and climbed inside. She leaned back against the headrest and closed her eyes, put both hands on her lap and drove one set of nails into the back of the other hand. "Take me home," she snarled menacingly. "Take me the fuck home!"

Even without hearing her, Josh knew what Jessie wanted. A fleeting thought of Michelle's smiling dimpled face crossed his mind, and he chided himself for aching for some kind of normalcy, with chicken dinners and movies and happiness and none of this torturous game-playing avoidance bullshit.

He yanked open the driver's side door and jumped into the car, put the keys in the ignition and skidded out of Trudy's driveway, barely missing an oncoming car rolling down the street in the sleepy subdivision. Even that wasn't enough to bring Jessie out of her funk, though. She turned her head towards the window and fought tears all the way back to South Rustico, and Josh cranked the air conditioning and the tunes and elapsed into his own sulk.

At home, Jessie ran up the wooden steps, cranked open the screen door, let it clang shut obnoxiously and loudly behind her, and headed straight to bed, even though it was hot as hades. She'd been to hell already, what was an afternoon slumber in the heat? She was in the mood for self-torture anyway. The physical pain was less than the psychological at this point.

Josh paddled a kayak around in the bay for an hour and when he got back he was saddened to see that Jessie was sound asleep, still in her tank top and shorts, bare toes peeking out from beneath a light coverlet, head facing away from the door and arms wrapped around a soft pillow. He closed the door and let her be.

Later, Steve called to confirm plans for their trip to the island. Josh warned him that things were heating up in therapy.

"I'm glad you guys are going to be here for a while but I have to tell you, this is hell right now. She's not even talking to me as we speak." He rubbed his temple with his thumb and forefinger. He was sitting on the deck below the bedroom. Unbeknownst to him, Jessie was now awake. She could hear his every word. There was no breeze on that hot day to carry the sting of his truths away to the ether.

"Some days I don't know about all this," he was saying. "Steve, I'm getting calls every day about the film. The producers are calling me."

Jessie slipped off the bed and sat against the wall underneath the window.

"No, damnit, of course I don't want to leave her. But what the hell's the point of therapy if it's one-sided? She has to at least want to try; otherwise I'm on my own here. And out there—well, the world is passing me by."

Upstairs, Jessie brought both hands up to her face and dug her nails into her forehead. Then she got up and went off to the nearby washroom, struggling to contain a new fear, unable to look at herself in the mirror as she passed by. She couldn't stand to hear anymore. She'd heard enough.

On the deck downstairs, Josh ended his call with Steve and listened to the ocean tell its tale of heartbreak and woe, earned over centuries of other lovers' lives. He didn't go up to bed until midnight and, when he finally crawled in next to Jessie, he lay awake for hours, lonely and missing Michelle.

Next to him, Jessie's tears had long since dried but her breathing was uneven. She was awake, and missing Jacob's earnest songwriting and passionate lovemaking. When Josh touched her, yes, there were triggers, but she could see in his chocolate eyes that he was afraid. So what if he was telling the truth, and by getting to the bottom of Deuce's abuse, Josh could work around that? It would still never be the same. Jacob was intense, and he'd met Jessie after the stalking and forced confinements of that awful summer. He and Jessie had established a pattern of lovemaking based on a character Jessie created, one that hid those deep hurts that Josh recognized and suffered from in his own way.

It was a long night. When the sun came up, Jessie was downstairs emailing Jacob. Josh slept fitfully until eight o'clock, finally wakened by the mourning dove singing its plaintive song outside his window. He found Jessie seated at the kitchen island nibbling on blueberries soaked in yogurt and coated with granola. He walked around behind her and wrapped both strong arms around her shoulders. Laying his head on her back, he whispered her name.

"Jessie," he murmured, and she let the spoon sink to the counter with a tiny tinkle. Wrapping her fingers around his, she closed her eyes and soaked up the feel of his warm body against hers. After a few minutes, Josh kissed her cheek and then let her go. He sidled over to the fridge, eyeing her warily, and grabbed the orange juice.

"Kayak ride?" he asked.

"Yup. Okay," she answered as she picked up her spoon.

And they got another sunny summer day underway.

# Chapter Seven

Feeling rather uncharacteristically voyeuristic, Trudy had watched the brief interaction in her driveway when her celebrity client decided she'd had enough and ended their afternoon couples' session with a death ray stare and the slamming of the side door. Disheartened, although she knew Josh's request for intimate information would not go over well, given Jessie's very clear refusal to open up, period, Trudy busied herself by popping a Keurig English Breakfast Tea into the machine and releasing her frustration to the only creature within sight who she knew would listen.

"Oliver, I don't know why I agreed to this. All I really want to do is write my book in peace, drink tea, or maybe a latte if I need some self-torture, and go for runs. She's a child, that girl. Over thirty years old and she reminds me of a spoiled child."

She grabbed an antique porcelain teacup off a hook underneath the oak cupboard and whipped around to face the cat, who yawned indifferently from his coiled up perch on a nearby café chair. She softened. "I know, you're right. I am the professional here. I am the therapist. But I've been doing this for a long time, Ollie, and I'm tired. Hell, add to her problems the fact that love is practically impossible to sustain at the best of times, don't you think? At least, in my experience it is. And you've got me, the biggest non-believer on the planet, trying to tell them there's hope? Oliver, the chips are stacked up so high against these two that I can't even see my way through to the other side."

A wave of guilt washed over Trudy. She'd told Josh that she felt he and Jessie could make it. What business did she have doing that? She was a failure at relationships, and maybe at therapy too. Yes, she had helped a lot of people over the years, but some had not been able to escape their demons. There were suicides, marriage break-ups, and debilitating depressions. Somehow on this day, recalling Jessie's angry eyes, that was all Trudy could focus on. The failures.

Sipping her hot tea as Oliver got bored and settled his furry white chin on a soft paw for another round of mousey dreams, she was drawn out of her nose diving mood by the ring of her cell phone. It beckoned her back into the sunny office where the phone lay vibrating impatiently underneath a mature sprawling African Violet on her teacher's desk in the far corner. She grabbed it hastily, thinking it might be Josh wanting to continue the session.

"Hello?" she inquired, almost too eagerly.

A male voice greeted her, but it was slightly higher-pitched than she expected. It was a voice of calm, which Trudy needed at the moment despite the volatile history she and the man on the other end shared over the past few years.

"Trudy," Frank tossed out comfortably, "how's life on the east coast? I hope you're getting out for fresh lobster on a regular basis."

They used to do that a lot in the summertime on Prince Edward Island. The tiny province was a mecca for fresh seafood. Now, in late summer, you could buy the luscious lobster right off the boats when they chugged in off the north shore. A plethora of restaurants also opened up seasonally to cater to the high tourist demand for quality dining. With professional theatre and musical productions to choose from, tip to tip, east to west and back again, restaurants, outdoor activities, camping, sailing, swimming...well, there was no shortage of places to visit or things to do, and Trudy could well afford whatever her heart desired. But she was alone, if you didn't count the dozing feline on the chair in the kitchen. Her and Frank's divorce came with a slashing of their friends' list and a retreat into a safe haven—herself. So no, lobster was not generally on her list of social niceties this season. Nor was the famous Malpeque oyster, or quahogs or mussels. She felt a pang of regret and loss, which only intensified her frustration and confusion in working with Josh and Jessie.

She pictured Frank reclining on a sunny dais on the outdoor deck of his

Burnaby condo. In her mind there was a goblet of red wine in his hand, probably a full-bodied Shiraz, she figured.

"Hi, Frank," she said, and he knew her well enough to detect melancholy in his ex-wife's voice.

"What's up, Trudy?"

Plopping down on the Windsor chair behind the desk, Trudy fingered a nearby plant and sighed at the light layer of dust coating its leaves. She was cautious. No way was she going to reveal too much to the man who had destroyed her not all that long ago. "Just the usual," she said. "Trying to help a couple who, let's face it, Frank, don't necessarily want my help. Well, one maybe does but the other one doesn't. It's clear."

"Let me guess. Jessie's the tough nut to crack."

"Yep. Makes sense, really. Although I admit, I thought Josh would be a tough nut too. But he isn't. He wants to try, but his memories of a more normal relationship with someone reasonably healthy are getting in the way."

"It's early yet, Trudes. Give them some time. You know how this game is played."

"Yes, all too well." She couldn't keep sarcasm from edging her voice. "Maybe I am just tired of playing it." She took a long sip of tea and prepared for a lengthy chat with Frank by leaning back into the chair, nudging off her heels and placing her small feet up on the desk. "Are you being queried, Frank? Is that why you called?"

"No, not at all," he responded sincerely. "The Keatings are in touch with Jessie. They don't need reports from me."

"Well, if she talks to them the way she talks to me, then they aren't getting a very satisfactory update on her progress. Or they're reading between the lines and realizing she's still in trouble. Shit. Sorry. I'm saying too much."

"Let's talk about something else, then," Frank urged matter-of-factly.

Surprised, Trudy reacted with a shake of her head. *He wants to talk to me? Just…talk?* "Okay?"

"What's the weather doing there? I heard something about a heat wave on the radio."

*Ahhhh*, she thought. *Let's start safe. The weather.* It seemed like a good place to get reacquainted. Maybe there was hope in Camelot after all.

"It's bloody hot, all right. But you know what they say. After Old Home Week on the island, summer's over. And the climax to that, the big horse race, is this weekend."

They chatted a while longer, and Oliver the cat was surprised when he stalked into the jungle office at the laughter emanating from his mistress behind the corner desk. Even he could sense the easing of tension. He meowed for attention. He wanted to go outside and chase real mice, not dream mice. But for once, he had to wait.

# Chapter Eight

After their kayak ride, an ensuing swim and a simple lunch of mixed greens and fish cakes they'd purchased the weekend prior at the Charlottetown Farmers' Market, Josh drove Jessie down the country road to the seniors' home. She was glad to play guitar and entertain the residents for an hour, if only to get her mind off Josh's difficult request from the day before. Besides, he was hovering over her today, and she was tired of being treated like a fragile Faberge egg. She was cracked, yes, but not broken, at least in her own humble opinion.

After tucking her mother into bed for an afternoon nap, Jessie went down the hall to see George while Josh took the Gibson out to the car. She found the old man sitting in a deep plush wing-backed chair by the bright window in his tiny room. Around the room were photos of people who were obviously family and friends—black and white framed photos of children, a wedding picture, and…a picture of Jessie's father singing at a club gig in the early nineties.

A sharp intake of breath accompanied the realization that the man in the photo singing was her father. Jessie stared, tilting her head as if that action would bring her beloved dad further into focus. She had just left her mother's room. She wondered if Emily knew this photo was on George's wall and, if she did, was there ever a flicker of recognition? A patter of her heart? Any emotion at all? Also…Emily's walls and dresser were bare of images, of memories, of her past. There wasn't even a photo of Jessie present. Her dresser had a few small boxes for jewelry and odds and ends, that was all. Nothing Jessie recognized. And certainly no references to either her or to David Wheeler.

A thin trembly voice called Jessie back from her reverie. George was having an off day. He had not joined the others on the deck for music, even.

Jessie turned to see him sitting in the chair, almost encompassed by it, a threadbare afghan over his lap.

"Mizz Wheeler," he was saying. "Yes, that's your father. He was a good friend, you know. Not just a musician. He was the kind of guy who shoveled my wife's car out from underneath mountains of snow so that she could get to work. She was a nurse. She went to work for 6 a.m. I was an asshole of a husband who drank a lot of my stock at the bar. I wasn't much for early mornings." He added, "I don't think your Dad slept much."

"No," Jessie said remorsefully, remembering a dad who fell asleep in a nano-second when watching a movie with his daughter. "He didn't. He worried a lot, I think." She made her way to the single bed and perched tentatively on the edge of it, facing George.

"He had a wife and daughter to support?" He posed that thought as a question. Jessie caught the subtext and crooked her head at him.

"Are you telling me there were other things on his mind besides us? I mean, we didn't have much, but we were okay. We had a house, a car, food..."

Shrugging, George pulled the afghan up higher over his body, despite the overwhelming heat of the day. Leaning forward, Jessie frowned and tucked it underneath his armpits. She peered intently at him, narrowing her eyes.

"What?" she asked.

"Nah. It's nothing."

"George?"

He nodded towards a white banker's box sitting on the floor near the door. "My son brought that in yesterday. It belongs to you, Jessie."

She whipped her head around and stared at it, wondering what secrets lay inside, wondering when she would have the courage to look. Her heart quickened.

George spoke from behind her, his mind taking him back to the music and friendship of years gone by. "You look like him, you know. Your father."

Slowly, Jessie let herself turn back to the old man. He seemed not much more than a skeleton, encompassed by the big chair. "I remember that he was funny," she said. "He made us laugh a lot."

"He was, indeed," George agreed. He regarded critically the short sundress Jessie had donned for the trip to the nursing home. "He wouldn't like his daughter wearing that dress, though."

That comment earned a rare smile from Jessie. She blushed and looked down at the hem, which barely covered the top of her thighs. "Ah George, it's the trend these days. I'm just doing what everyone else is doing."

"Don't you get tired of that? Following the crowd?"

Nonchalantly she replied, "Sometimes." A vision of her fiery red and then lavender hair in Scotland in the Jacob days crossed her mind, and George took note as her spirits seemed to sink.

"What?" he prodded.

"Oh, it's just hard these days, is all," she shared, her own voice thin now. But it was almost as if she was desperate to talk to someone she could trust. Trudy was still new, a risk, and Josh was, well, still a stranger in some ways after all their time apart, after the way they had both changed…after what they'd suffered these last few years.

Compassionately, George leaned forward and laid a hand over Jessie's, which she was resting on the bed next to her. "I've heard your story, Jessie. I know that despite success your life has not been easy. But you're here on the island with a man who obviously loves you, you don't have to worry about money like your dad did, and you're healthy, right?"

"Yeah," she said, thinking that Trudy would likely not agree on that last point.

"If you've got your health, you've got everything. Trust me." He sat back.

Pondering the gorgeous lush scenery outside her unlikely friend's window, Jessie watched as a hummingbird vibrated so fast at an attached feeder that it appeared to be floating, some mystical force holding it up so it could get nourishment from the colored sugar-water within.

George continued. "Why are you so sad?"

Her shoulders sank as, in the hallway, Josh paused unseen outside the room.

"I'm just feeling a little lost, that's all," she responded tentatively. At his friendly encouragement, with her father looking over her shoulder, Jessie felt awash with feeling and a need to let go of some of the emotions threatening to overload her. "When I was going through all that shit—oops, sorry—all that difficult stuff, the stalker and then having to leave…well, feeling like I had no choice but to leave…well, all I could think about was Josh." She lifted a hand to her throat and fingered where the engagement ring hung for so long, a constant irrefutable reminder of what she had given up and what she'd wanted back. "Now it's like I have him back, and I'm grateful, every day I'm grateful, George. But it's like we're going down different paths now. We want different things. We've grown and changed, not all in good ways, especially in my case."

She looked up at the old man who was watching her so carefully, his eyes boring into her soul as he remembered a kind friend and father to this girl. He wondered what David would want him to say to her. But for now, he listened.

"He's asking me to give him something I don't feel like I can give. As if he thinks it will bring us closer together. But I feel like it will tear us apart, and we're only just barely hanging on as it is."

"And you think it's a deal breaker. If you don't give it to him."

He voiced the thing Jessie refused to even allow herself to think. In the hallway, Josh sank against the wall.

"Yeah," she whispered. "Maybe. I think so."

"Then give it to him and let the Heavens sort out what it will mean." George leaned forward and clasped her small hand again. "If there's one thing that life has taught me, that your father and Emily taught me, it's that love is worth hanging on to. And it's worth fighting for. I'm pretty sure the Heavens would agree."

Jessie smiled again, just a little. George reminded her of Katrine, another unlikely friend who wasn't afraid to tell it like it is.

"Do you love him?" he asked, waving a skeletal hand in the air to help make his point.

"Damn straight I do," she answered with a sigh. "More than anything, George."

"Then look at me. Come on, take a good look. What do you see?"

Jessie paused. "A life well lived."

He smiled, a toothless grin. She was a chip off the old David Wheeler block, no doubt about that. "What else? How about an old man whose life flew by in the blink of an eye? Who had love but who took it for granted which, by the way, was something your father never did."

"And my mother?"

"She didn't either, Jessie. But she suffered for love."

"What? What the hell's that supposed to mean?"

He gestured towards the box. "When you're ready, open that box. But maybe give yourself a little time to let this island heal you first, Mizz Wheeler. Because you will need some reserves of strength when you open it. Trust me."

Reflecting on this man and his secrets, Jessie sat on the edge of the bed and chewed her bottom lip thoughtfully before rising to tuck the blanket a little tighter underneath George's bony armpits. "Thanks, George. I like coming to see you. You are a fountain of wisdom, my friend."

"I'm a safe place to hide, Jessie. Open up to your fellow. He seems like a good sort. He'll understand."

She frowned and stood back, admiring the man for who he had been, and for his long ago friendship with her father. "I'll try. Bye, George." She bent and kissed his sallow cheek thoughtfully. "We'll talk again, okay?"

"Don't wait too long. I'm dying over here."

She grinned. "We're all dying, George."

"Some more imminently than others. Or haven't you noticed?" He looked at her skirt again. "Damn, I wish those skirts were in style in my day."

"Hey! I thought you didn't approve."

"Oh, I approve." He narrowed his eyes again. "Just not on you. David Wheeler's little girl."

Laughing, feeling lighter than she had in days, Jessie stooped carefully to pick up the banker's box, and then she gave a little wave to George and then to her dad in the photo on the way out. *David Wheeler's little girl.* Oh, how she loved the sound of that. By virtue of knowing George, suddenly she had some roots worth clinging to.

Exiting the room, she did not bump into Josh in the hallway. He'd left after her confession that things were not the same with them anymore. He felt the same way, but it hurt to hear Jessie voice it. She found him leaning against the SUV, one knee bent like Jacob used to do. Jacob…seemed like he was on Jessie's mind a lot lately. Too much…

Josh took the box from her arms and, without speaking, went around the vehicle to the driver's side, put the box behind the seat, and climbed in. He started the car and flipped up the air conditioning as Jessie slid in, looking up at him questioningly. It was a silent ride home, then Josh left the car running and climbed out. When Jessie set foot on their summer home driveway's dried red clay, she paused. At the door to the house, he finally spoke.

"You have half an hour," he said, his voice taut. "I trust you'll speed all the way to Trudy's."

She swallowed. Not that Jessie had forgotten the appointment. It was just that after yesterday she didn't much feel like going. *Fine,* she thought, as he disappeared inside. *Fuck you and the horse that brung you.*

She sauntered around the vehicle wishing she had the nerve to run inside for a pee break. But she had the feeling Josh was watching from the window. So she took the seat behind the wheel that he'd just vacated, and she cranked a hard left. At the end of the long driveway, though, she didn't turn left towards Charlottetown. Instead, Jessie swung to the right and headed towards Cavendish, the busy north shore resort area, the same direction from whence they had just come. The seniors' home was not far down the road from Cavendish, just west, in fact.

That was the first day since the day at the Frosty Treat that the local radio announcers started serious 'Jessie and Josh' alerts, which were kind of a lark for the locals but not so much fun for the visiting celebrities. But that was a thing that was done on P.E.I., alert the locals and tourists to visiting celebs. Sean Connery, Tom Cruise, Bonnie Raitt, Robin Williams, Ron Howard and Kevin Costner had all been spotted on the island over the years. Dion Phaneuf and Elisha Cuthbert were summer residents. Now Jessie and Josh were added to the list. After all, when a woman decides to go driving to kill time, eventually she needs to stop for gas and a pee. And so she is seen, and remarked upon. But people were kind. Apart from a few autographs and healing hugs from people who knew her story, she was left alone.

At home, Josh's cell rang a half hour after Jessie's scheduled appointment was to begin. He was marinating steaks for dinner, his heart a mess after hearing Jessie's confession to George, of all people, and after receiving yet another phone call from the producers courting him to do the upcoming film.

He recognized Trudy's number right away, and grabbed the phone hastily. What if Jessie had suffered a panic attack? Shit, she had their vehicle...

"Trudy?" he asked quickly, and the therapist almost regretted calling him. She could hear the panic in his voice.

"Josh," she said evenly, knowingly. "I don't suppose your intended is anywhere near you?"

He felt sick. "Fuck," he exclaimed under his breath, but Trudy got the jist of his expression anyway. "She didn't show up."

Pause. "No, honey. She didn't."

"Whatever," he said, shoving the dish with the steaks in it further back on the counter with a squeal as the glass dish protested its proximity to the ceramic countertop. "I don't need this shit."

Trudy was a voice in the wilderness. Her talk with Frank last night had opened her heart enough to want to continue on this strange journey. "Josh, this is not uncommon behavior for someone who is starting out on such a difficult passage in her life. Don't be too hard on her. That's not what she needs right now."

"What she needs is a good solid kick in the arse."

Despite herself, Trudy smiled. Although Josh's reputation was on the mend, he had been known for his temper, a temper that Trudy doubted really existed. She could not see the gentle soul she was getting to know ever raising any kind of a violent hand to Jessie.

"No, honey," she urged. "She needs love and hope and patience right now. You know that."

"All right. So what do you suggest I say to her when she gets brave enough to show her ugly mug back here?"

"When are your friends arriving?"

"Tomorrow."

"Then you're going to buy some time. Stick to safe neutral conversations and don't trigger her if you can help it. Enjoy the company of your friends, let the impact of yesterday's request sink in over time, and just love each other. Try to come in for your own sessions and let her decide whether to come in for hers or not. I'll try calling her too—I tried today but lo and behold, no surprise, she's not answering—but I'll keep on her all week and hope that she comes around. I'll hold her to it, make her accountable."

"Fine." She could hear the frustration in his voice.

"Josh?"

"What?"

"Let me be the heavy, okay?"

He was silent as he digested the impact of that request. He was already the heavy, and he knew it. "Okay."

Jessie rolled in at one thirty in the morning. Josh was pacing and ready to call the police when he heard the growl of distant music, first, and then the purring engine of the SUV as it rolled to a stop outside. He climbed into bed and feigned sleep. He was in a very bad mood and did not want to exacerbate things that night with a knock 'em down fight. But he was pissed.

The song on the SUV radio—John Lennon's *Imagine*—played itself to a soulful finish before Jessie turned off the vehicle and climbed out, the banker's box from George in her arms. She set it inside the door, where it sat untouched. Inside, she puttered around a bit, opening the fridge door and feeling her heart sink at the sight of a dinner plate, saran wrapped for preservation, awaiting her return. He had grilled steak for her, complete with mushrooms and onions and a baked potato. There was even a barbecued ear of corn cuddling up to the steak. *Shit,* she thought. *Damn.*

She settled herself in the computer nook and opened her email. Sleep was still not on her mind, although she stifled a few yawns here and there. Scrolling through her emails, she found a brief note from Jacob and her heart roared into life as the day's loneliness grabbed hold of her heart and gave it a sudden twist.

*Jacob.*

The note's brevity touched her heart more than its written message, for Jessie knew what was underneath. He was missing her too.

*Hey Jessie, just wanted to let you know that recording is going well. We're almost done and Charles is releasing a song in September. John Paul is here working on the album with me. Hope the east coast is being good to you. Jacob.*

She ran his name over her tongue. *Jacob. My musical soul mate.*

Jessie started to type.

Upstairs, Josh could hear the click click click of the keyboard. Every tap shattered his attempt at peace and tranquility. He had spent the entire late afternoon and evening wondering about her, worrying, fighting with his conscience and the desire to split to do the film in Virginia. It was late, the middle of the night in fact, and where was Jessie? Downstairs clack clack clacking on the damn computer. Each clack sent his blood pressure up another degree. He rolled out of bed in his striped cotton boxers and scratched his head as he padded softly down the stairs. He could see Jessie at the computer, hunched over the keyboard typing emphatically. Although it was wrong, his conscience screaming that he was only asking for trouble, he crept softly up behind her in his bare feet, close enough to read what she was writing, and—to whom.

*Jacob. She is writing to Jacob.* Although they never made any kind of pact or agreement, it was implied that neither Josh nor Jessie would make any overt attempt to contact their exes. But here she was, some distant Jessie who Josh did not know or understand, writing—*are those tears on her cheeks?*—to Jacob.

Josh focused his tired red-rimmed eyes on the text.

*It's just that I feel so far away from him these days...and he has this perverted need to know what kind of games Deuce McCall played with me. I don't want to go there. It's over and done. Jacob, I miss you. I miss writing music with you, I miss our inane conversations, I miss hanging out at the pub with you and John Paul and Katrine and Charlene, too. Tell them all I said hello. I'd invite all of you to the wedding but at this point I am just not even sure if there's going to be a wedding.*

She was further than that in her writing but by then Josh's eyes were filling up and he couldn't see any more of the written word coming from Jessie's mind through to her fingers. He moved, and she jumped when she caught his reflection in the laptop's screen.

Jessie whipped around and sat facing Josh, in complete and utter shock. His shoulders were slumped. There was something about seeing him that way, in his boxers and bare feet with very tired sad eyes that tore at her heart. Slowly, she screeched the chair backwards on the hardwood and rose to face him.

"Were you reading my email?" she mumbled with less confidence than she needed at this point.

He just stared at her. That was enough response.

"I—I went to the drive-in," she said. "The movies. A double bill. My dad used to take me there." She chuckled, just a little, a forced attempt at lightening the suddenly very dismal, dark mood. "I can't believe it's still open, actually, after all these years…" Her voice faded away.

"Jacob?" he finally asked, unbelieving. "Seriously, Jessie?"

She wanted to fade away into the pine floor, to hide, to disappear. But she had to face him.

"I just needed somebody to talk to. To vent to. That's all."

"Oh, so the old guy at the seniors' home wasn't enough?"

*Oh,* Jessie thought. *That explains Josh's mood from earlier today.* She pressed her lips together and raised her chin stubbornly.

He spoke again. "So…Trudy's not good enough?"

Jessie refused to answer, but from her sunken expression Josh knew Trudy's counsel was not an option for Jessie anytime in the near future.

"What the hell, Jessie?" he pleaded, fearing an explosion if his blood pressure shot any further upwards. He tried to contain himself. *I am not supposed to be the heavy,* he reminded himself, but at almost two in the morning, after Jessie's lengthy disappearance and then this email to Jacob, that request seemed entirely unreasonable, even futile. "Talk to me," he demanded angrily.

She let loose. "Talk to you? Talk to you? Okay, Josh. I'll talk."

"Well, that'll be a fucking miracle!"

She fired a speeding bullet from her eyes directly to his. "Okay, you asked for it, well here it is. You want to know what Deuce's little games were, well fine. But let me just say that things are already fucked up between us when it comes to the bedroom, Josh, because you are already holding back, and if you think knowing what Deuce did, what he demanded of me, is going to change that, then you're sorely mistaken. It's going to make you see me in a totally different light, and I'll bet you won't even be able to bring yourself to touch me anymore! So you want to know what it is about Jacob right now? Well, let me just tell you, Josh," she was spitting out his name now, "when I was with Jacob it was *after* Deuce McCall. And I was someone else. And so he had no idea about that disgusting part of my history, he had no idea who I really was, even. And so, that first night when I made love with him—and, by the way, Katrine was a pretty spectacular part of that, well—"

She halted suddenly to see if that startling revelation achieved the desired shocked effect. It did. The blood drained from Josh's face.

Jessie continued her rant, uncensored and completely unfiltered. She raised her chin further, defiant and desperate to hurt him in order to protect herself. "Well, let me just say it was the best fucking orgasm of my LIFE!"

She marched forward and pointed a finger dangerously close to his face. "And you know something else, Josh? Someone else who wasn't afraid to touch me the way you are? Your good friend Stephen, in fact. Also a very nice orgasm."

Josh managed a low "*Jesus,*" and then he was completely speechless. He wasn't stupid, he knew something intimate had transpired between Jessie and Stephen. And of course he knew she and Jacob had sex, hell, they were a couple for a while. But for her to spit out their names to him like this? And to cry out, with fire blazing from her eyes, that she had enjoyed fantastic orgasms with these guys? Orgasms that apparently he couldn't quite manage…well, he was terrified of hurting her, the whole Deuce-touch thing. That was why he needed to know. That was why. But maybe it was too late for them. The ghost of Deuce McCall still haunted them, hovering over them when they made love. And in all likelihood, knowing what Deuce had done to her could indeed just make things worse. Perhaps.

But for now, the aching sting of Jessie's reveals was doing its job. Josh couldn't speak, and as he shook his head from side to side in disgust and confused wonder, dumbfounded at her audacity and apparently limitless capacity to hurt him, he slowly wheeled around and headed back up the stairs to their bedroom.

Behind him, Jessie gasped and reached out for him, but one hand just floated there in the overheated oppressive still night air, its downward arc finding nothing, no Josh, no retrieval of those nasty words, no hope.

She sank to the floor as he disappeared above. Burying her face in her hands, Jessie finally let great heaving sobs consume her. *What have I done?*

*What have I said? God, I am stupid—stunned, even.* But she had to fire back. If she told him about McCall—well, then, things would likely disintegrate entirely. If they hadn't already.

In the morning Josh found Jessie asleep on the overstuffed white couch in the front sun porch. He tiptoed past her and took the SUV for the day. Spending a miserable day alone touring lonely country roads through patchwork farmland and quaint fishing villages in the eastern part of the province, he landed nervously home just before Steve and Sophie arrived in their rented Mazda at seven p.m. that evening, and somehow he and Jessie managed to be civil enough to host their friends for the week.

Until their second last night on P.E.I.

# Chapter Nine

Steve and Sophie were prepared. Their friends were adjusting to therapy and its inherent issues, but the Vancouver couple knew Josh and Jessie were both survivors. Steve's arrival injected humor and a sense of lightheartedness into a tough and inevitable situation. Sophie's quiet, wise demeanor was a bright light. Somehow their presence alone was enough to settle the volcano of the last week or so at least enough to allow for certain civility and social graces. As the pressure around them decreased, both Josh and Jessie were able to function on a level that, if not wholly outgoing and loving, was at least somewhat amenable.

They did love each other, and through the mist and haze of hurts and anger, on a base level they understood that. Throughout the week of meal preparations, touring, kayaking, dinners out and bicycle rides through beachside parklands, they managed to address each other cordially and occasionally lapse back into the casual touching and handholding of long-time couples. It was almost as if they pushed the nasty thoughts awakened by counseling aside, with the exception of the two days during the visit when Josh quietly said his goodbyes and drove into town to see Trudy for his scheduled sessions. Jessie just turned her head away on the days when Josh asked if she was going. After that he just quietly fumed and stayed out of it. He wanted to keep the peace as much as possible while Steve and Sophie were their guests.

Two nights before the end of the visit, the boys went outside to build a bonfire on the beach while the women cleaned up the dishes. Sophie had become a good friend to Jessie throughout the week, and the small blonde opened up a difficult conversation after watching Jessie stand at the kitchen window staring at the silhouetted figures outside who were dropping logs on a budding fire.

"Jessie, honey, you've dried that plate about six times." Smiling, she took the earthenware dinner plate from Jessie's hands.

"Oh," Jessie said, startled. "Sorry." She surrendered the dish to Sophie and then reached for a glass on the nearby wooden Ikea rack.

"Anything you want to talk about?" Sophie offered helpfully.

Jessie looked at the glass in her fingers. She concentrated on wiping a particular spot away. "Nah," she said. "Just the usual." A thought crossed her mind and she set the glass down on the counter with a small thud before regarding Sophie critically.

"I don't know what he's told you guys, but I know I'm not making this easy. I just don't know how to fix it, that's all. It's like no matter which way we go with this it's bound to explode in our faces."

"The Deuce stuff."

"Yeah, of course the Deuce stuff. But also just with us trying to get back on track. It's like...too much water under the bridge, you know?"

"Are you worried?"

Jessie looked wistfully down at her bare pink toes. "Hell, yeah."

Taking the towel from her hands, which Jessie had started twisting into a knot, Sophie rested an arm on the counter and faced her friend. "Don't be," she said reassuringly. "Just don't give up."

"Easier said than done." Jessie grabbed the towel back out of Sophie's hand and retrieved another dripping glass from the drying rack.

"No," Sophie said, a hint of anger coloring her singsong voice. "I don't accept that."

Eyeing her warily, Jessie intoned, "Sophie, I'm not giving up. I'm just saying that I've lost control of this...situation. It's like the water out there in the bay, one step too far and you're way in over your head! Well, hell girl, I'm there, and the riptide's got me by the balls!"

"Then swim sideways until you're free, Jessie! Don't let it carry you out to sea. Stop fighting the current. And just to clarify, you don't have balls."

Setting the second glass by its mate on the counter, Jessie couldn't suppress a grin. Meeting Sophie's trusting eyes she countered with, "I guess what I am saying is that some of this play is in his court."

"Meaning what, exactly?"

"Meaning that he might be asking for more than he can handle. And by getting it, he's calling a play that just might not succeed. That might sink this team." She was trying to be strong, but Jessie could feel her bravado fading. Exhaling slowly, she grabbed the next glass on the rack and wiped at it furiously.

Sophie took the glass and towel and set them both on the counter. She grasped both of Jessie's hands and told her the only thing that was a guarantee in such a fucked up situation. "Whatever happens, Jessie, Steve and I are your friends. We're here for you. Don't forget that."

"I know, Sophie, thank you. Feeling's mutual, you know."

"Good. Because I would be honored if you would stand at my wedding. Steve and I both, actually. Bridesmaids, or whatever they're called these days."

"Soph..." Jessie could feel the flood starting. She didn't trust herself to speak so she just shook her head slowly, touched that Sophie would even consider her for such an honor. Her eyes told Sophie exactly what she was thinking.

The small blonde leaned in and squeezed her friend's fingers. She fixed her eyes on Jessie and spoke intently. "The past is the past, Jessie. Let it go. But let me say one thing—you and Steve leaned on each other for a reason, back then. I trust you now, implicitly. With my life—with my man. But the reason that both of you needed each other then is out there on your beach building a sweet fire for us to roast spider dogs and marshmallows on, and you know something? All he really needs is love and understanding. And so do you. One of these days your riptides will spit you both out and you'll land in a heap in the middle of that sunny beach, laughing and spitting out salt water, all the stronger for having ridden a current that for a while seemed out of your control. Trust me on this. But in the meantime, promise me you'll hang on. He needs you, Jessie. And you need him. *We* need you! We're already planning family holidays with the kids with you guys, for Heaven's sake!"

"Well, in that case," Jessie laughed. Rarely was Sophie ever so dramatic and vociferous, especially in Steve's gregarious company. "I promise!"

Hugging her friend, Jessie was surprised to note that Sophie held on for a few extended moments. When she let go, the smaller woman's eyes were blinking back tears. "You know, Jessie," she said honestly, "we're really rooting for you guys. If anyone deserves a chance at lifelong happiness, it's you two."

"Thanks, kiddo," responded Jessie sincerely. "And you as well. I already gave Steve a lecture about women and the need for chocolate."

Laughing, the two women finished up the dishes and then grabbed light sweaters for the cool August evening on the beach. Jessie filled her arms with graham wafers, marshmallows and Dairy Milk chocolate bars; Sophie opened the fridge and, in the meat drawer, found a dozen all-beef frankfurters for the spider dogs. In the other hand she grabbed a box of a dozen vodka coolers Steve had stashed there earlier. She and Jessie would share a few; the boys would stick to soft drinks. One thing was for certain. Josh maintained his discipline when it came to avoiding the liquor trap. And although he was fine with having some alcohol around him, it helped when at least one friend abstained along with him. Jessie drank wine with dinner sometimes, but rarely coolers or any other drinks. Tonight, with Sophie, was a rare and special occasion.

On the way out the door, Jessie reached for one of Josh's zip-up hoodies, grabbing it off a wooden hook where he kept it for easy retrieval. She took a deep breath and followed Sophie out the sliding glass door onto the deck, across the small lawn, and then down the wooden cliff stairs to the beach below. Josh met her at the campfire and shot Jessie a grateful look when she handed him the hoodie. The August nights on P.E.I. sure did cool down quickly. He was already shivering.

The boys had set out the camp chairs they'd been using all week, and the four friends settled into a relaxing evening of friendship and laughter. The girls got a little giggly after a few bottles of the grog, and Steve's steady influx of dry wit and sarcasm had them rolling on the ground while Josh shook his head and made them all spider dogs out of the roasted hot dogs he had cross-slit at the ends so that when heated they separated, in the end looking very much like spiders. It was an amicable group, very much like old times, until the s'mores had also been made and consumed and the fire dwindled in the moonlight, its glowing orange-red coals echoing the earlier sunset.

At that point, somehow the conversation turned to Jessie and Josh. It seemed safe to go there then, after Jessie had mellowed from the coolers, with the security and safety of old friends cocooning them underneath a twinkling sky dotted with hope and a pale crescent moon.

Josh started it. Maybe he needed the haven of third parties in order to broach the subject and he knew their friends were leaving soon. He also knew their attempt at therapy for Jessie was an unmitigated disaster, and the angry comments she had spit at him after he spied the email to Jacob had sent both of them spiraling into a never-never land. He needed some resolution before…well, before he left for the film shoot in two days, a few hours after the bubbly presence of Steve and Sophie also emptied their summer home of safety and warmth.

The segue way had been easy, almost handed to them by the stars themselves. Steve was talking about his wedding to Sophie, and he threw out that they fully expected to rearrange their schedules to attend Josh and Jessie's wedding as well—soon.

Josh responded as he stared at the fiery coals simmering and spitting in front of them. The words came almost without prior thought, preceded by a grunt, and they shocked everyone at the campfire. "Hang on to your britches, cowboy. You're gonna be waiting a long time."

Silence overtook them. Even Steve was quiet. Josh felt like shit, but he was tired of all the wedding talk and his capacity for patience on these tenuous days was at its limit. He tossed the stick he'd used to roast the spider dogs and marshmallows into the fire, pushed back his chair, and rose. Without a backwards glance he shoved his hands into his jeans pockets and strode off down the beach away from their little group. After a stunned moment Jessie mumbled an apology to their friends and, with a feeling of trepidation, she took off after him, her bare feet feeling the sting of the cold sand as she mowed through it trying to keep up.

Steve and Sophie sat in silence behind them, their eyes betraying their worst fears as the bright sparks from the fire rose into the air and burst into gray ash.

"Josh!" Jessie called. "Josh, come on. Don't walk away from me."

She called him a few more times before he finally stopped, turned, and greeted her. "I'm sorry, Jessie. It's just…all this wedding talk…I'm happy for those two, I really am, but I've got so much on my mind these days… I'm sorry. Really."

Somehow she knew he was telling her more than just that he was sorry for bringing their happy evening to a bitter end with such a dramatic statement. Jessie knew Josh inside and out—her heart started to pound as she sensed that more was coming. Intuitively she wondered if she could handle it before the words were even uttered.

"Jess…you're not even trying."

She blinked at him, willing herself not to disappear again, the way she did so often these days, it seemed. "What…what do you mean?" But her voice was weak, thin. She knew damn well what he meant.

He waved a fist in the air. "You won't go to therapy, you're writing lovesick emails to Jacob, you talk more to an old man than you do to me. You're telling me I suck in bed, and you refuse to talk about McCall. How the hell am I supposed to marry you? Someone who quite obviously doesn't want me." His voice broke as the emotion of the last months, years, caught up to him.

Standing there underneath the moonlight, he never looked more vulnerable to Jessie. More alone. He, too, was bare feet, and his jeans were rolled unevenly up at the cuffs. The hoodie was baggy over a green T-shirt with a yellow ribbed neck. To her, he looked like a little boy. It broke her heart. She reached out to him.

"Josh, you've got it all wrong. You know how I feel about the McCall stuff, we've just reached a standstill on that whole issue. The counseling…I'm just not ready. I'm not up for it, okay? It's too much."

"Okay, so you're just going to hide here in this house on the beach, I dunno, maybe get a bunch of cats and live here alone? Is that your plan? Is that what you want? To hide from life?"

The truth of that statement rocked Jessie to the core. *Um, yeah.* That was exactly what she wanted. A vague memory of a discussion with Charlie about choosing to be alone crossed her mind but she pushed it away. She was tired of the entertainment biz rat race. She needed a break. Just a break, that was all. To regroup, to relax, to figure out how to cope. But she wanted Josh by her side, in the kayak, on the beach, in her bed where she could let her fingers fall softly against his stubbly cheek, and kiss him tenderly before drifting off to sleep. She was deeply sorry about the orgasm comments—they slipped out before she had time to filter them. They achieved their desired effect—they hurt him, badly. But only now would Jessie find out how badly.

He was starting to tremble, and now it wasn't from the cold. The backdrop to his emotion was the roiling ocean—the waves rolled over and over themselves, crashing, accentuating, in crescendos that reached maximum impact and then suddenly disappeared before being replaced with more loud crashes. The effect on Jessie's frazzled nerves was abrupt and distracting, but to Josh it was shattering.

"Jessie," he started, and by the red coals Steve stood, prepared to stand by whichever friend needed him most after this impending altercation also climaxed like each ceaseless wave. Sophie eased herself out of a chair behind him and placed her hands on his waist and her chin on his shoulder blade, as if the bare emotion playing itself out a few yards down the beach couldn't touch her if she shielded herself this way.

Josh continued, trembling, but making an effort to raise his voice so that he would sound stronger than he felt. "Look. I need you to do this. You need to do this, the counseling. Therapy, whatever you want to call it. It has to happen, Jessie, it's not an option. Which also means that the Deuce McCall bullshit also has to come out into the open."

"Why, Josh Sawyer," Jessie spat back at him, raising her chin in defiance. "Why am I thinking that sounds like a threat? Like there's an *or else* attached in there somewhere?" She stood rooted to the beach, her bare toes digging in and hanging on for dear life.

"Because there is," he cried back to her. "There is, Jessie, a big fucking *or else*. The biggest, in fact." He took two steps towards her, and the moonlight shifted on his face so that he almost looked eerie to her. Jessie stepped back, frightened, and although Josh was instantly sorry because he knew well her fear of men and their tempers and strength, he had to finish what he had to say. But she saw the sorrow cross his face when he realized he needed to be cautious with her, treat her like eggshells, which she despised…but which both knew was absolutely necessary. Because Jessie was a damaged soul and there was always the ever-living fear that she would one day burst. Again.

He spelled his fears out for her, in case there was any doubt. "This is the thing. Every day I live in fear that you will decide you've had enough. Every day I ask myself a thousand, no a million times—is there going to be a wedding? Are we going to get those happily-ever-afters everyone says we deserve? Do we deserve them? Do we? Every day since you told me that I don't satisfy you the way Jacob did..."

Behind them, both Stephen and Sophie cringed. *Ouch.*

"...I question whether we can make things right again. Am I making your skin crawl, Jessie? Cause sometimes I feel like I am. But then I ask myself, is it me she is cringing from, or is it a memory of Deuce McCall? And it's this game that goes around and around and around in my head until I think I'm going to fucking go crazy! And you get this distant look in your eyes and sometimes I think you're going to go so far away—again—that I'll never be able to get you back. Every day, Jessie, every day I pray and hope that you will go see Trudy, because at least on those days I feel like there's that hope you're always talking about, or that you used to talk about, but that you obviously don't seem to believe yourself. And so every day that you *don't* go see Trudy I think *oh shit, we're backsliding here.* And then I catch myself watching you for clues and wondering, is this the day she's going to leave me again? Disappear into the ether? Forever, maybe? Do you have any idea what it's like for me, to live with a noose around my neck, knowing you have one foot out the door, wondering when you are going to disappear again?"

He was crying then, and it was painful to watch, this grown man who looked like a little boy in his faded jeans and frumpy hoodie and the stalwart moon lighting him as if he were a character in one of his films.

"And then you went away again, you took the car and said you were going to Trudy's but you didn't, and you didn't call or text, and then when I found you at almost two in the morning, what do I find? You, writing that stupid email to Jacob instead of climbing into bed with me. You, telling me how much I suck instead of holding me and telling me you love me. Every day, Jessie, every day, I am just waiting for you to disappear completely again. Every day I am wondering if this is the day you're just going to run away again! How can I live like that? How?!"

He teetered there in front of her waiting for an answer that he knew wouldn't come. Jessie was there, in the present, he could tell that about her stance and the clenched fists at her sides, her body hunched forward as if ready for a fight. She was still wearing the afternoon's shorts and tank top underneath her own hoodie, and she was shivering—from the cold away from the fire or from the heavy emotion, he didn't know. But Josh was so tired and dead from the effort loving her took that he had no desire to reach out and hold her, to consume her with his own warmth. He let her shiver.

She had no idea how to respond. So she bit her lip and remained silent, a 'Jessie special.'

Finally, sick of her and her thick brick walls, like the sand castle they'd built earlier that month on the beach, only much harder to destroy, Josh stormed past her. He was two steps by her when he stopped suddenly and turned to face her. When their eyes met there was only an emptiness inside his, sparked with little remnants of a dying anger. Inside hers was a yearning for something she had no idea how to have.

"I'm not like you, Jessie. I don't want to hide here. I want to get back into the world of the living." He paused before delivering the final blow. "I took the film," he stated. "In Virginia. I leave the day after tomorrow."

"No," she countered, stunned. "No, you can't."

"Oh yes I can," he defied her wishes outright. "And I will. Watch me."

He left her there, alone in the moonlight, but he had the presence of mind to stop at the campfire and grab some of the evening's detritus into his arms, wishing it were Jessie he was holding instead. Sophie followed him, her arms also full, and Jessie watched numbly as the odd little twosome made its way back into the shelter of the cozy old farmhouse. After the door slammed, she let her eyes drift back to the campfire. She was almost surprised to see Steve still standing there, patiently waiting as all good friends do.

Jessie stumbled hopelessly back to the diminutive circle of diminishing coal-light. The glow now was barely even visible. They sat, and Steve handed her a Strawberry-Kiwi cooler before picking up a long stick and poking the coals to restore some heat.

Jessie uttered her remorse. "I guess that's that," she said, twisting the top off the cooler.

"He just needs some time," Steve responded, heartily flipping over a big log and watching as new flames took a death grip hold underneath the burning wood.

"Did you know he took the film?" she asked, her voice small.

"Nah. I only knew he was thinking about it. But I'm not surprised." He studied her, compassion for Jessie evident on his lean face and in his tender eyes.

"I guess we didn't hide it as well as we thought then, eh?" She took a big swig of the cooler.

Steve smiled affectionately. "Not so good, no. But thanks for trying." He switched chairs, moving next to Jessie where he could take her hand and hold it tight. "Listen to me, little girl. This is not over. Let him go do what he needs to do, and you make things right on your end."

"Oh, fuck," she muttered. "Et tu, Brute?"

"Yes, damnit," he said. "You're fucking right. I've met Trudy. She's got her head on straight. Josh will be away, we'll be gone, you can just let the tears come and empty that vessel of yours in the ocean with no one watching. But I'm warning you that Soph and I will be calling every day. We may not be here, but we plan to keep an eye on you."

Wrapping both hands around the cooler bottle, Jessie collapsed her head onto her lap. As her shoulders started to shake, Steve dropped the stick back on the fire and wrapped an arm around her. He pulled her closer and held on tight, closing his eyes as he caught his breath on the familiar lavender scent in her hair.

"Hey, hey," he murmured. "He's not going anywhere. You'll see."

"He can't," she sobbed. "He can't, Steve. Don't you see? After everything, after all that...he just can't."

"Then don't let him," he whispered in her curls.

"It's not that simple," came the small muffled voice from his chest.

Steve kissed the top of her head. "Oh yes it is," he murmured, sending a silent prayer to the twinkling Heavens above. "Yes. It is."

They stayed that way for a while, then Jessie finally sat up and finished her cooler with Steve at her side, his arm around her and soon his jokes to keep her company and raise her mood and, along with it, her hopes.

Above them, Josh walked out onto the upper deck at the end of the upstairs hallway between the two bedrooms—the larger one where he and Jessie slept, and a guest room across the hall where Steve and Sophie slumbered. It was dark on the small eight by ten deck, but Sophie heard him go and so she padded softly outside in her boxers and sweater to keep him company. Together they watched as their partners—*two old sometime lovers*—cuddled closely together in the moonlight on the beach beneath them.

"Sometimes I think I'll never be as close to her as he is," Josh said quietly as Sophie eased into a relaxed stance by the rail next to him.

"I hear you," Sophie offered. "But I trust him. Now."

Pondering the comment Jessie threw in his face less than a week before about her intimacy with Steve, Josh wondered if Sophie knew. As if she could read his thoughts, Sophie spoke.

"It took me a long time to accept her again, Josh. As she is, broken and confused. But she's worth it, you know?"

"I notice you didn't say you trust her. Just him." He peeked down at Sophie beside him.

She shrugged. "It's not that I don't trust her. It's more that I don't have to. That's your job."

He smiled wanly. "Ah, the wise Sophie emerges. I knew you were in there somewhere, m'lady. Behind Steve and his need to entertain, that is."

"They have a bond, Josh. You and I have to accept that. Personally, I think they're lucky to have each other. And so are we, actually, to have those two in our lives as such good friends. They're always going to be close, they've built a history together during some rough times when all they thought they had was each other. Their love for you built their relationship. You know that, right?"

At his hesitant nod, she added, "They'll bring our two families close together. Our kids will be like brothers and sisters."

He ducked his head and a sad glow spread across his face. "Kids, huh?"

Sophie hooked an arm in his. "You bet. Lots of 'em."

"So what happens when ten years down the road one of us couples is fighting, huh? And those two seek each other out again."

Sobered, Sophie paused and reflected before responding. "It won't happen. Not what you think, anyway. Like I said, I trust him, Josh. And what we have grows deeper and more profound every day." She punched him lightly in the arm. "It does for you two as well. You just can't see your way out of the storm yet."

"Sophie," he reflected, a frown on his face as, below, Steve pulled Jessie close again and kissed the top of her head, "I'm not sure I ever will."

His friend's fiancée squeezed his arm tighter as they stood at the rail and listened to the ocean's relentless call to arms. To Josh it was as if it was saying *I am Jessie, hear me,* the same as on that horrid lonely Christmas day when Jessie had been gone more than a year and they didn't know if she was dead or alive. Would he still want her back if he knew how difficult their journey would still be? *Damn straight,* he told himself. *I think.*

"It's late," he said, and gave Sophie a little kiss on the top of the head also. *Steve is lucky,* he thought. *He has a woman with her head on straight.* Instantly, he chided himself. Jessie had a damn lot of baggage, and so did he, as a result of his association with her. But then again—he remembered the night at Charlie's Club so long ago, when this pretty girl with the short little black dress and tipsy high heels looked into his eyes and told him to have hope. Only now the situation seemed twisted, reversed, warped. They were both in the garbage now, but could barely, if at all, see beyond the fish brains and other smelly crap.

"Nite, Josh," Sophie whispered, and then she followed him off the deck. Her heart ached for him, but there was nothing anyone could say or do that would really help. This couple was going to have to find their own way through the mess.

After a bit Steve climbed into bed beside her, reeking like a woodsy campfire, a scent she adored and cozily breathed in while hugging him to her chest. "Love you," she sighed, smiling into his skin.

In the larger room across the hall, Jessie took her time brushing her teeth. She leaned against the doorframe while she dragged the brush slowly back and forth across her teeth and watched Josh breathe in and out on his side of the bed. She didn't know if he was awake or asleep, although if all bets were out she would have guessed awake, but ignoring her. After a bit she slipped off her shorts and the hoodie and climbed into bed behind him. She snuggled up against him without a word or any hesitation—he was her man and, despite their troubles, she loved him deeply. Besides, the hurts he carried were all her fault. Although that was a great burden to bear, she knew it beyond a shadow of a doubt to be true.

When she touched him, and inclined her knees in close to his and her belly and chest against him, he pulled away, hunching his shoulders over so that he was leaning away from her. *Yup, he is awake, all right.*

Jessie called his name into the dim moonlit room. "Josh..."

He stilled, but didn't speak.

"Just so you know," she said, her small voice determined. "I'm not going to give up fighting for you. Ever. Ever ever ever. Forever and ever."

She brushed a hand down his bicep and onto his forearm, then interlaced her fingers in his. She buried her face in his chestnut hair and breathed him in. "Ever," she whispered.

Because it hurt less to let her in, even just this little bit, Josh let his fingers open ever so slightly so that hers could fit inside, then he closed his fingers around hers and pulled her arm in closer.

Still, when Jessie awoke two hours later with yet another interminable nightmare, she found herself alone in bed. She hauled a homemade quilt over her trembling body and nudged it up around her ears, wondering where he was but afraid to ask. She cried herself to sleep only to awake with another nightmare as the sun peeked up over the horizon, canvassing the half-empty bedroom with the pink and white stripes of a summer dawn.

When she finally padded downstairs she found Josh making pancakes for all of them. She looked at him expectantly as she slid onto a stool by the kitchen island, the quilt wrapped around her shoulders in the cool early morning August air.

He didn't meet her gaze as he slipped a cooked homemade apple pancake onto a plate in the oven where it stood a better chance of staying warm. "I needed some sleep," he said.

*Oh,* she thought sadly. *The nightmares. Of course.* She sat straighter and glowered at him. "Well, Steve and Sophie are leaving tomorrow. We have a spare room."

He raised his eyes to hers then and, at his knowing look, she remembered that he, too, was leaving her. Well then. He would get lots of sleep. Even the five a.m. set calls would be better than dealing with her nightmares. Jessie sank further into the quilt, her eyes travelling to a safe place on the hardwood floor. Josh flipped the radio on to Hot 105.5 so that the silence between them wouldn't be so deafening.

That day, Steve and Sophie's last day on the island, they toured a local tourist attraction called Woodleigh Replicas, filled with miniature models of British castles and houses and overflowing vibrant colorful country gardens. Jessie strolled arm in arm with Sophie, and they laughed and chatted about what life would likely be like in L.A. for Sophie as the wife of a sitcom star. Her optimism and obvious love for Steve was humbling, and Jessie found herself captivated by this warm woman who she knew she would miss terribly the next day and the days afterwards.

Behind them, the boys sauntered along the asphalt paths admiring the miniature Shakespeare's cottage and wondering at how a place like this ended up in P.E.I.

Steve took the opportunity to counsel Josh, knowing it was likely their last chance to talk alone before departure time early the next day.

He poked a finger in Josh's chest. "Get your shit together. Don't be an ass on this film, it's not an escape route."

Josh grimaced and put a hand on his chest where Steve's finger had roughly jabbed at him. "Ouch," he growled. "Who said anything about an escape route?"

"It's in your eyes, damnit! I'm not stupid! Jessie's not stupid! You can't wait to get the hell out of here."

"Oh, fuck off, Steve, you don't know what the hell you're talking about." Josh turned back towards the pretty cottage, feeling like a giant imposter standing over the fake home of one of the world's greatest writers.

"Damn straight I do," Steve frowned at him. "Don't forget what she gave up for you, Sawyer."

Wheeling around to face him, Josh glared back at his friend. "Don't tell me to remember what she gave up for me. I see it and feel it every damn day." Whether he was talking about the spleen he himself had lost was questionable, as it wasn't something Jessie gave up for him. Yet his own losses were intertwined with hers. But everybody seemed to forget that—it was always Jessie, Jessie, Jessie.

"Fuck, Josh, get it together, man. She's healing. It's not going to happen overnight, give her time. Don't go away and do something stupid."

At the lowering of Josh's eyebrows, an awareness hit Steve like a rock. "You're planning to. You're planning to fuck her over." He felt an explosion rising in him, and Steve curled his hands into fists.

Josh glanced over at the girls, who were admiring a clump of pink roses twenty feet away, oblivious to the boys' exchange. He looked a little guiltily back at Steve. "You weren't here the night she told me how much I sucked in bed. Maybe I just need to get my confidence back. Maybe I just need to be with someone who doesn't cringe when I touch her, or who looks at me like her skin crawls when I'm near her."

"Geez, Josh, don't be stupid, there's no coming back from that shit."

A hard stare silenced him. Steve knew exactly what Josh was thinking.

"Oh no?" Josh asked icily. "Isn't there? Steve?" He said his friend's name spitefully, with distaste.

Frowning, Steve was silent. But he and Josh locked eyes and a lot was said, albeit it was unspoken in words. It was the first time the men actually acknowledged between themselves the intimacy between Steve and Jessie a few years earlier.

"Jesus, man," Steve finally said firmly. "Let it go. Get your shit together, and hang onto this girl with everything you have in you." He echoed Charlie's old words before he spun around to catch up to the girls and swing Sophie around by the waist. "Don't fuck it up, Sawyer."

A sentimental longing imbued Jessie's attempt at a smile as she watched Steve and Sophie frolic in the P.E.I. sun. She wrapped her arms around her own waist as if to stifle some unseen pain in her belly, then she glanced over at Josh, who didn't move until he noticed her spot him standing there towering over Shakespeare's home. He caught up to Jessie and grasped her hand, intertwining his fingers in hers, but they didn't speak. Instead, they followed their friends silently out of the diminutive castles and cottages towards the parking lot and reality, and then they drove home to freshen up for a final evening of togetherness on the island.

# Chapter Ten

Although the foursome attracted a reasonable amount of whispers and stares, the *Drifters* stars and Sophie were accustomed to others' curiosity and so, after finding metered parking, they hoofed their way down Queen Street in Charlottetown towards quaint Richmond Street, where they slid into seats at Pat's Rose and Grey Restaurant. It was eight p.m. by the time they arrived, and Jessie noted with pleasure that a live band was scheduled to take a small stage at nine. This felt normal to her, because it reminded her of her childhood on the island. She and her mother were always cherished guests at her dad's restaurant gigs, at least when an underage gal was either permitted or, in the case of George's bar, covertly sneaked in.

Downtown Charlottetown was an historic affair, its primarily red brick Victorian office buildings and cedar-shingled homes reminiscent of earlier times when wooden shipbuilding during the *Age of Sail* was the biggest industry on the island. The small city of 35 000 once hosted Canada's 'fathers.' Delegates at the celebrated 1864 Charlottetown Conference, these men planted the seeds that birthed a nation. As a result, these days many tourists flocked from cruise ships and from the small local airport, keeping the economy flowing with millions spent in gift shops and restaurants. It also didn't hurt that Lucy Maud Montgomery's red-haired literary orphan, 'Anne of Green Gables', was also a well-loved island figure. Her fictional home, the famous Green Gables itself, was a must-see for most visitors to Prince Edward Island, and many made lots of stops in both Cavendish and Charlottetown during their time on the island.

At the corner of Richmond and Queen Streets, Steve pulled Sophie down onto a slatted wooden bench and together they posed next to a life sized bronze of the nation's first Prime Minister, unruly-haired Sir John A. MacDonald. Josh snapped the couple's photo with his iPhone and then, because he was trying to act normal and fit in, he took Jessie's hand and she collapsed onto his lap for their turn at the photo op. The two of them huddled underneath the Father of Confederation's bronze arm as if he could bond them in the same manner he once united the country of Canada.

For Jessie, it was a chance to let her body relax into Josh's. Closing her eyes, she nestled her face into his chestnut hair and let her left hand linger on his neck as her thumb brushed his cheek. She exhaled slowly, praying they would soon find solid ground beneath their feet again.

Groaning softly with the pleasure of holding her, Josh, too, took advantage of the short respite and wrapped his arms tightly around the familiar body. As much as he knew he needed a break, he was already missing Jessie. To the delight of fans that recognized the famous couple, they kissed tenderly, oblivious to anyone or anything but their need to connect before the next day's imminent parting. Anything to hold them over just a little longer, to give them the strength they needed to go on.

Pat's Rose and Grey was a Charlottetown landmark recommended by the older woman from whom Josh and Jessie were renting the South Rustico farmhouse. Collectively, Jessie and Sophie drew in their breaths when they entered. Painted high on the walls surrounding diners in the dimly lit old apothecary/soda fountain-turned-restaurant were faint full size unicorns, gray on an aptly rose-colored wall. The unicorns danced around the patrons, their graceful bodies whimsical and delightful as if crying out a message to those within the hallowed walls—*life is a childlike fantasy, hang onto your dreams and your lovers.*

The legendary eatery, famous for fresh hot breadsticks and homemade carrot cake with mile-high cream cheese icing, once hosted poet Milton Acorn on a regular basis. It was warm and inviting, and Jessie visibly relaxed once within its revered walls.

An excited host seated them at a deep booth with high backs for optimum privacy. Jessie scuttled over to the inside, against the wall, with Sophie across from her. Immediately the dark wood and plush aged-velvet cushions reminded her of the dark pub in Scotland where she often hung out with Jacob and the crowd. These cushions were a deep plum-burgundy, like magnificently aged Bordeaux. A thin gold thread wound this way and that throughout the cushions, in curlicues and waves, so she told herself to 'let it go,' that this wasn't at all like the booth in Scotland, and anyways that was a long time ago and it was over; when in fact she had only left the country five months ago, and ended things with Jacob himself not much later.

Her memories were mushy bruises on a fallen grape, barely detectable to an uninitiated observer. To Jessie, the bearer of such discoloration, whether they could be seen or not, the soft parts still hurt.

Frowning, she brushed a hand over the opulent cushion beneath her butt, her mind fighting for recall, but she forced herself to focus on the fanciful unicorns bouncing gaily above her instead, for Josh's sake. He had laid it out straight last night. He needed her to try to live in the present.

Hot breadsticks with melted butter and honey were recommended by their young waiter, a boy who introduced himself as Jarrett, and who spoke with dramatic flourishes of long fingers and a thick western Prince Edward Island accent that was likely an evolution of 1811 Ireland brogue blended heavily with Acadian French. The girls ordered a bottle of Pinot Grigio to share, and Steve treated himself to locally brewed Gahan beer, Sir John A's Honey Wheat Ale, an ode to their historical bronzed seatmate from outside. Napoli pizza for the women and rich hearty pastas for the men were ordered, and they settled down to wait, their moods tentative and already filled with longing for the old days when they could hang out together with Maggie, Carter and Sue-Lyn also in tow.

"What," Jessie said, a slow smile etching the sadness away from the corners of her eyes. She was responding to Steve's prolonged quiet contemplation of her.

He grimaced and sat back against the booth. "Sorry. I was just thinking about you being alone here after we all pull out tomorrow." He avoided Josh's hard stare, and it struck Jessie funny that Steve had the nerve to mention that Josh was leaving her too.

She shrugged and countered. "I'm used to being alone, Steve. I'll be fine." That, too, was in its way meant as a dig at Josh. Steve met her gaze and between them the old friends spoke legions, but then Steve glanced over at Josh, who glared at him before shifting uncomfortably and twisting around sideways to observe the band setting up at the far end of the restaurant. When Josh turned back to the table, his eyes were shooting daggers at Steve. Sophie wrinkled her eyebrows in consternation and, at her look, Jessie followed and let her eyes drift eastward to rest on Josh. *What the hell?*

She laid a hand over his on the table and let her thumb move over his fingers in soft reassuring touches. Whatever had transpired between the boys was their business. Jessie didn't want any more drama on this, their last night together with Steve and Sophie—and themselves—for a while.

Their breadsticks arrived steaming hot fresh out of the oven, and they settled into the business of dividing them and ladening them with butter and the recommended honey. Jarrett spoke. He couldn't help himself; he was almost dancing as he cleared his throat. Jessie looked up at him, a mouthful of delicious breadstick revealing that she was as ordinary as anybody else on the planet, despite her fame and success in the entertainment business.

"Miss Wheeler, I hope you don't mind but I just wanted to tell you how much I look up to you."

Coloring, Jessie glanced downwards and put a finger to her mouth to make sure she didn't spit out the breadstick. She swallowed before trusting herself to speak. The others sobered. They knew how their girl felt about herself, and although it was humbling to know she believed she had just stumbled into her life, and that she had no ego to speak of, it was even more humbling to know she also had very little self esteem. But she also had good manners. She smiled up at the young waiter.

"Thank you, Jarrett. What do you do? Are you a student?" She doubted he was a fulltime server, he was young and they found that most establishments they visited had students employed for the summer months.

"Yes," the dynamic dark-haired boy answered, his right hand punctuating the point with a sudden flourish. He was solidly built, with a few extra soft spots here and there, and Jessie guessed rightly that he studied Arts, the deduction made also partly because of the beautiful artistic establishment in which he was employed. "I am a student in the Performing Arts program at Holland College. It's a local school."

"Ah. So you're into theatre, then?" Jessie laid the rest of her breadstick on a side plate in front of her and wiped her sticky fingers on a napkin. She knew Holland College was a busy campus. The Performing Arts program had been mentioned in the local news, as it was in its infancy catering to musicians and musical theatre actors. "Do you sing?"

Shifting his feet nervously, Jarrett grinned at his unbelievable luck. He was serving Jessie Wheeler and her beau! And another of the *Drifters* actors as well. What a night! And Jessie was nice, social. Like everyone else, he knew her story, or at least overtones of it, but that was far from his mind at the moment. Right now she was just a person like everyone else, albeit a pretty special one, in his mind.

"I sure do!" he enthused. "I had a part in 'Anne of Green Gables,' the musical, as a kid. My mom's a Lucy Maud fan," he added in an unimportant off-handed sort of way. "In the spring our program at Holland College did the 'Wizard of Oz.' I didn't have a great part, just a munchkin, but it was still a blast." He puffed up his chest, proud.

"So what are your future plans?" Jessie asked with genuine interest.

He shrugged and his face fell a little. "I don't know. Toronto, maybe? I'd love to do some auditions and stuff for the big musicals. Maybe even some film or television," he added, speculating. "Not sure. It's stiff, the competition. I'm a realist, I know what I'm in for."

He was obviously a smart cookie. Jessie felt her heart twitch as he spoke. Jarrett was so earnest. So many people sought fame, stardom, parts in the 'big shows.' She had what others desired, but she didn't earnestly want it. Sitting next to Josh, she could feel his thoughts permeate her brain as well. *Why would you want to give up what so many others so deeply desire?*

During the brief discourse, Steve had been staring at the table. Now he solemnly regarded Jessie, reading her mind as well. She looked over at him and their eyes locked. Across from him, Josh had one elbow on the table and was lightly chewing a fingernail. Humbled, he too looked up at Steve. They all had to remember not to take their own success for granted.

Jessie's voice was a little pinched when she spoke, but still, she was sincere. She was the ultimate role model for wannabes like Jarrett. Kind, she took the time to listen and to encourage, despite her own issues. "Promise me one thing, Jarrett."

"Sure. Anything," the server said enthusiastically.

She paused and smiled before continuing. Her caring pale blue eyes spoke legions to Jarrett as she peeked up at him from underneath long eyelashes. "Don't be too focused on the prize at the end. Enjoy the journey. Each and every day. And never lose the joy."

Jarrett nodded thoughtfully and then his plump cheeks broke into a grin. He beamed at Jessie. "You got it," he responded eagerly.

"Promise?"

"Promise." As he backed away from the table, he knew he had found a soul mate in Jessie Wheeler. She clearly understood fame and dreams and, although she maybe believed in such things as dancing unicorns, she proved to him that she also knew there were more important things in life than money. Jarrett was humbled to see, just before he continued on his journey which, that night, consisted of serving pasta and breadsticks, that she took Josh's hand, brought it to her lips, and kissed the backs of his fingers.

Later, after the plates were cleared and the breadsticks long gone, Josh rose to excuse himself for a 'ten one-hundred break' in television and film parlance, or a 'bathroom break' in the lives of normal human beings. Just before Josh left their table, Jarrett approached again.

Nervous, the server sucked in a breath before speaking directly to Jessie. "I've been elected to ask if you would consider playing just one or two tunes. The band rocks but you can only take so much John Hiatt, Stevie Ray Vaughan and Tom Waits. It's all we hear every time these guys play which is, like, three nights a week. From like, nine to one." He exhaled before adding, with a flourish, "It's cool if you're not up for it. I mean, you're out with friends and all, and I guess music is probably work these days, right?"

He gestured behind him to the band, which was currently rocking a Stones ballad. The lead singer, a lean forty-something guy with three-day stubble and long curly salt and pepper hair, had his eyes glued to the foursome's table. Jessie had to lean forward and crank her neck around the corner of the bench seat in order to meet his gaze. She looked up at Josh. After the Charleston concert she hadn't played for him since the two got back together. She did play, but it was when she was alone, when he was in the city for counseling or out kayaking without her.

Josh's heart caught in his throat. He shrugged at her as if to imply that he didn't give a shit. But inside he wondered if the universe was sending him a message. He was a sucker for Jessie when she sang. And of course, for her, a green light went on. She communicated best through song. Her face softened at the opportunity to speak to Josh this way.

She smiled and nodded at the enthusiastic waiter. "I'd be honored," she responded honestly. "Music is everything, Jarrett. It's never work. It's the key to *life*." She winked at him as she slid out of the booth.

By the time Josh got back from the washroom, she had one of the band's spare acoustic-electric guitars in hand, and was seated on a high wooden stool behind a microphone. The restaurant was humming as the regular Pat's Rose and Grey house musicians settled themselves around her. Jessie humbly spoke to them away from the mic, and they prepared their capos and settled into their positions to accompany one of the world's most beloved singer-songwriters in a long, narrow little legendary restaurant in historic downtown Charlottetown.

He would have had to crane his neck to see Jessie from the booth, so Josh remained standing and leaned over the back where Steve and Sophie snuggled together, waiting to see what she would play. This girl, so troubled and hurting, was divine under the soft gauzy lights of the dim venue. Her expression was peaceful—music did that to her. Pleasing others the way her father once did gave her a sense of purpose, of belonging in a world that had turned dark and foreboding, robbing her of her childhood at a young age, and of her self-love as a woman years later.

She adjusted the mic, glanced up, and found herself locked in Jarrett's excited gaze, his eyes already shining with unshed tears. Her hopeful baby blues twinkled happily in his direction.

"This song is for Jarrett, our amazing server tonight." An experienced pro, Jessie waited until the cheers and whistles died down before continuing. "It's for Jarrett, and for the rest of you out there who like to dream once in a while."

Then she started to pick the first few notes of "Somewhere Over the Rainbow", a song she was famous for interpreting in her own original profound way. Accompanied by the musicians flanking her on guitar, bass and drums, she carried the patrons away on a magical journey into a world that contemplated dreams. The kitchen staff took a break, the servers stopped serving, it seemed even the unicorns stopped their dancing and strained their heads to watch and listen. Josh crossed his arms on the back of the bench seat, and rested his chin on his hands. He almost wished the film was not happening now, but it was too late to change his mind. Plus, he knew from experience that this moment in time was an illusion, a fantasy. That the Jessie on the low stage was a fragment of the real woman he loved and cherished, that the music, as surreal as it was, was itself really just a dream.

Others were crowding into the restaurant for the chance to partake of the magic. Beckoned by staff and diners with fast thumbs to text with, they arrived breathless. Cell phones recorded the enchanted performance.

The cheering was loud and enthusiastic, and there was a surplus of tears by the time Jessie ended the tune. She won that audience over on the first note. Now, she took them to a place where those lucky patrons could barely breathe.

She was staring at the floor, distant, while the cheering continued. For an instant Josh was poised to help her. She was in that far away place from where he lately often feared she would, like her mother, never return. But then she raised her head and peered across the dimly lit space at him, a sad smile expressing the angst she felt about what she was about to tell him through the power and majesty of song. She strummed a few notes on her guitar, turned and whispered a key to her homemade backup band, and then leaned forward to speak into the mic.

"Josh," she started slowly, her voice low, and the audience was reaching for more tissues before she finished breathing his name. They, like Jarrett—like everyone, it seemed—were aware of the very heavy price these two had paid to be together. What they did not know was how exacting that price still was, how much it still controlled the couple. Perhaps the unicorns knew, in their fantasyland, but if they did, they weren't telling.

Jessie continued, her own diaphanous eyes suddenly misty with the emotion of it all—the recent fights, his angry words, his inevitable choice to leave tomorrow. "Josh," she whispered his name again, even lower this time, as she tried to preface the song with words she wanted him to remember. Then, struggling, she switched gears and spoke to the assembled crowd instead, all the while holding Josh's gaze. "This is a song I recently wrote for the man I am going to spend my life with. For the man I am going to marry." She paused and smiled bashfully while the whistles threatened to blow the roof off the place. "For the man I am building a future with." Her voice broke as she added, "For the man who will be the father of my children."

She did not take her eyes off Josh as she began to strum and then sing. As the band picked up the tune, Josh had to fight to remain upright and not succumb to where he wanted to be, which was lying in a puddle on the floor. He let himself soak up her essence as she sang to him a song of love, sung with absolute certainty that they would be together forever. Still, he knew his girl well, and he could see that the misty eyes he was lost in that night were troubled and afraid, mostly at his acceptance of and response to the song, he figured. But her message in the lyrics was clear. Would it change anything? Would she try the counseling again, as he demanded? Who knew? But she was doing what Jessie Wheeler did best. Through music, she was telling him that she loved him.

Would that be enough? No. By now Josh knew—and that was the heartache of having to stand there in the midst of all those people, captured by some of their cell phone cameras once again—that this was all a farce, that her singing about love to him was not enough. That yes, she loved him but *love* was not enough. She needed to combine action with love. She needed to do more than sing to him. This new knowing broke his heart and, if he was not so absolutely entranced by the dreamlike place and the vision and music of the woman he so desperately ached to love and to have really love him in return, he would have raised his hand and said *so long.* Like Moses, Josh would have stilled the voices around him, and swept through the center of that great wave of people who put their lives on hold to bear witness to Jessie and her fairylike mysticism. He would have emerged from that false cocoon into what he knew to be reality, without Jessie by his side. But as it was, he rooted his boots to the trembling ground beneath his feet and forced his own anguish to remain buried inside as Jessie finished the song, returned the guitar to its owner, shared hugs and thank you's, and cautiously made her way across the floor to where he stood.

As she got closer he could more clearly see that somewhere along her journey across the floor, the blue eyes had lost their sparkle and were instead dim and lined with terror—of what? *That the verity of the song didn't matter. And that I won't return after the film shoot,* he supposed. Perhaps she was also afraid of the knowledge that what she had cried out to him the night of Jacob's email was a wound as deep as Deuce McCall's blade. Deep inside, Josh also hoped that by now she harbored a fear of the truths that haunted them, that if she didn't accept Trudy's help, their love would indeed not be enough.

She balanced herself in front of him.

Expressionless, Josh reached out and ran his fingers through her hair. She was as adorable as ever, in a red patterned sundress that ended mid-thigh, the ubiquitous dusty brown embroidered cowboy boots, a faded jean jacket. Tomorrow at this time he would not have access to her. He wrapped both arms tightly around her and felt a choking sob rise in his throat, but he fought it. He could not break down here, now, in front of all these people who thought they were witness to a great love's survival.

Steve sensed his friends' pain. He knew what they were going through, how high the price they were paying each and every day. With a great sigh, he hoisted his long legs out of the cozy booth and encircled Josh and Jessie with his own version of great love. Sophie joined them, and the good friends stayed in the safety of their huddle until Josh managed to get his emotions under control. They were a tight-knit group of people who had met on the set of a television project, and who would now do anything for each other, even if it meant just offering a comforting presence in a crowded restaurant on a late summer's eve.

They were unified that night in their knowledge of the universe's power to bewitch them and, after their huddle, they wiped their eyes and got on with life. The boys paid the bills, and Jessie left Jarrett with one final hug and a light brush of her lips on his cheek.

As the group emerged back out onto homey Richmond, harsh streetlights illuminating the way back to their SUV, Josh once again grasped Jessie's hand. But he walked quickly, so that she had to scurry along to keep up with him. Behind them, Sir John A's bronze likeness sat frozen, and inside Pat's Rose and Grey the unicorns eyed their backs with suspicion and warning. As they exited, Jessie had found herself shivering under the mythical creatures' stares. Somehow the unicorns' dance was slower and less mystical than before. Peering closer, she had taken notice that their paint was peeling.

At home in the beach farmhouse bedroom, Josh drew Jessie to him and, with sober liquid brown eyes, dared her to let him say goodbye with an intimate touch. She stared hard at him before letting the denim jacket drop to the floor. She gripped the hem of the sundress and slipped it up over her head, then slid her cool hands underneath his vintage cotton shirt and forced open the pearl snaps. She let her hands memorize the feel of his hard chest, but she was angry about it because his leaving reminded her of a time years before when she also had no idea whether this was a permanent good-bye.

So she pressed hard on his skin, and moved quickly, as if by waiting and taking it slow it would just draw the pain out further. She leaned into him and caressed his nipples between her thumb and forefinger, and he instantly hardened to her touch.

Josh reached a hand around behind Jessie and unclasped her red lace bra, then tilted her chin up so he could tease the determined lips with his tongue. He was too tired of their bickering and the strain on their relationship to linger on the possibility of triggers or of not satisfying her. Instead, he just went for it, and cherished the fact that she, too, was not holding back.

Roughly, he pushed Jessie slightly away from him so that he could thrust a hand down her panties. She parted her legs and arched her back as he slid two fingers inside her, and Jessie's ragged *ahhhhh* furthered his own arousal. Josh cradled an arm around the small of her back as her legs threatened to give way, then he urged her towards the bed. Jessie recovered her wits enough to pull at the button on his jeans. She struggled with it before it finally let go, then quickly she unzipped him but he was on top of her on the bed in an instant and so the jeans remained at his hips.

His tongue found hers and then he pushed her head back and brusquely drew his lips down her neck and onto her breasts, where he sucked on a nipple while he reached down to position himself where he needed to be in order to enter her. But her panties were in the way and so, his own breath coming hard and fast, he slid down her belly and removed them before roughly parting her legs and tasting her, licking her, driving her around the bend before moving back up her body and entering her.

He thrust hard against Jessie, not caring what Deuce did or didn't do, nor did Jessie seem to care then and, as she crushed him against her body, her back arched and moans increasing, he came loud and hard inside her. He rocked back and forth enough to let her finish her own explosive orgasm before he rolled off the bed without meeting her eyes. Then, wordlessly, he sidled into the bathroom to clean up and brush his teeth.

Shocked and lonely, Jessie lay on her back for a moment and ran a hand thoughtfully over her belly before rolling over onto her side and crunching herself up into a fetal position. When Josh was done in the bathroom she took her turn, and then she joined him in the darkened bedroom for a night of confused dreams and, of course, the inevitable nightmare, which she suffered through alone amongst a veil of tears while Josh forced himself to ignore her plaintive whimpering cries by pressing a knuckle against his eyes.

He needed a break and, that day, he would have it.

*But by the Lord Tunderin' Jesus,* borrowing an expression used by the Newfoundlander at the corner store yesterday when Josh dropped in for milk, it wasn't going to be fucking easy.

# Chapter Eleven

"I am so pissed at you right now," Steve said bluntly, dropping his leather suitcase into the back of his and Sophie's rental for the trip to the airport.

Josh regarded him cautiously. Steve didn't appear angry. In fact, despite his sharp words, the lithe actor casually rested an arm against the car and leaned on it, then studied Josh without apparent malice. Instead, he seemed rather resigned.

Toeing the red clay underneath his boot, Josh's shoulders slumped. "It's okay. I'm actually kind of pissed at me too." He was thinking about how he'd treated Jessie the night before, making love and then ignoring her as she struggled to gain control after another terrifying nightmare. He was a shit, plain and simple. And later that day he would be leaving her to fend off her demons alone. What kind of partner was Josh? *Selfish,* he thought. *Fucking selfish.*

"C'mere, man," Steve said, pulling his friend close and treating him to a serious hug. He patted his hands on Josh's back before letting go. Sniffing, Steve met Josh's eyes. He could see the fear in his friend's face, in the way he stood there like a lost puppy, praying for Steve to tell him that everything was going to be okay.

Resting a hand on Josh's shoulder, Steve spoke, his voice firm and sure. "Look man, it's done now. Just go and rock the film, and come back here and make things right. She's strong, she'll be fine."

His eyes gave another instruction to Josh—*don't do anything stupid.* Josh nodded, and shoved his hands in his pockets just as the screen door slammed behind the girls. Josh turned to look as Steve dashed forward to help drag Sophie's big suitcase down the wooden steps.

"What the hell's in here, Sophie? The entire beach?" Sincere joy skipped across Steve's tanned cheeks.

Her blonde hair pulled back in a casual long ponytail that she'd fastened with a leather hair clip, Sophie flushed happily. "I couldn't go back to Vancouver without, let me see, a bottle of beach sand for Kayla, lobster stuffies and Anne of Green Gables rag dolls for my nieces, and—"

Steve cut her off. "Clothes for Sophie." He grinned mischievously and raised an arm in a blocking defense as she swatted him.

Jessie took the high road and nudged herself in under Josh's arm. He raised it so that she could snuggle closer. Regardless of his reasons for taking the film job, they were both feeling the angst of their impending separation, and watching their friends pack up their car was a reminder of their own parting later that day. Besides, neither wanted to see Steve or Sophie leave, either. Despite all, the foursome had enjoyed a leisurely fun week in the small sunny east coast province.

The car packed, Sophie put her tiny hands over her mouth as tears filled her eyes. She faced Jessie with her feet planted solidly on the P.E.I. soil as if she meant to ground herself there and stay forever. Jessie slipped out from underneath Josh's arm and covered the three steps to her friend. The women held each other tight.

"Sophie," Jessie whispered sincerely. "I'm going to miss you so much."

"I know," Sophie agreed. "I'll miss you too, Jessie. Take care of yourself, okay? Call us. Lots."

"I will." Releasing her, Jessie smiled, her own eyes wet with unshed tears. "You're the best."

Sophie leaned in for one more hug. "So are you, girl. And don't you forget it."

It was early, but the sun was already threatening to overheat the island. Shimmering waves of heat bounced off the car's waxed finish as Sophie turned to hug Josh. Steve rested an elbow on the car and ran a hand through his long blonde curls as Jessie crossed her arms and tipped over an ankle, cocking her head as she watched him.

"You know," she said, "the sitcom doesn't know what it's in for, casting you."

He grinned at her, honest emotion interrupting his power of speech.

"In fact," she continued, "L.A. doesn't know what it's in for." Her lips curled up in a wide smile.

He shook his head from side to side as he removed his arm from the car and grabbed her in a big bear hug and spun her around.

"What am I gonna do on that set without all you *Drifters* folks around to drive crazy?" he asked. "Especially you, little girl." Neither of them brought up the fact that Jessie hadn't been on *Drifters* during the season three shoot, or that because of her mysterious absence a pall hung over the cast and crew during that entire term of production.

Jessie snuggled into him and buried her face in his hair, breathing in the familiar goat's milk soap scent of her good friend.

Steve laughed at her and lifted her chin to face him.

Wanting to bury herself in the familiar warmth of the flecked green eyes and the safety she found within, Jessie had to choke back her own threatening emotion. This was going to be a tough day. Steve saw her eyes melt from bright and happy to liquid pools of sorrow, and he frowned.

"Listen," he implored her as Josh held Sophie under his arm and watched, uncomfortable at the obvious connection between his girlfriend and his best friend. "Someday we'll work together again. We'll get on Jonathon to produce another western."

"No, not another western," she choked, in an attempt to brighten up. "The corsets. Ugh. I don't know how women wore those things."

He laughed. "Then something contemporary. Maybe a...I dunno. Something about vampires. Or zombies."

Groaning, Jessie melted back into his safe embrace. They held each other for a few minutes, eyes closed, before Steve finally looked up and met Josh's uncertain wide brown eyes. Sighing, he released his grip on Jessie and gently placed both big hands on her shoulders.

"All right," he asserted. "Lecture time." He took a deep breath. "Either one of us will call you or you will call us. Every day. Capiche?"

She nodded, swiping at a loosened tear. She could not muster a smile. Jessie adjusted her footing, her flip flops dusty in the building heat.

"I will expect entire descriptive paragraphs on each and every sunset as seen from that spectacular back deck of yours."

"Hey," she mumbled feebly. "F. Scott Fitzgerald I am not."

"I'm not asking for the dream, little girl. Just the reality." He leaned forward and kissed her firmly on the forehead, letting his lips linger there. "Miss you," he managed, before turning abruptly and heading towards the driver's side door, reaching into his plaid shorts pocket for keys as he moved. "C'mon, Soph. We've got a plane to catch." His voice was low and husky.

Frowning, Jessie wrapped her arms around her belly and hunched over. She mustered a hint of a smile for Sophie, who touched Jessie's forearm and squeezed it.

"Bye," the pretty blonde whispered softly before climbing into the passenger door that Josh held open for her.

Then the car was chugging up the lane, Steve leaning on the horn and waving out the window, his heart a stone despite the excitement of landing a great job on a new sitcom.

Left alone in the hot driveway, Jessie gazed at Josh with despair. He was next.

Josh waited until Steve and Sophie were out of sight before running his hands over his stubbly cheeks and thinking vaguely that he needed a shave. Wheeling slightly to the left, ready to go back into the house, he froze when he spied the woman he loved standing alone, staring at him as if she were once again memorizing every feature. His arms dropped to his sides.

Nearby, a fat bee buzzed from wavy pink petunias towards a patch of yellow sunflowers, sucking out the sweet nectar and reminding them that it was still summer, and that although it would be a scorcher of a day, there were still things to treasure about the season. The flowers at the front of the verandah were always such a welcoming, homey sight. When Jessie returned from her sojourns each day, she always felt her blood pressure return to normal with the flowers' welcoming embrace. She felt safe here, at the cozy cedar shingled island beach house. But she knew the house would feel empty without Josh. The question was, for how long? Would he return, or had he had enough of her and her troubles?

He spun fully around on one heel then, and clomped his way back up the steps past the flowerbeds and the gaily buzzing bee, and swung open the screen door without a backward glance.

Slowly Jessie followed, but she held onto the wooden rail and studied the bee for a moment first, wondering what it would be like to buzz from flower to flower and not have to worry about things like pleasing and loving someone. Eventually she made her way inside and started to clean up the breakfast dishes. Upstairs, she could hear Josh running water and going about his usual daily morning routine of shaving and brushing his teeth. Later, she heard the radio click on and Hot 105.5 blare over the crashing of the waves outside. *He must be packing,* Jessie thought as she tucked the last of the juice glasses into the dishwasher. *Maybe we can go for one last paddle before he has to leave.*

After a bit she heard Josh's heavy footsteps on the stairs. She was plunking away at her guitar by then, trying to fill the empty hours with something, anything.

"Hey," he said, and when she looked up she saw that he was already in his travel clothes—jeans and a long-sleeved shirt, and black cowboy boots. *Oh,* she thought. *So much for one last kayak ride.*

That added to her cranky mood. "Huh," she huffed, a touch of sarcasm coloring her voice. "You could at least try to hide the fact that you can't wait to get out of here." She leaned over and set the guitar down on its stand, leaning the neck carefully into a padded holder. Jessie was sitting on the arm of the big white chaise, perched precariously almost, as if prepared to get up and run at any moment.

He shrugged. "I don't see any point in delaying the inevitable, Jessie. This is hard enough as it is."

"Oh," she remarked with disdain. "Thanks for at least pretending."

"Pretending what, exactly?"

"Like you care."

He crossed his arms and planted his boots into the pine floor. "Care about what?"

An icy glare silenced any more remarks from Josh. He waited for Jessie to speak.

A waterfall of hair slipped off her shoulder and blocked her face from Josh's view as Jessie concentrated on pushing back a cuticle on one of her fingernails. Shortly, she accosted him. She shook the hair back over her shoulder, a stark flicker of anger blazing in the icy blue eyes Josh loved.

"I understand why you need to do this. But just for the record, I don't want you to go." She dropped her hands to her lap.

The nerve in his cheek twitched as Josh fought for words to come forth and smooth this over. There weren't any. He reached for the suitcase at his side and unzipped the cover for the extendable handle. Pulling it open, he started to walk towards the door, his voice trailing behind him. "Can you give me a lift or should I be calling a cab?"

Resigned, Jessie uncrossed her legs and rose from the arm of the couch. She followed Josh out of the door and locked it behind her. He was already in the driver's seat when she climbed in next to him.

"Your flight isn't for three hours, Josh. We could have at least gone for one last kayak ride."

"Better to be safe than sorry." He snapped down the signal indicator and turned left at the end of the long laneway.

"This is Charlottetown, not Vancouver." She glared at him. "The airport is practically in a farmer's field. There's a cow in the entrance, for God's sake!"

His lips turned up just a little then, as he acknowledged the truth of that statement. There was indeed a cow inside the arrivals gate, albeit a life-sized fiberglass cow advertising a local ice cream company.

"Whatever," he said abstractly in return.

In twenty-five minutes they were at the Charlottetown airport. Josh swung over to the curb by the departures entrance. Jessie's heart pounded and she forced her fingernails into the back of her left hand. He was already out grabbing his bag, so she opened the passenger door and walked around back. Josh slammed the rear hatch shut and faced her. Already someone had spotted them and was pointing enthusiastically.

"Get in the car, Jessie," he demanded.

She forced herself to swallow past the lump in her throat. "In a minute," she retorted defiantly.

"Jessie." His voice was rising as he telegraphed a warning. Josh was not up for an altercation here, under curious public eyes.

"No," she breathed, her voice small. "I'm not going anywhere until you talk to me."

Grabbing the handle of the suitcase, Josh pushed past her. He stopped a few feet away but didn't turn to face her when she cried out behind him, "I am trying, Josh! I'm trying, can't you see that?"

He stood still. Onlookers hurried by, those who realized there was a famous couple in their midst trying not to stare.

"Don't leave mad, Josh! Please—don't leave mad!"

He grabbed his sunglasses from his face and squeezed a forefinger and thumb into the corners of his eyes, his head hanging.

From behind his back Jessie heard him say, "You don't communicate, Jessie. At least not to me."

She was stumped. The hell she didn't. "Josh, I sang that song for you! Last night. Come on, cut me some slack here!"

Finally, interminably, he turned, his shoulders squared against her and fire blazing from his eyes although Jessie could see that the chocolate brown flickered in the sun. Evidently sorrow was etched there as well.

Sunglasses in hand, he waved at her as he spoke. "You, Jessie Wheeler, are more than just your music. A helluva lot more."

Then he turned on his heel and left without even a good-bye hug. Left standing by the SUV shocked and bewildered, Jessie almost collapsed. But she sensed people staring at her and so, despite the overwhelming urge to run past people and seek him out inside the small airport, she trailed a hot finger alongside the vehicle and stumbled to the driver's door instead.

Josh didn't hear the door slam, but somehow he felt it, and it jarred him back to reality. In line to check in for his flight, he whipped his head around to see if he could see their car outside the glass entrance, but all he spotted was a family laden with bags on a cart making their way inside, golf bags and a small child trailing along behind them.

"Fuck, Sawyer, what did you do?" he muttered mournfully to himself. "Jesus." He couldn't even believe that he left her the way he did, especially with the knowledge that Jessie was going through such a rough patch. What kind of partner was he? But he couldn't get past the email to Jacob…and what she had spit at him about the orgasms. Those wounds were still very raw.

On some base level he understood that she was still the Jessie he knew and loved—somewhere in that troubled skin she was hiding, waiting to be found. They just needed a short time apart. *Tough love,* he told himself as he inched forward in the large line-up. Unfortunately, such drastic measures also meant that he had to hurt, too.

Steve and Sophie were long gone by the time Josh got past security and into the waiting room. He sat alone, his head down, ignoring the curious stares of people around him. He fingered his boarding pass and passport, and wished to hell he could sink into oblivion and disappear forever. Stubbornly, he turned off his phone after Jessie's first text, which was simply *I luv u.*

Then his flight was called and, as he flew away from the land of the bright red mud, instead of feeling the instant relief he expected, Josh Sawyer hung his head in shame.

# Chapter Twelve

For most of that interminable sweltering hot August day, Jessie drove. She motored to the small city with the quaint inviting name of Summerside and then kept going west, following colorful signs that kept her on the scenic North Cape Coastal Drive route. She travelled on a two lane country road above red sandstone cliffs for most of the trip, past the famous black and white striped West Point Lighthouse, past the adoptive childhood home of singer Stompin' Tom Connors, and right to North Cape where she parked the SUV underneath monstrous windmills that scared the crap out of her as giant blades swooshed above her head.

She stepped over shallow waves at the beach, clutching flip-flops, and lifting her sundress so the salt water wouldn't soak it, but she kept daring herself to wander further and further out to sea so that when the waves crashed by her on their way to renewal, they drenched her anyway.

She found herself laughing as she played in the waves, but it was artificial. Jessie was numb again that day, alone and lost, a drifter in the brisk Atlantic Ocean. She wondered if riptides could grab her from a standing position, but she doubted it, although she felt the force of the waves threaten to yank her feet out from under her. A defiant stubborn part of her begged the rational part to keep on going until she was completely soaked, until the cool ocean could tear apart the pain in her soul and rip and destroy it into a thousand—no a million—tiny fragments, and disseminate those lost parts of her in a riptide, sending them out to the deepest parts of the ocean where, once again, no one could find her. No one would know where she was again. She could disappear for real this time. Forever.

She bent over in the waves and, clenching the flip-flops to her thighs, finally relinquished the hem of the already waterlogged dress, and cried heartlessly into the salty spray.

"God," she cried over and over the thunderous bellow of the crashing whitecaps, "Can't you hear me? Why aren't you listening to me? Why did you give him back to me just to take him away again? Why? Why?!"

Overhead, white and gray seagulls watched her curiously as they rode the breeze and played joyously in the summer sun, their wings almost still as they harnessed the wind. On shore, tourists and visitors wandered the white sand beach and climbed on the gritty sandstone rocks as, above them on the furthest western point of the island, dozens of windmills harnessed an incontrovertible power, the same wind in which the seagulls rejoiced and which hid Jessie's cries from the world.

She sobbed until there was nothing left in her belly but dry heaves. Jessie stayed and tottered there, buffeted by the cool waves again and again and again until her legs trembled; until her tired spirit was cleansed and baptized by the unremitting spray. She had not received an answer from God and so, angry and spent, she dragged her soaking wet body back to shore, to the beach, and then to her SUV.

She whipped the steering wheel to the right and headed back down the coast towards home, on the north side of the island this time, still following the North Cape Coastal Drive signs, until she found a vacant field. She eased the car over to the narrow shoulder and ground to a sliding halt, then slipped out and hoisted open the back door. Lifting out a quilt she and Josh had taken to various beaches on the island—and once to a seemingly deserted field of fragrant clover where they made love boisterously before a threatening low rumble from a farmer's tractor had them running to their car, laughing—she spread it over the grass and then rested her weary body and soul on top. Roughly, she yanked her dress over her head, slid off her underwear and let the hot sun dry her off in the nude. Wet, the dress was uncomfortable, and she had no change of clothes, so she laid it out to dry before lying on her belly, elbows jutting out to the sides and face resting on her arms. Jessie was beyond caring if anyone saw her. Anyways, the spot seemed deserted. After swatting away a few pesky mosquitos and one annoying 'daddy long legs,' she settled into a restless slumber.

By the time an overhead jet startled her awake, the sun was on its way to rest, and a nonchalant white and black cow was staring down at her, chewing its cud and wondering what this strange creature was doing hanging out in its pasture, all sprawled out like that.

"What the hell!" Jessie hollered, jumping up and grabbing her sundress. Her heart raced as she reached down and plucked up her panties as well, and then clutched them to her chest, but the cow didn't seem to be a threat. It just looked rather amused as it chewed away on some grass, watching her.

With one eye on the cow, Jessie pulled on her panties and then slipped on the dress. She was tipsy—sun-drunk—and well roasted, as she had neglected to care enough about herself that day to even consider applying sunscreen, but the sundress was mostly dry except for a spot here and there, and the SUV awaited with its air conditioning, so she didn't give the sunburn a passing thought. She would deal with it later, would smother herself in lotion before she settled in at home for the night. She grabbed the quilt, waved a goodbye to the cow, and headed for her car.

*Home. Ahhh.* With a twinge, Jessie thought about the empty house awaiting her, and she fought the devastating emotion that welled up in her belly yet again. She wondered whether Josh had arrived at his destination yet and, silently, before twisting the key in the ignition, she willed her iPhone to speak to her. It didn't. There was a message from Steve announcing his and Sophie's departure from Toronto, where they landed and changed planes partway through their trip, and a voice mail from Dee asking her to call, saying that she was just 'checking in', which she did periodically. But there was nothing from Josh.

"What an ass," Jessie mumbled to her new cow friend as it abstractly studied her from inside its fenced-in paddock. Instantly sorry for calling Josh an ass, Jessie scrolled to the iTunes App on her phone, tapped her 'favorites' playlist and then the shuffle icon, and plugged the device into the car's stereo. She plunked the auxiliary 'line' button in the SUV's dash and cranked up the volume. In terms of her geography, Jessie was still pretty far up west—she had at least an hour's drive ahead of her, and the succession of low growls emanating from her belly were a reminder that she had not eaten anything since breakfast.

A half hour later she pulled into one of the island's more popular dairy bars, this one in the small farm and fishing village of Richmond, and ordered a chocolate milkshake, fries and a cheeseburger with the works minus relish. The lady working the window was obviously not a Jessie Wheeler fan, so Jessie was able to relax and just be anonymous as she wolfed down her treats in the parking lot, haunted by memories of her little family's happy trips to the ubiquitous P.E.I. dairy bars.

"Hey dad," she mumbled, as David Wheeler's calming presence flitted across the slide show in her mind. Then the white banker's box she had brought home from George's tiny room at the nursing home shoved her dad aside. With Steve and Sophie visiting, Jessie had conscientiously pushed the thought of the box and its contents to the back of her brain. Her eyebrows furrowed as she pondered what could be inside. Maybe now, with Josh away, would be a good time to have a peek.

Stuffing a french fry in her mouth and following it up with a swig of the milkshake, Jessie suddenly smiled to herself. One thing about everyone complaining that she was dropping pounds was that she could eat this kind of food and not be concerned. She laughed outright. Maybe she would eat like this every day while Josh was gone. The smile turned instantly to a frown. *While Josh was gone.*

*Well. No matter.* Jessie finished her junk food, dropped the packaging in the proper round iron green and white striped compost and waste bins outside the low framed boxy dairy bar, and started the car. With her belly full, she felt content to watch the sun go down in her rearview mirror and listen to tunes as she drove. But when Jessie arrived at the narrow country lane that led to their rented farmhouse, she drove right past. The car seemed to have a mind of its own. By the time she flipped on the blinker to signal a turn onto the Charlottetown bypass, traffic had thinned out to almost nothing. It was pitch black outside, although the sky was alight with the sparkle of twinkling stars and mysterious planets. But Jessie's dark mood, cleansed by the cathartic cry under the windmills at North Cape, and a belly full of junky dairy bar food, had crashed again. She did not want to be alone. Ballads on the iPhone had lowered her spirits further, reminders of Josh and of the tumultuous past few years. The day had given her a helluva lot of time to think. She had Josh's voice bouncing around in her head—*you're not trying. Counseling is not an option. It's a necessity, a deal breaker if you choose not to go.*

She didn't call ahead, but Jessie also didn't hesitate. Gasping for breath to help swat away the haunting, stifling crap floating around her brain and threatening her sanity, she hit the brakes and plowed to a stop in Trudy's driveway, whipped open the door of the SUV, and jumped out.

A warm light beckoned her from the therapist's office window. Trudy was likely up late working on her book. Stepping up to the side entrance that clients used, Jessie raised the knocker and ungracefully pounded on the door. A light breeze had come up after the sun went down. It caressed her knees and shoulders. Inadvertently she shivered, but the wistful fragrance and light touch the breeze carried from Trudy's English country garden was lovely and soothing on her hot skin, so Jessie embraced it.

She teetered backwards when Trudy cautiously opened the door.

Shivering, Jessie crumpled into herself as Trudy peeked outside and searched the shadows for her late night visitor. Clad only in a wrinkled sundress and sandy flip-flops, Jessie's sunburned arms were wrapped around her belly. Her hair was a tangled mess and the sea-pearl eyes were red-rimmed and swollen. Upon seeing Trudy's kind eyes searching, assessing, Jessie started gasping for air, harder and harder now, and her hands flew to her mouth as her sore knees buckled. Trudy was the only person Jessie really knew here on the island, besides her and Josh's landlady, but the kindly older lady had a large family visiting and, besides, it was Trudy who demanded that Jessie face her problems, her past.

It only took a second for Trudy's surprised demeanor to soften. Letting the screen door close lightly behind her, she tiptoed forward and wrapped the trembling visitor in her arms. The girl was a quaking, timid ball.

Trudy held her up, her own eyes surprising her by filling with emotion as she considered what she knew had transpired this day to bring Jessie to her door at ten-thirty at night, a mess, something the cat might have dragged in. She smiled as Oliver, as if on cue, rushed past her and stared expectantly from his arrogant pose in front of the closed door.

"Okay, honey," she whispered to Jessie, her voice already a healing beacon, like a lighthouse, in the evening summer breeze. "Let's go in or Oliver will never forgive us. His Highness doesn't like to be kept waiting."

One arm around Jessie, Trudy opened the door with the other and all three stepped inside. Oliver padded off to his food bowl while Jessie sank to the floor in the narrow entryway. A box of tissues rested on an antique stand nearby. Trudy grabbed the whole kit 'n caboodle and handed the box to her evening guest, who accepted them gratefully and blew heartily into a tissue.

Trudy slid down the opposite wall and waited.

"I'm sorry to come here so late," Jessie started, sniffling. "I didn't know where else to go." That admission almost started the waterworks again, but she fought her demons and held her ground. She needed to find some reserves of strength within, and the woman with the reading glasses shoved on top of her head across from her, lit by the glow of a warm orange lamp in the hallway of her jungle-like office space, was shooting her a kind, steady look that read *you can do this.* Trudy's existence alone, for Jessie, was strength personified.

"Did something happen, Jessie?" The therapist knew damn well what had happened—Josh took the film. But she needed to hear this from Jessie.

After firing her an unfiltered *guessing you know as much as I do* glare, Jessie shrank further into the wall and stared at her toes. "You know he's gone, right?" She uttered the words without emotion, letting them hang unfettered in the semi-darkness.

"Yes, I know," Trudy responded simply.

Jessie looked up. "Why do I feel like there's a *what the hell did you expect* couched in there somewhere?" She could feel her temper building. Raising a hand to her hair, she started twisting a ringlet, fast and furious. She bit her top lip hard enough to draw blood.

Frowning, Trudy countered. "I'm not passing judgment, Jessie. I would never do that. But I'm also not surprised."

Letting go of the unruly ringlet, Jessie sighed and closed her eyes. "Neither am I," she admitted. "But I still wish he hadn't gone. I wanted him to stay here and 'fight the good fight' with me."

"But that would have been hard to do from his point of view, Jessie. It takes two to tango."

"Yup. I know," Jessie answered, lightly touching her arm, which was starting to feel very hot and uncomfortable, a reminder of Jessie's angst-filled western sojourn.

Trudy noticed. She hopped up and disappeared for a minute, returning with a bottle of green aloe-vera gel. "Here," she said. "This will help."

Wrapping her fingers around it, Jessie whispered a grateful, "Thanks."

Once again sliding down the wall, Trudy waited while Jessie squirted some of the soothing gel onto her sunburnt arms and then legs and rubbed it in.

"I do want to do more film, you know," Jessie offered quietly. "He thinks I don't, but I really do. And music," she added sadly.

"So…?" Trudy left the question hanging.

Jessie replied matter-of-factly, still rubbing in the gel so she wouldn't have to meet the older woman's trusting eyes. Her answer was frighteningly honest. "I'm afraid to. I'm afraid I'll have a panic attack on set or stage or…or something."

Glancing upwards, she handed back the aloe-vera before settling back into the wall and nudging a trailing vine from the nearby stand off her shoulder. "Acting is harder than people think. You need to reach deep inside yourself to connect with the emotions of the character you're playing. I'm afraid I'm going to tap into something I can't handle." Her eyes flickered and dimmed and Trudy thought she was going to space out, but Jessie managed to hang on.

"I can help you with that, Jessie," Trudy offered calmly. "If you'll let me."

Regarding her carefully, Jessie pondered the gesture. "Do you really think so, Trudy?"

"Yes," Trudy smiled, reaching across and taking Jessie's hand. "I do. In fact, I know so. But you have to do your part."

"That's what Josh said."

"Josh is right."

Jessie bit her lip again. "He's going to be gone for eighteen days." She studied Trudy to see if the therapist might give away any clues as to whether Josh might have indicated he intended to stay away longer, but the therapist didn't blink.

"Then that will give us time to get some serious work done before he returns," is what Trudy said instead. Jessie allowed a small smile to escape her lips. She liked the sound of the word *returns*.

"You really love him."

"Yes."

"You want him to come back."

"Yes." Studying her fingers, Jessie stifled the urge to lift a hand and chew on a nail. "I told him I would fight for him. For us. That I will never let him go."

A deep ache clenched Trudy's belly. *I should have done that with Frank. I should have fought for him.* She cleared her throat before responding. "That sounds like a good plan, Mizz Wheeler."

"Trudy? Do you think he'll come back?"

"Yes," Trudy said, letting go of Jessie's fingers. "I really do." She hoped she was telling the young woman the truth, that Josh would return when he was ready. Her sessions with Josh revealed a man conflicted about a lot of things, but not about his love for Jessie. That was irrefutable fact, and it ran deep.

"Are you a tea drinker?" Trudy asked out of the blue, her eyes brightening.

Puzzled, Jessie answered, "No. Coffee." She shrugged. "But maybe I could learn to like tea. Probably I should make the switch one of these days. Tea's better for you, right?" Focusing on something as normal as tea helped ease her mind, and a small sigh settled across her body. Just a smidgen, her shoulders relaxed.

Trudy slid back up the wall and reached out a hand to Jessie. "Come with me. It's not fancy, but it'll do." She led the way to the kitchen, flicked on the overhead light, and hit the power button on the Keurig. Spinning a little wheel next to it, she gestured to Jessie. "Choose."

Relieved that a cup of tea meant she could buy some time with this kind woman and not have to go home to her empty farmhouse just yet, Jessie picked out a lemon ginger blend. They sat at the kitchen table with their steaming mugs, surrounded by Trudy's plants and knick-knacks, collected over years. Jessie couldn't help but grin at a menagerie of cat figurines displayed on a 1980's oak buffet. Lined up on a lace doily, poised in the coveted center of a middle shelf, were two Siamese cats with holes in the tops of their backs—salt and pepper shakers! Trudy won Jessie's heart a little more with that not-so-surprising revelation.

"So this Frank guy," Jessie started, hesitating at Trudy's suddenly guarded expression. "I saw a picture of a nice-looking man in your waiting room. I'm guessing that's Frank?"

"Yep," Trudy nodded. *Oh well, it's not like this is a normal appointment,* she thought as she considered her profession's rather strict code of ethics. Besides. She spent all of her time with a cat. Trudy was enjoying some female companionship for a change. It was cozy sitting here in her kitchen drinking tea with a…*friend*?

"So what happened? Why aren't you together?"

Frowning, Trudy responded, "Well, that's a little abrupt, isn't it? Do I do that to you?"

With a small giggle Jessie replied, "Maybe. Sometimes." She lifted her lips to the edge of the comforting tea and sipped carefully. "Often," she added.

Settling her teacup on the table and wrapping her fingers around it, Trudy answered truthfully. "I got caught up in my work. He was a do-er. It got to the point where we wanted different things, I guess. Now he's out in Vancouver sucking the marrow out of life, and I'm here with His Highness over there." She gestured to the cat that lay curled up beneath their feet, striped tail wrapped possessively around his slumbering body.

"Vancouver, huh?"

"Yes. He's a therapist too, but he plays music on the side. In various incarnations. He got wind that you and Josh were coming here, via Charles Keating." She shrugged.

Jessie sighed. "I miss Charles. And Dee."

Trudy took a chance. "It must have been hard when you were away."

Stiffening, Jessie paused. She didn't respond and, instead, wrapped her hands around the warm mug and focused on the trail of steam that dissipated quickly into the cozy kitchen.

Continuing, Trudy gently added, "We'll talk about that another day, okay Jessie?"

Exhaling slowly, Jessie nodded, eyes downcast. "Okay." She looked up. "How come my life is so full of opposites? The music, the good things, success, money…yet everything is so hard. Bad things happened. Jacob killed Deuce and ended so much bad but he almost killed Josh—he could have, you know?"

At Trudy's shocked expression, Jessie added with a shrug, "We'll talk about that later, too, okay?"

"Yes…okay…"

"Jacob means so much to me, Trudy. And I know that's one reason why Josh left. Because he thinks I want him back, maybe. But I don't. I miss the music. I miss him. But I miss everyone else too, these days—Katrine, JP, Charlene…Charlie, Kayla, everyone. Not just Jacob."

"I get that. Jacob represents a time for you when you were anonymous, when you took a little reprieve from the world. He was your shoulder to lean on for a little while."

"My crutch, you mean." Sorrow etched the lines furrowing Jessie's forehead.

"You hurt him."

"I used him, I think. Or he thinks…" She drifted off, unsure.

"Did you?"

"Maybe! No. Hell, no! At least that wasn't my intention. I needed him, Trudy. And by the way, I think this whole fall-in-love-breakup-have-to-let-go-completely-thing sucks. FYI. Couples ought to be able to remain friends after things fall apart."

Scrunching up her face, Trudy cocked her head sideways and eyed Jessie. "I agree. But there's this little thing called a heart that can get in the way. 'Specially with the new relationship." She said that last part quietly, so that Jessie had no choice but to groan and agree.

After the tea was emptied into their bellies, balms for their souls, Trudy made them both fresh cups. Their chatter about relationships and men reminded Jessie of the long talks she, Maggie and Sue-Lyn often shared around the *Drifters* camp in the old days. Longing took hold of her, and she bit her lip at the frustration inherent in the inability to ever go *back*. But on the plus side, it was such a relief to share long buried honest thoughts with someone like Trudy, a woman who it was apparent had suffered her own hurts in the game of love, and whose position as therapist made her a non-judgmental listener.

Their talk lasted until Jessie was so tired she started to slur her words, and Trudy packed her up and sent her on her way. Trudy didn't prod Jessie in any direction in which the girl obviously was not ready to go. But what they did was establish a trust between them that opened the door for future chats, a safe place in which to start the road to healing.

As Trudy walked Jessie to the door, she pointed to the cell phone Jessie was clenching tightly in one hand. "Anything?" she asked.

Shaking her head despondently, Jessie replied, "No." Tossing her hair out of her eyes with a shake of her head, she peered intently into Trudy's trusting face. "What if I lose him, Trudy?"

Hesitating, because many others before Jessie had posed this question, and sometimes—as in her own life—the outcome was not what was desired, Trudy answered carefully. "You do what the rest of us do. You put one foot in front of the other, and you breathe in and out. That's what you do, until the worst of the pain passes. And you learn to wrap him in light and let him go. You'll be fine." She hugged Jessie tightly. "Now," she demanded, "drive safe going home, watch for skunks, don't drive too fast, this isn't Vancouver..."

Jessie laughed and returned the hug.

"...And come back tomorrow. Hear?" She brushed Jessie's hair away from her face.

"Yes. I hear. I heard." Saluting her, Jessie pushed the door open. The cool August evening welcomed her, dancing around her legs and skirt. "See you tomorrow, Trudy. And...thank you."

Safe at home in half an hour—she didn't see any skunks but she did witness a little family of some kind of night animals, hedgehogs maybe, a mom and three little ones all trundling in a line behind—she climbed into bed, exhausted, a genuine smile creasing her face. It was not at all the way Jessie expected to feel that night, alone in the big old farmhouse devoid of Steve's laughter and Sophie's wisdom and Josh's chestnut hair falling over his cheek as he grilled steaks on the barbeque. But, as the ocean's comforting call rocked her into a land of dreams filled with butterflies, she was grateful for Trudy's presence and calming wisdom in her life.

When she awoke at seven, the sun already high in the sky proclaiming yet another beautiful day, she felt more rested than over the last few months. No nightmares had assaulted her and, even though it was just one night free of bad dreams, it was a start. She climbed out of bed with a yawn and a big stretch and reached for her cell phone. There was a message from Josh, finally, brief but reassuring—*safe and sound.*

"One day at a time," she announced to the empty house before scratching her belly and plodding into the washroom for a pee. "One day at a time."

# Chapter Thirteen

Josh's milk-run flight to Virginia was melancholy but otherwise uneventful. In Richmond, Manny, a slender twenty-something mop-topped kinda guy, was waiting for him, reclining against a van whose cranberry finish sparkled brightly as it embraced the pale waves of heat rising from the pavement.

A wilted sign scrunched in his hands, Manny stepped forward when he saw Josh approach the arrivals curb parking area. With a black Sharpie, the young guy had scrawled a single word on the sign, *Harley,* the show's code word for arriving actors and crew.

"Transport," he decreed staunchly. "I'm your driver. Manny. Best way to make a living. Drive, nap in the van, drive. Who needs real sleep, anyway? Don't even really need digs. Just a place to shower, that's all. Can't offend the ladies. You know the drill."

As the young driver grabbed Josh's bag, Josh let his eyes glide over the faded blue and red sleeve tattoos running the length of Manny's skinny arms. Manny's tats were easily visible underneath his black tee and ragged denim vest, and a wide leather belt held up his baggy stonewashed denims which otherwise would have likely melted down to the ground after a few steps. Raising his eyebrows at the scruffy host who would accompany him for the seventy mile ride to Charlottesville, the city the production company was using as a main base for their film, Josh was in some ways thankful. Judging by Manny's effusive introduction, Josh figured at least the conversation would flow, even if it did end up being a little one sided.

During the ride, Josh let Manny's animated voice fade in and out as he considered what he had gotten himself into. In his view, he was extremely fortunate that the producers and director—the director being a newbie with one hot Indie Sundance premiere to his credit—wanted him bad enough to wait til the last minute before deciding to go with someone else for the part. The ringer was twofold. Josh's success in *Drifters* and the few features he shot on hiatuses between seasons and then after *Drifters* shut down earned him both the experience and the accolades required to build up his acting resume to a point where he was now highly desired in the film biz. On top of his skill as an actor, though, he had some extras going for him that gave him an edge over other leading men. One, his hair was still longish and layered—not as long as on *Drifters*, but wild enough to play a rogue member of a motorcycle gang. Two, he was an experienced and confident Harley rider. The part was the lead, not the villain as in most of his recent films. Needless to say, Josh's stomach fluttered with excitement once he left Jessie and her woes behind in pastoral P.E.I. This was a good role, and it would elevate his career dramatically. The director, Thomas Scott, came with high recommendations, and the production company making the movie was trusted and well qualified.

As Manny rattled on about the cinematographer, locations, cast and crew, and how thrilled he was to be one of the locals hired on the production, Josh's mind slipped to Jessie. He knew he had been exceptionally hard on her, but he honestly felt like she needed a kick in the pants to prompt her into gear. Yes she was depressed, but she had found some peace when she buried Sandy and Rachel together, and then reunited with Josh. But even though her healing island was the medicine she needed in some ways, it was also working against her. It was too easy to hide there, to distance oneself from the real world. She had not done a film, or any acting for that matter, since *Drifters'* season two. She had a few in mind, or so she told Josh and Deirdre, but so far she had not committed to anything. Instead she spent time kayaking or soaking up the sun, visiting her mother on the good days, and picking away at her guitar. On the bad days, she took to napping more and more and for longer stretches, skipping meals, and generally resisting any attempt to go out. True, she had done better with Steve and Sophie around, but prior to their visit Josh occasionally found her wandering the house, her small hand hanging on to a door frame as she peered in first one room and then another, until she had the whole house covered. When he finally asked her what she was doing that last time, her eyes were vacant, distant. She had turned to him in a ghostlike mirage, and explained that she was just grounding herself in the house, reminding herself that it was a safe place, that no one could hurt her there.

Josh knew instinctively that she wasn't just talking about Deuce McCall. Jessie meant everyone—the world. Her triggers, fueled by a lack of restful sleep, had increased to the point where she was terrified of having panic attacks. Josh knew this to a degree, but he really had no idea how entrenched this fear had become. Jacob's presence in Jessie's life, and the quiet time being 'normal' in Edinburgh had settled her to a point, but the return to Vancouver, the traumatic climactic showdown with McCall, and the loss of Jacob were too many changes, especially with the constant clamor of the media to know the truth, to keep her and Josh in the public eye. They were martyrs, of a sort. As a couple, they represented hope for many others in the world. But nobody except for Josh—and maybe Trudy, to a point—understood just how much of a toll Jessie's past was thrusting on them this summer. How difficult it was to love each other with so much crap hovering overhead.

Eventually Manny pulled up to the hotel where the production team was housed. Deftly, he hopped out, opened the back and grabbed Josh's bag. It was a warm late summer evening with a hazy gray sky overhead, and hints of pink and orange kissed the landscape as the sun began its daily descent. Looking around and taking stock, Josh felt himself relax further. This part of Charlottesville was very pretty, its architecture like many other ubiquitous post American Civil War Federal buildings—red brick, white columns and broad steps that led folks inside to banks and local government services.

"I'll be back to pick you up at seven a.m.," Manny was saying as Josh silently observed his surroundings.

His comment jarred the actor awake. *Crap.* There was a downside to film work—early mornings. Yet seven was likely going to be late, a sleep-in, he knew from experience. Most set calls would likely be much earlier, as the producers and director would be hoping to cover a fair bit of script each day. Lighting and blocking always took longer than anticipated, slowing down work and making for long days.

A smile flitted across Josh's lips. He grinned wholeheartedly at Manny and grabbed his bag with his left hand, reaching out with his right to shake the driver's skinny paw. "Thanks, Manny. I'll be ready." Yawning, Josh wheeled around and sauntered off into the busy hotel. Scanning the lobby, he spotted the reception area and made his way to the counter to check in.

Later, upstairs, he ordered room service for dinner—a side of grilled asparagus with a red pepper and chicken Alfredo—and unpacked his bag, hanging up his vintage shirts and refolding T-shirts and jeans to place in drawers. He swung around to the washroom and set his shaving kit on the counter. Removing his toothbrush and toothpaste, Josh stood in front of the mirror and stared at his tousled reflection while he brushed his teeth. Ennui hit him then, and he picked his cell up from the bed where he'd tossed it earlier, and he searched for messages from Jessie. There were three, all standard *how's it going* types. Just as he was about to type back a response, a knock jarred him away from the phone.

Two of the producers were at the door with the young director. Introductions were made and then Josh was invited down to the hotel bar to meet some of the other cast as well as the cinematographer and production designer. It wasn't long before everyone was acquainted and swapping war stories from previous productions. The only references to Jessie were the basic *how is she doing,* and *give her my regards.* After the Coupland interview, it seemed the truth about what happened to her and the irreversible choices she made seemed to be everyone's business.

By the time Josh yanked down his jeans and climbed into bed, he was exhausted. Overall, he was happy with the personalities working on the film, although he knew that once the long grueling days began, so would the emergence of true artists' gripes and stripes. However, it was a good group overall, Thom Scott had some great ideas, and Josh was thrilled to be a part of it all.

The bed was comfortable, but it felt too big. Expansive. Empty. Josh rolled over onto his side and grabbed a pillow to hug. In the end he decided to wait to text Jessie in the morning, telling himself he didn't want to take a chance on waking her with a jarring text message. Still, it was her face and sad eyes that flitted back and forth across the invisible screen in his mind all night long. He tried to push her away but she just kept coming back. By three a.m.

Josh had to fight a searing pain in his belly. It erupted with every breath as he pictured the pleading desolation in Jessie's eyes as she stood haltingly by their rented SUV in the parking lot of the Charlottetown airport. Shock waves reverberated in his stomach as he was reminded of leaving her alone the way he had. He was an ass, and he knew it, but he was also very, very tired. Of everything.

A wake-up call jarred him to life at six. Not wanting to be late on his first day, Josh crept out from under the light covers and whipped open the heavy drapes. The Virginia sun almost blinded him, but it achieved the desired effect of waking him further to face the day. He ran a hand through his tousled hair and yawned as he studied the unfamiliar skyline. Nestled in the heart of the Blue Ridge Mountains on the banks of the beckoning Rivanna River, Josh was pleased to see that outside his window lay a lush green landscape, a velvet blanket of trees. Instantly remorseful when he caught himself thinking Jessie would love this place, he backed away from the country view and opened a drawer in the large suite. He plucked the first pair of jeans off the top of the pile, and then a fresh pair of boxers, and threw them on the bed. His shower was warm and restorative but he skipped the shave. The night before, the production designer had asked him to hold off. Today they would determine as a team whether he should shave or remain scruffy, and whether they would trim or color his hair.

Manny was true to his promise. He was waiting downstairs, chatting with another cast member, a tall willowy longhaired blonde with welcoming eyes and a ceramic thermos held lightly in her hand. She moved gracefully forward to greet Josh and then they followed Manny out to the van and headed towards their set, which was a restored airplane hangar a few miles outside of town.

It was then that Josh finally took the time to text Jessie. Sitting in the back of the van as the Charlottesville landscape slid by his window, he sent her a simple note, which became his general pattern over the duration of the busy shoot until, about halfway in, the tide turned.

# Chapter Fourteen

"Nothing like getting paid to ride a Harley," Manny remarked casually to Josh as he handed him a traditional black flame spoiler half-helmet. Chuckling, Josh buckled the strap under his chin. He was having a blast. Nine days into the actual shoot, and they were shooting a road scene today. There would be a mélange of shots—longs, wides, mediums, some from a camera car with the bike mounted on a trailer in back, and some with Josh's bike mounted on the side. There were six principal cast working on the bikes that day, and although their work was well choreographed, it would take some finagling and patience, especially given the almost explosive roar of the engines, to bring it all together and get the shots the director wanted.

Manny was taking a break from napping in the van and was hanging out on set. As one of the drivers, he was stationary at the moment, since all cast was already on set and the squirrely girls in the office hadn't yet beckoned him to run errands. He was a fairly chill guy, Josh had discovered. Despite the first impression of faded tattoos and a fairly unkempt appearance, it was readily apparent that the young driver had his head on straight. Most nights after shooting, the boys chatted over dinner. Manny made it his business to fill Josh in on film set gossip regardless of whether Josh wanted to hear it or not.

Tightening the now fastened helmet strap underneath his chin, his newly highlighted blonde hair straggling out from underneath both sides of the helmet, Josh grinned. He was having the time of his life on this show. His part was intense. His character, an Afghanistan war vet, was helping a friend fight for civil rights in a backwards town where 95 % of the population was Caucasian. Of course, there was a girl involved—the willowy blonde. Discovering her to be a happily married mother of two, Josh was relaxed in her company and was enjoying working with her. Even the few always uncomfortable lovemaking scenes somehow managed to be fun and easygoing.

However, there was one woman who piqued Josh's interest from the start. Melanie, crew for on-set hair continuity and styling, was a thirty-something gregarious redhead with a perfect body that she loved to flaunt. She wore mainly jeans, always a size too tight, with a wide studded belt, black boots, and tight fitting low cut T-shirts, most with arcane and inappropriate suggestions that blazed from her 38 DD chest. A tiny diamond in one nostril was accented by five more on each ear, and her hair was spiked in all directions. Even her clunky black motorcycle boots screamed rebellion. In short, she wasn't really the kind of girl Josh would ever find attractive, but there was something about her outward personality that he found enticing. Perhaps it was her confidence and complete self-assurance. At any rate, he found Melanie intriguing, a little wild even, and Josh side-stepped her carefully as Steve's admonishing voice echoed in his head, *you're going to fuck her over, aren't you?*

Now, Josh sucked in a breath as Manny begrudgingly ducked out of the way so Melanie could make her way over to Josh. She stood beside him and the big bike, her legs parted and lips pouting while she tucked Josh's hair in and around the black helmet. Her dark eyes fizzled into his as she teased strands this way and that. She was allowed to touch him but she lingered too long and stood too close, and even had the audacity (according to Manny's Christian upbringing, as he told the other drivers later) to lean forward and whisper something highly inappropriate in Josh's ear, according to the quick blush that bloomed across his face. She liked to tease, and after nine full days of shooting, Josh was finding her attentive and interesting, not distant and sad. And so he stopped fighting his conscience and soaked in her presence.

When she was done fiddling with his hair and letting her fingers graze his cheeks, Josh didn't attempt to disguise his pleasure at watching Melanie's perfect tiny runner's butt saunter away. From beside him came a quiet voice.

"I'd keep an eye on that one if I were you, man."

His defenses rising, Josh shrugged. "She's harmless." But he was lying, and Manny picked up on that. Already the driver had deduced that something was amiss in the Sawyer-Wheeler camp, but there had been no mention of a break-up amongst the cast and crew, so Manny was on the alert but keeping an eye out for his new friend.

"Just watch your back," Manny countered. "She'd sleep with Horace. But she's definitely got her hooks in you."

Horace was a three hundred and some pound teddy bear that at one time had really and truly belonged to a biker gang. He was working as the set's advisor on this film. Josh caught the guy's eye and gave him a wave before tossing a leg over his Harley. The advice from Manny was unsolicited, and Josh was uncomfortable being on the receiving end. Still, he knew the young driver was right. But—whatever. What happens on a film set stays on a film set, right? Revving up the bike as if the roar could wipe out his uncharitable thoughts, a sudden image of Charlie flashed through Josh's mind. True, the old playboy had settled down over the last few years. He was married now, expecting a baby, and absolutely devoted to Jane, his pretty pixie-blonde wife. But there was a time when he had been a thoughtless ass, a cheater extraordinaire. To Jessie, in fact.

*Shit,* Josh grunted, pondering the invitation Melanie had whispered in his ear while she was teasing his hair. *I'm not that guy.* But part of him wanted to be. Part of him was experiencing a rebellious freedom as the leader of a fictional biker gang. Part of him wanted to touch a woman without fear of triggers and resistance, without a look that said *my skin crawls when you touch me.* Or *the best orgasm I ever had was not with you.*

Revving the bike again, Josh could feel Manny's eyes on his back. Early on, Manny had made a quick reference to Jessie, as had many others on set. But something in Manny's ever changing flecked hazel eyes, and the unexpected wisdom underneath, told Josh that somehow Jessie meant more to the guy than to some of these film types. He later found out that Manny's sister had once been sexually assaulted by a cousin. *Leave it to Jessie,* Josh thought when Manny had revealed that little bit of info. *She's everywhere. She's everybody's fucking hero.*

With a quiet nod to Manny, Josh followed the instructions of the first assistant director and he revved the bike up again and rolled it across the gravel parking lot to his first position. He was thinking about Melanie's whisper, her seductive offer, and his body tingled with the sudden promise of it, of the pleasure of feeling the electric tingle of his hands on her bare skin, for starters. He pushed Jessie from his mind for the thousandth time that day alone, and let the wild breeze generated by the Harley's speed carry him away with each and every shot.

Between shots he wrangled with the notion of toying with Melanie. Yes, an affair with her would have its repercussions, but maybe Jessie needed a bigger wake-up call.

Angry at himself for wanting what he shouldn't have, and pissed for even considering hurting Jessie any further, Josh was glad for the freedom the bike and the day's shooting schedule gave him, because he wasn't much in the mood to face Manny's searching eyes and judgment, or Melanie's temptations, for that matter. He needed some time to think.

~

"I think I'll go for a swim when I get home," Jessie told Trudy as they walked arm-in-arm towards Jessie's SUV, where she'd carefully parked it in the therapist's driveway. The rain that poured from the Heavens all through their afternoon session had finally dissipated, leaving the fresh summer rain scent of earth-washed renewal floating in the air. The sun was peeking out from behind a slate gray cloud and the hot wind, now just puffy gusts, seemed to be abating. Waves of misty heat were rising from the soaked pavement. It was another muggy day, and Jessie knew the ocean would beckon her when she arrived back at the farmhouse. This time of year, in late August, the north shore Gulf water was about as pleasant as it would get. Islanders were experiencing one of their warmest summers ever. Rainfall was down and the farmers were complaining, worrying about the lack of rainwater to keep their potatoes hydrated. Yet the tourists and residents of the province were thrilled as they enjoyed their favorite summer pursuits of camping, biking, swimming and lounging about the beaches, and agreeable evenings munching on s'mores in front of crackling bonfires.

With a hug, Trudy acknowledged Jessie's spoken desire to cool off with a swim. "You deserve it, kiddo. Good work today."

"Not easy," Jessie managed, fighting back the overwhelming emotions that today's unearthed sordid memories created. An afternoon of recalling Deuce's manipulations and learning the tools to manage the pain of that terrifying and lonesome time of her life was almost more than Jessie could bear. But she got through it. She survived another day, and somehow setting those loathsome memories free were indeed lessening her heavy load.

"Hey," she tossed in, grasping Trudy's hand, which was a breakthrough in itself—the comfortable acceptance of touching another, and being touched in return. "We've already broken some of the rules. Let's go out to dinner tomorrow. My treat."

A grateful smile tickled her lips, and Trudy's eyes lit up. "Do you like seafood?"

"Damn straight."

"Fine. What time?"

"Well...my session's in the morning tomorrow, right? So that will give me time afterwards to go home and have a swim maybe, do some songwriting...shower and change...let's say six." She brightened. "Hey! Why don't you come to the farmhouse for a glass of wine, then we can go out from there. We can drive into Cavendish and 'play tourists' or maybe go eat at that old Victorian house in Kensington—The Home Place?"

"It's a deal," Trudy replied happily. Jessie was proving to be good company, surprisingly, and any awkwardness the women felt at the beginning of their sojourn together had simply faded into oblivion over the past nine days.

She watched as Jessie steered her vehicle out into the quiet street. Jessie turned to wave goodbye to Trudy before scooting off towards her summer home. The girl had certainly proven that she could be disciplined when her heart and mind decided to work in concert. The afternoon's session was decisive, and Trudy could see the weight begin to rise off the singer's shoulders.

"Who do you cry to?" was the first thing Trudy had asked earlier that day after the women settled underneath the office foliage into the wicker chairs, with steaming antique teacups of chamomile tea carefully clasped between their fingers. Jessie had chosen a Wellington pattern of fine bone china, in pleasing pink cherry blossoms accented with green leaves. It seemed apropos in Trudy's verdant office, and brought to mind images of Dee and her love of gardens.

Taking a sip of the hot liquid, Jessie pondered Trudy's question and thought for a second. She was getting used to this therapy thing, and the comfort level established with Trudy over the last many days was making it easier not to withdraw.

Trudy threw in another query while Jessie reflected on the first. "Can you lean on your friends? What do you imagine would happen if you leaned on your friends?"

"They're actually great," Jessie replied honestly. "Pretty much all of them. They're good listeners."

"And Josh?" Trudy noticed a stiffening in Jessie's demeanor upon the mention of Josh. She knew the communication between them since he'd left was relegated mostly to brief texts and the occasional quick phone call. But she wondered if there was more to Jessie's physical reaction to this question.

"Josh..." Jessie said simply, her eyes dimming and leaving Trudy's gaze and wandering to the window. But she didn't fade. Instead, Jessie turned back to her therapist and revealed one of her biggest fears. "I'm mostly afraid to tell him things. We stick to safe subjects."

"Do you know why you do that, Jessie?"

"Yeah."

Trudy waited.

"Because I feel like if he knows the truth about me, about who I was as a kid, or what Deuce did to me, then he won't like me anymore. I don't even like me, actually. Much."

The revelation was not a surprise to Trudy. Self-loathing was often the case amongst survivors of child sexual abuse. But it saddened her to think that an internationally beloved superstar like Jessie Wheeler, someone who achieved great success, was still filled with so much self-hatred that she dis-associated from those around her, including herself at times.

"That must make you feel lonely."

Shrug. "Yeah. I guess."

"What do you do when you're in a bad mood?"

"Around who? Josh?"

"Anyone. Your producer, your manager, your fans...Josh..."

"I guess I go away from them. Go sleep or write a song or something. Or go for a drive."

*We are validated when we are understood,* thought Trudy. "If no one knows who you are, bad moods included, then you must feel alone with your sadness. There are probably lots of parts of your personality that you are afraid to share because of fear of how people will react, eh Jessie? You feel you need to keep up the good stuff—the singing, the acting. To please people."

"I guess so." She hadn't really thought about it. She just lived it.

Leaning forward in her chair, the teacup balanced in her fingers, Trudy continued. "I'm going to help you show me those parts of your personality that you feel you can't show your friends."

The rest of that afternoon she helped Jessie see behind her self-created mask. Trudy became a guide to help her through. She knew the easiest way to break through her patient's defense was to show that she could be comfortable getting close to her pain, rage, and despair. At times, Jessie still slipped away into a daydream. To get her out of it, Trudy either called her name firmly or moved her chair closer, startling Jessie. Both techniques worked to refocus her client's attention and effectively kept her from drifting. By now Trudy clearly knew that Jessie zoned out when the painful experiences were too much to bear.

Jessie still sank into explaining her problems as if they were all in the past and were thus fine, and that she was making lots of progress. But when Trudy asked specific questions, Jessie's expression often changed, revealing that the problems were as real and current as the hot tea in her pretty antique cup.

At one point after Jessie faded off Trudy called her on it, gently and nonjudgmentally. "It looks like you may have just relived some things a little there."

Glancing up into Trudy's warm eyes, Jessie responded, "They still come and go sometimes—the feelings." It felt good to be honest for a change, with both her therapist and herself. She wondered if she could do that with Josh, if she could come clean that way. Her stomach hurt when she thought about it. She still felt it would be too much for him, that he only wanted the *good* part of her, the singer, the actor, the popular Jessie.

Occasionally Trudy watched Jessie fade out in front of her but made the decision not to interfere. After a period of silence Trudy would speak. "I think you needed some time because what we were talking about was too hard to bear." Maintaining strong but sympathetic eye contact was part of her training. It helped Jessie readjust, which she did by shaking her head and focusing her eyes.

Gradually it got easier and Jessie found herself able to speak in longer sentences as she worked with Trudy to understand and make sense of her life. The chaotic, disconnected thoughts that bombarded her, especially at night, resulting in mental disintegration, started to settle as she and Trudy developed a pattern of trust between them.

# Chapter Fifteen

On set in Virginia, a magic hour—golden light—shot was scheduled for later in the day. The actors had a break while the camera was moved. Then, when the A.D. called them to set, they lined the bikes up at first position to wait for their cue to roll. The shot was planned to capture the motorcycle gang from behind in a long, distant frame as the Harleys moved as one around a curve in the rolling Virginia countryside. The first two takes were a breeze, and Josh found his mind wandering as the wind coursed through the longish hair peeking out from underneath his half helmet. Powering the heavy bike in the lush countryside of Virginia in the company of his new friends was a genuine rush. The sense of renewal that accompanied his growing comfort in the rogue character he was playing fed his need for independence. But it was a false need that played on his fears, on the feeling that he was inadequate in Jessie's eyes, and in his own inability to care for her and minister to her. His glance kept changing during that last shot. The camera was behind him, so although he watched the road, Josh also let his eyes lose focus here and there. The long day would soon be over, and Melanie was very clear in her intentions.

Josh surrendered, and let his mind wander.

~

Jessie dropped her beach towel on the sand and didn't bother to straighten it and position sandstone rocks at each corner to keep it from blowing in the breeze, as she usually did. Instead, she dropped one large sandy red rock on the center of the towel to make sure it was anchored enough not to blow away, and then she headed down the beach for a walk.

The storm had passed and refreshed the air somewhat, but it left in its wake a mostly gray sky and a still gusty wind that blew the slate clouds so quickly that Jessie felt if she hitched a tail to one she could parasail above the Atlantic, and study the red and green patchwork land beneath her as she flew along. She could go from tip to tip on the island, which was roughly, from Tignish in the west to Elmira in the east, 274 kilometres. Floating up there, high above the farmers tending their potatoes, the fishermen with rare coveted tags hauling in massive tuna, and the families at Shining Waters Park in Cavendish in the dying dregs of their summer holidays, Jessie would be invincible. No one could hurt her anymore.

Sometimes she did hitch a tail to a cloud, on stage, or within a cast on a production. But always there was a price, lack of privacy being the main one. Still, her success did enable her some benefits, the least of which was financial security that brought with it its own ability to hide.

The puffy wind was still strong enough to blow the sand around. Jessie had left her sunglasses on a vintage rosewood sideboard at the house since the early evening light was diminished, so now she wrapped a hand over her eyes to keep the sand from biting. It felt like a spatter of tiny insects attacking her, and she didn't want to get any in her eyes or she knew it would feel like she had sandpaper underneath her eyelids. With a last backward glance at the towel to make sure it was secure, she headed down the beach towards a large wet sandbar where the whipping frenzied sand would be less pervasive. She would dip her toes in there.

Glancing out to the ocean on her left, she was awed by the waves. They weren't the biggest she'd ever seen, but they were cresting high enough to look like fun. She and Josh had spent hours on the beach one day their first week here, by turns lying on the beach soaking up the sun, interspersed with bouts in the waves, ducking and diving and playing and laughing with glee as the waves sucked their feet out from under them and crashed over their heads. Recalling the exhaustion afterwards, she figured that a good romp in the waves just about equaled a day at the gym.

She slid both fingers under the band of her red bikini top and pulled it out a little to adjust it. Comfortable with her body image, although Josh and Dee constantly reprimanded her for being too skinny these days, she was still grateful for the private beach. She could see tiny figures way down the beach, perhaps a father, child and dog, it appeared from here. But mostly the beach stretch where she and Josh hung out was for private home owners or cottagers, only, and her landlady was very strict about placing signs and monitoring the property against curious travellers. Jessie and Josh's stay on the island had become public, and some in the area were clueing in to where they were living, but for now she was alone and, for the most part, felt safe.

Curls whipped around her shoulders as she stopped and bent to peer closely at a pearl-blue shell. Jessie was feeling Josh's presence in the wind. Sometimes he did that, just popped into her brain for no reason. Absently she wondered if it meant that he was thinking about her. He was on her mind a lot, of course, but this thought seemed to just pop in there suddenly while she was looking at the shell. Jessie paused, straightened, and fought a sense of panic. For no apparent reason, she suddenly sensed that something was amiss in his world today.

Sighing, she continued her slow plod down the beach. She would try to contact him later, although she found most of his communications brisk and terse. At least he did take some time the day after his arrival to send her an email. In it, after he described the area in Charlottesville where he would be shooting, and mentioned that the producers had asked him to highlight his hair blonde, which Jessie found rather tantalizing, he was very clear that he was still feeling at a loss in terms of their relationship. The paragraph was to the point:

*I feel like we are going in different directions, that we want different things, and I don't know how to make that work. Trudy is wise and can maybe help put this in perspective, but I can't help but wonder if we rushed back into things too quickly, after what happened with McCall, and with you being away, and both of us in other recent relationships. I love you Jessie, but you have to meet me in the middle here. Maybe we should think about where we both want to go with 'us' before we commit ourselves further to something that maybe has just changed too much to succeed.*

The email hurt Jessie deeply but she understood his position clearly. She also found herself wondering if it was really just Josh's own self-preservation kicking in. They could make the film thing work. If he wanted to do films, then so be it, she would find a way to support him in that, even if it meant constant travel and time apart. At least he would be feeding his soul and career ambitions. And maybe someday (she would not have said this two weeks ago, but Trudy had a way of settling her mind and giving her hope) she would sign onto another project as well, and ease back into her life as an actor and singer. But underneath Josh's printed words was the subtext that he didn't know if they could work as a couple. Meaning intimacy, sex, all the things Deuce stole from her, the horrid distasteful things that were not an issue with Jacob because initially she was someone else with him, and he didn't know. But with Josh. . .well, the bad things were so apparent that they filled his sad brown eyes with fear every time he touched her.

The walking was slow and cumbersome as her toes dug into the sand. She sidled to the left, closer to the water where the sand was wet and where the walking would be easier.

Again, Josh popped into her head in a more urgent way. She paused, frowned, grabbed a ringlet in her hair and started twisting, and considered going back to the house. *Seriously, is something wrong?* She could feel it in her bones, running up and down her spine with the heavy breeze, threatening to suffocate her. Hesitating a moment longer, Jessie decided she was just worried about their relationship overall. She dug her toes back into the sand, close enough to the smaller wavelets dying on the beach now that she jumped with the sudden shock of the cool water reaching and then caressing her bare feet.

The tide was out, so the sandbar she decided to wander onto was now clearly visible, jutting out between pools of now shallow water, inviting her to navigate it. It was unexplored territory. There were no footsteps before hers, just virgin wet sand, and little ripples here and there that her toes enjoyed scrunching, bringing a diminutive curved smile to her lips. Jessie's thoughtful pale blue eyes were sparkling in the new sun that kept trying to peek from behind the large leaden clouds. She was enjoying the freedom and peacefulness that nature laid at her feet each and every day when she came home to the old farmhouse and wandered its age-old beach. Still, something was nagging her about Josh. She faced the wind so that it whipped the curls unmercifully around and behind her shoulders, and so that with each new gust she had to lean forward a little in order to remain standing. Then she turned her head to the side and stared at the tiny pile on the beach where she'd dropped her towel. Beyond it she could see the highest gable of the farmhouse over the small cliff. Awaiting her there was her cell phone. She could text Josh when she got back.

*Hmmmm, getting back...* one foot in front of the other, Jessie stepped cautiously out into the cool waves, towards the house. She was a ways out on the sandbar now; surely the salty water around it wasn't very deep. After all, there was another sandbar further over towards the farmhouse that she could easily reach in minutes. The sand back on the beach was hard and the wind whipping it made walking uncomfortable. Swimming would be much easier, and quicker.

She yelped as a frigid wave crashed over her warm body. The temperature of the water was probably about twenty degrees Celsius, she figured, which was really pretty good overall, and she shivered in the rapidly cooling evening air. Another reason to swim. Yes, it would take a few moments to adjust to the water but likely it would be warmer than the air temperature at this point, considering the cooling wind. Soon Jessie was swimming. She was strong, and at first she enjoyed the waves and she laughed as she dipped and dove and played in and around them on her way back towards her waiting towel.

But then when she reached for the sandy bottom it wasn't there, and she began to dog paddle breathlessly as another wave crashed over her—*geez, they just keep coming, I can hardly catch my breath*—but she stifled an initial panic and focused on the towel, her comforting destination. Another incessant, powerful wave caught her off guard. Shaking her head after it passed and wiping fingers over her face to clear her vision, she turned steely eyes back towards the sandbar near the farmhouse.

"It's not so far, Wheeler," she asserted out loud to herself and to the swooping gulls overhead. "Just keep on swimming."

She dug both arms into the ocean and forged ahead.

~

In Virginia, the director asked for a second take of the last shot just as the day's fatigue was sinking profoundly into the actors' bodies. Cast and crew were all in need of a hearty meal, a few good beers, and stimulating conversation. But this was solid paid work. In good spirits, the cast revved the bikes up back at their first positions and Thom Scott, perched behind a video monitor where he could eyeball the camera angle, shouted *Action*! The First A.D. relayed the call with a wave and, as Josh pondered Melanie's tight tee and warm sensual hands, he revved the bike harder and pointed it down the road. Tired, his mind wandered during the simple shot as his body ached for a touch from the smoldering eyes of the on-set hair gal. In his mind he had already replayed the images and sensations he would expect to feel in her company many times, and every nerve on his skin was reacting more intensely the closer the production got to wrapping for the day. It seemed to him that Melanie's eyes smoldered every time he glanced at her and, after an initial shyness, he started meeting her steady gaze, smoldering right back. This morning was the first time she had versed any concrete desires, and Josh had to admit that the thought of being with this adventurous sensuous woman with all the right curves was driving him right around the bend.

He had it all figured out. They would join the others for steaks in the hotel restaurant, and despite his past relationship with alcohol and substance abuse Josh decided he would need some liquid courage, so he planned to have just one beer. He knew she would save him a seat at the table. Every night since day one he would arrive in the hotel's dining room to find her blistering gaze on him, and she would raise her French-manicured fingernails and pat the seat next to her, aligning her body alongside his and occasionally resting a hand on his thigh.

After dinner he would join her in her room, which was on the floor below his alongside some of the other crew who flew in with the production company for the shoot. Josh could see his hands on her body; he pictured pulling her top over her head and running his fingertips over her skin. Her hands would burn when they touched him, he knew that already, because even through his jeans he could feel himself yearning for her, Melanie's every touch electric and sizzling as she inched her fingers higher up his leg and towards his crotch. Last night at dinner she had gotten brave enough to let her slender fingers rest there, on his thigh but gently rubbing downwards. They were at dinner with everyone else and Josh thought he might explode there and then. It was torture and, *whatever,* Jessie would never know.

Still, the struggle continued. Could he do this to the woman he was supposed to marry?

"Hell, I need it," he muttered to himself as he piloted the heavy bike further down the road.

He pushed thoughts of Jessie away again as a small smile lit his face. He could hardly stand the anticipation of putting pressure on Melanie's hand and pushing her hard down onto him. And then later…? A full-sized grin crossed his face. But it was clouded in anger towards Jessie and her hateful comment, and a tear stung his eye as he thought about what he felt willing to do to erase that.

"Fuck, Jessie," he spat aloud angrily, hanging his head at her ability to haunt him from so far away as the production assistant at the end of their route waved an arm, signaling to the bikers to turn around and head yet again back to first positions.

~

"Fuck, Josh," Jessie was muttering to herself as she fought to breathe after yet another wave crashed overhead. If Josh hadn't been on her mind, she would not have tried to take a shortcut home. But he was in her head, taunting her, and now she was in a fix.

She realized, as she caught a glimpse between waves of her towel pile on the beach, that she was not making progress. In fact, Jessie was losing ground. It hit her like the next relentless wave—she was in a rip current, or a riptide as the locals called it. It wasn't a tide though, it was a current, and she should have known better. Both she and Josh had taken a peek at the National Park website advising tourists to be cautious in their swimming adventures, especially on the north shore of the island where rips were common. Jessie knew, damnit, she *knew* better than to go swimming this deep alone, after a storm, between sandbars! Rip currents were common in these conditions as the tide tries to carry the water back out to sea and uses a break in sandbars to do so. Swimmers drowned every year in riptides, mostly because they used all their strength to try to swim against them, then finally gave up and sank beneath their watery depths.

"Fuck!" Jessie cried, spitting salty water between her lips, to the waves and to the seagulls. "*Fuck!*"

Well, at least if this didn't turn out well she could stop worrying about Josh. About her career. About her past. About everything. She chided herself for being so dramatic. She knew a few things about rip currents. Hell, she knew a few things about surviving. She flipped over on her back and paddled her legs and arms just a little to help her stay afloat. The waves continued to buoy her but she managed to steady her mind and rest a little. She was losing energy while still being rather quickly thrust out to sea. The rip would spit her out deep past the sandbars, unremitting in its attempt to end her earthly struggles.

As she fought the good fight, Jessie remembered what Sophie told her not so long ago as they were drying dishes. Something about her life these days being like a riptide, and that she was caught in the middle but if she swam sideways she could likely get out. Well, damnit, she thought she had been swimming sideways all along, but now Jessie started swimming sideways with gusto. She knew the current wasn't likely very wide, but even so, she was still way past her comfort zone. It was a terrifying feeling trying to tread water and stretch her toes down far enough to feel the ocean's sandy bottom, and grasping only water. And in her mind was Josh, raging at the beach that night, angry with her, telling her she wasn't trying. Well, she was damn well trying now, and she fought back tears as she stroked hard to ease her burden. Hell, she was seeing Trudy and things were going okay, but she still knew that she disappeared now and again. The therapist was always scratching her chair and moving it or calling Jessie's name to bring her back. So things were slow, but they were gaining *some* momentum.

The biggest thing that was holding her back was the desire to let Josh know any of the details about McCall, that was clear. But damnit she did not want to go there. Another formidable wave hit her, and Jessie went under and came up the other side gasping, just as yet another mighty onslaught of water crashed over her, barely giving her time to catch her breath. What a feeling, struggling out here with no foothold in sight, and no one to pull her in. This was Jessie's fight, and it had to be fought entirely on her own. Well, the McCall thing—with the next wave came a realization. *What if I don't have to tell him? I mean, he'll still know everything but at least I won't have to say it. Would that be enough?*

*Huh.* There *was* something she could do to maybe meet Josh on a level playing field. There was, after all, the stalking journal she wrote that entire awful summer. She could give him that, if she had any idea where it was. Well. She had some idea.

Jessie's arms and legs were numb, both from the cold which was seeping in, and from the struggle. She flipped over on her back again, fighting back the tears because they would only deplete her energy further.

"Josh!" she cried to the spirits that floated on the wind. "Josh!"

She prayed desperately that somehow he could hear her, and that he would listen.

~

Back at the starting point, the wheel a little shaky at such a slow speed as he maneuvered for position, Josh looked over at Melanie. She was a flirt, all right. Her tight cleavage from the v-neck T-shirt was highly visible as she leaned in towards another of the cast, spraying hairspray to lock a loose strand of hair in place, which was entirely unnecessary as they were riding in the wind anyway. She brushed her breasts against the guy's arm and Josh chuckled as his heavy cast mate turned an interesting shade of pink. With a grunt, Josh steered his own Harley in between two other large bikes and waited until Melanie could make her way down the line of cast to him. In the meantime, the young director sauntered over to him, a clipboard in his hand.

"Sawyer, great job, love the look, this time let's try bringing up the speed a bit. I need this shot to pick up on the hair blowing." He spied Melanie and rolled his eyes as she spurted another spray onto the other guy's hair. "A little more speed will give us the look we want." Thom was speaking with the urgency of a busy film director who just spent the day calling out direction and actions, fine tuning lighting and shots, and generally trying to make a good film that would make or break his career. He was only about twenty-six, Josh figured, which was young for the level of success he had already attained, but a prime age for an expensive first big studio feature. The guy was great, though, understanding and patient, and he clearly knew what shots he wanted.

Thom rubbed a thumb and forefinger across the stubble on his chin and cocked his head at his star. "This time let Hank get ahead when you start out, then before you get to the curve give it the gas and pull ahead of him."

"All right," Josh agreed companionably. The tingling anticipation of Melanie's touch was undoing him. At this point he would do anything to get the shot over with, hell he'd stand on the bike seat in the wind if the director wanted.

Thom went on to give Hank the new action and Josh crossed his arms and leant on one elbow on the bike handle as Melanie sidled forward.

"Hey, gorgeous," she said, teasing him as she reached out and fingered his layered hair. He swore his hair even sizzled when she touched him—she was that kind of woman. A tattoo towards the top of her breast peeked out at him, a rose, he thought, and Josh wondered where it ended and whether he would find any others on her body that night. At the same moment, a sharp pain shot across his gut but he fought it, pushed it aside again. Its name was Jessie.

Melanie saw the flash of doubt in his eyes as they flickered from deep brown to a dimmer shade. She shifted her balance to one hip, legs once again parted. "What?" she pouted. "Having second thoughts?"

"Hell, no," he responded after a momentary pause. "It's just a little harmless fun, right?" Not yet 100 % sure, he slipped a hand over to her behind and gave it a little squeeze in order to reassure her. Without losing eye contact, Melanie let her fingers trail from Josh's hair down to his neck and shoulder to rest finally on his broad chest.

"Can't wait, soldier," she breathed as he swallowed uncomfortably.

*What the hell am I thinking?*

Around him, Melanie's attention was attracting stares, not for the first time, on the shoot. Josh lifted a hand up to his helmet clasp as his fling walked away, her butt swinging intentionally from side to side. Loosening the buckle under his chin, Josh avoided the others' eyes, but he could feel their disapproval and he could almost hear the whispers.

Then the A.D. called *places, please,* and soon, with a mighty roar, he slipped the bike into gear and joined the fake motorcycle gang for its last run of the day.

"Damnit!" Jessie was thinking about Josh, and mentally saying her goodbyes to Charles and Dee too, as she fought the roiling Atlantic under the subdued dreary sky. She was tiring quickly now, and not making any progress that she could detect. She thought of that fishing boat full of partiers she and Josh had seen so long ago now, it seemed. Maybe they would come by and help her out. But the waves and wind were mighty. No partiers would be out drinking leisurely on a small boat on a hoary evening such as this.

In her struggle she told Josh all the things she would tell him if she had him back.

*I miss you I need you I'm trying I'm sorry I love you I miss you I need you I'm trying I'm sorry I love you I miss you I need you I'm trying I'm sorry I love you I miss you I need you I'm trying I'm sorry I love you I miss you I need you I'm trying I'm sorry I love you*

Somehow she thought Josh heard her words, and she felt him reach out to her upon her last and final thought amongst the waves that day. *I will not give up on us, Josh Sawyer. I will fight for you.* A calm took over her mind and body then, and she felt her stubborn fears and interminable worry subside. Then, as quickly as she found herself embroiled in a struggle for life, the battle was over.

~

He didn't pay enough attention to the road on the last take. Just as Josh made up his mind firmly to definitively move ahead and see where things might go with Melanie tonight, the speeding bike hit a loose patch of gravel and started to go down, the other riders cruising closely behind like a momentous train that couldn't stop.

Suddenly, the universe seemed to be telling Josh what it thought of his crass decision. Instantly, his tires started to wobble as the loose gravel sucked him in. He went ass over teakettle as the bike spun out in a 'rear steer' manifested by excessive speed, fatigue, inattention and an inherent Harley related problem of reduced traction and lateral control. Steadying the bike was not an option. Throwing his arms over his head to try to prevent another huge motorcycle from squashing his brains all over the road like a watermelon was about all Josh could do as he hit the pavement and rolled. He was an experienced rider, but he was out of his element at the end of the long shoot day with his mind distracted by lust. He paid the price.

The paramedics that had been standing by all day were already packed up. This was said to be the last take of the day, the 'window shot' as it's known in the industry. But the medical team was at Josh's side in minutes. He was lucky. The other drivers saw the 'Harley Wobble' start once Josh hit the gravel, and they knew he might go down. They managed to veer around him. Yet he was hurt, knocked out solid, in fact.

Taking all precautions, Thom Scott sucked in his breath and frantically, finally, waved *Wrap*. The emergency team eased Josh onto a backboard and transported him to Charlottesville's Martha Jefferson Hospital. He woke en route to the wail of the ambulance siren, and panicked when he realized he was completely strapped down onto a gurney and couldn't move. The first person who crossed his mind was Jessie.

~

Jessie made it to her beach towel before she broke down completely. The fight with the ocean took twenty minutes of her life, twenty minutes of struggling against the waves in the heat of the rip current, twenty minutes of begging and fighting the 'big fight.' Burying her face in the windblown sand-covered towel she sobbed, grateful and relieved that God gave her the grace to continue the battle for a life she now wanted more than anything. She cried for Trudy, she cried out of lonesomeness and love for Charles and Dee, and she cried for her friends, who she was desperately missing these days. But mostly, she cried for Josh.

Eventually she gathered her wits about her and stumbled, exhausted, up the beach towards the welcoming farmhouse. It was getting dark but she'd left a few warm glowing yellowish lights on inside and, like all good spirits, they beckoned her, called her, and nurtured her when she collapsed on a kitchen stool inside. Then she leveraged her aching body off the stool and hauled herself on her knees hand over hand up the stairs to the second floor. An intense shiver started at her toes and crawled its way up her body, and her dripping hair left droplets behind, a knowing trail like that of Hansel and Gretel's ubiquitous bread crumbs.

Upstairs, Jessie ran a steaming bath, stripped off her wet bikini top and bottom, and perched on the edge of their bed to text Josh while the tub was filling. She was not ready to speak to him yet, she was shivering so hard she doubted she could speak at all, in fact.

*Babe I luv u* was all she said in the text.

Then she climbed into the hot bath, disappeared into the bubbles, and thanked God for the chance to fight another day.

~ ~

In his trailer at the production's base camp, Josh's phone vibrated unheard. Ten minutes later, wardrobe gathered his day clothes and gave them to Manny to transport to the hospital. Inadvertently Manny saw the text, and his heart sank for the girl who sent it. He shoved the phone deep inside Josh's jeans pocket and threw the bundle of clothes on the front seat of the van before piloting it out of the gravel lot towards the city.

It was a few hours before Josh was cleared for release from the hospital. X-rays determined that nothing was broken, but he had a few bruised ribs, and a lot of bruised arms and legs. Road rash also left its mark on his face. Nasty cuts and scrapes marked him, *a scarlet letter in some ways,* he later thought. A rude bump to the noggin topped off his earnings on the bike that day.

A cheer erupted in the hotel's dining room when he arrived, escorted by Manny and one of the show's producers, a gray-haired executive who unwittingly reminded him of Charles Keating in his gray tailored suit and cranberry silk tie. Slinky Melanie greeted Josh most exuberantly. But this time he hesitated before he took a seat next to her.

Eyebrows were raised around him again that day when Josh spoke to the server.

"I'll have a beer, please. Guinness." And, for the second time that day, Josh ignored the whispers.

He settled into his steak and fries while the others drank, sincerely relieved their film would not be marked with a fatality. Melanie snuggled closer, occasionally touching his thigh but being careful not to apply too much pressure—yet.

Josh took a healthy pull on the hearty Stout and thanked God for the chance to fight another day.

# Chapter Sixteen

Drained, Jessie climbed under the covers. A welcome warmth was weaving its way up her body from her toes, and she had a sense of victory, fight and courage in her mind, but an empty hole in her heart. Her text to Josh had not elicited a response and, after her battle with nature, she really needed to hear from him, to touch base and make contact. She snuggled deeper underneath her woven coverlet and added the cozy quilt, which she hauled up to tuck in under her ears. Burrowing deeply, legs pulled up to her chest, she sighed and drifted off to sleep.

~

"Look," Manny insisted, shoving his hands deep in his pants pockets so as to avoid the desire to point an accusatory finger in Josh's face. "If I had Jessie Wheeler I sure as hell would not be messing around on her."

"I'm not," Josh argued, leaning a sore shoulder against the wall by the hotel's first floor washrooms.

"The hell you're not," retorted the driver sharply, reminding Josh of another voice not so long ago, that of his good friend Steve before he left P.E.I.

"Look, you don't know what the hell you're talking about, man."

"Uh yeah, actually I think I do. And I think you're better than that."

"I haven't decided anything."

Embarrassed that his attraction to Melanie was so apparent, Josh lowered his eyes and stared at the institutional geometric pattern on the carpeted floor. Since the accident, he had time to contemplate the possibility that a fling with Melanie might in fact be a really shitty thing to do. Period.

"Why would you even consider it?" Manny was pleading, now, unmercifully.

In a small voice Josh retorted sharply, "I have my reasons." He shuffled his feet. His obstinate angry desire to cheat on Jessie was rapidly diminishing, especially with the voice of reason standing there across from him, coming from a young friend he barely knew but who still, for some inane reason, seemed to care.

"Aw, come on, Josh. Don't fuck around on her. Jessie's like…"

Suddenly pulling his shoulders back and raising his eyes to bore holes into Manny's urgent expression, Josh spat, "Jessie's what, Manny?"

"Dude, you know what she is…" Now the driver was almost whining, begging.

Josh's heart pounded. *Yeah, I know. Ouch.*

Manny continued. "She's a breath of fresh air, she's magic, she's surreal… her music *changes* people. It *heals* people."

Detached, Josh watched his new friend as Manny spoke decidedly about a woman he did not even personally know. Yet there was the same old look in his eyes, a twinkling and a light that magically appeared in most people's eyes when they spoke of Jessie Wheeler. Josh shook his head, astounded. Had he gotten so deep into the forest that he could no longer see the trees? No. He knew Jessie better than anyone. He just wasn't sure if he had the strength to hold her up.

Manny stopped talking then and regarded Josh. The actor was standing there with his feet a shoulder's width apart now, his chin raised defiantly, curiously. He, too, had his hands shoved in his pockets. But there was something else about him, about his countenance. The shoulders were a little slumped, and he looked tired. The large white bandage on his cheek didn't help reduce an overall aura of sadness. And his eyes were glistening. He didn't speak, so Manny filled the overwhelming pause.

"She sent you a text. I—I couldn't help seeing it when I picked up your stuff at the set. You've got your phone set to show alerts when they come in, you should change that if you don't want others to see it. Wardrobe is always clamoring around your trailer."

Josh hung his head. "I saw the text."

"Then why, Josh? Don't be stupid. I mean—is it true? All that shit she said to Shawna Coupland?"

Josh paused. He shrugged sadly. "Yeah. It's true."

"She gave up a lot for you, then."

"Yeah," Josh cut in quickly, standing straighter, defiant. "But she also made some shitty choices." He stared hard at Manny. In a whisper he added, "It's so fucking hard, man. To rebuild something that was almost entirely destroyed." His eyes were pleading for Manny to understand. "I don't expect you to get it."

"Well I understand one thing, Josh." A quizzical expression crossed his face.

Josh waited.

"I understand that you could have been killed today. But you weren't."

"All the more reason to seize the day," Josh said sardonically. Not that he really believed it.

"I think your vision of seizing the day is different from mine." Before he stomped away, sorry he'd ever decided to work with actors, some whose egos appeared too big for their britches, Manny had one last thing to say to this guy he'd made the mistake of admiring upon his arrival in Virginia. "If it was me, I'd be on the phone calling my girl and telling her I love her back. Not screwing some mixed-up woman who thinks sex is a substitute for love. See ya around, Sawyer."

He brushed by Josh abruptly then, bumping shoulders with him and causing Josh to cry out. Every part of his body hurt, rubbed raw by the asphalt and gravel he rolled across hours earlier. He half-heartedly hoped a little endorphin rush, combined with the beer, would be enough to erase the ache.

Melanie cruised out of the ladies' washroom and took him by the hand. She was already half in the bag. "C'mon, handsome."

The elevator door closed behind Josh's back because he couldn't bear to face any more stares from the crew, some of whom were hanging out in the lobby laughing and saying their goodnights to each other. Melanie kissed him, her arms wrapped around him, all the way up to her floor. Her tongue thrusting again and again inside his mouth, deeper each time, weakened him further.

Yet, in the hallway upstairs, outside her room, he pulled her back. "I can't do this, Melanie." But his body was a traitor. It was screaming *Just do it!*

She hesitated for a brief second, then drew him closer and kissed him even harder, running her tongue back and forth across his upper lip before suddenly thrusting it deep inside again. Josh heard himself moan and, embarrassed, he tried to pull away. He knew that part of the draw towards this woman was because he hadn't been able to muster that kind of heated passion for Jessie lately. But he also understood there was a reason for that, and if she would just try, maybe they could find the old Josh and Jessie again. His eyes hurt and his sore head and ribs were pounding.

When Melanie slipped a hand tantalizingly down the front of his T-shirt, Josh winced. The anticipation drove him insane as he waited for her to go lower and then lower. And soon enough, she was there. He parted his legs as he moaned again and buried his face in the unfamiliar spiky red hair. His breath was already starting to betray him, coming in faster and faster ragged gasps as she massaged him, and then he took a chance and slipped a hand underneath her tight top and let his fingers brush her breasts. She felt strange. Different than what—who—he was used to. He shook his head to dispel the unwanted thought.

Melanie reached for her keycard and opened her door, then pulled Josh tight against her and kissed him with an intensity that shocked him, that reverberated throughout his body as they leaned against the doorframe, the door at her back.

"Oh Jesus I want this," he groaned, but his feet wouldn't move.

"Then come on," Melanie said, confident she could convince him that what they were doing was right, that it was going to feel like Heaven once they were between the sheets with no one watching, and no clothes to hinder their lust. "What are you waiting for?"

She grabbed his belt and briskly undid it, and then just as hurriedly undid the button and slid down the zipper, as if she didn't move quick enough to suck him in she would lose him. She thrust her hand inside his boxers and he almost melted then and there.

"Oh God I want this too," she was whimpering to him, and Josh let himself feel her hand on his skin for a few moments, but when she started to rock him back and forth he knew he was reaching a point of no return. Gently, he removed her hand, and the glistening brown eyes deepened in fear and sadness as he released her and backed away.

"I'm sorry," he whispered, but it wasn't really Melanie he was talking to. It was a girl who loved him, who had given up everything for him, who believed in him, who missed him and who he knew wanted him home.

And he left Melanie standing there, pissed and cursing at the door as he did his zipper and buckle back up and strode hastily to the stairs. He didn't want to risk seeing anyone in the elevator and, as he took the stairs up to his own floor, two at a time despite the aching pain in his legs and ribs, Josh managed to stifle his sobs. But once he was safely inside his room, he collapsed next to the bed and cried like a baby.

He almost died that day. He could have died. In more ways than one, Josh Sawyer had almost lost it all.

~

Jessie's cell finally rang at 3:20 in the morning, Prince Edward Island time.

"Josh?" She didn't even have to see the display. Who else would be calling her at this inane time, in the middle of the freaking night?

"Jessie." He was crying.

"Hey, babe." She was half asleep but waking up fast. Concerned.

"I almost…I almost…" He was slurring the s's so that they came out as sh's.

He paused and tried to focus.

"You've been into the bottle a bit, eh?" She felt a rising panic but she quenched it.

"Bottles. Little ones. Mini-bar. Jessie, I…"

*Jesus,* she thought, suddenly fully awake. *Who stocks the mini-bar in the room of an actor known to have fought the demons of substance abuse?* She cursed the Virginia production under her breath. "Nah, look, it's okay, look it's one night…" She attempted to calm him. "Are you okay though? Josh?"

Her understanding helped a bit. He quieted. "Yeah, yeah, I just…Jessie… I almost slept with someone, Jessie." He broke down completely then, the truth finally out in the open. "I'm sorry. I was so angry—it was stupid…"

Closing her eyes, Jessie slid to the floor and wrapped an arm around her belly. After a moment of silence she lifted a palm to her forehead and pushed hard. "But…you didn't?" *I'm going to die for real this time,* she thought as a new aching numbness overtook her.

He was silent for a moment. "No." He was calmer now. "I just—we were at dinner, a bunch of us. This one woman—she keeps hitting on me and—I admit, I've been hitting back. At the hotel…" He almost dissolved again. "Things heated up, you know, but I didn't Jess, I walked away."

"Before the point of no return, huh?" She was panicked but trying to make light. Her throat was dry and she felt a bile rise in her belly.

"No. After. But it didn't happen, you know?"

"Ah. So you limped away."

"Jess…"

She cut him off. "No, look, I get it, okay? I know where we left things."

Silence. After a moment to steady her breath she continued, "How much did you have to drink?"

Over the phone came a heavy sigh. "A few little bottles of your old favorite. Jim Beam."

"Ah well at least you've got style, Josh Sawyer. If you're going to go off the wagon, you might as well go with tradition."

"I'm not planning to do this again, Jessie, I just…" He hung his head in his hands. "I couldn't think, you know?"

"Yeah," she whispered softly. "I do know."

That hit home for him. Suddenly Josh had an even greater sense of Jessie's own personal struggle.

She continued, "Josh, I don't care what you did with that woman. I want you to know that no matter what you choose to do I'm going to fight for you. I'm never giving up on you—on us. Ever." She interpreted his silence as that she needed to convince him more. She had no way of knowing that her man was in fact sobbing with relief. He thought his stupidity that night might in fact be the last straw.

Jessie sensed that he was crying again and it broke her heart not to be able to help him, to hold him. She softened.

"Babe. Look, when this shoot is over just come home, okay? I've been trying…I've been in to see Trudy every day since you left. Every day, Josh."

He perked up and the sobs stopped. He was surprised. His voice was gruff, weary. "What?" It was like a beacon in the darkness to hear that. It was a quaint white Prince Edward Island lighthouse, showing him the way. Suddenly he realized that, for some reason, Jessie sounded different. Her voice was different, not so small. It had some substance to it, despite the middle of the night phone call.

"Yeah," she added. Then, more brightly, "We're actually going out for lobster tomorrow. Me and Trudy! She's pretty cool." She sounded surprised herself at the way things were turning out with her therapist.

"Isn't that like…breaking rules or something? Crossing a line?" But she heard relief in his voice.

She laughed. "Hell, yeah. But I've crossed so many lines in the past few years that I don't even know where they are anymore. She's lonely. It's summer on P.E.I. We need a good feed of fresh-off-the-boat lobster. It doesn't get any better than here. Right outta the ocean." A deep breath accompanied Jessie's next remark. "Hey Josh? Look, I really am trying. I've been thinking about something…about…the things you're wondering about. With Deuce."

Josh was quiet as he took that in. Maybe he had no right to pry into her personal pain that way. After all, who says couples have to know everything about each other? Yet, in their case, the not knowing was causing problems that Josh was having difficulty overcoming. He thought about his accident on the shoot. No way was he telling Jessie about it. She avoided the rag bags and generally the internet. She may never know, especially if the production's cast and crew kept their lips zipped shut. Why worry her? What would be the point of that?

"Jessie, it's okay. I've been selfish. Let's just let it go for now, okay?"

"No, listen for a sec. I've figured out a way I can tell you. In a way I can handle."

In the darkness, with the blue glow of the television lighting the glaring white bandage on his cheek, Josh raised his chin and cocked his head. God, how self-centered he'd been. Jessie was just trying to put one foot in front of the other these days, to breathe in and out, in some desperate attempt to survive a past she'd tried to outrun for so long it had consumed her when it finally caught up. How could he be so demanding of her? He sank lower into the carpet, and hung his head in despair.

In Prince Edward Island, Jessie listened to his breathing and the deep sighs telegraphing Josh's angst. She knew he was angry at himself for all kinds of reasons tonight, plus he was on some level not in his right mind after the lure of the mini Jim Beams. But she felt she needed to give him some fuel for the fire, some genuine sign that she was trying. "Charles is going to send you something. I'm going to ask him tomorrow. I mean today." She glanced at the nearby clock. "It's like…a diary of sorts. Okay? You can read it on your own time. Actually," she hesitated, thoughtfully tracing a moonbeam's pattern on the floor by her toes as she pictured him in a hotel room alone, despondent and sorry. She wished she could reach out and pull him into her arms, comfort him, whisper to him to just hold on a little longer, that it would all be worth it in the end. She finished her thought. "I think what you should do is stay another couple of nights. Maybe not there, in that hotel…"

In Virginia, Josh winced as he followed her thoughts, which were *what if the woman he was with tonight decides to stay too.*

Jessie added, " Just find someplace quiet and do some reading. And get angry, Josh, and throw things around, I don't care, I'll pay for the damage as long as it's not to a living breathing person." She forced a chuckle as he raised his eyebrows, wondering what the hell kinda diary she was sending him, knowing in his heart it was her tale of that awful summer with McCall. He barely heard her as she finished. "Then come home, babe, okay? Just come home and we'll go see Trudy and she'll help us sort this shit out once and for all."

He was quiet. He didn't want an extra few days away from her. He wanted to be home with Jessie now.

She filled the pause. "Look, this book, it's going to arrive before the end of your shoot. Bury it, okay? Don't even try to go there while you're working, Josh. Pull it out after the wrap party and go into hiding. Call me if you need to but just promise me one thing."

"Anything, Jessie," he whispered. "Anything." This was a grand gesture on her behalf, and in his heart Josh knew it was also a force that could rip them apart—and that she was well aware. He ached for how afraid she must be to share such awful memories with him, and suddenly he was also afraid at just how bad those memories would be, at how the power of the written word and its truths could tear them apart.

Her voice was tiny again, childlike, terrified. "Please baby…please after you read it…just come back to me." A tear threatened to squeeze out of the corner of her eye but she fought against it, using her fingers to squish it away. There was no more time for crying. Now was the time for strength, a new strength, rebuilt one childlike wooden block at a time, piled high with care and precision in fingers just learning this game of life anew. She could be strong—Trudy was teaching her that. That even if the shit was piled so high she couldn't see over the top, she could plunk her sore feet into hip waders if she needed to, and one mushy step at a time she could—she would—get there, over the peak, over the mountain of crap, and on the other side she would find all the good things. Joy, love, family, friends, self-love, even. And so could Josh. Her heart lifted at the thought of finding her way with him at her side. She could see no other way.

He heard the smile in her voice when she spoke again, stronger this time. "We're gonna do this, Josh. We're gonna figure it out, you and me. You just… you take as much time as you need and you call me when you're ready to be picked up at the airport. I'll have Trudy on standby and hell, we'll move into her place if we need to. I'll get the local indie coffee shop to set up an intravenous, for God's sake. Just come home."

He laughed. He'd often thought they could make millions by inventing a caffeine-drip. "All right, Jessie Wheeler," he said confidently. Whatever was in that diary she was sending…well, no doubt it would suck, but maybe it was the lowest rung on their ladder and, after reading it, they could work their way back up, together. "I'll see you in about two weeks then."

"Yay."

"Yay?"

She grinned. "Yup. Yay. I miss you, you nerd."

"Hope you're being careful around the water. No swimming alone and stuff."

She caught her breath and scrunched her body up tighter. "Yeah, sure. It was windy tonight, though. Big waves…" Her voice drifted off as she recalled the terrifying battle with the riptide. But it wouldn't do to worry him. Not tonight.

"Jessie?" His voice was fraught with warning. But she could hear a slow drawl in his voice…he was tiring, the alcohol in his system wearing him down after an emotional day.

"It's nothing," she said quickly. "I just played in the waves, that's all. It was fun," she lied. She added lightly, "Hope you're being careful on that big bike."

He grimaced.

"Go sleep, Josh. I'll see you soon. And Josh…please…keep an open mind about the journal. It was a bad time and you can think I made shitty choices if you want to, but I did what I had to."

*For me,* he thought.

She read his mind. "You can stop thinking I did it just for you. I'm selfish, Josh. I wanted you back with no restrictions, no fear hanging over us. It's done. Let's move on, okay?" She added hastily, "With Trudy's help."

"All right. Jessie…this diary you're sending me…Charles has read it? And Matt, I'm guessing?"

"Yeah. They found it after I took off. I left it in my bedroom, between the mattress and box spring. Kinda hoped no one would find it. I started it because I read somewhere on the internet that you should keep details about stalkers, a record of sorts…I kept hoping I could nail Deuce, take him to court and put him behind bars, you know?"

"Has Charlie seen it?"

"No. No one else knows it exists. For obvious reasons. Well, Dee, I guess." She cringed at the thought of Deirdre reading the horrid details painstakingly recorded in the awful journal. "Don't ask me if I was ever planning to tell you about it. I wasn't. I didn't see the point. But now…well, I hope it answers some questions for you. But I am afraid, Josh."

His sleepy voice was small but steady and firm. "Don't be, little one."

Jessie's heart leapt with joy.

He continued. "I'll be coming home. Save some lobster for me. And Jessie…"

"Yeah?"

"Thank you."

"Yeah."

"Stay out of the water on windy days."

She smiled. "Yeah. Thinking I might." Then she tossed in, "Stay away from Temptation Girl."

"Done. Over with." He added, "Sleep well, little girl. Dream of me, okay?"

"You bet, Josh."

"Love you."

"Love you back."

A lengthy pause filled the phone line with promise as they contemplated the *I love yous*. What a simple grace, to hear those words again, to once again know they were the utter, wholesome truth. After a bit Josh whispered, "You can hang up now."

"Um hmmm." Then, "Can't."

His laugh warmed her heart.

"Okay. I am taking the phone to bed with me."

"Me too. 'Night Josh."

"'Night Jessie."

When she heard him start to snore, Jessie finally hit the 'end' button on her cell. She lay awake for a while, hugging his pillow and aching for his touch. But her spirit was soaring, despite the ever-present fear of his reaction upon reading her stalking journal. She was glad she wrote most of it in a business-like manner, with most of the raw emotion removed. Still, she knew there would be parts of it that would devastate him. But she prayed he could get past those entries and remind himself that Deuce McCall was gone from their lives, that these truths were part of the healing they required in order to move forward as a couple.

The ocean's gentle lapping snuck inside the open window of the old farmhouse, accompanied by a fresh calm breeze that happily buffeted the curtains, teasing them. Jessie drifted off to a golden land of childhood wonder, where Josh, Sandy and her dad built sandcastles on the beach together under the warm glow of a summer sun as she watched in blissful happiness from a nearby brightly decorated beach towel. The waves were benign now, the storm had moved on to other unsuspecting victims. The peace was welcome, the sleep deep, restorative and good.

# Chapter Seventeen

Trudy didn't realize just how much she missed female company until she had Jessie in the car with her, laughing and telling tales of life on her various film sets. One thing about Jessie's patient, quiet nature—she was always an observer. With her flip-flop clad feet childishly up on Trudy's dash (she asked permission and Trudy thought *what the hell, don't sweat the small stuff),* Jessie was the happiest the therapist had seen her. Funny what hope and a little understanding could do for a person.

"So we're shooting in Surrey, on the outskirts basically of Vancouver, on one of the first films Charles produced, actually, cause he's usually a music guy, and we're in this park. It's gotta be forty odd degrees Celsius, people are melting, literally. I was worried about the distance to the bathrooms. We were mostly on this trail deep in the woods. I was drinking all this water but I guess I just leached it out in sweat so in the end the bathrooms weren't a big deal. But then one of the crew, this sweet little gal from wardrobe, comes running down the path screaming. Guess what she was screaming, Trudy?"

Turning her head to fix her gaze on the older woman, Jessie's eyes were lit with glee as Trudy steered her vehicle down the Trans-Canada highway by Victoria-By-the-Sea, a quaint south side village mostly inhabited by artists and craftspeople living in colorful tranquil cedar-shingled Victorian homes. Beyond her, Jessie could see the calming waves of the Atlantic cozying up to the shore. Two bright dots caught her eye—a yellow kayak followed closely by a red one, their paddles zipping easily through the salty water on this calm day. Butterflies danced in her belly as she anticipated Josh's imminent return. It was mid September, and kayaking days on P.E.I. would be short-lived as the seasons changed. But first, she had to finish her story. Trudy was smiling widely as Jessie almost danced in her seat.

"Bear! She was screaming bear! Well, I've seen some professional crews, but this one rocked. First, everyone looked at me because I was alone in the shot, and all of a sudden there was this pressure to make the next take count, I mean really count, it had to be the *one,* you know, because all of the women on that crew—and a few of the guys, too, although most pretended they didn't care but I knew better—wanted the hell off that trail." She was laughing at the memory, and Trudy could feel Jessie's radiance from across the car. "So I'm standing there trying to look non-plussed, but I can feel everyone's eyes on me and the director, who was this short French guy who I barely understood on a good day, starts hollering for the assistant director to call the rolls, and buddy jumps behind the camera and after this little song and dance I hear *Action!* So I am trying not to look behind me where ostensibly this bear was seen, and I am more focused than I've ever been but I catch Charles' eye—he wasn't always on set, but this day he happened to be there—and I start to laugh." She slapped her thigh, barely able to keep hysterics at bay as she remembered. "And I laughed and I laughed and I laughed. Everyone's eyes were wide and afraid, but Charles was laughing too and so the whole crew burst into laughter with the exception of the gal who cried bear in the first place. I swear Trudy, it took us a good hour to get through that take and Charles was laughing so hard he had to leave set but eventually the director called *cut, print* and you have never seen a crew pack up so friggin' quickly! They were outta there in seconds flat. That was back in the Charlie days, before my big music tour, before *Drifters.*"

She smiled wanly up at Trudy as the kayaks disappeared into the vastness of the ocean behind them.

"I never did see that bear. I smelled it, though. Pretty rank, in case you're wondering what bear smells like, since you'll never see one here on the island." Suddenly her countenance changed and Trudy wondered what caused it. Jessie deflated, frowned, and looked out the window towards the rich copper and green farmland on her right. Row upon row of verdant potato plants caught her eye, peppered here and there with white farmhouses and welcoming driveways. In her lap her hands squeezed tightly together, but she refrained from driving her nails into the back of one hand, as she usually did when something triggered bad memories. Jessie was remembering her first meeting on a lonely road at the bottom of a mountain with Deuce McCall. It was the last time she smelled a bear so closely watching.

She turned back towards Trudy, who reached out a hand and wrapped long fingers around Jessie's.

"Okay?" she asked.

"Yeah. Just…old stuff," Jessie said. "Gone and done now." She shrugged. "Geez Trudy, is everything going to be a trigger now?" She peered sorrowfully up at her new friend.

"'Course not. But when something creeps in there," she tapped Jessie on the noggin, "fill it with light and let it go. Like we practiced."

She was rewarded with a genuine smile.

They continued down the highway almost alone, as most tourists had departed for home and school, their children tired out from the sheer joy of blessed days in the outdoors. And most islanders were at work, so it was a quiet drive punctuated with content black and white dairy cows, mellifluous farms and abandoned swing sets. They passed another little village on the way—Bedeque, where Jessie had spent the first years of her life in the loving embrace of David and Emily Wheeler in a one and a half story century home. It was from that home's sun porch where they'd often watched pink and orange sunsets blossom over the famous William Critchlow Harris designed church steeple across the road; and where they slurped ice cream cones after a casual stroll to the village store on the corner. Trudy raised an eyebrow at Jessie but the singer shook her head. They passed the exit to Bedeque and Jessie told herself she would bring Josh there someday, to revisit the old memories and maybe plunk down behind the barn like that sun kissed evening so long ago when she was seven and her father told her that music had the power to heal.

Ten minutes later they reached the small city of Summerside, turned west onto Water Street and cruised down to where they'd finally decided to eat that night, at a little pub called the Deckhouse, where they could sit on an outdoor deck overlooking the harbor. The women hunkered down under expansive table umbrellas with chilled bottles of Bud Light Lime and feasted on succulent fresh lobster. Both were surprised at this new easy friendship and, as the colorful spinnaker sails hoisted by local sailors on their weekly race brought the boats to safe harbor beyond, Jessie and Trudy relaxed, avoided talk of therapy, and genuinely enjoyed each other's company.

~

As the nights cooled and farmers started plucking bursting harvests from P.E.I.'s fertile red soil, it came time for Josh to arrive home. Jessie grew increasingly tense when his film shoot ended and he quarantined himself to read her stalking journal. But he called just before he holed himself up in a small hotel in Virginia Beach, where he randomly planted himself in the need for complete privacy. He swore not to have to take Jessie up on her offer to pay for the damages his temper caused as he read the journal and, as the two days he stayed there ticked along, he managed to keep that promise, but it wasn't easy. Long walks and a pre-emptied bar fridge saved him as he read long ago truths uttered on the page in Jessie's distinctive cursive handwriting.

When he finally closed the journal that had been the complete undoing of Charles, Dee and Matt when it was first discovered, Josh sat for hours in a deep comforting wicker chair on the small balcony of his hotel, overlooking sunset surfers as they straddled the waves on the beach below. He pinched his bottom lip and let the numbness that encompassed him when he first started reading completely fill his body and spirit. He would need some time to process this. But he would go to Jessie on her little eastern Canadian island where by now the red and burnt-orange leaves would be starting to lose their grip and fall to rest on dwelling places on the ground, and where the farmers' markets would be bursting with ripe produce for harvest dinners. And he would hold his girl and tell her in no uncertain terms that it was over now, and they could start to rebuild once and for all on a secure foundation.

And he would marry her before the beach got too cold for a barefoot wedding, in front of their friends and family, and life would go on.

The day he flew home, Jessie was waiting in the SUV in the short-term parking lot of the tiny Charlottetown airport. She listened to one of her own tunes play on Hot 105.5 as Josh's small plane dipped from beneath a fluffy white cloud and fell below her line of vision behind the airport terminal building, its props whirring as it brought her man safely back to her. She didn't want to go into the building where her emotions would be laid bare for everyone to see. And so she fiddled with the car keys and tapped a nervous hand on the open window on this seasonably warm September day, and waited for the text announcing his arrival.

*Home,* it said simply, and she smiled. *Well, that's a good sign.* They hadn't spoken since before his self-imposed quarantine, before he read the awful truths.

She answered *in parking lot.*

Soon she spied him leaving the terminal building, the object of many excited and curious stares. Jessie grinned as a brave fan approached him with paper and pen. He smiled a little crookedly, still shy from such attentions, and signed a few autographs before grabbing his bag and stepping off the curb, his eyes scanning the parking lot for his girl.

After a moment of exhaling in sheer relief that he had indeed come back to the island, which for a time Jessie believed may never be the case, she placed her left hand on the door handle and eased her way out of the vehicle, silently hoping the fans would stay away so she could gain some sense of Josh's feelings away from awkward stares. She was lucky. Maybe on some level their fans sensed this reunion was sacred, for now they stayed away.

Crossing her arms and cocking her head to one side, Jessie regarded Josh carefully. Besides the usual faded blue jeans and loose vintage pearl-buttoned shirt, he was wearing polarized sunglasses that hid his real countenance from her. She frowned as he drew closer—there seemed to be an ugly healing gash on his cheek—when had that happened?

Josh stopped a few feet away from Jessie. He assessed her the same way—carefully. She was as adorable as always, large curls blowing this way and that in the scattered wind, as if they couldn't make up their mind where to land. She brushed them away with one hand and grabbed the skirt of her short red print sundress with the other, and then she hauled off her denim jacket and tied it around her waist to keep her skirt down. She stepped forward then, one brown cowboy-booted foot in front of the other, and paused directly in front of him.

Tentatively, Jessie reached out and let her fingers trail down the scar on his cheek. Embarrassed, Josh grabbed her hand and pulled it down, as he had done after her show at the Orpheum when that famous photo was taken so long ago when they first got together.

"It's nothing," he whispered, then he pulled his sunglasses off and plopped them atop Jessie's head to keep her hair somewhat in place so he could peer deeply into those haunting diaphanous blue eyes. Her expression was curious but at the same time he could see that Jessie was trying hard to remain in control. Something was different, there seemed to be some peace about her today that wasn't present when he left her at the departures gate more than three weeks earlier. It helped to see her this way, calmer, steadier. It eased the agony that consumed him, brought on by her frank written tale of a horrifying stalking.

"Okay?" she asked softly, that one word filled to the brim with a thousand unspoken ones.

"I will be," he whispered honestly.

To her, Josh was different now, too—a changed man. The scar on his cheek bothered her—she would get to the bottom of that at some point. But it was more than that. There was no way he could read her stalking journal and not morph into some different version of himself, like a child who first realized life was not eternal here on this earthly plane. That the foundation beneath his feet could shift without warning. Josh seemed older. Tired. His eyes were searching hers, seeking the truths of experiences he now knew were real, but which he achingly wished were not.

Slipping her hands up underneath his shirt, Jessie leaned into a warm embrace that she prayed would be reciprocated. It was, and as his arms wrapped tightly around her neck, both prayed that this time they could hang on, that nothing could come between them, not even a sinister telling of a frightening past both knew they could never forget no matter how many times they tried to push it under a rug.

Briefly Jacob flashed across Jessie's mind as she pushed hard on Josh's shoulder blades, rubbing her fingers across his skin as if she could meld inside him. She breathed in and buried her face in his neck, and he felt a tiny smile light up his insides as her hair tickled him. He wrapped his arms even tighter around her, afraid to let go; oblivious to the stares of others as passengers from his flight were scooped up by loved ones.

"Little one," he breathed back at her. "It's good to be home."

Jessie leaned back and swiped a fist across her eyes as she buried herself in his loving gaze. "Home, huh?" she said.

He grinned back. "Wherever you are. That's home, to me."

She nodded. This was good. Very good. "Okay," she breathed.

Josh frowned. "We're off to see Trudy, then?"

"Yeah. Okay? Just to get this over with. I want it over with, Josh. I'm trying, but I feel like we need to climb this hill right away so we can move ahead."

"All right then. Let's do this thing."

A worried glance flitted across her face and Josh frowned. "What?"

"I can't let go," she whispered.

He laughed outright. Then Josh reached over and brushed yet another stray lock away from her cheek and leaned in for a tender kiss, which brought on a hunger that made both think of calling Trudy and rescheduling. As his tongue brushed against the underside of her top lip, he felt her squirm and moan, just slightly.

"Oh God," she said. "Please, take me now." The remark was accompanied by a sincere joy lighting Jessie up from within.

"Rrowwwwrrr," was Josh's response before he scooped her wildly up in his arms, to the delight of the not so discreet observers in the small parking lot of the Charlottetown airport. Laughing, Jessie let him deposit her on the passenger seat of their SUV, but she leaned out the window and grabbed a fistful of his shirt and pulled him towards her for a lingering sweet kiss before he could get too far away.

And that was the photo that graced the front page of the Charlottetown newspaper The Guardian ('we cover the island like the dew') the next day—Jessie half leaning out of the vehicle's window, both arms around Josh's neck, his arms around her waist, as they kissed tenderly after their time apart.

No one watching had any idea what the evening had in store for the couple—a painful re-hashing of age-old events that tore them apart not so long ago, a necessary exercise on the road to well-being, an exorcism of sorts.

But at least Josh and Jessie now had the basis they would need to survive. They had a deep enduring love built on the seeds of a shared loneliness and a sense of unworthiness, and then on a sincere and beautiful friendship. Even the bad building blocks were now a part of their shared experiences. All they would need now was Trudy's guiding light to bring them home.

Josh steered the SUV carefully out of the parking lot as Jessie laughed and waved at a few carloads of cheering observers, sinking into the seat with a faint pink blush across her cheeks. She did what she often did in the car, planted her feet on the dash. Grabbing Josh's hand, she brought his fingers to her lips and kissed him tenderly.

"So glad you're here," she murmured. "So glad."

Josh rounded the rotary at the Brackley Point Road and the airport disappeared behind them. They were only about ten minutes from Trudy's place but he took the long way around, grabbing them some coffees from Timothy's on busy University Avenue before heading out to the difficult session with their therapist. Before he pulled into Trudy's driveway, he kissed the back of Jessie's hand as well. "No more fucking up," he said quietly to her. "It's you and me, kid. Always and forever."

Trudy heard them drive up, but when they didn't enter, she slipped a finger through the office blind and peeked out. What she saw was a couple very much in love, foreheads pressed together and eyes closed, hands around each other's neck. Occasionally a head came up for a soft kiss. Trudy smiled and lifted her cellphone to her ear.

"Hey, Frank? It's them but they might be a moment. Any last minute advice?" And she sank backwards into the wooden chair behind the old teacher's desk in her indoor garden sanctuary as trickling water fountains bubbled happily nearby.

She crossed her ankles after laying her feet on the desk, and chatted comfortably with her ex until the door opened and footsteps announced the arrival of her celebrity clients.

Then it was time for business. She tapped the 'end' button, and stood.

"Shall we begin?" she asked Josh and Jessie, who stood nervously at her door hand in hand, ready and waiting for Pandora's box to be opened, but supremely confident they could handle its tempestuous contents. Cautious smiles flitted between them, and they took seats in the wicker chairs as Oliver snoozed in a swath of cat-filled sunshine at their feet.

Trudy leaned back against the desk, and the long-awaited much-feared session finally began.

# Chapter Eighteen

"Josh, turn your chair to face Jessie. Jessie, you too. Face Josh." Trudy waved a graceful arm towards the couple and nodded her head in encouragement. "This is a conversation the two of you are having. I am just here to mediate, to help if you get stuck somewhere along the line, okay?"

Nervously, Jessie swallowed. Josh nodded and a quiet "Okay" echoed in Trudy's jungle sanctuary.

"Jessie?"

"Yes, okay." Jessie pulled her chair a little closer to Josh so that his knees encircled hers. She reached across their little bubble and took both of his hands. Afraid of what he was thinking, of what terrors this session would unleash, she held on tight as she settled their hands on her lap, brushing a thumb across his fingers as she mentally prepared herself. Glancing upwards, she relaxed a little when she spied a new confidence flicker across his eyes. She felt supported, as if Josh was telepathically reaching across the distance between them, telling her that he had figured some things out, that he was determined they could, and would, survive their troubles. She took a deep breath and waited.

Trudy set them on a path. "Josh, you know Jessie's been coming to see me regularly over the last few weeks."

"Yes." He didn't take his eyes off Jessie, who he thought looked terrified. A tiny smile creased his lips, highlighting his dimple, and he gave her hands a squeeze.

"She's been working very hard. But there are some things the two of you still need to figure out. And there are tools I can give both of you so you can start to manage more on your own."

"Okay."

"I'm going to start by asking you where you would like to begin."

This time it was Josh's turn to look nervous. He swallowed. "With the journal." His voice came out low, raspy. Still, his eyes did not leave Jessie's, even though she flinched and looked away.

"All right. Tell Jessie about the journal, then. How it made you feel, whatever thoughts you'd like to share with her."

"Well, I want her to know I read it—all of it." He looked up at Trudy, who gestured to him to look back at Jessie, whose shoulders were slumping as she tried to focus back on Josh. He could feel her hands start to sweat. Jessie resisted the urge to pull away and drive her nails into the back of her left hand. She bit hard onto her bottom lip instead.

Josh continued. "Jessie…I'm never going to understand completely why you couldn't come to me when all that crap started with McCall…but I'm glad you let me read your journal. I'm glad you thought to keep it…I know how hard it was for you to share all that with me."

She blinked nervously but managed to keep her eyes on his, although she was wearing her mask and her pupils were darting a little from side to side. She was silent.

He waited for a response that didn't come. Trudy gently jumped in to help.

"Josh, how did reading the journal make you feel?"

He didn't hesitate. "Angry." A nerve twitched in the side of his cheek.

"Why?"

"Because it…it detailed a summer where I was excluded, where I wasn't given the choice or chance to help. A summer where Jessie was harassed, where she…had regular sex with someone who terrified her, who…" He couldn't continue.

"Who what, Josh?" Trudy's voice was smooth, controlled. But she sat on her hands to keep her clients from noticing her own trembling nerves.

"Who…hurt her so badly years before." He watched Jessie carefully to see how she was handling this. She pulled her hands away, finally, and crumpled them in her lap.

"Who killed someone she loved," Trudy said softly.

"Yeah, I understand why she excluded me." He looked up at Trudy for help. Jessie was staring dejectedly at Oliver, who was snoozing peacefully nearby, oblivious to the angst flooding the small room. "But it still makes me angry. And sad."

"Talk to Jessie, Josh. Make her listen."

He sighed and placed a finger under Jessie's chin, tilting her face upwards so she had to look at him. "Jess…I can't promise you I'm ever going to get over that anger. The journal…Jesus, at one point he tied you up and left you for hours…and you know what really bites about that? I know what I was doing that day. I was shooting, hanging out with a cast and crew and likely thinking about you. But I had no idea…" His voice broke, and he pushed back the chair with a screech, stood and faced the wall while he tried to regain control.

Trudy pulled on her own chair and settled it close to Jessie. She grasped a hand in hers while Josh took a moment. "Honey," she said, "tell Josh what you thought about that day."

Her eyes glistening, Jessie looked up at Josh's back. He turned around and faced her, the age-old sorrow etching his face, picking away at the confidence with which he'd so hopefully approached this session.

Jessie's voice was low, childlike, matter-of-fact. "I thought about you. About the good times. About getting through that day and seeing you soon at my concert."

He remembered the concert, the night Deuce beat her so badly. He remembered the little interplay he and Jessie shared that night, when she teased him about running away. He melted further and reached an arm out to her. "Jessie," was all he managed.

Trudy patted his chair. "Come. Sit."

He did, wiping the corners of his eyes as he did so.

"Josh, the thing we need to do now is identify triggers. This is what this is mostly about, right? You wanted to know the details so you would be able to identify triggers in your lovemaking. So the two of you can move forward with confidence and enjoy being a couple without fear of hurting Jessie or setting off an anxiety attack, raising…unbidden memories."

He nodded, and his eyes drifted to Jessie, who was staring at the floor again, her face still a mask. But she was here. She was trying. He sat slowly.

Trudy placed Jessie's hand on Josh's knee, which jarred the singer back to the here and now, and Josh covered her hand with his. He entwined their fingers together and inhaled deeply.

Jessie spoke, quietly. "Josh, you should know that there have been lots of times in my life when I've had to do…things…I haven't wanted to. The triggers don't just come from Deuce."

He knew she was talking about sex. He listened carefully.

"Like…that was the reason I left P.E.I. in the first place…my stepfather, you know?"

Josh cringed, but the admission wasn't a complete surprise.

She continued. "On the Downtown Eastside, well I had my guitar and singing for money and that helped but still…before that…I know I did some things…although to be truthful it's just a hazy blur. I don't really remember exactly." A shadow passed over her face and once again she looked away. Her voice was small when she spoke again. "It's just that I learned how to handle it a long time ago, you know? And Deuce wasn't…necessarily cruel… not really…not all the time. Sometimes, I guess."

She gestured absently into the air and shook her head.

"What I don't get, Jessie, is…" Josh started cautiously, afraid he was going to lose it again. These waters required judicious navigation or together they would sink to the murky bottom. He took her chin in his hand again and forced her to focus on him. He leaned forward. "What I don't get is what possessed you to think I was worth any of that. Why would you go through that hell…for me?" The brown eyes were liquid pools of pain as Jessie melted in front of him.

"Oh Josh," she breathed, her voice trailing off as she slowly shook her head from side to side. "Don't you see?"

She held up their hands like a trophy in between them.

"There was never any question. This"—she nodded at their entwined fingers—"this is everything. Your touch, it's everything. The way you look at me…" She smiled softly, sadly. "This is the thing, Josh. Charlie never looked at me the way you do. After Sandy…I never thought I would find anyone who could love me again. Really love me. Sometimes I feel like…like…" She was struggling, gesturing in the air again, searching for the words. "Like nobody out there *really* loves *me.*" She pointed to herself. "*Me.* Not the singer. Not the actor. Me. Plain old Jessie Wheeler from Prince Edward Island, Canada." Her voice was breaking.

Josh stared at her, incredulous. He looked over at Trudy and saw a similar astonishment flicker across her face. Their eyes met—both were amazed that this woman, an International superstar, a worldwide celebrity, could be filled with any level of self-loathing. But tears were slowly creasing their way down Jessie's pink cheeks. Slowly she hung her head and started to sob, staring at a peeling painted toenail.

"Jessie, you're loved everywhere. Your music affects people, it moves people!"

She peeked up at him from beneath long wet eyelashes, her face set, determined. "My *music*, Josh. My *acting*, the characters I play. Not *me!* If they really knew me they wouldn't like me."

"What, so Charles and Dee, Steve, Sophie, Maggie, everyone? Me? You think none of us who have gotten to know you really like you?"

Jessie cut in quickly. "You know that's what I mean! My own mother hated me! I got in the way of her perfect little romance with my dad, and then he died on his way to my birthday party! She didn't stop my stepdad from climbing into my bed! And then...what Deuce did...I'm like the plague or something! Dirty."

"I don't accept that."

Jessie stopped and reflected. Her life on the Downtown Eastside was in some ways a painful blur, so soon after Sandy's murder, but she remembered some things about it, and lately she was remembering more and more as Trudy helped her start to let go of the bad and replace it with the good. It was like as some of the bad was erased more moved in to take its place. What would Josh think of her when he understood the truth about her life there? About what she did to survive?

"Josh..." she whispered, "why do you think I'm hanging on to you so tightly, huh? Why do you think I am so afraid to let you go?" She shook her head and bit her lip again, and the nails dug this time into the flesh above her wrist. "Why? Because I see all this in you too. You feel the same way about yourself, on some level, at least. So maybe what I really think is because of that, you, at the very least, can accept me for who I really am."

She hit a nerve. Josh tensed and stared hard at her. His cheek was twitching rapidly as a steady pounding started in his head. His hands were clenched now on the sides of his chair.

Trudy held her breath.

"So who do you really think you are, Jessie?" She barely heard him.

Her eyes settled into an ice-blue stare back at him. "A whore." She let that resolve in his addled brain before continuing. "So you see, all that crap you read about in the stalking journal...it wasn't so hard, really. It's who I am. The music is just a cover."

Josh whispered brusquely back. "Don't give me that bullshit. You're just a scared little girl whose mother was so torn up over losing her husband that she couldn't see to help her daughter deal with the pain of losing her daddy. You did what you had to in order to survive." He leaned forward as Jessie started to sob again. The pain overtook her. Josh placed a big hand firmly on the side of Jessie's head and kissed her cheek. His body was shaking now, too, as his grief finally overcame him—grief for Jessie's own pain, for her survival tactics, for who both of them thought they really were, in their hearts. "I don't care what has made you who you are, Jessie. I just know I love you. I love you! *You!* The singer, the actor, the girl...all of you. And so does Dee, and Charles too, and don't get me started on Steve..."

That drew a sodden chuckle from Jessie.

Trudy rose carefully and turned her back. So many women came through her doors filled with self-loathing. Hell, she came through the door into this office every day filled with self-hate. Why else did she quarantine herself in this jungle, hiding amongst the ferns and blossoms and tricklings of the mini water fountains? Why else did she let the man she herself loved walk out of her life?

She heard a shuffle behind her and turned back around to see Jessie climb into Josh's lap and wrap her arms around him. He was crying openly now too and holding his fiancée close as Jessie curled herself up into a little ball in his arms. Trudy had to lean in a little to hear what Jessie was saying to him. The girl was begging, her fear overtaking her in this safe place amongst the verdant fawn and fern.

"Please Josh, please...don't go away. I need you. I've been so scared..."

He was murmuring back to her, his face buried in Jessie's hair so Trudy couldn't make out his words of comfort. Slowly, Trudy tiptoed by them, resting a soft hand on Jessie's back for a moment as she passed. She left them alone and went into the kitchen where she robotically placed an English Breakfast tea pod in the Keurig, then leaned back against the counter and let her own tears fall. She would call Frank tonight, not to talk about Josh and Jessie for once, although she was always careful not to divulge any personal confidences. She would call instead to talk about *them*, about herself and her own man, and the time they were losing when they could simply be together, loving one another again.

At least a half hour passed before Trudy heard the door to her office creak open. Then they were facing her, Josh and Jessie, hand in hand, their deepest fears released, their faces tear-streaked but their eyes buoyant on some deep layer below all the *sad*. Trudy smiled. They looked like two children who snuck peeks at their Christmas presents; happy despite the fact they'd unlocked some powerful secrets and upset their parents.

Josh broke the silence. "What's next? We work on the triggers?" His soulful chocolate eyes searched Trudy before he glanced over at Jessie. He grinned when he saw the look on her face—her eyes were narrowed playfully and her lips were curved up in a wide butterfly smile.

She cut in before Trudy could respond. "That's easy," she said easily. "The triggers can wait. For now—we plan a wedding."

"What took you so long?" was Josh's immediate response as he laughed openly and gathered his girl into his arms, lifting her off the floor and twirling her joyously around.

Soon Trudy joined them and they enveloped her in their hug as well. She was already planning her words to Frank. She would start with, "I need a date. For what, you ask? A wedding, in fact. You heard me! A wedding!"

Happily, she let herself believe that it would be the start of something great, not just for Josh and Jessie, but for her—and Frank—as well.

# Chapter Nineteen

The first thing Jessie did after climbing into the SUV was call Deirdre. She found her in Chicago.

"Dee!"

The older woman pulled a large earring from her ear so she could place the phone closer in order to better hear Jessie. She was hoofing it down a sidewalk in the windy city and beeping horns and whooshing buses were winning the battle over the cellphone.

"Jessie? How are things on your little island?" She ducked underneath a bright red and white striped awning and poked her left hand over her ear in order to drown out the city's incessant cacophony.

"Good, Dee. Josh and I are wondering what you and Charles are doing next weekend. A week and a half away…"

Jessie could hear Dee's smile through the phone line. "Are you coming back to Vancouver or are you inviting us east?"

"East. No more waiting, Dee. We're having a wedding!"

Immediately Dee's radar went up. She knew Josh had taken off to do a film over the last few weeks and she discerned from Jessie's mood over that time period that things were not necessarily A-okay in the Sawyer-Wheeler camp. What changed? Besides, Dee wanted to throw a crazy big party—she was a good manager, but a week and a half was not a lot of time to pull together a celebrity wedding. But then again…Jessie deserved this. And hell, why make her wait a second longer to marry someone she loved and should have long been married to by now?

"Bring it on!" she hollered over the roar of a passing delivery truck.

Jessie was laughing wholeheartedly now, the earlier cry and snuggle with Josh a catharsis the two of them had sorely needed. She felt cleansed and ready to start anew. "Okay! We'll sort some things out and I'll call you later, okay?"

"Wait, Jessie, hang on for a sec…are you still there?"

"Yeah! Yes, I mean."

"Jonathon called me today. Did you get the message that he's flying in to P.E.I. tomorrow? He wants to see Josh. He heard about…I don't know, something went down on set in Virginia, I think."

Jessie frowned and glanced over at Josh who, tapping along to the radio which he now played at a reasonable volume with Jessie in the vehicle beside him, was oblivious.

"What went down?" Jessie asked Dee nervously. Suddenly she felt a little sick. Jonathon had no professional association with Josh's latest film. If he was flying to their little island because of something that happened in Virginia it was because…it was because of his *personal* association with Josh.

"Honey, I don't know exactly, he wouldn't say. Something with the bikes I think, I don't know. You'll have to ask Josh. But for whatever reason, Jonathon had a little panic attack or moment of clarity or something and… well, maybe he just wants to see Josh, I don't know. We all had a bad scare…" Her voice trailed off.

*And Jonathon is Josh's real father,* Jessie thought.

Dee finished Jessie's thought. "I think he just needs to see him, honey. Anyways his flight arrives around one. He's renting a car and I gave him instructions on how to find you. Can you plan to be home?"

"Yeah, of course," Jessie answered. "We'll be at the house." She wrapped her fingers around Josh's and smiled a little nervously up at him. More secrets?

After they hung up, she pushed her curious thoughts aside and then called Steve to give him the good news and to beg him to get the time off to celebrate with them. Charlie was next as Josh piloted the SUV down Route Two towards the South Rustico turn-off. The guys were ecstatic and promised to sort out their schedules in order to make the wedding. The other calls could wait. Jessie laid her head against the back of the passenger seat and grinned over at Josh.

He smiled warmly back at her. "What?"

"You sure about this? Marrying me?"

He slipped a hand along her thigh and snuck a finger up under her short skirt. "Yeah," he winked. "Although I did consider the whole 'why buy the cow when you can get the milk for free' deal."

"You pig!" Jessie squealed, hitting him. "Give me a break! Anyways, I make more money than you! You will do all right by marrying me. And no I'm not interested in a pre-nup."

Sobering, Josh grasped her hand tightly. "I'm marrying you, not your money, Jess. You. And I am doing okay on my own, anyway."

"I know, Josh, I just—I don't care about that stuff." She looked out the window at the robust leafy green potato plants zipping by them. In the distance ahead she could see the ocean, whitecaps dancing gaily on the waves, mirrored by fluffy white clouds above.

"Me either," Josh echoed. Then, "Should we pop in to see your Mom before we pack it in for the night?"

Nodding, Jessie brought up her visits to the seniors' lodge while Josh was away. "George is like a twenty-eight-year-old in a ninety-year-old's body. He's a big flirt."

"You wanna marry him instead? Is that what you're saying?"

Jessie laughed, soaking up the light in Josh's eyes as she snuggled into the seat, his right hand clasped firmly against her body. "Maybe if we were the same actual age at the same time! Anyways…now that you're home maybe we should open that box he gave me. I thought about doing it while you were away but with counseling finally going good I just didn't want to go there. Alone."

Frowning, Josh interjected. "Let's give it a few more days, Jessie." He glanced at her, and she could see the wheels turning.

"Ah. You don't think I can handle it."

"For today you have enough on your plate. Remember what Trudy said before we left—building blocks. One at a time. From the bottom up."

"Okay," Jessie acquiesced. "But soon. I need to know what's in there."

"Fine. In a few days, okay? Or maybe after we're officially married. For now let's just do some kayaking and spend some time together. Plan our wedding." He smiled warmly over at his girl, his eyes twinkling happily.

"Okay. Josh?"

"Yup?" He slowed the car to let a couple of cyclists on bicycles cross the road by the Oyster Bed Bridge turn-off.

"Let's visit good-ole Emily Wheeler tomorrow. I kinda want to go home with you right now."

A pink flush bloomed across Josh's cheeks. This time when he looked over at Jessie she was shyly pink as well. He would have stopped the SUV then and there on the side of the road, but they weren't far from their summer home, so instead he pressed on the accelerator and headed for a big comfy private bed instead of a claustrophobic car seat or a scratchy field of clover. For the millionth time after reading her stalking journal he thought about the grace God gave him to be the man who had the power to erase Jessie's hurts—well, maybe not erase them, but at least ease them somewhat. That he could touch her lovingly, and show her what true love between a man and a woman felt like, instead of a brusque rough touch from a man—or men, in her case—that left a trail of deep unwanted scars.

"Love you," he whispered earnestly to her as he turned onto their driveway, sheltered by trees already losing their summer hues and turning vibrant shades of reds and oranges. His brown eyes searching her baby blues melted Jessie completely, and she almost moaned in anticipation of feeling his touch on her skin in the way that only lovers crave.

She didn't need to respond with words. Her happy smile—on the smoky side—said it all.

Inside the house, Josh lifted Jessie and pressed his lips gently to hers. As her lips parted she let her tongue run across his upper lip; he leaned into her and pressed a hand against the back of her head to keep her still, to show her how much he wanted her by pressing his body against hers, by forcing her mouth open wider.

Still connecting in that intimate way, he set her on the bottom step that led upwards towards their bedroom, and she rested both arms around his broad shoulders and snuggled with a sigh into his neck as he trailed his lips along her shoulder. He pulled off her denim jacket and it floated softly to hang over the banister as Jessie turned and locked her fingers in Josh's, leading him upstairs to where they could love each other in peace in a way they hadn't really been free to since before Deuce McCall made his fateful appearance at Agassiz.

Jessie smiled at him when she got to the top of the stairs, then she let go of his hand, reached forward and undid the top button on his jeans, rubbed a hand firmly over him, then backed off and pulled the sundress up over her head, swatting his hand and teasing him when he tried to touch her. She turned again and headed into the bedroom as Josh undid his shirt, slipped it off, and followed the woman he loved onto the bed. He pushed away thoughts of what he'd almost done in Virginia with Melanie, and of what Jessie had cried out in anguish at him about her time with Jacob. This was about he and Jessie alone, and despite the ever-present ghost of McCall and her stepfather, which he had suspected but never had the guts to ask her about, Josh touched Jessie lovingly, wherever he wanted to, and she helped him along, her gaze rarely leaving his.

It was all worth it now, today. With Trudy's help they were both exorcising their demons, the awful deeds and loathsome feelings that haunted both of them for so long. Josh was instantly concerned when he saw tears slowly creep down Jessie's cheeks, and he backed off a little, suddenly afraid, but she placed her palms on his cheeks and shook her head slowly from side to side.

"It's all worth it now, Josh," she whispered. "Everything. I longed for you..." Her voice was thick with emotion as she brushed back the piece of hair that teased her from the first time she saw him at Charlie's Club. She was on her back on the bed, and he was on top, so the piece of hair kept falling forward and brushing her cheek. She laughed and kissed his sore cheek above her. "Josh..." She relished the simple way his name passed between her lips. "I'm so in love with you."

His own eyes glistening from the heavy emotion of the day and everything that got them there, Josh kissed her softly just beneath one eye, then he let his lips trail downward. He slipped one nipple between his lips and teased her with his teeth as she arched her back and leaned into him, urging him on. This was Heaven, this is what she dreamed about, even with Jacob by her side. Life felt complete with Josh, everything was finally the way it should be. This was real.

He slipped further down then and flicked his tongue against her, holding her still while she cried out in pleasure. He pulled down her panties and urged her orgasm on further, and she begged him to go inside, to start moving there, to make their love complete and perfect.

When he came she was already exploding, riding the wave, loving him and this freedom he seemed to have discovered by finally letting go of her hurts, by trusting that she would let him know if he touched her in the wrong place or if Deuce's memory was too close by. They sobbed together then for the second time that day as Josh rocked Jessie and held her tight against his chest as their bodies settled. They stayed that way for a long time, locked together, finally together joyously and euphorically, knowing they were finally on a proper uphill climb, that their wedding date was set and their friends would soon be arriving, and that yes, in the end, *this* was everything.

~

"Spider dogs?"

Josh wandered up behind Jessie on the beach as she nudged another chunk of campfire wood onto the fiery teepee she'd built in their pit. Already the kindling and newspaper stacked below the carefully placed wood was catching fire, spitting little bits and pieces of local community news into the air. It was late—midnight, but she was out here on the beach starting a fire, her hair pulled back in a hasty ponytail, faded jeans and a comfy navy blue hoodie keeping her warm on this cool late September evening as she puttered around the fire, nurturing its growth.

"You know, we coulda tossed a frozen pizza into the oven. Or I could make you a peanut butter and jam sandwich." Josh crossed his arms, grinning at her, his eyebrows raised. He shivered and rubbed a forearm as Jessie turned to face him.

She frowned at his simple white T-shirt and bare feet. She was always worried about him getting sick without his spleen to even things out. Approaching him in the sand, she wrapped her arms around him. "Go get a sweater or a fleece or something. You're freezing. I'll keep the fire going."

"Couldn't sleep? Need a bigger orgasm? I could call Katrine." He winked and Jessie's face flamed red. At least he could joke about her 'Jacob' comment now.

She shot him a look of utter embarrassment and warning. Josh sobered.

"Seriously Jessie, it's after midnight." His voice was cool now, serious, and as he peered into her solemn eyes Josh realized there was more than roasted hot dogs on her mind this night. Above them a gray cloud drifted in front of the luminous textured harvest moon, giving a Halloween-like shadow and cadence to Jessie's late night ministrations. She leaned into him and wrapped her arms around his waist, laying her head against Josh's chest. His heart was beating gently, and she couldn't help but sigh. She would never let herself forget the long months without his touch, his heat, his energy. He was her light source, her raison d'etre. He was her everything. It was time to eradicate the past.

The silver-orange moon emerged from its hiding place, and Josh inhaled deeply at its simple beauty—enormous, perfectly round, it hung there over the beach and bay as if it was a Christmas ornament placed by God for their enjoyment alone. It was quite literally an awesome sight to behold. Maybe that was why Jessie was on the beach in the dark of night, to sit back and behold its beauty. Josh wouldn't put it past her. She was, after all, an artist who knew to stop and appreciate such gifts from the amazing world surrounding her.

But no, his eyes flickered to a place on the sand where the moon and smoky fire combined to illuminate a dark spot near the fire pit. Lying there as if it were already forgotten was Jessie's stalking journal, the gentle breeze and Jessie's footsteps delicately embracing it with minute grains of sand that, combined, almost had the power to bury it altogether.

"Ah," he said, nodding slightly as Jessie followed his gaze.

"We're planning our wedding," she whispered as she gently peeked back up at him, one hand now looped over his belt at his waist, the other reaching up to caress the rogue layer of hair threatening to hide his cheek from view. "No more bad stuff. We need to let it go." Jessie brushed her lips against Josh's neck as he took in the verity of the situation. She intended to burn the stalking journal. It wouldn't eradicate the demons it contained within, but by symbolically destroying it, maybe it would help to ease the psychological ache its physical presence carried.

He wrapped an arm tighter around her waist and another around her head, his big hand keeping his girl safely against him where he could protect her, and keep her safe. "Okay," he breathed into her ear, his belly clenching at the horrid truths the simple leather notebook had so recently revealed to him. "Let's do this."

But first—there were more tender kisses to share in the light of the glorious harvest moon. Lips to touch with loving fingertips, cheeks to caress with the backs of hands, trails to create with kisses in each other's hair. There were *I love yous* to share, eyes flecked with moisture to peer deeply into... then Jessie pivoted in the sand and, without letting go of Josh's hand, she bent down and retrieved that terrible lonely summer—the journal—from where it lay half-buried in the sand.

Josh took it from her and opened it. He ran a finger over a page and then flipped to another and did the same. He could see the words, painstakingly formed in Jessie's familiar hand, but in the moonlit darkness he couldn't make them out and he was glad of that. He knew what they said—all the same thing, *I am lonely, I am hurting, I am lost.* The words imprinted there were the same that lay buried beneath her eyes early every morning when she fought haunting nightmares, or when he caught her looking up at him when they sat on the deck after scoffing down grilled steaks—the times when he thought she was looking out to the whitecaps on the gulf, when in fact she was memorizing him, remembering a horrific time when the fates conspired against them as lovers. Those stares were almost vacant, sad, empty, so lost was she in the *bad*. Josh hadn't seen that look much today—a little, in Trudy's jungle. But not at home when they made love. Instead she was happy, lighter, her soul beginning to heal and fill with the *good*.

Josh closed the journal and spoke quietly to Jessie. "It's over," he said softly. "You're stuck with me now, kid."

A tentative hand gripped the journal and Josh watched as a thousand emotions crisscrossed the face he loved to touch, to brush with his lips. For a moment he thought she might collapse with the weight of the words within, but she didn't. Instead, Jessie let her lips curl up just the littlest bit and, as she looked up at him, his heart skipped a beat when a little light glimmered in the pale blue eyes. *Hope.*

Jessie took a deep breath and then grasped Josh's fingers in her right hand. She held the journal up with her left and together they stepped towards the now blazing fire. Moving the old memories towards her belly, she nodded at Josh to do his part. He took hold of it with his right hand, a firm grip to tell it just who was boss, and then he let Jessie lead the way.

"Three, two, one," he heard her whisper, and then she looked over at him. Their eyes met and he nodded. They leaned over the fire and together tossed Jessie's sad little truths onto the crackling flames. Josh pulled her close as they watched it burn, consumed by a gentle crinkling and sputtering of an innocent campfire. With it went Deuce McCall, and Jessie was saddened for the man, despite his power over her life. In the end, he was just a man who was lonely and ill. Still, she hoped by burning the journal that his presence in their lives—in their bedroom—would continue to fade. She whispered a silent prayer that he was no longer tormented, that wherever Deuce's spirit went it was managing to find peace.

"Okay?" Josh asked tenderly, breaking through her thoughts as the journal's edges curled up and the paper within disintegrated the factual account of Jessie's horror.

"Yeah," she whispered as she snuggled deeply in her man's arms. "I will be, Josh." She smiled up at him. "Thank you for understanding."

He thought of the time she had approached him at Jonathon's birthday party and thanked him for understanding how things had to go down that awful summer. At least this time it made sense. At least now he understood more. Was he still angry? Yes. He always would be. But he was learning to forgive, and burning the journal was one step in the right direction. They would be okay. He and Jessie would be okay.

"Josh?" she asked him, her eyebrows knitted together now with concern he didn't expect.

"Yeah?"

"There's one last thing. One more—secret—we need to deal with before we get married." She was shaking her head slowly now from side to side. "We need a clean slate. We need everything to be out in the open, on the table. Everything."

Josh frowned. Suddenly he was afraid again. "The box?" he asked. "From George? Did you sneak a peek at it while I was away? Or what? I don't know if I can handle any more secrets, Jessie."

"Not that," she said, her shoulders sinking enough for him to know that this, too, was a biggie. "The box can wait til after we're married. Whatever shit's in there, it's got to do with David and Emily Wheeler and, if you're willing, we can deal with that together. No, it's...something else. But I'm not the one to tell you." She thought about Jonathon's impending visit, which she had yet to share with Josh. In the excitement of the wedding and calling everyone, plus their surreal evening of lovemaking at the farmhouse afterwards, it had completely escaped her mind. Laying the fire while Josh was still asleep upstairs earlier, she was reminded that their old producer would be arriving the next day. And Jessie had decided enough was enough. The secret she carried with regards to Josh's paternity was huge; not insurmountable, she hoped, but it would be an emotional roller coaster for Josh to have to deal with. She would be there to help him through it, but by God it was time for Jonathon to tell him, for all their sakes. Regardless of Jon's plans and intentions, Jessie was going to make certain this particular truth would find its way to the surface.

"Look, Josh, I forgot to tell you something Dee said on the phone today." She knocked him gently in the rib—on his good side—and her lips curved up in a teasing smile. "You were too busy helping Lynryd Skynyrd with the vocals for Sweet Home Alabama. We're having company tomorrow."

"Oh? Charles and Dee? And I'm not a bad singer myself, you know. I did that song proud." He winked and she laughed.

"Yeah, remind me to invite you on stage some day. No, Jonathon. Alone, I think."

"Huh. Okay." He shrugged.

"Seems like a long ways for him to come just for a visit. Don't you think?"

"Yeah. I guess..." Josh looked at Jessie curiously.

"Dee said it had something to do with the Virginia shoot. Something he heard about."

"Look Jess, I didn't sleep with that woman, or anyone else. Not that Jon would come here because of that anyway. Huh."

"Did something else happen?" She let a finger trail gently over the scar on his cheek. "Why the scar?"

"It's nothing. It'll give me some character. I'll get all the villainous parts from now on. Grrrr." He raised his fingers like little claws and grrrred adorably at her.

Jessie laughed. "I don't care how many scars you have on you, Josh Sawyer. Inside *or* outside." Sadly she lifted his T-shirt and bent down and kissed the healing scar on his side.

"Do that again," he pleaded, his eyes twinkling. Then he bent down and whispered in her ear. "Or even lower, if you feel the need." He winked at her and the sound of Jessie's laughter filled his soul. Nothing could hurt him now. He was invincible with this amazing woman by his side.

"God, I love you," she laughed wholeheartedly, letting his T-shirt fall back down around his waist and cuddling him tighter. "And yes, okay, I might feel the need when we go back inside. And if there's something else that happened in Virginia that might explain Jon's presence on the east coast of Canada tomorrow, then feel free to share it with me."

She saw a dark shadow flit across his chocolate eyes then, and he glanced away for a second. He swallowed. Shrugged. "Nothing. Just laid down my bike, that's all." He looked back at her. "Earned me a little trip to the ER. Nothing that would bring Jonathon here."

*Like hell,* Jessie thought, her blood pressure suddenly rising as fear trickled down her spine. Jonathon's visit made sense then, at least if the accident was...bad enough.

"Jesus." She let her left arm drop from his waist and turned towards the fire, sickened. It must have been bad if Josh was brought to the ER...if... if Jonathon was coming here to lay eyes on his son. "When?" She bent over double, fighting the urge to get sick. Would the bad shit ever end? Would they ever be able to just live without worry? Without fear?

"Jessie," Josh started softly. "It was the day I got drunk and called you. The day I almost...the day I was considering being stupid. I figure it was the universe telling me to smarten the fuck up." He laid a hand on the side of her head and turned her back up towards him. She straightened and Josh felt sick at the fear in her eyes. "Look, I'm here, aren't I? I laid the bike down on some gravel when we were coming around a turn. The other guys were smart and on the ball, they swerved around me. It wasn't so bad, a mild concussion and some bruised ribs, a little road rash..." He touched the scar on his cheek.

Her voice back at him was childlike, scared. "Jesus, Josh. Don't bad things come in…" Her voice trailed off.

"Jessie, you can't think that way. Anyways we've had way more than—"

"—Threes?"

Silent, they watched each other digest the fear. Josh shook his head. "After all the shit we've been through I refuse to believe that the universe or whatever the hell you want to call it is conspiring against us. We're here, together, and we will not give in, Jessie. We will not live our lives in fear. Look, if anyone out there understands the need to live our lives in the moment it's us, little one. It's us."

She nodded but in the beautiful moonlight Josh saw that her eyes were glistening.

"I'm just so tired of being afraid," she whispered.

"That's why I didn't tell you," he said. "I didn't want to worry you."

"No," she pouted firmly. "No more secrets, Josh. From now on we share everything. We tell each other everything, no matter how much it sucks." She thought about her fight with the riptide. Swallowed. *Well. Everything from here on in. The riptide is in the past.*

"All right," he agreed. "So what's this other thing then, the one that can't wait?"

"Tomorrow," Jessie murmured. "Tomorrow. For now there's…" She raised her eyebrows at him and undid the top button on his jeans, then looked down, tantalizingly. Then she dropped her hands and ran towards the house, her voice trailing behind her, "Spider dogs! They're in the fridge!"

Jessie squealed as Josh laughed and gave chase, rolling his eyes. Already the last big solemn secret was forgotten. They had spider dogs to roast and eat, and marshmallows for s'mores to float lazily on sharpened sticks and brown over the fire too, and then there was that undone top button on his jeans to attend to.

The sun was arcing upwards over the eastern sky when Josh and Jessie finally snuggled in for a few hours sleep. They'd barely woken and showered before Jonathon's rented Honda sedan eased its way up the dusty driveway and then, after lengthy hugs, lemonades and chitchat, they settled on the sunny deck, protected from the cool breeze, and another necessary truth was released.

# Chapter Twenty

"Is it something about *Drifters*? One of the crew?" Josh asked nervously, watching Jonathon fidget with his refilled lemonade glass. "Is Giselle okay? Hell, are you okay?"

Uncertain how this was going to go down, Jonathon glanced up and apprehensively eyed Josh. "Yeah, I get that this is a little sudden. My visit, I mean. Considering I expect to be back soon for a wedding, I hear?" At that, a small grin escaped his lips and he looked over at a beaming Jessie who was perched next to Josh on a lime-green cushioned wicker loveseat, across from Jonathon in a matching chair. "That is, if I've ingratiated my way onto the guest list?" He wiped a sweaty palm through his long white locks, and Jessie couldn't help but notice that Josh had, somewhere along the line, picked up the same nervous habit.

Blushing, Jessie tightly squeezed Josh's hand, and then she focused on a spot on the deck. It was hard to be nervous for Josh and Jonathon with the excitement of the wedding so quickly approaching. But this afternoon's meeting with their old producer was certain to be momentous and memorable. Jessie had called Jon after his plane was scheduled to land, while Josh was in the shower. She wanted to know his intentions, and if her instincts were right (and they were), then she felt Jonathon's task might be eased somewhat if he knew Jessie was already privy to the secret about to be unleashed here, today.

Josh thoughtfully responded to the wedding comment from Jon. "Yes, sir," he said quietly. "There is indeed going to be a wedding." Part of him was terrified that whatever Jonathon needed to say today—and it was obvious from the older man's fidgety behavior that something was up—might stand in the way of his and Jessie's long awaited nuptials. As if the wedding actually happening would be nothing short of a miracle, given everything that so far had plopped itself heartlessly in their way. He wrapped his own clammy fingers more tightly around Jessie's. With a sideways glance at her staid countenance, though, he realized that whatever was up today, she knew. She was in on 'the secret', as she called it herself last night at their cleansing campfire. His heart started to pound as Josh realized this was big. He bit his bottom lip anxiously and shifted in his seat, straightening, but never letting go of Jessie's hand. God, if he had his way he would never let go of her hand again.

"Get on with it," he demanded almost too coolly. "I'd think maybe you were here to ask us about shooting a sequel to *Drifters*, but you're not in business mode. Are you sick?"

"In the head, maybe," Jonathon responded. He had no idea how to start this conversation. He glanced over at Jessie again, and Josh's eyebrows knitted together in curiosity. What the hell? It was as if Jonathon was appealing to her for help.

At that, Jessie tried to pull her hand away from Josh. She thought maybe Jonathon was signaling to her for privacy, which she completely understood. She got up to go, but Josh looked panicked, and he wouldn't let her fingers go.

Jumping in, Jonathon waved an arm, signaling for her to sit back down. "No Jessie, it's all good. Stay. Please."

She swallowed nervously and sat again, this time with a knee curled underneath her. She leaned against Josh's shoulder and rested her right arm on his thigh. In the pause before Jonathon spoke again, she lifted that hand and pressed her palm against the left side of Josh's face so that he turned his head towards her. She could see the fright in his eyes, and she leaned in to push her lips against his soft mouth. Her eyes closed for a moment as she sent him strength that way, and then she looked up and into his own brown eyes. He heard her loud and clear as their thoughts bounced across the space between them, and Josh nodded. Whatever this was—the purpose of Jonathon's visit—it would be okay.

Across from them, Jonathon's heart lurched as he remembered a deep shared love with a woman thirty years ago, a woman he knew before meeting his wife, Giselle. A woman who also made music, albeit in a symphony orchestra back in Vancouver. A woman who resembled Josh in the way she laughed, cried, and hung her head shyly, sequestered by long layered chestnut hair.

"Josh," he started, leaning forward towards the wicker coffee table between them, resting his elbows on his knees. He gestured absently with his hands. "I knew your Mom. We were…good friends. For years."

"She was Giselle's friend," Josh said calmly. "I remember her taking me to yours and Giselle's place one weekend, when…" His voice got quiet as he remembered the reason why his mother dropped him off at Jonathon's home. Wes had attacked him in the midst of a knock down screaming fight with Josh's mother. At eleven years old, a skinny freckled boy had no chance of defending his mother against a full-grown man with a nasty temper and a hate-on for his own kid. In the haze of buried memories, Josh recalled standing on Jonathon's doorstep in a mist of fog and fear, his mother's fingers like vice grips digging into his bicep as he stood there holding a beat up duffle bag and wondering why she had thrown pajamas into it. When the door swung open, Giselle was facing them—it was the first time Josh met her, in fact. She took one look at Wes Sawyer's wife and pulled the two of them inside. Josh was sent to watch television while the women talked, and then his mother was on her knees hugging him and crying before she rose and walked proudly out of the room where he was watching old reruns. The Partridge Family was just climbing into their colorful bus after a gig.

After that, Josh recalled Giselle making him a dish of vanilla ice cream with green crème de menthe liqueur drizzled over the top. She was a gentle lady of exceptional class, and he liked her immediately.

When Jonathon came home that night, Josh remembered standing and facing him, clenching and unclenching his fists. After the fight with his father, which he didn't understand, he was less than welcoming towards the presence of another man. He thought Giselle was his mother's friend…not Jonathon. He always thought that, despite a few hazy recollections of seeing Jonathon around the house when he was very small.

Jonathon continued. "No, Josh. Your mother never knew Giselle. Not until that weekend, anyway. I was…in love with your mom. Wes was away a lot, you see."

As Josh grew increasingly uncomfortable with the direction the conversation was going, he squeezed Jessie's hand harder and harder. She moved her right hand over to cover their clasped hands, and then lifted them and kissed his knuckles. He didn't notice. His ears were burning and humming loudly as he looked quizzically at Jonathon. The older man continued.

"Josh, I…well, your mom got pregnant…and as much as I begged her, she refused to leave the great Wes Sawyer. I didn't get to raise my own son. Wes did. And he was a piss-poor father to you. Damn near killed me." He turned his head away, the emotion of all those years now catching up to him.

Josh was white. But thanks to Jessie's tight grip, he managed to stay seated. "Oh. Hell." He leaned forward—still not letting go of her—and rested his head on his arms. "Jesus."

They were all quiet then as the men struggled to retain control of their emotions, and as Jessie quietly observed the two men she loved desperately. How Josh would handle this news was anybody's guess, and both Jonathon and Jessie had spent hours guessing, Jessie over the last few years, Jonathon over the last thirty-two or so years.

Predictably, when Josh's faint voice eased out from under his hands, muffled, the heartache was evident. "So that would explain how I got the part… Billy." He refused to raise his head. He couldn't look at his old producer. It was as if it was suddenly all a lie—*Drifters*, playing the lead. Especially so soon after *the Black Death.*

"Son," Jonathon leaned forward and touched Josh's left arm, but his son recoiled and pulled away.

The hurt flitting across Jonathon's face broke Jessie's heart. She rubbed her fingers gently over Josh's fisted knuckles.

Jonathon tried again. "Son…you didn't *get* the part on *Drifters.* It was written for you."

At that, Josh finally looked up into eyes that closely resembled his own. At hair that was long and layered, like his, albeit snow white. At a man who was peering intently at him with great love and respect. "Wh-what?"

"It was written…I wrote it…for you. Long before we ever put the show into Development."

His voice hushed, Josh asked again, incredulous. "You *wrote* Billy for me?"

"No, Josh. Not just Billy. *Drifters*."

"But I was…I was lost…*the Black Death*…"

"Hope, Josh. I just kept hoping. You were young, you were trying to figure out things that didn't make sense to you. I just kept hoping. And then…" He looked over at Jessie and smiled.

Josh finished his sentence. "And then Jessie came along." He smiled back at Jonathon, then leaned back in the wicker chair and unclasped his fingers from Jessie's. He lifted his arm and wrapped it around her shoulders, then leaned in and kissed her. Looking into those shining blue eyes, he grinned broadly. "Well, figures the two of you would have something in common." His voice was thick with emotion. All of a sudden there were two people in his life who had believed in him all along. As weird as it was…all of this… Josh was incredibly humbled. There were a lot of questions, there was a lot of shit to process, a lot of shock to absorb, but…this was surreal.

He let his gaze drift back over to Jonathon, who seemed visibly relieved that Josh was smiling and that the cat was finally out of the bag, as it were. "I had no idea," he said, idly waving his left hand in the air. "None. Not that it was you, anyway." He blushed and looked down, then wiped the stray lock of hair out of his eye. "I mean, I guess I figured out pretty early on that Wes had a hate-on for me, but…well, I admit, even on *Drifters* I had no idea. You took a helluva chance." His voice broke, then. "On me, I mean."

Jonathon shrugged. He was still leaning forward as if he was so close to his son now—and all those lost Christmases, birthdays, school functions, you name it—that he could almost touch him…hug him…but it was still too soon. "I didn't take a chance, kid. I watched you from a distance. You were just like me—a good rider, a good actor…you aced that Disney film. I wasn't worried. Besides, in the end we did audition you, remember?"

"Jesus, this is a lot," Josh muttered, letting go of Jessie finally. She laid a hand back over his thigh as he leaned on his hands again and looked down at the cracks in the planking on the deck. Then he stood. He held his hands up in front of his face, palms towards Jonathon. Then Jessie rose as well. "I just need some time, okay? To process this. I mean…Jesus, Jon, Wes was an ass to me. Always. So like…why?" He was incredulous. "Seriously, why? If you were my real father, then how could you stand back and let that happen?" He rested his hands on his hips then, facing Jonathon, and Jessie held her breath as Jonathon sagged before them and wrestled with the question. But then he was overcome…how could he explain to his kid the agony of having to let go?

Hesitating, Jessie stepped forward and took Josh's right hand in her left. Her own right hand snaked around in front of her own body to rest on his belly. "Josh?" she asked quietly. She didn't know if he heard her because he was studying Jonathon then, intently, maybe comparing features, trying to understand…everything. His eyebrows were narrowed, his cheeks popping with color, his lips pursed and his jaw clenched. She had seen that look before.

Jessie jumped in, louder this time. "Babe," she said, forcing a finger to his chin to turn his head and make him look at her. "I think I know why."

Silence. Then he said, in a steady voice, "I'm listening."

She sighed and tilted her head. Her lips turned down just slightly. "Your mom loved Jonathon. But she had Zach, and Wes was—is—a powerful man. For whatever reason, she couldn't leave him. But by having you…and keeping you…she got to keep part of a man she loved." She brushed her right hand down his arm, over the strong bicep and tender fingers.

Interjecting, Jonathon added, "She wanted to leave you with me. That awful weekend, when Wes was so hard on you. And I wanted to keep you, Josh, God I can't tell you how much I wanted to…" He broke down then, and sat back down on the wicker chair. He buried his face in one hand, embarrassed, remembering.

Josh settled his eyes on the man, and then turned to Jessie. "You knew… you knew this…"

Then it was her turn to fear his reaction. But there was no more running away for her. She loved this man—the man she planned to marry—and she would fight for him. She would also be honest with him, as painful as that might be.

She gulped. Nodded. "Yes." It was a whisper, and Josh could see the fear in her wide blue eyes. "I think Charles and Dee were hoping I would think… I dunno…it was a long time ago. They told me the night I told them I loved you…that I couldn't marry Charlie."

"They thought you would think I was a hack, that I got cast on *Drifters* only because of Jonathon."

She smiled then, widely, knocking his trepidation solidly aside. "Josh," she said firmly. "As if. You might recall we were at the end of shooting season one at the time. I *knew* you weren't a hack. And I was already head over heels in love with you, so there. Take that and shove it in your fruitcake."

She placed her hands defiantly on her hips and her twinkling eyes dared him to challenge her.

He wanted to but she was so cute and silly standing there after such a lame comment that he couldn't help himself. Josh laughed, causing Jonathon to look up, somewhat hopefully. "I guess it was a long time ago," Josh said, and then he grabbed Jessie and hugged her tightly. "Okay then," he whispered. "Okay."

Josh turned to Jonathon as he stood. The older man looked tired. Jonathon shrugged his shoulders. "Life is short, kid. I just wanted...I needed...after I heard about the accident on the set in Virginia, and then the whole thing in June..." He glanced at Jessie, who cowered closer to Josh, "...well I guess I just needed some time...some actual time...with my son. With you knowing you are my son. And if you hate me for it, for not telling you, well then I'm sorry. But it was your mother's wish, not mine. And all of a sudden I am pushing seventy and I just couldn't stand it anymore. You not knowing. I needed you to know. I know it's damned selfish, but that's the goddamned truth. And for what it's worth...I'm goddamned sorry."

Josh's life flashed before him like a movie screen. Every shot involved Wes. Wes staring at him at dinner with something akin to loathing in his eyes, Josh, shrinking under that awful glare; Wes not showing up at the premiere of the Disney film; Wes playing cards with Zach, laughter; Wes tenderly carrying little Kayla up to bed; Wes hitting Josh; Wes hitting Josh; Wes and his black box theatre hookers, Josh crying on satin sheets; Wes hitting Josh. But there was another film playing there too, an old one that was somewhat buried under the other. And in it was a sadness that Josh sometimes saw at play in his father's...no, Wes'...eyes. Occasionally there was a flicker of a smile accompanying that. Then Wes' eyes would dart across to Josh's mom, and the sadness would be even more profound. In his heart Josh now realized that the indomitable Wes Sawyer had his own share of the old pain. For how difficult must it be to be in love with a woman who in her heart most likely truly loved someone else? And then…to raise the love child of your wife's lover?

Josh could see now that Wes likely did the best he could with what he had to work with. It would be weird to see the man again. But maybe now they could 'shake' on a fucked-up past and let bygones be bygones. Maybe now they could approach life as adults, with a new knowing that would let things go easier between them.

Josh stepped forward then, around the coffee table, and he took a hold of Jonathon's shoulders. He nodded. "Okay. Okay."

Then Jessie ducked her head and left the men alone on the deck as the afternoon sun started its cool descent into the west, leaving its magnanimous trail of pinks and oranges glistening in its wake on the serene bay before the old cedar-shingled farmhouse. As she left them to their tears and tales of joy and heartache, she entered the kitchen and spied, off in the corner, the white bankers' box gifted by George at the old folks home.

She sighed. One more secret. One more.

Silently, as she opened the fridge door and pondered what to throw together for dinner, she hoped it, too, wouldn't be a biggie.

*Fuck, yeah,* she thought. *No more surprises.*

She pulled some pepper steaks out of the fridge and reached for the marinade. As she turned, it seemed George's box was looking at her, its white cardboard sides glaring in the fading light.

Her heart sank. *Oh, damn,* she thought. *Just damn.*

But for now that could wait. There was steak to marinate, vegetables to prepare, and some healing to do with the man she loved. She happily expected it to involve a great deal of tender cuddling.

She smiled, and peeked through the patio doors at the guys. Jonathon had his hand on Josh's shoulder, Josh had his hands shoved in his pockets, and they were grinning like two fools at each other.

Jessie started to whistle a new tune, and then she waltzed over to the door and hollered at Josh.

"Start the barbecue, will ya? I've got me some steaks on the go."

# Chapter Twenty-one

Speckled sunshine filtering through lazy clouds dappled the asphalt on the edge of the runway at the old Summerside air base. Built in the early nineteen forties as part of the British Commonwealth Air Training Plan to train up pilots and flight crew during the second world war, the base was now used for a myriad of purposes—the Atlantic Police Academy, air cadets, various Aerospace businesses. The runway was still used for training and private aircraft and recently an International Air Show brought back vivid memories of screaming jets and puttering aircraft engines. Canada's Snowbirds and the American Aerobatic Team the Blue Angels thrilled delighted spectators. Today, though, it was quiet at the old air base. Quiet with the exception of a few screaming women running up and down the asphalt dragging helium balloons behind them, that is. Chased by Kayla's man Paul, Jessie, Kayla and Sophie were playing tag on the runway with the pure delight of children, passing time in each other's joyous company while awaiting the arrival of the Keating jet, which was expected within the hour.

Watching them from the edge of the runway as they rested on the open tailgate of the SUV, munching on apples plucked from trees earlier that afternoon from Arlington Orchards, fifteen minutes west of Summerside, were Josh and Stephen, swinging their legs and relishing one of life's serenely happy moments. Parked behind them were other rentals driven by Steve and Paul—they expected a full load of guests today.

"Damn, who knew," Steve was saying, somewhat dazed, referring to Josh's visit from Jonathon, who would be arriving on the jet with Charles and Dee.

"I sure as hell didn't," Josh replied. He glanced sideways at Steve. "Jessie did, though."

Raising his eyebrows, Steve looked over at his friend.

Josh shrugged, waving the apple idly in the air. "I'm not thrilled about that, but I see her reasons for keeping that secret. Besides, she's had other things on her mind these last few years."

"So what about Wes, then? Where does that leave him?"

"Can't say I really know," Josh answered honestly. "He's coming to the wedding. I guess we'll have to find some peace over the whole thing. He and Jon have always been civil the few times I've seen them together, so I guess that thing about time healing old wounds is true. Maybe they found some peace in the knowing they both loved my mom, I don't know. She was a pretty special lady."

"She was good to you? A good mom?"

"Yeah. The best. Always trying to make up for crazy ole Wes, I guess." He took a bite out of his apple, pondering his mom and wishing she could somehow be at his wedding. "She would love Jessie, I know that for sure."

Steve grinned, watching Jessie try to catch her breath on the runway, ducking and diving away from Paul, trying to protect her balloon from him. It glinted in the warm sun as boisterous shouts punctuated the air. "Who doesn't?" He added soberly, "I don't think I've ever seen her this happy, Josh. Something tells me the right man won."

Ducking his head, embarrassed, Josh smiled under the waterfall of layered hair that fell over his cheek. "Who would have ever thought things would turn out this way? Especially after she took off. It just seemed like I was living in some hole, going through the motions, telling myself everything was okay. The hole was so deep I didn't even notice it. But when she came back in March..."

"She has that kind of power. Over everyone. She's just one of those magnetic people you can't help but want to make things better for."

"Yeah, she's all that and more." Josh sighed, wistful. "Definitely my mom would have liked her. She would approve."

Frowning, Steve asked a question he'd been wondering about. "Speaking of wedding guests, and women loved by more than one man..."

"Jacob," Josh said simply.

"Is he coming? To the wedding?"

"He's been invited." Josh thought about the awful comment Jessie threw in his face earlier that summer after he read the email to Jacob over her shoulder. "What am I supposed to do? I trust her. We're sorting things out. Trudy's a huge help. Not saying it's going to be easy, but we've already agreed they're going to continue to work together. Playing each other's shows, recording..." He squinted up into the sky as a steady engine announced the appearance of an approaching jet. "I think it will be harder on him, anyway."

Steve was silent as he considered that. From the runway came a squeal of delight as Jessie spotted the jet in the distance. She started jumping up and down, her balloon forgotten. When Paul snuck up behind and grabbed it, Jessie elicited more high-pitched squeals as Sophie and Kayla ran to her aid. Steve shook his head. "She's like a child, sometimes."

"Just catching up on a lot of lost years," Josh said quietly, a tiny smile creasing his lips as he tossed the apple core on the grass beside them for the squirrels to picnic on later. "I just hope I don't have to watch over my shoulder for Jacob my whole life." Thoughtful, he rubbed his palms on the thighs of his jeans, drying off the apple's moisture and the nervous sweat that thinking about Jacob induced.

"Nah," Steve cut in, a bit too quickly. "He helped Jess through a hard time. He's a good guy, Josh. He knew from the start she was attached to someone else and I'm pretty certain she never let go of that. Jesus, the night of her concert back in the spring she was a mess. She was with Jacob then but all she could think about was you—*Is Josh coming to the concert? Please bring him, Steve.* She's lost without you. I don't see Jacob ever being a threat. We'll find him a good woman and that'll take his mind off her."

"He probably won't even show up." Josh eyed the jet as it taxied to a landing. Jessie was jumping up and down again, waving her arms at the plane. Absently Josh thought Dee would be thrilled to see her girl so joyous.

He looked around at the open fields and the expansive blue sky. North of them, Malpeque Bay twinkled in the late afternoon sunlight, its waters crystalline diamonds sparkling for their enjoyment. "I love how open this place is. Simple people and a landscape where you feel like you can breathe.

Not claustrophobic. At night you can see the stars so clearly…thousands of them. There's no light pollution, at least not out in South Rustico."

"I'm sensing a 'but' in there somewhere," Steve interjected.

"No, I love it here, really. I mean, it's starting to cool down and I'm wondering what winter would be like, but still…Jessie's at peace here, at least this last little while she's been doing great."

"So what's the 'but'?"

"But…offers are coming in regularly now. For more films. And I want to do them. Hilary's bringing some new scripts for me to consider."

Steve patted him on the back. He knew the best was yet to come from this man. "You'll have your own Oscar before you know it, cuddling up there on the mantel next to Jessie's two."

"Well, she'd get some more of her own if she would go back to work. She hasn't done any acting since season two of *Drifters*."

"Too soon for her, maybe."

"Yeah, I know, and I don't want to push her. Besides, both of us working at the same time means a separation, and neither of us want that. Not after everything."

"Is she looking at anything?"

"Yeah, she's narrowed down a few but I can see her heart's not in it." He turned to Steve. "She's actually considering helping out an independent filmmaker here on P.E.I. Some local gal from Summerside who studied film at Vancouver Film School. She wants to make a film about a hockey player and a bar singer…something about a missing child and second chances. It's a good script, I've read it. Jess would star in it and Exec Produce it. She's met the filmmaker, through Trudy, actually."

"When would it go to camera?"

"If Charles helps them sort out the financing they would go to camera in late winter or spring. But it means Jessie would spend most of the winter here. Which would mean…"

"You would spend most of the winter here."

Josh shrugged. "I can think of worse things than being hunkered down with Jessie in a remote location all winter." He smiled and a pink blush spread across his cheeks. "This is a cathartic place. And it's her home. Regardless of where we end up, I expect at the very least we'll be spending some time in the summers here."

"You'll figure it out," Steve added. "And leave it to Jessie to want to help out a local filmmaker. You gotta love that girl."

Ten minutes later the jet was safely situated on the runway, and its door was opened and steps secured. Dee was the first to appear. Jessie practically ran up the steps to hug her.

Watching her as he and Steve sauntered closer to the happy group, Josh couldn't keep a permanent grin from lighting up his own eyes, despite the nervous fear that Jacob might be on this flight. But soon all the passengers were on the tarmac, and Jacob was not amongst them. Josh slipped an arm around Jessie's waist as she shyly handed her welcome balloon to Jane, whose belly had grown substantially as she and Charlie's new baby was making its presence known. The baby was due in a few short months, and its parents were ecstatic.

Josh shook Charlie's hand warmly and then leant to the side to brush his lips against Jessie's temple. He could see her trying to covertly look up the steps of the small jet, and despite the ecstasy of seeing those who were like family to her, he also easily sensed her dejection at Jacob's glaring absence. She was trying to brush the thought aside, he could tell, or at least hide it from him, but Josh figured he may as well accept the fact that Jacob meant a lot to her, and always would, as hard as that would be for him.

"Hey," he whispered to her as Charlie and Jane accepted warm hugs from Kayla and Sophie, who were marveling at pixie-haired Jane's belly, "maybe he'll fly in with the others."

Jessie's face was pinched as she looked up at Josh, embarrassed. "I'm sorry," she mumbled. "There's this new song bouncing around in my head and I was just thinking it would be cool to work it out with him, that's all." Her cheeks were a rosy red.

"As long as you're not fixing for one of those wild orgasms," he replied drily, with a wry grin.

From beneath long eyelashes came a quiet voice. "You're never gonna let me live that one down, are you?" Pouting, Jessie placed her hands on Josh's hips and stared at the tarmac.

He laughed and wrapped both arms around her shoulders. "Nope."

"Never?"

"Uh uh." Then he laid his palms on her cheeks after a happy sigh passed between them. Josh looked deeply into Jessie's soft blue eyes. "Okay. Maybe. I love you, little one. Let's go visit with these wonderful people." He could see Jonathon pacing nervously near Charles, watching him with what he thought were surreptitious sideways glances. He ought to go say hello and dispel any nervousness that still lingered after the producer's recent admission. "We're getting married in a few days. I'm the happiest man on the planet right now, and I'm guessing Jacob isn't. But hopefully he will mellow and still show up, maybe on the flight with Katrine and John Paul."

"And Charlene." She was still pouting.

Josh's heart skipped a beat. She was pretty cute in her faded jeans and printed empire top floating lazily over her hips. The pink cardigan overtop made her seem even more childlike, despite the fact that she was a grown woman. He shook his head in wonder.

"I love you, Jessie Wheeler. And don't you ever forget it."

He was rewarded with a smile as wide and genuine as he had ever seen on his girl's buoyant face. Her eyes sparkled like the shimmering water in the nearby bay.

"Not likely to. Love you back, Mister Sawyer."

Cheers broke up the sweetness of their lingering kiss, and hollers of 'get a room, you two' tickled their eardrums. Finally, Josh took Jessie by the hand and they strolled over to Jonathon and Giselle. Jonathon, too, had a light in his eyes, one that in his case none of the group had ever been privy to, and Josh found himself wondering why secrets were kept between people over years and years; secrets that could provide happy times and the creation of wonderful memories instead of lingering sadnesses and everlasting regrets. He pumped Jon's hand proudly, but Jon grabbed him for a hug instead, and Josh felt his heart bursting with emotion, happiness, and a long sought after peace. With Jessie's arm still around his waist, and his biological father's arms around his shoulders, a cheerful buzz from close friends and family nearby, life was about as perfect as it could get.

Finally.

~

The next few days were filled with remaining wedding prep. Dee was in her glory handling the myriad of tiny details, and she and Jessie argued happily over odds and sods like centerpieces for the tables and where to sit Jessie's mom, Emily, and the elderly Wheeler family friend, George. For the dinner and dance they booked a local restaurant not far from Josh and Jessie's rented summer home, the Dayboat. The days were cooling off and although Jessie hoped for a warm enough day to hold the actual wedding on the beach, they needed a venue where they could bring in a hired band and serve hot food. The Dayboat was perfect. Weathered gray cedar shingles and a large outdoor deck overlooked a pretty river, and it was only about twenty minutes from Charlottetown, where most of the guests would be staying on a secure floor at the Delta Hotel. They had also prepared for a cool or rainy day by booking St. Augustine's church in South Rustico, a quaint historic white church with gothic elements where the excited locals had gotten used to seeing celebrities amongst their Sunday morning congregation.

The day before the wedding, Josh and Jessie found their farmhouse filled to the rafters with a steady stream of happy well-wishers. All day they entertained friends who were flying in from all over the world—Priya, Benjie, Erin and Keira from Jessie's usual dance troupe, Janet the publicist, Christian and other regular musicians who played with Jessie, many of the old *Drifters* cast and crew, various directors and producers, and various extended family and friends.

The reunions were sweet; everyone was happy for Jessie and Josh and a union that seemed perfect and well deserved. The day remained dry until evening, and although it was now too cold to swim in the Gulf, the kayaks were in and out all day and Josh had even rented a small Bayliner pleasure boat and a couple of Seadoos with which to entertain their wedding guests. The barbecue was going all day, the men taking turns grilling burgers, steaks, and shish kebabs, and the women were busy trying salads out of local celebrity chef Michael Smith's cookbook, and keeping the drinks coming. People dropped in and out between touring the island's red sandstone cliffs and white sand beaches, and shopping in Charlottetown's quaint historic district.

That night a gray mist settled over the revelers. It soon morphed into a serious Prince Edward Island drizzle, damp to the bone and urging folks indoors. Josh piled some wood into the cozy wood stove as everyone relaxed in the open concept room and swapped stories in little huddles here and there. Josh found a seat at the kitchen island next to Steve, Charlie across from them, as they watched their women chat excitedly about the plans for the next day. Josh didn't hear the doorbell chime the first time, but then it rang again, followed by a tentative slow opening of the screen door.

Jessie happened to look up at Josh then and she saw him straighten apprehensively. Following his eyes, she wheeled around and spotted Katrine, John Paul and Charlene at the door. With a sharp intake of breath she was up in a second, squealing happily and welcoming her Scots friends with unbridled glee. Behind them, hands in his pockets, shyly appraising Jessie's tanned arms and shining eyes, was Jacob. He watched her welcome their friends before meeting her gaze and nodding nervously.

Jessie cocked her head to one side and smiled a little sadly at him. But her eyes were indeed shining when she spotted him, and she couldn't fight the tears welling up in her soul.

"Jacob," she breathed, reaching for him. "I didn't think you were coming!"

"Neither did I," he said, letting her hold him and slowly raising his arms to encircle her. They held each other tightly, for old times sake, as Josh, Steve and Charlie looked on from the kitchen island across the room.

Jacob felt their eyes on him and he looked up, wary, and met Josh's steady gaze. Jessie followed his glance, even though she could tell by how quickly he stepped back from her that Jacob had spotted Josh. Her fiancé was watching the little reunion carefully, his body tensed, and she could see him swallowing nervously. Josh shifted his eyes from Jacob to her, though, and a tiny, trusting smile lit up his face.

Jacob nodded a greeting to Josh before turning back to Jessie. "You should know...the only reason I decided to come was because he called me."

"Wh-what?" she asked, surprised. She looked curiously back over at Josh, who was saying something to Steve at his left as he leaned his elbows back on the counter. "Seriously? He called you?" She crossed her arms and grinned, which helped Jacob relax.

"Yeah. Seriously. He seemed to think you wouldn't feel your wedding was complete without your ex drooling close by. Maybe he needs a stand-in for the wedding night or something." He threw his hands up in front of his face, anticipating a thwack from Jessie that never came.

Instead, she grabbed him and held him close again. "Told you he was kind. And good."

A lump formed then in Jacob's throat as he thought about his time with Jessie—mostly as Annie, and of the split-second when he thought about eradicating Josh from their lives altogether. Jessie could see the difficult feelings flicker through his eyes, turning them from a deep warm blue to a de-saturated icy pale.

"Babe," she said, breathing in the scent of green apple she loved and missed. "I'm glad you're here. I'm glad about everything, with you." She touched his stubbly cheek with the back of her hand and peered into the sad eyes. She shook her head slowly from side to side. "No regrets, with you. You still mean everything to me. You know that, right?"

Jacob tilted his head and looked deeply into the baby blues he still loved. His spirits lifted when he realized that the old lingering ennui Annie Hayden carried—and then Jessie after that—was not at the surface that day, the day before she would marry Josh Sawyer, the man whose ring she'd worn around her neck for so long.

"You're happy," he said, as if it was a surprise to him—a good surprise.

She smiled genuinely, and nodded, still clutching his damp denim jacket at the elbows. She reached up and undid his buttons from top to bottom as she always did.

Watching, because he couldn't tear his eyes away from Jessie and a man he knew she would on some level always love, Josh felt uncomfortable, as if he were witnessing an intimate tender moment that belonged only to her, and to Jacob. There was a current at play between the two, and Josh had to fight his fears and instantly quell any jealous thoughts threatening to undo him entirely. He had to remind himself that she was marrying *him*. Not Jacob. She came back to Canada *for him*.

He felt a pat on his back—he flipped himself around in his seat just as Jessie was pulling Jacob's jacket off. The two had still not looked away from each other, although neither was speaking except the volumes through their eyes, and Josh was feeling rather unsettled. After turning away from them, he glanced up at Charlie, who wasn't grinning playfully, as usual. He felt Steve soberly turn towards Charlie too, across the kitchen island from them.

"Jesus," Josh muttered, fingering a glass of cranberry juice Charlie thrust between his fingers. "Please tell me I won't have to look over my shoulder for him my entire life."

"Jacob belongs to a part of Jessie's life when she needed him, Josh. Accept that, and let it go." Charlie was like a wise big brother, which Josh appreciated right about now.

"Sucks," he murmured in response. "Seeing her with him. Brings back all the old jealousy."

"So why'd you call him and ask him to come?" Steve was with Josh when he made the awkward call the day before.

"That's easy," Josh said. "For her."

"Glutton for punishment." Charlie's eyes were a little more playful now, the glow from the fire flirting over his face.

"Nah. I just want her to be happy, that's all."

Katrine eased by them and smiled at Josh before winking seductively at Steve. He raised his eyebrows and couldn't help from eyeing her tight little butt as she opened the fridge door and poked around for a cooler. Her spiked hair now featured green and burgundy tips, and her bangs, pulled down over one eye, were royal blue.

Steve tapped Josh on the elbow. Thanks to Josh's fears earlier in the summer, Steve knew about Jessie's threesome with Katrine and Jacob—and he couldn't resist. He leaned into Josh and whispered, "How happy do you want her to be? Sure you didn't bring that little Scots group here for another reason?"

Groaning, Josh buried his suddenly beet red face in his hands.

Katrine found a raspberry cooler and leaned forward on the counter next to Charlie, who was eyeing the boys curiously.

"Don't you worry 'bout Jacob, Josh. Dis girl, she was a lonely shell in Edinburgh. Dat ring of yours, she wore it 'round her neck like a noose, even wit Jacob. I look at 'er now, she one 'appy woman. Tomorrow she marry you and den the two of you, you go make babies and live 'appy ever after. You deserve it, no?"

With a typical graceful Katrine flourish, she grasped Josh's fingers in hers, lifted his hand and let her lips delicately linger on the knuckles. Then she raised her eyes to him, smiled warmly, and glanced over to Steve, who was watching with interest.

"You let me know you and your woman need to, 'ow you say, spice up your sex life? I like a man wit yellow hair." She bent over the counter and twisted a finger in one of Steve's blond curls. Winking, Katrine reached behind her and pinched Charlie's butt. He jumped and yelped, then stared at her in surprise.

Katrine was laughing when she sauntered over to Jane and Sophie, where Kayla had pointed the guys out with a laugh. Her eyes glinting, it was all Katrine could do not to burst out in hysterics. She settled by Sophie on the couch and cuddled up to her, eyeing Steve seductively, who had turned his head back around to watch her. The girls had a good laugh at the boys' expense as Jessie joined them, wondering what all the fuss was about.

"Good Lord," Steve exhaled. "Damn, Josh, maybe you should get in on that, after all."

"Not my style," Josh said, taking a sip of the cranberry juice and eyeing Jacob, who was nervously making his way over to the fridge for a beer. "Keeping Jessie to myself, thanks very much." *I hope,* he thought as Jacob yanked the cap off a bottle of Guinness and turned to face him.

Charlie eyed Steve and then sidled over and leaned in to talk to him as Jacob settled across from Josh. Thrusting out a hand, Jacob was relieved when Josh accepted the offer of friendship.

"Thanks, man," he said. "For calling me, I mean. I wouldn't have come."

Josh thought carefully for a second before responding. Then he looked up at Jacob, and spoke his mind. No more untruths or hidden agendas. He may as well be frank. "I'm not so sure I'm glad I called." He wasn't being mean, just truthful. He shrugged.

Jacob was quiet as he pondered the man Jessie loved and ached for in Edinburgh and then later in Vancouver. "Yeah well, I can't help you with your demons, man. I'm too busy fighting my own." He took a deep pull on the soothing Irish Stout and leaned his elbows on the counter so that he was more at eye level with Josh, who was still watching him carefully.

Then, glancing downwards, he picked at a puddle on the counter with his forefinger. Josh spoke from beneath a curtain of layered hair. "Yeah, well, I suppose I should at least be glad you didn't shoot me when you had the chance." *Might as well get that out in the open too,* he thought. He looked up when Jacob didn't respond, and then Josh chuckled. His remark had the desired effect—Jacob was gray.

"She told you?"

Now it was Josh's turn to pale. He sipped on the juice, slowly, his eyes not leaving Jacob's panicked expressive baby blues. "Nooope," he said. Then, "Seriously?"

Shrugging, Jacob eyed him back. "What'd you expect?"

Josh laughed wholeheartedly then, surprising everyone. He raised his glass to connect with Jacob's beer. "All right then. I had a lot of time to think about…that night. I realized you likely had a pretty clear shot at one point. Maybe I should ask what kept you from killing me?"

"Huh," Jacob said, surprised at Josh's reaction. He figured the guy easily hated him, and why not? He didn't think his admission would clear the air, in fact he thought if Josh ever found out, he would likely keep Jessie as far away as possible. Jacob's eyes drifted over to Jessie, who was watching them with amusement.

He smiled at Jessie before nodding at her and glancing back at Josh. "Her."

*So we are two simple guys on the same path,* Josh thought. *He loves Jessie enough to care about making her happy.* He grinned and their glasses clinked together. It was enough to raise Jacob Ryan a little higher in Josh's esteem, and the other way around as well. But Josh couldn't resist one further dig.

"So, I s'pose I oughtta be careful about leaving my drinks lying around then. Unattended." He raised his eyebrows at Jacob, who relaxed visibly and laughed heartily this time.

"Yeah. I mean, I would if I were you. But then again…" He winked at Jessie, who grinned broadly back at him as she threw an arm around Maggie, who floated over to her after a conversation with some of the *Drifters* crew. "Maybe it's me who should be on my guard."

Josh turned and saw the wide smile Jessie aimed at Jacob. She saw Josh twist around, though, and she shifted her glance towards him. She winked at him and he smiled back. It was all Josh could do not to get up off the stool, go over to her, grab her arm and haul her upstairs where they could be alone. He didn't much care about getting married, he just wanted *her*, period. But then again, there was something awesome and wonderful in his and Jacob's shared goal of wanting to make this often troubled girl happy. And watching her sitting mid-way across the room from them, with trusted girlfriends by her side, and Dee and Charles close by—people she loved all gathered in this lovely quaint old weathered farmhouse in her home province with her wedding scheduled for the very next day...well, it was clearly obvious that she was, indeed, happy.

So Josh let her be. But it wasn't long before she drifted to his side to hear what he, Jacob, Charlie and Steve were groaning and hooting about. Jessie wrapped her arms around his shoulders from behind, nuzzling her lips on Josh's warm neck underneath the layered chestnut hair. He reached a hand up to entwine his fingers with hers as he laughed along with the boys, and couldn't help but think that this evening was absolutely unequivocally surreal.

Jessie smiled softly and let the warm fuzzies envelop her as well. Now, with Jacob and their other Scots friends here, the wedding would be perfect. She closed her eyes and breathed in Josh's musky familiar scent, which mingled with the wood smoke and a room filled with good friends and the best of times, and she was *glad.*

Just before she, Jacob and Christian bowed to demand and settled in to play some music, she bent further towards Josh and whispered into his ear, "I mean it, Josh Sawyer. I am so in love with you." Her eyes remained closed as she pressed her body against his, and the others noticed him bow out of their conversation momentarily as his eyes got a little smoky—not from the wood smoke—and he turned his head just slightly so that he could lay a hand gently on the side of her cheek and lift her face up to touch his lips gently to hers. Then he leaned his forehead against hers and closed his own eyes. They stayed that way for a few moments and then when he found his voice he whispered back to her, "Thank you, Jessie Wheeler. For following me out to the garbage, I mean." He swallowed, all of a sudden the emotion of their turbulent lives catching up to him in this cozy farmhouse where the sound of the gentle lapping waves outside blended with the softly falling rain and the happy voices within its gabled walls. He added, "And for loving me. I love you back."

Her eyes flitted open and she looked deeply into Josh's before leaning in for one last kiss.

When she let go, they both had happy hearts because they knew beyond a shadow of a doubt they would be together again, that they had a whole lifetime to revel in the sweet glory of each others' presence, and regardless of what happened to them in the past, the *now* was truly all that mattered.

And most of all, as Josh watched Jacob pull out his guitar and Jessie excitedly start to show him the chords for her new song, Josh knew a few other things for certain. One, that Jacob was indeed a good guy; two, that Josh could trust Jacob; and three, that in some weird way he, Josh, had given Jessie a great gift by calling Jacob and encouraging him to come to their wedding. For she obviously shared some deep connection with the guy and it was in her very essence, because it had to do with the love of music.

And music, no matter how you looked at it, was inextricably intertwined in Jessie Wheeler's soul.

~

Before the night was over, Josh had to steel his nerves for one more reunion with a guy he didn't relish seeing. Wes Sawyer arrived without a girlfriend in tow, for once. Accompanied by Zach, Hilary, and his sprouting grandchildren, the older man was beaming. He seemed to be mellowing with age, and Zach's youngest, Lana, was clinging to his hand, which pleased the man inordinately. As the family stepped into the bustling farmhouse, Kayla rushed at them and her dad squeezed her tight. Josh couldn't help but feel his nerves crunch around his belly. He glanced over at Jonathon, who was watching him apprehensively.

By then Jessie was half sitting, half leaning on Josh's lap at the kitchen island while Jacob and Christian pounded out a rousing Pogues' tune in the far corner. John Paul was in on the action, too, and the old farmhouse was practically bouncing on its foundation. Jessie turned around to Josh and eyed him carefully.

He shrugged and answered her unasked question. "Jon said they talked a few weeks ago, before Jon's visit here. So yeah, he knows I know. Kayla and Zach are in on it now too, I hear. Guess I was the last one on the list to check off."

Grudgingly, she pulled herself off his lap. "Okay then. Let's go say hi, at least." Sensing his hesitation, Jessie took his hand and led him over to where the group was being soundly hugged and greeted by the other wedding guests.

Wes stepped through the throng and smiled down at Jessie—he was a tall man, an imposing seasoned actor with broad shoulders and an almost aristocratic presence. He gripped her small hand in his and pulled her towards him in a gracious hug.

"What took you so long to marry my son?" he asked, fondly peering into her eyes.

Jessie grinned shyly and glanced down at her feet. She wondered what Josh—and Jonathon—would think of the reference to Josh as his son. Technically, Josh was raised as Wes' son, but the ground had shifted beneath both men's feet. She supposed it would seem to Josh now as if he had two fathers, in a way. Her thoughts wandered to her own dad, David, and Charles Keating. Well. *Having two fathers is not such a bad thing.* She smiled up at Wes.

"So glad you could come," she exclaimed honestly. "As you can see, we're having quite the east coast kitchen party!"

Lana, sleepy from the journey, pulled at Jessie's top then. Stooping down to chat with her at eye level, Jessie brushed back a piece of the little girl's wispy brown hair. "Well, hello."

Clutching her old faded and worn pink bunny baby blanket, Lana leaned forward into Jessie's arms. Jessie could feel her eyes watering as she stood and held the little girl. The small arms laced themselves around her shoulders. Josh lifted a hand to brush Jessie's neck, and then he bent forward and whispered to Lana.

"Sleepy, little girl?"

She nodded, and her eyes closed. After a little peck on the forehead, Josh left his niece to Jessie's care and forced himself to look up into the eyes of the man whose name he himself carried, like an anchor, he used to think. Now he felt somewhat more comfortable with the name, for some strange reason. Seemed that with Jonathon's startling admission, the universe had balanced him somehow.

"Hey," he said. "Thanks for coming all this way on such short notice." Neither man reached out to grip the other's hand, or to embrace each other as father and son should. Instead, a thousand trillion tiny thoughts worked their way through their uncertain minds, and Josh could see Wes' mouth working to form words that couldn't seem to make their way through the curtain of fog that years of confusion and hurt and deceit left hanging like a veil in their lives.

Josh could feel Jonathon's stare against his back and he wished this strange reunion with the man he'd thought of as his father for so many years was private. He felt Zach clap him on the back as he ushered one of his young boys through the throng of people who were making the farmhouse dance with unbridled gaiety.

Then Josh took the high road and eased things for Wes. After all the years feeling unloved and sometimes even despised by who he thought was his father, and the nasty headlines those few times they came to blows, all Josh could think to say was, "I mean it, Dad. I'm really glad you're here."

Struggling with emotion then, because Wes really had no idea if he would be welcome at this party or in Josh's life any more, the older man nodded and said simply, "Thanks."

It was one of those words that carried everything within, all the years of pain, of staring into the eyes of a child whose eyes were those of another man whom Wes' wife loved.

It was Josh who reached out and grabbed Wes' hand then, gripped it tightly, and by that simple move assured the Sawyer patriarch of acceptance and understanding. Years ago Josh would not have responded this way. Instead, he would have turned the other way and avoided Wes altogether. But Josh would be marrying Jessie Wheeler the very next day, and the beauty and understanding she brought into his life, despite her own years of suffering, made him a better man. And so he started to relax while Wes swiped at his eyes, unable to hide his own relief, and even Kayla and Zach grinned stupidly at each other when they spied Josh grab Wes and pull him into a welcoming hug.

When Matt and Julie landed at the door with their daughter, along with Arnie and his wife in tow, the evening was complete. Dee rolled her eyes at Jessie, laughing, while Jessie squealed with delight. Mary Helen, too, was there—she and Arnie were the only friends of Jessie's from the Downtown Eastside who were flown in; there were others but Arnie had his own special place in Jessie's life, one that was largely unknown even to her at this point, because those two years were still primarily buried deep in Jessie's psyche. The exceptions were moments when she played guitar for money or food, or when she stared up at Arnie's water-stained ceiling from underneath an old afghan on a sagging couch on the nights too cold for outdoor sleeping.

Sometimes when she was in Arnie's presence Jessie could feel the fog from those years lifting a little, and no more so than on this night when her soul seemed more ready than usual to let in a little of the old darkness, if only because she was happy and perhaps her spirit felt she was ready, especially with Trudy's gentle coaching and listening over the past few months. Tonight Josh caught her more than once watching Arnie with a quizzical eye, and he reminded himself to ask her later what that was about. Or perhaps a chat with Arnie himself was in order. After all, he was also the man who aided Jessie in her undercover escape a few years ago, and Josh wanted to shake the man's hand, stare deep into his eyes, and beg him never to keep such secrets from him again. Josh was about to become Jessie's husband, and as far as he was concerned they were only formalizing a love that already inextricably intertwined he and Jessie. From now on he wanted in on her secrets—her life from the past, future issues that might rise between them…he loved her, and someone who had the power Arnie did to respond without question to Jessie when she needed help, was someone Josh wanted—needed—to know.

But for now he went back to his kitchen perch, always a watcher, and Josh settled comfortably with Lana in his arms now, surrendered reluctantly by Jessie because once again she was begged to sing and play for the assorted crowd.

So as Jessie plopped herself down by Christian at the grand piano, John Paul took a break, and Josh watched as Jacob leaned in towards Jessie and whispered conspiratorially, his blue eyes twinkling merrily as his comment brought forth hearty laughter from Jessie. Josh snuggled Lana in closer and fought the confusing mélange of feelings that taunted him—a new dad, an old dad, a life that now amazed and humbled him, a sweet little child in his arms and Jane in the distance, her own belly growing with child. And as he watched Charlie bend over Jane and lay a hand on his wife's stomach, Josh felt truly and utterly blessed, despite the twisty turny emotions swirling around in his addled mind.

He shook his head slowly from side to side in wonder and then the night became even more surreal. He heard the first chords of the song Jessie played for him that day not all so long ago at Pat's Rose and Grey Room in Charlottetown and, as she looked up at him and smiled—glowed, really—he bent his lips to Lana's hair so nobody could see through to his misty joy. How Jacob could sit there and accompany her while she played that song was a mystery to him, but it was only a fleeting moment, because as the song took hold the entire throng of revelers quieted, as they always did when Jessie's husky voice filled the room, and then all eyes flitted back and forth between him and Jessie as she sang, confident and sure.

Her voice broke near the end and she had to look back to Jacob and Christian and silently plead with them to play a few extra bars, because suddenly Jessie, like everyone else in the room, was overcome by emotion. Nobody earned the right to be happy as much as Jessie and Josh, it seemed, as least that night it was all about them, and so as she sang of a deep enduring love for her man, to her man, it was all she could do to hang on and finish the song.

This time, when she did finish, her eyes on Josh and Josh alone, she signaled to him the way she did at his birthday party in April earlier that year at Charles and Dee's home and he thought *screw it*, and raised his wet cheeks from Lana's hair and signaled back—two fingers at the corner of an eye, a trail down the cheek, a touch to the lips, and then a graceful flourish.

It was a late night for everyone, but the next day there would be a wedding—on the beach, they'd agreed, since it was forecast to be unseasonably warm—and tonight, there was loving to be done, so, when the last guest parted, Josh took Jessie by the hand and led her yawning up the stairs to their bedroom, where he showed her in no uncertain terms that Deuce McCall no longer hovered over them, frightening him into a fear of touching her, and he whispered, "Jessie Wheeler, I can't sing to you the way you sing to me, but I love you just the same, and I promise I will always be here for you."

He placed his hands on both sides of her cheeks the way she did with him back on the night she spied McCall in their group photograph at Agassiz, and Josh implored her to hear what he had to say. "I can't wait to start this next part of my life as your husband, Jessie, with everything life brings us—children"—he grinned widely at her sweet blush—"careers, family, friends… even the bad stuff, Jessie…" She frowned but he raised her face back up to him, her hands resting gently overtop his, "There will be some, Jess, you know there will, but together we will handle it, okay? You and me. Always and forever, remember?"

And she nodded then and whispered, "Yeah. Always and forever. You and me, Josh."

Josh pulled her close and wrapped his arms around the woman who would, the very next day—or later that day if you looked at the clock—become his wife.

And he was glad.

# Chapter Twenty-Two

Digging her toes into the sand, Jessie giggled to herself. She gazed adoringly up at Josh as Charles graciously delivered her to him.

Swiping at his own glistening eyes before joining his wife of almost forty years, Charles reflected on the wedding. Who knew he and Deirdre would be so blessed—challenged at times, yes, but ultimately blessed—when Jack Deacon delivered the quiet little waif to their North Vancouver home so many years before?

Sophie stood next to Jessie, with Maggie, Sue-Lyn, Jane and Kayla alongside, in periwinkle blue dresses Dee wrestled from a designer friend at the last minute. Alongside Josh was Steve, next to him were Zach, Charlie, Paul and Carter. The men wore cream linen suits with white button down shirts; the cut of the boys' suits echoed the Gatsby-esque F. Scott Fitzgerald era. Tears-of-paisley tangerine linen ties were perfect on this warm October day, although Josh's shirt was already unbuttoned at the neck and his tie loosened. Everyone was bare feet, including the bride, who reached up to Josh's tie and gave it a gentle yank so that it loosened down his neck just a little bit further. She hooked both hands over his belt buckle, her favorite place to touch him in mixed company so that the backs of her fingers could glean whatever energy she could get from him, this man who was about to become her husband. Her diminutive bouquet's fragrant fresh scent tickled Josh's nose and he smiled at her as she peeked shyly up at him.

Jessie, in a gossamer cream silk fitted A-line gown with satin finish, also a throwback to the twenties, poised gracefully there, facing him. Typically rogue, Josh grinned at her choice of dress length—the dress was worn above the knees in the front but was slightly longer in the back so that it brushed the backs of her thighs. Its pleated cross-halter style fastened at the neck so that it was backless; Josh instantly ached for a private audience with her so that he could brush his fingers along her back and let them rest at the top of her butt, where the dress teased him mercilessly. Emerald deco diamond encrusted earrings and a matching bracelet were gifts from him the night before—this morning Dee had added a similar twenties emerald diamond encrusted ring that caught the sun and glistened brightly. Later, for their dinner and dance at the Dayboat, Jessie would slip on handcrafted matching comfy Emmy shoes with a four inch heel—hand beaded, they too were an exquisite cream silk throwback to the roaring twenties.

She carried a small bouquet of white roses and baby's breath. Before the priest started the ceremony she glanced over at her mother, tucked into a wheelchair by Dee and accompanied by George and two favorite kind (and lucky!) long term care nurses from the seniors' home. A child's innocent smile caressed Emily's face.

Jessie's soft blue eyes drifted up to Josh and she inhaled deeply. He knew what she was thinking—she was wishing her dad were there, too. He knew, because he wanted his mom at their wedding as well. But the two long gone parents were likely hovering around in spirit, Josh and Jessie had decided the night before, and so the couple settled their nerves and waited for their lives together as husband and wife to begin.

The service was simple, the priest's eyes alight at the opportunity to marry a celebrity couple whose well-publicized hardships were proof that adversity could be overcome, should folks choose to work hard in loving one another instead of giving in to the darkness. Weddings have a habit of breaking people down, and this one was no exception—Frank was the first to lend Trudy a Kleenex, with Dee and Lydia right behind.

Josh and Jessie chose traditional vows, and they got through them okay until Jessie's turn to say, "I, Jessie Wheeler, take you, Josh Sawyer, to be my husband." At the word husband, her voice broke, and everyone held a collective breath until she could get going again. On their make-shift altar of an eight-by-eight foot one-foot high stage, she licked her lips and fought the urge to break down altogether. Was this real? After everything, was Jessie marrying Josh today? It seemed too good to be true.

He helped her out. Josh tipped up her chin so that Jessie had to look into his eyes. He'd learned to do this when Jessie lost focus or simply needed him, and Trudy encouraged him. It was a way of asking Jessie to refocus, and it was a tool—a delicate gesture—that always seemed to bring her back from wherever distant, dark memory she wandered off to. In the white wooden folding chairs the guests were perched on in the sandy congregation, Charles grasped Dee's hand tightly as they prayed for Jessie to get through her vows. Now, their girl gazed lovingly at Josh as he whispered something affectionately to her that only they and the priest could hear. It elicited a smile from both Jessie and the priest, and then a little laugh from Jessie as she got back on track.

"I promise to be true to you in good times and in bad, in sickness and in health. I will love you and honor you all the days of my life."

Josh got through his okay, too, in the end, and when the priest finally introduced them to the assorted guests as 'Mr. and Mrs. Josh Sawyer,' there was a rousing cheer heard down the beach at neighboring homes, where the mostly empty summer homes—cleared out for the new school year and impending cooler season—were once again filled as those who'd gotten wind of the celebrity nuptials aimed binoculars and long lenses, trying to get a peek.

Matt kept a wary eye out even though he had Susanne, Dan and Ulysses in place. Matt also hired a local security firm to police the long driveway to the farmhouse as well as the Dayboat. They decided not to be overly concerned about the fishing and power boats suddenly peppering the water or the fly space overhead—yes, word had leaked about the wedding but Matt and Charles agreed that there were only so many reasonable precautions they could take. They did have security on boats in the bay, and Ulysses was in touch with the airport to at least be prepared for any action in the skies, but overall, besides curious locals down the beach and on the road, it was a low-key affair.

Josh and Jessie accepted gracious hugs from Sophie and Steve and then the others, including little Lana, who made a perfectly divine flower girl and who stood by her daddy quietly and happily wide-eyed throughout the wedding, in awe of Jessie in her glamorous gown.

Then it was time to wander excitedly down through the middle aisle of the guests and accept hugs from everyone. Dee grabbed Jessie and held her at arms length.

"Exquisite, my dear," she breathed, little black trails of mascara leaking underneath shining eyes.

Glowing, when Jessie finally turned from her, the first person she saw was Jacob, shuffling bare toes in the sand, hands buried deep in his pockets. She wandered slowly over to him, Josh's eyes discreetly watching her back, trusting, yet still wary.

Jessie took Jacob's wrists and pulled his hands out of the pockets. She wrapped them around her and urged him into a warm embrace. It took Jacob a moment to respond, but when he did he exhaled and held her tight, burying his face in her neck. They held each other longer than they should have, given the occasion, but there was so much they needed to say to each other, and in this case they had to do it with touch since time wasn't on their side. For a moment Jacob forgot where he was, and that Jessie was no longer his. The past informed his move—an old intimacy took hold—and he let his fingers slip across Jessie's bare back to where the soft silk dress met her flesh, and then slightly inside so that he brushed her breasts. He felt her tense and then Jacob pulled away when he remembered she was no longer his—she never was, really—and he looked up to see Jessie turn her head delicately to the side in time to spy Josh start towards them, his jaw working a little from side to side as he reacted to an intimate moment that no longer belonged to Jacob.

But Steve was watching, too, and his firm hand shot out and gripped Josh's bicep tightly, and when Josh whipped his eyes over to him and tried to pull away, Steve shook his head ever so slightly from side to side, *no*, as his expression also telegraphed a warning.

Jacob couldn't see Jessie's eyes then, but he could see Josh's, and he saw him instantly soften as somehow Jessie's thoughts bounced over to him.

Steve was in awe, humbled. For in that moment Jessie's calm and loving demeanor towards Josh managed to instantly settle him, a man whom years before would have been on Jacob in a second, fists flailing.

When she turned delicately back to Jacob, Jessie was smiling, her eyes a soft blue floating on the glorious beauty of her wedding day. She still had a gentle hold of his hands.

"Jacob," she whispered, shaking her head just slightly as she cocked her head lovingly at the man who helped her through a tough time, at the man who set her free of her old nemesis, Deuce McCall.

His lips curved up just a little as he looked at her. "Sorry," he mouthed, glancing up to see that Josh was easing off, the recipient of effusive hugs from Maggie and Sue-Lyn. Then Jacob's lips turned down and Jessie was sorry to see they were quivering just slightly. He turned away for a second to try to get a grip.

Laying a palm against his usual grizzled cheek, Jessie spoke carefully. "Babe," she said. "You and me will always have a connection. You know that."

He turned back to her and eyed her seriously; his baby blues a saddened glimpse into what hurt that day. "I know, Jessie." He struggled to regain control. "It's just hard, you know. I miss us. It's hard to be here." He looked up at Josh again, and met his adversary's eyes as Josh peeked around behind him again to spy on the two. Nodding towards Josh, Jacob spoke again to Jessie. "It's not really fair for him either, I guess."

Jessie shrugged. "Tough. You're a part of me, Jacob. We make great music together. I love you dearly, and Josh knows he has to accept that. I want you in my life."

"I want you in my life, too," he responded quietly, his eyes boring holes into hers, communicating clearly to Jessie that he wanted more than he knew he could have.

Shoulders sinking just slightly, Jessie sighed and leaned forward. She let her lips brush his ever so softly, and once again, behind them, Josh tensed.

"I'll always love you, Jacob," she whispered. "You set me free." She implored him to understand and, after a moment, he nodded.

"Okay," he exhaled. "I'm here for you, Jessie. Always." He smiled then, which encouraged her a little. "Annie."

Well, they would always have Edinburgh, and music, to make things go easier between them. Jessie squeezed his fingers and kissed one set of knuckles before turning on her bare heel and wandering back over to Josh while

Katrine stepped in to Jacob and slipped an arm around his waist and laid a head on his shoulder.

In front of the house later, after pictures of the wedding party on the beach, Josh took Jessie by the hand and faced her. They were getting ready to climb into their SUV for the short ride to the Dayboat Restaurant where their dinner and reception were taking place, but Josh felt the need to clear the air first.

"Hey," he said, gently turning her to face him. "I'm sorry about that—when you were with Jacob. I trust you, but it's hard to see you with him. And he's obviously feeling pretty shitty himself today."

Jessie shrugged. "He shouldn't have touched me that way, Josh. Old habits, you know…" Her voice trailed off. "I don't blame you for being pissed."

"He's a good guy, Jess. I know that. And I'm glad he was there for you when you needed him, but I am sincerely hoping he figures out the boundaries soon if he's going to be working with you." His eyes were earnest, pleading.

"Hey," she said in response. "It's me you have to trust. I can handle Jacob."

Josh nodded. "I know." He leaned in closer and brushed his lips against her ear. "I'll spend the rest of my life trying to give you a better orgasm if that's what I need to do."

She laughed, and the sound of her happiness was a balm to his soul. It was genuine, real, and all the years of worry and sadness etched on Jessie's face were disappearing into the abyss of old memories and unhappy places, being replaced with new starts and sincere joy.

"Or two or three?" she asked, "in a row, maybe?"

This time it was Josh's turn to chuckle. "Hey, I'm game to try!" Then, conspiratorially, he winked at her. "Shall we invite Katrine?"

"Uh, negative, Sawyer." Jessie grimaced. "I'm not planning to share you with anybody ever again." She wrapped a hand around the back of his neck and drew him closer for a languorous kiss. Slipping her tongue along the underside of his top lip, she smiled when she felt a delicate shiver course through his body.

"Um, do we have to go through this whole dinner and dance thing?" he asked. "Not sure I can wait to aim for those four or five orgasms."

"Thought it was two or three."

"One can dream..."

Stepping out onto the top step as the screen door slammed neatly behind them, Deirdre spied the newly married couple engaged in their intimate conversation. She took her husband's hand and gazed fondly at Jessie, whose spirit was radiant on this, a day she roundly deserved.

"Charles, I don't think I've ever seen her this happy."

Charles watched the couple thoughtfully while Matt and Julie reclined against the steps nearby as their daughter ran onto the lawn to join Zach and Hilary's gang of ruffians in a game of tag.

"One day at a time, Dee." At her curious look, he shrugged dispassionately. "Sure. There must be something in this Prince Edward Island air. She's glowing."

"Somehow I don't think it's the air," Matt broke in, grinning as Josh slipped a hand down Jessie's back and urged her closer for another round of intimate whispers and delicate kisses. Matt slid his own arm around his wife's waist and pulled her closer, too. There was something about Josh and Jessie's happiness that encouraged all the couples present that day to cherish their partners even more. It was like a check-in for their own relationships, a reminder that the ground can easily shift beneath one's feet and so each moment was worth treasuring, each partner worth loving.

As the newly minted Sawyers slipped into the backseat of their vehicle for a chauffeured ride to the Dayboat, the guests made their way to the cozy weathered gray summer restaurant as well. The musicians from the late August night at Pat's Rose and Grey Room were set up to entertain, and Joe Kelly, Jacob, John Paul and Christian were also prepared to play some tunes, their guitars and the grand piano in the corner tuned and waiting patiently for the dinner to end and the evening's festivities to begin.

There were the usual jokes and toasts and wine. Jessie stuck to one glass out of respect for Josh, but there were others in the wedding party who didn't take long to start slurring their words. Jacob preferred local P.E.I. Brewing Company beer but he, too, was cautious. The last thing he wanted was liquid courage or false bravado. Despite his own feelings, he was genuinely happy for Jessie and didn't want to mess up her wedding to a man she obviously deeply loved.

Jacob's devotion and admiration for Jessie, and a promise to Josh to respect their union, was sealed in stone as dinner was drawing to a close. He stepped to the microphone as he adjusted his guitar over his shoulders, and called the room to attention as JP and Christian took their places behind him along with Joe Kelly and the back line band hired from the Rose and Grey musicians. He cleared his throat as Jessie and Josh looked over to the small stage, surprised and touched, although at first both were a little wary.

"Jessie," Jacob said, his voice gravelly and, at first, a little uncertain. "I had no idea what to get you for your wedding to this guy. In fact I didn't think I'd be coming here at all, and as much as it sucks to watch you marry some low brow *actor*"—he grinned as everyone in the room responded with tentative boos and laughs—"when, let's face it, you could've had a *musician* to serenade you every night..." His face colored a little as he recalled a lot of very good nights in Jessie's company. "Well, it just seemed to me that it made sense to write you a song." He cleared his throat again and wiped a sweaty palm on his black jeans, which were as dressy as Jacob felt prepared to go on that weird day. "Actually," he looked nervously up at Josh and met the solemn brown eyes Jessie loved, "to write both of you a song. To wish you well."

As Josh leaned an elbow on the table and dropped his chin into bent fingers, wondering about this intimate, personal wedding gift, Jacob looked down and fine-tuned his guitar a bit more before glancing back to Christian and counting in the rag tag band. The song was a waltz in three-four time, a sweet sad piece that in essence was Jacob's only way of telling Josh that he understood about having to let Jessie go. That he did wish them well in their union, and that also he was entrusting this woman he loved to Josh's enduring care. In those moments, as Jacob's husky voice filled the space, Jessie never loved Jacob more. It was a sincere and delicate gift, partly because it was his signal that he was truly letting her go, as difficult as it would prove to be. Grasping Josh's fingers and holding them tightly under the table, she sensed that Josh was relaxing as he, too, recognized that Jacob was speaking clearly through his music. Touched, Jessie's eyes glistened as, when the final chords rang solid and true, Jacob looked up and smiled sadly. His glance shifted over to Josh, who frowned just slightly as he acknowledged the pain of letting go, and then the two men nodded quietly at each other across the room, overtop the heads of their friends and family as everyone stood and cheered.

Charles, of course, smiled conspiratorially at Dee before leaning in to whisper, "Might have to cut a new EP. That's a keeper."

As the evening moved on and the laughter in the Dayboat increased along with the uptempo tunes and touching ballads, Jessie took her turns at the mic. It was a thrill for the local musicians to back her up, and a thrill for her as well to play here in her home province for the people close to her who she once almost entirely shut out of her life. It was a day of reckoning, an evening of hope and promise and of trust, Jessie thought, as she fondly watched Trudy happily zip around the dance floor in the arms of her ex-husband Frank.

She needed Jacob once again that night.

Halfway through her old ballad, the song for Josh she'd written after finding him in Charlie's garbage, Jessie lost her voice. Suddenly everything caught up to her once again, as those old hurts and bad memories seemed to do now and again, and she found herself overcome. The song started out okay—amongst cheers and hurrahs—but then Josh himself was standing opposite her, twenty feet away, his hands deep in his pants pockets, jacket discarded, shirt untucked, linen tangerine tie loosened almost to the point of being completely undone. One ankle was turned over on its side and his head was cocked as he watched her sing to him. The old electricity buzzed through the room on an invisible wire between them as the other couples in the space gathered their lovers close and fell under the spell of Jessie's voice.

Josh's soulful chocolate eyes flickered in the twinkling fairy lights dotting the room as he silently cocked his head and watched his girl sing to him, and there may as well have been only the two of them in the Dayboat that night, their wedding night, because each other was all they saw despite the couples slowly weaving back and forth on the rustic pine floor between them. It was all there, the heartache, the loss, the lonely summers and lost Christmases, the tears shed on the cold tile of bathroom floors, the red dress covering Jessie's nakedness the night she clearly told him to leave her be, the agony of wonder and worry when she disappeared...Deuce McCall's beatings, the horrid secrets of the stalking journal, the fear Jessie carried within her that Trudy helped her understand and let go at a point when Josh wondered whether Jessie had anything left in her to convince herself to try to heal. They were both on the same wavelength then, and as Josh stood alone on the dance floor amidst the gently waltzing couples, he swallowed back the pain of all those years and nights of aching loneliness and watched as she did the same. The band hesitated for only a brief moment before picking up a few extra instrumental verses, as Jessie's voice broke and trailed off, the emotion too much on the night when Josh finally became hers forever.

So Jacob stepped forth, cursing under his breath but grinning just the same, and he bent forward and gave Jessie a sweet chaste kiss on the cheek before urging the mic from her fingers.

"Go, you dweeb," he told her in no uncertain terms, his eyes sad but a steady calm underneath. "Go."

Jessie broke her glance away from Josh just then as somehow she realized where she was, but the spell was only broken for a second. She kicked her heels off her feet and left them by Jacob's side as he took up the balance of the song Jessie wrote for Josh, a song everyone knew the words to, and Jessie stepped to the center of the dance floor and let herself sink into Josh's welcoming safe embrace.

She didn't sing again that night, and the couple hardly noticed another soul as Jacob, and then Joe Kelly, too, did what they did best, as they mixed it up with the locals and held a kitchen party wedding night each would remember fondly for the rest of their lives.

Josh and Jessie's wedding was what weddings should be—a dedication to each other that would never be broken, a celebration with friends and family of a union that would, beyond the shadow of a doubt, last forever. It was too long in coming, but real and true and heartfelt and agonizingly beautiful, and it lasted as all good things do, well into the night as the truly well deserved Sawyer-Wheeler happily-ever-after finally began.

# Chapter Twenty-three

The next day at noon when Charles and Dee arrived at the summer home on the beach, the weather had cooled into a crisp October Prince Edward Island autumn day. It was as if the Gods of the changing seasons waited until the beach wedding was over, then they moved in with the promise of ripe apples and root vegetables like squash and turnip, and even turkey and all the trimmings, which was only a short few days away in the Canadian tradition.

Dee sauntered over the rustic floor and slipped an arm around her new son-in-law's waist. Josh was elbow deep in dishwater, scrubbing happily, his indigo blue T-shirt as wrinkled as his faded denims, bare toes peeking out from beneath the hems of the jeans, his layered hair still wet from a recent shower. He smelled innocently of ivory soap and Dee caught herself wondering for the umpteenth time why she ever doubted this man's love for Jessie in the first place. She gave him an extra squeeze as Charles yawned and settled himself at the nearby kitchen island. Dee grabbed a dish towel and picked up a platter, then turned around to lean against the counter and smile over at Charles as she chatted with Josh.

"Get any sleep?" She winked at Charles who grinned back at her. *They* certainly hadn't gotten much sleep.

Josh colored instantly and ducked his face a little lower. "Uh..."

"Now that you're married, you realize we'll be expecting grandbabies."

Charles threw in his vote. "One a year. At least. Or maybe the occasional set of twins so Jessie can double up and take on some new film projects."

Eyeing him sideways, Josh smiled carefully. He and Jessie had gone over some scripts before the wedding, and she was still talking about co-producing with the island filmmaker who wanted to make the hockey film, but nothing was set in stone just yet. Besides, they promised each other they would try to coordinate their schedules so as to spend as much time as possible together. Once things settled and they moved back to Vancouver for the winter they could sit down with his manager, Hilary, as well as Charles and Dee. But Josh promised himself that, as hungry as he was to work, his family would always come first. He had learned that lesson the hard way with the recent film he shot in Virginia.

Tentative steps started down the stairs, and Josh turned around to see Jessie, pink cheeked blooms on her still sleepy face, beaming down at them. Soon she was hugging Charles, and then Dee, and then her arms were around Josh, who didn't hesitate to wrap his soapy hands around his new wife.

"Hello, Mr. Sawyer," she whispered into his neck.

"Hello back, Mrs. Sawyer," he smiled back at her, eyes shining.

"Get a room," they heard from the front door as Steve wandered in, Sophie by his side.

Soon the house was filling up again as guests came with gifts and treats in tow, sleepy-eyed and happy. But before the brunch dishes were done and the day's events got under way, Dee spied the white banker's box George had given Jessie at the Clinton seniors' home. It was gathering dust, unopened, tucked into a corner underneath the stairs, where Josh had placed it to help make room for the expected guests.

She elbowed Josh as he swiped at the last dish, which was Jessie's favorite chipped earthenware mug with violet lupins hand painted on the side.

"What's in the white box?" she asked curiously. In truth she was wondering if it was filled with all the scripts she'd been sending Jessie to go over in the hopes that the girl would choose a few to consider working on.

Hesitating, Josh answered, "You know that old guy George from Emily's nursing home? The old friend of Jessie's dad?"

Her brow wrinkling with a new curiosity, Dee nodded. "Yes. What about him?" She handed Josh the dish towel so he could wipe his hands dry.

"He gave Jessie the box and told her not to open it until she was good and ready. Seems there are a few more family secrets she has yet to uncover."

Dee groaned. "No. No more drama. I refuse. Except fictional drama. That I encourage."

"I hear ya, Dee." Josh turned and leaned his butt against the counter while he dried his hands so he could watch Jessie bouncing gaily over to the door to welcome Arnie and Matt and their gals. "I kinda don't want to mess with this right now either. I'd sorta like things to remain on an even keel for a while."

As if she could sense something new and sinister in the air, Jessie looked back over her shoulder at Josh and Dee. Both were watching her, frowning, and she shivered as her eyes narrowed at their serious countenances. She shrugged her shoulders as if to ask 'What' before twisting back around to Matt's little girl and enveloping her in a big hug.

Josh sighed and turned back to his new mother-in-law. "Whatever it is, Dee, we'll figure it out together this time. She promised me. She's not going rogue again."

"So obviously you haven't looked inside yet."

He shook his head and leaned both elbows back on the counter, the dish towel falling limply beside one hand. "Nope. Said we would open it after the wedding."

She shot him a sardonic look as Carlotta came in with an armful of fresh produce from a local farmers' market, her man hauling a large pumpkin behind her, which he was enthusiastically promising to carve up for the kids.

"I see," Dee said.

"I'll keep you posted."

"Okay." Frowning, she stared hard at the box.

"Don't even think about it," Josh implored her nervously.

She grabbed the towel and flicked it at him before throwing her hands up in resignation. "You know me too well, Josh Sawyer."

Then more folks entered the happy home and the day continued in the spirit of a new start for Josh and Jessie. The box remained covered and hidden, despite Dee's occasional curious glance in its general direction, which also couched a *don't you dare mess up my girl's newfound happiness* vibe.

The next day, the guests either all piled back into transport to their various airplanes or went sightseeing, and an exhausted Josh and Jessie lay happily relaxing on their big bed in the comfy and spacious bedroom overlooking the peacefully lapping ocean. The newly carved pumpkin guarded the home's front entrance, a silly sneer on its orange face as it balanced on the top step.

The last thing Dee said to Josh before one last hug upon her departure when the new Sawyers made the drive to the old historic Summerside air base that morning was, "Let me know what you find in that box," so Josh felt its presence all day. It was now late afternoon, and the thought of what secrets lay within were bouncing around his brain like some old Atari ping-pong game.

He leaned up on one elbow and gently tousled Jessie's hair. She was lying on her belly, head resting on folded arms, a pink-patterned top flowing over the waist of her jeans.

"You awake?" Josh asked carefully. He didn't want to disturb her if she wasn't—she needed some rest after their crazy weekend.

"Mmmhmmm," she murmured contentedly. "Suppose I should get packing."

They were heading out the next day to eastern P.E.I., to the Inn at Bay Fortune, for a five-day Thanksgiving honeymoon.

Josh reached down and wrapped a big hand around her bare toes. She sighed as the warmth of his touch started a glow from the feet up.

"You're freezing," he said, chastening her.

"I refuse to wear socks," Jessie replied obstinately. "I refuse to acknowledge that we will soon be covered in snow."

"We'll be back in Van," he countered. "Not much chance of more than a few feet there, Jessie."

She blinked open her sleepy eyes and looked up at him. "I suppose at some point we'll have to go back," she said. "But I sure like it here."

As she said that, the wind outside their window echoed its agreement. The old house shook and the tempo of the waves picked up so that within the hour they were crashing against the shore.

"I guess if you guys get funding sorted out you'll be shooting by March," he said.

She shrugged, still dozy. "We'll see. It would be nice."

Josh let a forefinger trail down her cheek to pick up a wispy tendril of hair. Jessie's eyes narrowed.

"What?"

"Well, I was just thinking there's something else we need to do before we start packing."

"What?" she asked again, raising herself up on one elbow. "Put on socks? I refuse, on principle."

"Nope," he said, avoiding her eyes.

"Go see my momma? And George?" Jessie pulled herself up on one elbow and looked at him, trying to read Josh's thoughts. Whatever it was, it was something he was obviously uncomfortable speaking to her about.

He eyed her carefully. Concerned, Jessie sat up and crossed her legs underneath her, facing him. "What, Josh?"

"Dee saw the box, that's all," he replied nervously. "The white one from George. She was curious. Got me thinking maybe it's time."

"Oh." Jessie's shoulders sank and Josh hoped the mysterious box's contents wouldn't further deflate her. "I suppose we can't hide from it forever."

"I'm sure you're curious..."

"Hell, yeah. Scared too, though."

"Well, whenever you're ready, Jess. Let's not rush it."

"As if," she said, chuckling as she grabbed him by the hand and pulled him off the bed. "It's only been sitting there forever. Ooch," she added when her bare toes hit the cold floor. "Damn it." She bent over a nearby dresser and yanked out some pink knitted socks she found at a recent South Rustico arts and crafts sale. She sat and pulled them on while Josh grinned stupidly down at her.

"Charming," he said as she frowned, the big socks not exactly much of a fashion statement on her small feet.

"At least they match my top," she stated with gusto.

She padded out of the room wiggling her butt at him, smiling behind her as he shook his head and followed happily.

Moments later they were sitting cross-legged on a large braided rug in the old farmhouse's modernized open concept living room. The white box sat between them, its corners roughened and ragged and its lid swaybacked like an old mare, as if it was moved a lot before finding a home underneath something heavy during a damp humid summer.

Josh eyed Jessie warily. Six weeks ago he would have dragged the box out to the garbage to avoid her finding any new secrets inside, anything that might trigger the old haunted girl from the last few years. But now she was vibrant, happy, encouraged, and curious. Stronger.

Across the box from him Jessie smiled cautiously, a mischievous glint flickering across the surface of her sea pearl eyes. Josh acknowledged with a wry grin that she was also fairly adventurous. This box was a link to her past, to parents she loved and missed, to summers building sandcastles on P.E.I. and listening to her dad share his music in island clubs and pubs.

She clasped her hands together nervously and peeked up at Josh. "Okay," she said. "Let's do this thing."

Josh reached forward and removed the lid. Inside was exactly what they expected, musty paper—faded envelopes, yellowed newsprint. The box was about half full of assorted odds and sods. Atop all was an 8.5 by 11 sheet of computer paper upon which was marked in large bold permanent marker in cursive script *Emily and David Wheeler, Bedeque, P.E.I.*

Jessie inhaled slowly as she regarded the contents. What mysteries would she find inside? What about her childhood would be revealed to her here today, with the man she had just wed by her side to help ease any hurts?

Encouraging her, Josh removed the cover sheet announcing the box's contents. He grasped a bundle of envelopes in various legal and card sizes, tied up with a length of baling twine. He handed them to Jessie but she hesitated before taking them from him. Then she slipped a finger under the twine and undid it before laying the envelopes beside her, fanning them out so she could see them better, all at once. All were addressed to Emily Wheeler, to a post office box in Bedeque, Prince Edward Island. Wrinkling her eyebrows, Jessie picked up a limp legal sized envelope and closely regarded the return address—it was from a street in Peterborough, Ontario. The name scrawled there seemed to have been written in a hurry—it was hard to make out. But it seemed like Kilfoil.

"Hmmmm," Jessie wondered absently as she twisted a ringlet in her hair with the fingers of her left hand.

She eyed the inside of the box again before glancing once more up to Josh. Nodding at him, Jessie laid her hands delicately in her lap as he removed a packet of old newspapers and handed them across the box over to her. Jessie opened the first—it was a Journal-Pioneer, Summerside's daily news edition. The headline was about the Summerside Lobster Carnival's cardboard boat races, and the photo featured a sinking mass of soaked cardboard and a dismayed boater clinging to the sides for support.

Below the racer's grimacing face and the corresponding article, on the front page, was a smaller article titled *Musician's death suspicious.* Jessie gasped. She went on to read *Sgt. Michael Redstone, of the RCMP, announced at a press conference late yesterday afternoon that the recent death of local musician David Wheeler, whose car toppled into the Southwest River, is being investigated for reasons not being made available to the public at this time. "Wheeler's death is considered suspicious based on testimony by those who knew him as well as one witness to the event that took Wheeler's life, namely the scene where the car left the road."*

Shocked, Jessie looked up at Josh. He got up and inched himself over to a kneeling position behind her, and read over her shoulder.

"It's pretty vague, Jess. It says here only that the car may have been coerced off the road intentionally. Doesn't say why."

"Huh. Guess that substantiates George's thoughts." Jessie dropped the paper to her lap and pondered that strange twist in the age-old story of her father's loss. She set it aside and grabbed the next. Josh followed suit and opened the third. There were five papers in total, each a few days apart until the last, which seemed to be an addendum to the entire story as it was a few weeks newer than the first few papers. Increasingly each story was buried deeper in the small newspapers as time passed and other stories took precedence over the loss of the local musician *who left a wife and twelve-year-old daughter behind.*

The stories didn't reveal a whole lot more except for confirmation that David Wheeler was likely being given a message at the time of his death—that he owed a large sum of money to a local businessman whose name remained anonymous, and that apparently the incident was intended only to frighten him, to send him off the road with a warning. The RCMP was hesitant to provide details but the journalist writing the story had secured testimony from the witness who was quoted as saying *Wheeler wasn't supposed to roll the car and end up in the river.* The witness was apparently remorseful and apologetic. He identified himself as the person hired to coerce Wheeler off the small twisty, hilly country road in Clinton. He was the man who pulled out from behind a slow moving tourist and played a lethal game of chicken with a family man rushing home to his daughter's twelfth birthday party after a serene canoe ride. The witness refused to identify the businessman who hired him, to whom David Wheeler owed money. He also suggested that he was coming forward because "...*Scams like this are happening all over the place because big businessmen are using their power to hurt the average guy, and because this type of coercion is escalating in our previously peaceful province. Somebody got hurt, and I don't want to be a part of this any more. I want it to stop. It has to stop. David Wheeler was a good guy who found himself in a tough situation—he couldn't pay his bills based on his gig pumping gas at the local Esso. His music was really something but it was powerless to help. He borrowed from Peter to pay Paul. It got him killed.*"

The witness was not identified.

Jessie was astounded. She stared at Josh, who was watching her closely to see how she was handling this shocking information.

"Guess we'll be taking a trip to the seniors' home this afternoon to see George, eh?"

Frowning, Josh agreed. "I'm a little pissed at him, Jess. I don't mind admitting that I don't see what good this is going to do you, finding this out after all this time. What's it gonna do but raise old ghosts?"

Her voice was small. "Maybe this businessman they're talking about is still causing shit. Maybe George thinks I can do something about it—about him."

"Oh no," Josh warned, shaking his head. "You're not getting mixed up in any crazy local mafia shit. No way. I draw the line there, Mrs. Sawyer."

Shoulders slumping, Jessie looked back down at the yellowed newsprint in her hands. "He owed money," she whispered. "And you wonder why I don't care about money. All it does is hurt people in the end."

"Aww Jess," Josh said, taking her hand and lifting it to brush his lips against the knuckles. "You know that's not always true. Look at the shelters you and Dee built. Karma's biting this corrupt businessman in the ass. David Wheeler's daughter is out there helping people."

Sadly, Jessie let her eyes wander over Josh's big hand as he trailed his thumb over her fingers. She leaned into him and closed her eyes, feeling the heat of his body through his T-shirt. "It just sucks that money has the power to hurt people too. That's all I meant."

"Money doesn't have the power to hurt people," Josh responded wisely, lifting his arm to wrap around her shoulders. "The people with money do. Sometimes by choosing not to use it to help others less fortunate than themselves. By hoarding it, or by not spending it on African wells or soup kitchens or local children's school supplies or whatever. I don't suppose we're really any better than those people in some ways, Jessie." He thought about his big home in Vancouver and the Harley in his garage. "So maybe we should rethink some of our goals for the future, eh? See if there's more we can do as a couple."

"To alleviate our consciences you mean," Jessie intoned quietly.

"Hey little one," Josh interjected, turning her face towards him so she was compelled to meet his gaze. "You, for one, have paid your dues. Don't ever question the abundance the universe has given you. You are the most generous person I know. It's me who needs to step forward here."

"Well," she said. "First thing we need to do is sponsor some of those World Vision children. A whole mess of them." Her eyes were wide, hopeful.

Josh smiled at her. "Charles and Dee are already hinting at kids too, you know. So we'll get some of our own too, okay?"

Blushing, Jessie inched closer under Josh's arm. "And we'll teach them to be responsible. They'll write to the World Vision kids and send them stuff. For starters."

She spied the unopened envelopes at her side and her eyes narrowed. "But for now let's finish going through this box. Then I'm going to open these letters and see what other Wheeler mysteries have been hoarded for all these years."

The remainder of the box held packets of old printed photos as well as two old photo albums. One of the albums contained clippings from George's bar outside Summerside, the one where Jessie was allowed to go with her mom to watch her dad entertain to a usually full house. The clippings were of various artists who played at the bar, as well as sports teams—minor league hockey and baseball—sponsored by George's business. The second album contained more actual photographs, usually of a younger George, or David and his cronies either playing sets from the small corner stage or of them horsing around for the camera, beers in hand. One in particular caused Jessie to exhale in surprise and wonder. Josh leaned closer to her and stared at the photo before kissing her cheek tenderly.

"Beautiful," he murmured in her ear. "I see why George kept that one."

"It's perfect," Jessie breathed.

The photo was of her old family—she herself was probably around ten or eleven. Jessie was sitting on a stool, her back to the bar, hair in a messy ponytail, and her parents were standing on either side. David and Emily were leaning in towards each other, overtop their daughter, who was looking up at them, a smile as wide as her small face would allow, lighting up her rosy cheeks. Jessie's parents were holding hands and their expressions were telegraphing pure joy and love as they gazed adoringly into each other's eyes. David's hand rested on Jessie's shoulder. Below the arc of her parents' entwined fingers Jessie, too, radiated a simple joy, a rare happiness Josh was surprised to see on her face. Although she was happy now, with him, he knew it was a hard fought happiness and would always carry with it layers of pain from the hauntings her life's experience left embedded in her spirit, and so he was humbled to see this old Jessie from days gone by when she lived with a mom and dad on a simple island where, apart from financial worries, her family was at peace.

Slowly Jessie removed the photo from the sticky plastic holding it hostage in the album. "I'll get it copied and blown up," she planned softly. She stared at the images for a long while before sighing and placing the photo on the floor by her toes where she could stare at it at will.

Then it was time to open the letters. Josh kissed the top of his wife's head lovingly as she delicately opened the flap from the first letter. She was careful to check the dates first—Jessie wanted to follow whatever story held within in its proper sequence.

She was only a few paragraphs in before she realized what she was reading. For the second time that day she looked up at Josh in surprise.

"It's from my mom's mom," she whispered. A slow smile creased her face and she held up the letter as if it were a trophy. "Guess who all of a sudden has a grandmother? In Peterborough, Ontario, apparently. Who knew?" Her eyes fell back to the letter, hungry, searching.

Watching her read, her eyes alight with wonder at this discovery, Josh was apprehensive. For anyone, all of a sudden finding an extended family would be exciting and dangerous. What secrets led to family separations in the first place? Sometimes the old adage was true—it could be best to leave sleeping dogs lie. But for Jessie, an international star with millions of dollars in earnings at her disposal…well, reconnecting with family members she never knew existed could be harmful in a myriad of significant ways. But now was not the time to bring that up. Josh leaned further over Jessie's shoulder to see what else she was gleaning from the letters.

Then, she looked up at him with a mixture of trepidation and unbridled comprehension.

"Josh," she breathed. "You're not going to believe this."

"Uh oh," he muttered under his breath. "Here it comes." His eyes were guarded, afraid. If Jessie noticed, she let it go. Josh had long ago realized that she often forgot exactly who she was, who she had become in this crazy world. To Jessie herself she was just a person, not a world famous celebrity. For the umpteenth time since they opened the box, he frowned. "What?" he asked carefully.

A slow smile spread across Jessie's face, replaced with a thousand other emotions as she shook her head slowly from side to side, the letter in her hand almost a flag of truce as it wavered in the slight breeze her movement created. "Apparently," her innocent naïve hopeful eyes searched Josh's fearful chocolate ones, "I also have a sister."

# Chapter Twenty-four

They gathered up the remaining letters and cuddled up on the white leather couch to read the rest of the clues to Jessie's extended family. There were only certain truths written there, but one thing seemed certain—the way the letters were worded it did not appear Emily Wheeler ever wrote back or responded in any way. In the cursive neat script of Jessie's maternal grandmother was a tale of hidden secrets, for it also appeared in her diary-like style that no one from the woman's own circle—her husband or other grown children, perhaps—were even aware that the letters existed. Instead it seemed they were an attempt—and sometimes it appeared a perhaps futile attempt from the writer's perspective—for a mother to connect with a daughter. Jessie realized early on that obviously some outreach had happened from her own mother's point of view, for the address on the envelopes was consistent and specific. So Emily must have provided that one simple link and then just sat back and basked in the news from home without overtures to place her own mother's mind at ease.

"I guess I am not so different from my own mother," Jessie whispered sorrowfully later, when she and Josh talked about what they'd discovered hidden in the old cards and yellowed paper. "I shut her out, too."

"We don't know all the truths yet, Jess. People don't just take off and cut people out of their lives for no reason. Do they." His deep eyes searched hers.

Edinburgh crossed Jessie's mind. A solitary trip around the world. Caring for Chinese babies in Ningdu. She shook her head slowly. "Noooo..."

Josh changed tack. The afternoon's explorations had exhausted him and, judging by Jessie's own tired eyes he could see she'd had enough as well.

"C'mon. Let's pack. We'll have lots of time to ponder all of this at the Inn on Bay Fortune. For our honeymoon...in between snuggles, of course." He pulled her close and wrapped his arms lovingly around Jessie's shoulders. Breathed her in.

"We have to go see George. And my mom," Jessie pleaded, her voice muffled from underneath his layered chestnut hair.

"Dinner first," Josh said. "I'll start the barbecue."

He leaned back and placed both warm hands on either side of her cheeks, gazing soulfully into Jessie's confused sad eyes. "One day at a time with all this new stuff, okay little one? Promise me? No going rogue on me and taking off to Ontario."

She shook her head and placed her own hands over his, then sighed and leaned her forehead in to rest against Josh. "No. Besides, first I have to find out about what happened with this crap with my dad. I wonder if that businessman was ever prosecuted."

"Not sure what they would prosecute him for, kiddo. How could they ever prove, beyond someone's word alone, that the accident was meant to intimidate your dad?"

"Unless someone recorded a conversation I suppose it would be near impossible...well, let's go see what George knows and go from there."

With a final small hug, Josh stepped away and padded out onto the deck to start the barbecue. There was a chill in the October air, and as he twisted on the propane Josh felt the first real hint of the season's lull towards frosty mornings and the onset of cooler days. There were no pleasure boats on the water today, no brightly painted red or yellow kayaks, no undulating rhythms from the motors of white fishing boats echoing across the bay, no parasailers with their bird's eye views hanging underneath striped awnings as they floated across the horizon on lines from power boats below. Cottages were closing now in preparation for winter, their wooden ladders scaling the infamous red sandstone cliffs of P.E.I. now pulled up on shore to await the next season of happy swimmers and cottagers.

Soon he and Jessie would travel back to Vancouver, he thought, but first it seemed there would be a few details to wrap up here on Jessie's patchwork red clay and green carpeted island, where a multitude of potatoes were now almost all harvested from their comfortable hiding places beneath the rich soil.

As Josh pondered the changing of the seasons, which in some ways paralleled his and Jessie's life together, his wife was holding the refrigerator door open inside the old farmhouse, staring at the assorted jars and fresh harvest veggies inside, one hand holding a zucchini in mid-air. Jessie's eyes were distant, wandering, her mind unfocused. Suddenly she had two new goals, as if her father was calling her from where it was he now existed, in some far off plane or strange dimension. Feeling his presence in the home now, Jessie was calmed but curious, and she felt a strong pull towards George at the seniors' home, where perhaps some answers could be found that would let her father rest more peacefully. Her mother? Well, there were more secrets unearthed in Emily Wheeler's world today too, as if while Jessie's mom's mind slipped further and further away, her legacy would be passed on to her daughter, old hurts and secrets and a need for healing now Jessie's responsibility.

Josh slid his hand over the zucchini, removing it from Jessie's fingers and startling her back into reality. As she turned apologetically toward him, he reached past her and opened the meat drawer of the fridge, removed some pepper steaks, and shook his head laughingly at his new wife.

"Go," he insisted. "Read some more letters. Dinner's on me tonight."

As he removed the cellophane from the steak, Jessie smiled her thank-you and grabbed the white banker's box, pulling it towards a comfy seat on the couch. She leaned back into a pillow and read and re-read until Josh beckoned her for dinner. Even then it was hard to let go—the letters were entry into an unfamiliar world where she once belonged. Mostly they were matter-of-fact daily details from the lives of people she didn't know, as if they were characters in a script she was reading and considering becoming a part of. Occasionally there were tidbits about a half sister, about a woman much older than Jessie herself, a woman who, as a child, it seemed Emily Wheeler must have walked away from when she left Ontario with David. A woman who the Kilfoil grandmother didn't seem to judge Emily for leaving because her carefully penned letters were delicately worded as if to safeguard against strong reactions or feelings for fear of, what? Of Emily and

David cutting her off completely? Now and then Emily's mother asked about the new baby...then, as the letters went on, about Jessie as a child. By the tone, it seemed she never received responses. Instead, her questions were quite general. *Does she dance, like you did? Ballet?* Or *is she more inclined towards math in school? Or English?*

Absently Jessie realized the woman must have received notice of Jessie's birth, for she knew David and Emily had a girl. But that seemed about the extent of her knowledge. Did she receive a school photo every year? Maybe. But if so, the letters didn't reflect or comment on it.

After dinner, Josh tossed Jessie a hoodie and he grabbed the keys to the SUV. They left the dishes in the sink, rinsed but not washed, and Josh pointed the car towards Clinton where the pink and purple blossomed lupins lining the ditches were long gone, and where deciduous trees were now proudly heralding the change of season in primary colors of russet, red and pear-yellow. Before scooting home later they would take one last drive out to the town of Kensington for final cookie dough flurries at the Frosty Treat—the dairy bar would be closing for the season this weekend. On the drive home, Josh would take detours through heritage red clay dirt roads flaked with fallen leaves being buffeted about by the breeze. They would miss their island when it came time to board the plane, although in the back of his mind Josh felt the absence would not be for long.

They found Emily Wheeler first, in a common lounge, hands in her lap while other residents stared blankly at unknown artists on the Country Music Video station. Jessie grabbed hold of the wheelchair and slowly steered her mother towards her room. Josh wasn't far behind but he took the time to shake hands and greet some visitors who were excited to see the celebrity couple in their midst. Although he stayed and chatted to be kind, Jessie silently thanked him for taking the heat off her temporarily and allowing her to escape to privacy with her momma. Her blood was boiling as she stared at the top of her mother's head, wondering what life the woman had lived before her second daughter was born. More than ever, Jessie wished Emily could speak, could even become lucid for just a few short moments to answer the important questions Jessie read between the lines in the letters from her grandmother in Peterborough. Was the woman still living? Was there a grandfather still living? Or maybe two sets? Were there aunts, uncles, cousins? What about the half-sister, where was she?

Jessie remembered her Aunt Evelyn, the cheery lady who cleaned her up the night Emily threw a full ashtray in Jessie's face. Jessie had not tried to contact her, but she knew now that Evelyn would be the first person she would try to call after her and Josh's short honeymoon in eastern Prince Edward Island. Her new family out west—Dee and Charles and Charlie and Matt and all the *Drifters* friends and everyone else—were now secure and complete in Jessie's heart. It was time to step back and investigate the old family. Evelyn would be the key, if she were still living and in good health.

Jessie arranged her mom's wheelchair so that it faced her in the small room. She herself settled into a deep wing chair and sat back to watch Emily, to see if she could detect any glimmer of light in her mother's eyes.

"Guess you're better at secrets than I am," she finally intoned quietly as her mother turned her head sideways and gazed out the window towards the patient white and black dairy cows dotting the hill below the home. "A whole family, huh? The whole extended redneck she-bang."

Resting her forearms on the arms of the chair, Jessie watched and wondered about the suddenly mysterious lady withering away in this silent room where only the distant breeze, an occasional clink of china, and the hollow clang from the wind chimes outside a neighbor senior's window could be heard.

Moments later a tall shadow leaned against the doorframe.

"Anything?" Josh asked. One could always hope.

"Nada." Jessie said, resigned. "Not that I expected anything. Not even a blink or a shudder."

They stayed with Emily a little while before a resident care nurse stepped in and ushered them away, citing bath time.

Silently, Josh took Jessie's hand and they padded down the hall towards George's room. From here, Jessie expected more co-operation and participation. In the end she got more than she bargained for.

George visibly lit up when they entered the room.

"That was quite a party," he enthused, grinning. "Haven't been to a good old party like that since..." His watery gray eyes faded when he spotted the frown turning Jessie's lips downwards.

"I see," he said, leaning back in his wing chair and crossing arms that were all gangly elbows and knobby arthritic hands. "You finally opened the box."

Jessie settled on the bed across from George and leaned back on her left hand, studying him. Josh took up a stance against the far wall, near the framed photo of David Wheeler's band playing at George's long-ago club.

"So?" George asked in a voice saturated with age, timorous and thin.

"Just counting on you to fill in the blanks, George." Jessie was patient but she set her mouth in a firm line and waited.

"Which first?" he asked.

Jessie's heart leapt with anticipation. *Hmmm, so obviously he knows about my new-old family, too,* Jessie thought, cocking her head to one side and straining to get inside his head. She shrugged. "Whatever. We've got all night."

"I don't," George said matter-of-factly. He nodded towards the hallway, where rustling and voices were heard as residents were ushered back to their rooms in preparation for their nightly routines. "Bath time."

"So talk fast," Jessie countered. "We're going down east tomorrow for a few days and I want lots to think about."

Sighing, George leaned back in his chair. "Well," he said, "for starters, your mom gave me those letters as each arrived so your dad wouldn't know she had them."

"So you read them?"

"No. Not one. She confided in me over tea and biscuits. I guess I seemed safe, somehow." He frowned and something unseen flashed across the withered road map of his life, etched deeply in every line and wrinkle on the aged face. "Our chats became a ritual on the evenings she came in with your dad. She'd sit across from me at the bar while your dad and his friends set up. You would be either outside running around the fields with your dad's friends' kids or over with your dad handing him mics and cables." He grinned. "Doubt you do your own set-ups anymore, huh, kid?"

"On with it," Jessie growled.

Glancing up at Josh, George hesitated before continuing. Then he looked back at Jessie and pondered where to go next. "I don't suppose the letters explain why your parents estranged themselves from the Ontario clan…"

In response, Jessie shook her head. "Nope. They don't."

"Well, kiddo, first tell me this—did you read them all? In other words, how much do you know?"

"I know I have a sister. And a grandmother, of course. Not much else. The letters were mostly about day to day stuff, trivial things, I guess."

"Your sister was fourteen when Emily met your dad. It was a whirlwind courtship, a lightning-struck sort of love. Rather quick and, from what I gather her telling me, painful and difficult."

Jessie glanced up at Josh and blushed deeply. The apple didn't fall far from the tree, apparently. "Because my mom was married."

"She was. But obviously not happily. And the daughter was at an age where she was rebellious and cantankerous, and sided with her father whenever the occasion demanded it. So when your mom got pregnant with you..."

"Ouch," Jessie grimaced.

"Yes. Ouch. She knew David was the father and she also knew where her allegiances lay. But any attempt to leave her marriage was thwarted both by her husband at the time and by her own father. To the point where she ended up locked in a room on the top floor of an old stone farmhouse just outside Peterborough. In the end David put a ladder up to her window and snuck her out. Just like in the movies. He brought her straight to P.E.I."

"Without her daughter," Jessie whispered, shocked.

"With one of them," George responded quietly. "Although you weren't born for another month."

"How could she...?" It was too horrible for words. No wonder her mother always had a distant underlying anger, a cover for what must have been a terrible self-loathing, a horrid consuming sadness.

"She had no choice. By then she'd been locked in the room for over two months, Jessie. And there wasn't much hope of freedom. David —your dad—was terrified. He'd had no contact with her all that time, and he knew their baby was soon due. He took a chance—he knew from what Emily told him that she was often locked in the room when her husband disagreed with something she said or did. And the daughter—your half-sister—was brainwashed into agreeing with everything her dad said and did."

Jessie got up and walked past Josh, who reached out and brushed his hand alongside hers as she passed. From the other side of the bed she stood and faced George again, a distant look crossing her own puzzled features.

"But if my grandmother knew where my mom was, why didn't my mom's husband come looking for her?"

"I got word to Martha for her. They'd always had a fairly secure relationship but there was no way Emily could take a chance on writing back. So it was a one-way thing. Your mom lived in fear, Jessie."

A tremor swept across Jessie's face as a chill crawled up and down her spine. Inadvertently she wrapped an arm over her own belly. Would her children be haunted by fear too? Or could she and Josh end the vicious cycle that seemed to stalk the Wheeler women? She shook her head in disbelief at the parallels in hers and her mother's lives, and instantly two thoughts almost brought her to her knees. As she met the fear in Josh's own thoughtful brown eyes, which morphed from their usual solemn chocolate to a deep seated darker fear, Jessie wondered if their own love would end, too, in sudden and irreparable violence; and whether she would someday melt into the vacant space her mother's mind now occupied, unreachable, seemingly permanent.

"Jess," Josh offered hesitantly. "It's just a weird coincidence."

"I dunno." She shivered, and sat down on the bed, her back to George. Then, Jessie twisted around and faced the older man. "George, were my parents even married? I mean, how could they get married if she was already married and couldn't get divorced?"

"Honey," George said kindly, "as far as they were concerned, they were. They told everyone they were and Emily took David's name. What's marriage anyway, kiddo, a piece of paper, that's all."

"Geez, George." Jessie's shoulders slumped. Then she threw out, "What about my dad, then? And this businessman bullshit."

"No connection to Emily's husband or father in Ontario, Jessie, if that's what you're thinking."

"I wasn't. But thanks for clarifying that. Anyways...how do you know for sure?"

The old man seemed to shrink more into the chair. Suddenly he was ten years older and even more frail than when they'd entered the room.

Jessie's eyebrows twisted into a knot as, outside, a sweet old lady they'd met earlier in the summer started sobbing and crying *mommy* over and over.

"I know because I was the man who"—he swallowed—"who drove your dad off the road, Jessie."

As she stared at him in complete and utter shock and disbelief, a sudden rush of blood pumping in her ears, George added feebly, "It was only supposed to scare him, Jessie. Not kill him. I would never have wanted that… for…for Emily. Or for you. But I knew he needed to get his shit together, your dad. I knew that man—the businessman—was after your mother. And I knew your whole family was going to be in real trouble if David didn't get scared and get outta town. I wanted him to pack up and leave town. I wanted all of you away, somewhere safe."

"My dad owed the guy money." Her voice was weak, affected, scared for her good ole dad of years before. It was all she had in her not to cut and run. George was no longer a man of advanced years. Now she peered at him through a veil that only thinly disguised his long-ago middle age, an age when she might have been able to loathe him for such a vicious deed. Now she just felt sick. She squeezed her belly and prayed for a wave of nausea to cease.

"Yes, but the asshole didn't care about your dad paying him back. He wanted Emily. He didn't give two shits about the money. He just used it as an excuse to hold your dad hostage. I made up the story for the papers, about being hired to drive him off the road. I wasn't hired, I…I did it myself. I knew David's schedule that day, that he was hired to play at that wedding. I didn't expect he would stop to go canoeing, but then that was your dad, Jessie. He was a dreamer, the kind of guy who grabbed such pleasure when he saw it. He was utterly faithful to your mom but when it came to a sweet ride on a summer day on a perfect river—he went for it. So I waited on a hill and when I saw him packing up the canoe I drove down the road a piece. I was far enough away that I could gather some speed and…" He gulped.

"Jesus," Jessie heard from her left ear. Josh was shocked, too.

"Poor old George," Jessie whispered softly, tears trickling down her cheeks. "You killed your friend."

George stared at her incredulously. He half expected Josh to come barreling after him with fists blazing, but he didn't know the power Josh had gleaned from Jessie's gift of understanding and from her gentle nature. Nor did George expect Jessie to see his pain. He figured she would be far too focused on her own. He blinked and a single tear dripped down his almost translucent skin. "I did more than that, didn't I, Jessie?" he asked her knowingly. His voice husky, he asked, "Why did you leave when you were fourteen?"

After a pause, her shoulders sinking, she murmured softly, "I'm guessing you know why." She gulped, and heard a shuffle behind her as Josh uncomfortably changed his weight to his other foot. "The businessman...the man after my mother..."

George picked up. "He married her. He knew he had to take care of her, in the end. Someone had to." He struggled with the final words they shared on that sacred evening in the small east coast province. "I got lost in the drink more and more. So I was useless to her. Hell, I couldn't even face her, after what I...after. So he married her and she...told me what he did to you...years later...before she disappeared inside herself to wherever it is that people go when they can't take anymore."

"She told you." It wasn't a question. It was stated as a fact. Jessie was diminished in the new knowing that her mother was aware all along of the travesties her rich husband inflicted on her own and David Wheeler's young daughter.

"Yes."

Watching Jessie carefully for signs of trauma, Josh was silent but ready. He tensed.

"So why didn't she do anything?" The age-old question often battered and beat itself around and around inside Jessie's brain—still—after all this time.

George shook his head slowly from side to side. It seemed the answer would never come. Jessie slumped and turned away from him. From behind she heard the old man's small voice.

"I see your dad in my dreams, Jessie. I'm an old man now, every fucking inch of my body hurts. My sleep comes in short spurts because I can't breathe, every position hurts. There will never be any more sex, or love, and my food is so ground up and bland it ain't worth eating. My bowels don't work half the time and I can't even cut my own damn gnarly toenails. I want to die, but I don't. Every day I sit here and stare at the cows when I can't stand to look at your mother anymore and know how much I…how much I hurt her. And her daughter."

He struggled through raspy breaths then as the emotion got the best of him. It took him a few moments to speak but Jessie and Josh didn't interrupt. They let him find the words he needed to say.

"In my dreams he comes to me, your dad, and he doesn't speak, except by virtue of the pain in his eyes. He knows it was me, who ended everything for you that day. For Emily."

At that, George started to sob quietly. Jessie got up and went to him, and covered him carefully so she wouldn't hurt the frail skin, the skeleton arms.

George looked up at her, his eyes pleading, flickering from hope to despair and back again. "Do you know what it's like to live this way, Jessie? Dying more each day as the truth of your past comes back to haunt you? I watched you in your career, you know, I knew it was you out there in the movies and on the world's great stages, I knew it was you and for a while I thought I was glad, that it all turned out okay in the end. That Emily was in her safe place and you were rich and famous, so everything was okay. But then…"

He looked past Jessie at Josh. "Then I would see your photos and watch you in your interviews and movies and I would know that I was wrong, that nothing was okay. When you met this guy," he shrugged towards Josh, "there was a light in your eyes that was missing in all those previous photos and videos. And then…" He shook his head.

"I know," she whispered as she settled back down onto his narrow bed. "I'm haunted. Or cursed. Take your pick."

From behind her she heard Josh's short intake of breath. "Jessie…"

Without looking at Josh she raised a hand to stop him from speaking. "No. It's true." She pleaded sadly at George. "I wonder if I'll ever be able to live in peace, George."

The old man shook his head. "I'm sorry for what I did to your family, Jessie. But I want you to know that I hate myself every day for what I did."

"George," Jessie softened and laid a gentle hand over his. The skin was cold, the hand awkward as bits of bone protruded in odd places. "My dad loved you. My mother loves you. Hell, I love you, you old goof. Despite the weird part you played in my life, in my family's life...you also gave my parents, and me, some of the best memories and best times we ever had."

"There should have been more..." The tears kept falling as George stared up at Jessie from underneath the blanket, ashen, diminished in the big chair.

"Yes. There should have been, George. But there weren't." She hugged him gently so as not to hurt him, and her tears mixed with his. Leaning back and holding his cheeks gently between her hands, she smiled wistfully. "And now I don't see the point in torturing ourselves over past mistakes. There has been enough pain."

A staff member peeked her head into the room but backed out slowly when Josh put a finger to his lips and signaled her to remain silent. She would come back for bath time in a bit.

"I'm so sorry," the old man cried. "I'm so sorry, Jessie."

A bony hand clutched hers.

"I know," she sobbed back to him. "And that's enough for me, George. That's enough for me. Okay?"

After a few moments the old shoulders stopped quaking. Jessie eyed the fatigue in her elderly friend's eyes and she sat back again. She swallowed past the nausea that still threatened her belly.

"You can sleep now, George," she whispered softly. "You can rest."

This time when the rheumy eyes met hers there was a peace within. A small light burned deeply somewhere inside, met by the tiniest hint of a smile. But he was too tired to speak, so George just nodded, almost imperceptibly.

Jessie bent forward and brushed her lips tenderly against her friend's soft cheek. "I love you, George."

When she finally tore herself away from the man who loved her parents as much as she did, Jessie reached for Josh's big, comfortable hand. He was ready, and pulled her close to his side as they left the room. Both were reminded, once again, of the short time they would have together on this earth—a day, a week, a month, years? They didn't know. But in their hearts they were grateful for any time together.

Outside, before Jessie slipped into the passenger side of the car, she turned and looked tearfully up at her new husband. She placed a hand on his stubbly cheek and smiled through her tears. "I don't know where this life is going to take us, Josh, and I'm sorry it's been this hard for us to find a way to be together, but...as much as I have missed my dad all these years," she breathed deeply, "I'm glad. In the end, I'm glad. Every damn second with you is such a gift. I will never take you—what we have—for granted. Ever."

Josh placed a big hand over her small one on his cheek and closed his eyes for a second. "Nor will I," he said quietly. "I love you, Jessie Wheeler-Sawyer."

"Jessie Sawyer," she murmured, and turned his hand around so she could bestow soft kisses on his palm.

They leaned in close to each other so their foreheads touched, and Josh kissed his wife tenderly.

He heard a small voice. "Will it be okay, Josh? Will it? Do I need to be afraid of losing you every day? With every breath? With every parting?"

"We'll never be apart, Jessie. Even if..." He shook his head. But she understood what he was saying. She thought of her mother, who lived inside herself each day, every day.

"I wonder where my momma goes..."

He smiled. "You know where she goes. You've seen the peace in her eyes. She's happy there."

When they parted, climbed inside the SUV, and Josh pointed the car back down the lane, neither Emily nor George could see them leave. But both knew, somehow, in the muzzy worlds of ache and sorrow the past had wrought upon Jessie that, despite what the future would bring, one thing was certain. Josh and Jessie would take care of each other from here on in because they loved each other, and they'd fought hard for that love. They would not be carelessly throwing away the universe's great gift to them—each other. Ever.

# Chapter Twenty-five

"He didn't need to tell you, Jessie. I don't know what purpose it served George to tell you that it was he who drove your dad off the road."

"That's easy."

He turned to look at her. They were sitting in the screened-in patio of The Inn At Bay Fortune, in eastern P.E.I., where they were sipping ginger ale and waiting for their dinner to be served. They had already signed autographs and accepted congratulatory hugs from strangers who were thrilled both at the recent Sawyer nuptials as well as the famous couple's presence in the Inn.

Jessie glanced over at Josh. A wistful smile flickered across her face. "Forgiveness. He needed to let go."

"He doesn't know you the way I do, Jess. He didn't think you were going to forgive him so easily. He was afraid."

She shrugged. "Didn't matter. Maybe he thought that somehow by telling me out loud he would earn my dad's forgiveness. I don't know." She rested a forefinger thoughtfully against her top lip and tapped a few times. "Maybe just letting it out was enough for him."

"Well, I don't really appreciate him laying it on you." Josh spoke quietly, but his experiences with Jessie's post-traumatic stress made him a cautious man. He would watch her closely, yes, and help her as best he could, with Trudy's help, but still—there would be lots of careful tiptoeing around her in the days to come.

Eyeing Josh judiciously, Jessie paused as a young blonde teen placed fresh bread in a small basket on their table and blushed before turning on her heel and wandering slowly away, throwing a backwards glance towards the celebrities in her midst as if she could hardly believe their presence on her end of P.E.I. Idly Jessie reminded herself to offer the girl a photo-op so the girl's friends would believe her presence at the Inn.

"I'm not an egg. I'm not going to crack."

Josh grinned and picked up a warm piece of Guinness bread. He pantomimed throwing it at Jessie.

"Don't even think about it, Sawyer." Jessie reached for her own slice of bread as Josh buttered his with a pat of herbed garlic butter. "Anyways, I just mean that I know I have work to do to get better, but I'm sleeping better now and—"

"It's all the sex," he cut in mischievously, winking. "I'm tiring you out. Mrs. Sawyer."

Laughing wholeheartedly, Jessie ducked her head, embarrassed. The patrons in the full dining room all raised their shoulders a little higher and felt the world's pressures fall away. The sheer happiness of Jessie and Josh after their public trials and struggles was enough to raise the spirits in any room.

"I'm getting better, Josh."

He slipped a hand under the table and rubbed Jessie's thigh. "I know, little one. I love you for trying so hard. I just mean that this was information George could have kept to himself. That's all."

"And the box?" She raised her eyebrows at him.

He shrugged. "The box not so much. Except that now I know you'll go on a quest."

"Well, I need to let my dad rest. And George along with him. He'll go now, you know, Josh. I've heard that, that people can choose to go when they're ready, when they've tied up loose ends."

"He's an old man, Jessie. He'll die because his body is giving out on him."

"Whatever." She bit into her bread and chewed thoughtfully, staring out at the exquisite dappled sunshine highlighting the waters of the sanguine Fortune Bay. The glassy waters glistened eloquently beneath the rolling hill upon which the Inn sat proudly, its weathered cedar shingles and 1920's screened-in porch lending a pristine beauty to the lives of the lucky who managed a lunch, a night, a weekend in the tranquil eastern Prince Edward Island setting. A kayaker anxious to get in one last paddle before the winter snows turned the salt water to ice was puttering in the bay beneath them as Josh and Jessie chewed thoughtfully on their artisan bread. The boater's paddles dipped rhythmically beneath the diminutive cresting waves, rising and then falling methodically, like the beat from a metronome, one-two, one-two. Absently Jessie considered writing a song to the paddler's lonely but steady cadence.

"Yes," she said quietly. "A quest. I suppose I shall." She scanned the room pensively before letting her soft eyes land on Josh, who was watching her attentively. "There's a family out there somewhere that belongs to me. Roots."

Popping the last bite of his Guinness bread between his lips, Josh leaned forward and grasped Jessie's hand in his. The huskiness in his voice betrayed his fear. "Jessie, I just don't want to see you get hurt anymore. Enough already."

"I just want to meet them, Josh. I won't get my hopes up. I swear." She raised her fingers up in a two-fingered girl guide salute that, as she did it, she realized was some vestige of her lost girlhood come back to haunt her from some deeply buried memory.

Her eyes were wide, innocent. Naïve. Josh sighed. "Try to remember who you are, Jessie."

"I'm some random runaway homeless kid who got lucky," she bit off hastily.

Shaking his head, Josh stared at her in wonder. But he knew Jessie's refusal to believe that she had any special gifts was one of the reasons why he loved her so deeply. "Then remember who it is the rest of the world thinks you are, Jess. Look, I just mean that people will try to get things from you. Not everyone out there in the big old world can be trusted."

"Got that one covered, Sawyer. Been there, done that."

He grimaced. "Fine, then. I get that there's a family you want to meet. But I'll be by your side, little girl. Count on it."

"I am," she grinned. "Counting on it. Every second of every day, sexy man."

The server returned with a basket of gourmet mussels for her famous customers to share. Happily, Jessie used the supplied tongs to pick out a few.

She placed the shellfish on a plate, and then handed the tongs to her husband, who dug into the herbed delicacy with undisguised relish. He licked his fingers and Jessie tossed him a napkin.

"Redneck."

Josh laughed openly before obediently wiping his fingers on the linen.

Below them, in the sparkling bay bordered with the stunning red sandstone cliffs of their small island, the kayaker paddled around a bend and disappeared from sight. Jessie paused to reflect on their rare sanctuary, and on where she found herself, beside a man she loved with a need and desperation that frightened her. Slowly, she forked up a mussel from between its shiny black shell, and she closed her eyes as the flavor of garlic commingling with a hint of wine warmed her soul.

When she opened her eyes, Josh was smiling wholeheartedly at her.

"You break my heart, Mrs. Sawyer."

A pink flush crested the tops of her cheeks as a small smile lit up her face. Jessie managed to refrain from putting down her fork and crawling into his lap, where together they could watch the sun on its downward journey sink slowly back into the sea.

Wordlessly they ate their mussels delicately, savoring every bite. As Jessie finished each, she placed its gracefully curved shell inside another, so that she ended up with a big line of empty shells all snuggled up together on a plate. Their entrees arrived soon after the shells were removed. The sun drifted off without a care, just doing its thing as it did every day while fireflies twitted in the twilight outside the verandah where the diners sat in quiet reflection on the beauty the world could provide if one chose to see it.

Later, cozied together under a homemade quilt in the room they were told Canadian actor Colleen Dewhurst had once considered her Prince Edward Island bedroom, Jessie slipped her hand inside Josh's T-shirt sleeve, where she could soak up his essence and remind herself that she was no longer alone.

She yawned.

"Too sleepy to play?" he asked, his own voice heavy with fatigue.

"Too full," she whispered, settling her body in closer to him. "But I could be convinced. If you don't mind if I'm a bit sluggish, that is."

"Oh, I don't mind," Josh slyly whispered back. "Trust me."

"Somehow I figured you wouldn't." Jessie removed her hand from underneath Josh's T-shirt sleeve and slipped it up under the waist of the soft cotton instead. She relished the warmth she found there and, as she rubbed first his belly and chest, and then pressed her lips against his as he turned his head to face her, she cherished the gentle moan that escaped his lips when her hand glided gracefully down between his legs and urged him to action.

As their lovemaking increased in intensity, beneath them Fortune Bay echoed its want and need for their own treasures to multiply. But it wasn't money and gold the newly married Sawyers needed; instead it was solace in each other's company—in their bodies and in shared hearts and shared knowing. Life had a way of messing with perfection that both had already experienced wholeheartedly, and in that evening's intimate caresses it was telling them to believe and to continue to fight for survival, for the happily-ever-after they both deserved.

When Josh could stand it no longer and slipped himself inside the woman he loved that night, there was no second guessing, no remembrances of how she'd been so badly used and abused from the time she was twelve. Instead, there was love and tenderness and caring that left no room for doubt as to how deeply each cherished the other. When he came, she came too; afterwards he rocked her gently in his arms as she squeezed him repeatedly, and it almost physically hurt when he had to let her go.

They slept, restoring their faith in sweet dreams and, unknowingly, preparing them for the next stage of the fight that already preyed on them, that waited patiently outside the couple's honeymoon suite.

Outside, the stars sparkled in an immaculate night sky over the Inn At Bay Fortune and, somewhere around the quiet bend in the rustic narrow country road before the Inn, the kayaker doused his boat with fresh water to remove the salt, tucked his paddles into their corner of the garage for the winter, and trudged off into the night.

# Chapter Twenty-six

Trudy's goodbye at the airport wasn't as painful as Jessie expected, especially after the therapist surprised them with the announcement that she and Frank had reconciled.

"So from now on we'll spend the winters in Vancouver and the summers here on the island."

In obvious delight, Jessie squealed. She was indeed feeling better these days, yet in some ways she was afraid to let go of Trudy and her healing wisdom. Trudy would remain a constant help in the days, months, years to come and, beyond that, she was also now a good and trusted friend.

"So we'll see you in Van!" Jessie responded excitedly, with obvious relief, upon her friend's announcement.

"You bet," Trudy said, her own eyes twinkling with delight. She had received, from this sad, lonely woman, a dose of reality herself—a wake-up call of sorts, that life was meant to be lived with verve and gusto, and that true love was worth fighting for.

When they parted, and the Air Canada jet disappeared into the clouds, Trudy stood and reflected for quite some time. She pondered what Frank said to her that day so long ago when he called from Vancouver to ask Trudy to work with Jessie and Josh. "Your life will suddenly become very interesting," he had said. He had neglected to add, "And very full." Trudy was grateful, so the first thing she did when she whipped around on one heel and started past the fiberglass white and black dairy cow that stood sentinel at the arrivals exit of the Charlottetown airport, was whip out her iPhone and punch in a call to Frank.

Above them, happily ensconced in the main cabin of the jet, as far away from first class as they could get, Jessie entwined her fingers in Josh's and pointed out the Confederation Bridge. They could only grasp bits and pieces of it as the clouds wisped by beneath them.

"See? Like a snake," she said.

From the aisle seat of the small jet Josh leaned over her and peeked out of the small oval window, where Jessie's nose was delicately pressed. "Hmm," he agreed. "Looks neat from up here."

She turned and poked him in the ribs. "You dork. Everything looks neat from up here."

They watched as the patchwork farmland of Prince Edward Island faded beneath them, and although Jessie felt a certain ennui at leaving her beloved island province behind, she had an equal serenity in the knowing that she would be back, with Josh beside her.

"Babe," she said suddenly, turning to look deeply into the knowing chocolate eyes of her husband. "I admit that I'm in love with this place. For all kinds of reasons. But there's one thing P.E.I. doesn't have that I confess I'm desperately craving. And since we're landing at 4 p.m. Vancouver time, may I suggest we head there right away?"

"You and your perfect coffee!" Josh laughed agreeably as he settled some earbuds into his ears. One of Jessie's old films was playing on the in-flight entertainment system and he was keen to watch her in action with the strange sensation of having her sitting next to him as well. That was a feeling he had yet to become accustomed to, and as he relaxed into the seat and gripped her fingers, Josh felt a wonderful lightness in the knowing that there would be many more opportunities to watch her in action on screen, starting with the hockey film she planned to shoot soon back on the east coast.

As they landed many hours later in Vancouver and climbed wearily into the King Ranch pick-up, Josh was quietly pleased that Jessie seemed to embrace being back in the west coast hippie city. He pointed the truck towards their favorite coffee hangout and was surprised when Jessie told him to go to Revolver instead.

"What? Why?" Josh asked. ROAM was close to his home, where they could drop their bags before piloting the vehicle over to North Van for dinner with Charles and Dee. Revolver was in the city's downtown core, on the cusp of the somewhat sketchy East Hastings neighborhood, Jessie's old haunt in her homeless days. It was near the shelter she and Dee had built, though, so maybe she just wanted to slip by and say hi to her old friend Mary Helen, who managed the shelter. Or perhaps, Josh thought, unable to bury a sense of profound distaste, perhaps Jessie wanted to see Arnie Sylvester, the Downtown Eastside friend who'd aided her in her disappearance from Vancouver a few years earlier. Regardless, he obediently headed north on the 99 towards Granville Street. He glanced sideways at Jessie and saw a small smile flit across her face. She turned to him.

"New beginnings," she said, a slight pink blush tinting her cheeks. "We can hit up Rebel On A Mountain Coffee tomorrow." She took his hand and appealed to Josh quietly. "I haven't been to Revolver since Terri died. I just want to start fresh here, and work at letting some of those old triggers go, you know?"

"You got it, little one," Josh said, nosing the pick-up back into the outside lane after passing one of Vancouver's Car2Go vehicles, a tiny white and blue Smart Car consumers could rent to meet their temporary driving needs. The driver, a tiny Asian man, looked terrified to be driving—he was hunched over the wheel with his eyes glued to the road. Josh eased cautiously ahead of him and gave the truck a bit more gas to give the guy a wider berth. "Revolver it is."

Twenty minutes later he stood behind Jessie at the popular downtown coffee hotspot. His arm resting protectively but casually on her waist, Josh waited while she ordered an iced mocha. From somewhere in front of them, further into the narrow shop with its old wood and iron booths, he had heard an audible gasp when they entered. Jessie seemed to miss it; she was fixated on the scrumptious apple coffeecake in the cooler. Swallowing nervously because although Jessie was one hundred per cent comfortable in this part of the city, Josh would never be completely at ease here. At least, not with the level of fame and notoriety he and Jessie had earned over the last few years. Although he was now, for the most part, accepted by the world as her partner, there were still those who would likely question his role in her beating and disappearance. And here, near East Hastings, not all people were necessarily in their own minds. Josh clearly knew the dangers of drug addiction and he especially understood the darkness that accompanied the use of drugs. In this part of the city, all of the dangers lurking around each corner were elevated.

Apprehensive, Josh sought the source of the gasp. In the back of the semi-dark café a tall strongly built man with dark hair greased to one side over a shaved scalp, and a confident don't mess-with-me demeanor, appeared to be comforting a wiry bleached blonde whose long blunt-cut hair was highlighted with alternating pale pink strands. The woman, too, was tall and fit, but seeing Jessie seemed to have upset her. Josh wondered whether she was a victim of sexual abuse; many women who now knew Jessie's story, thanks to the Shawna Coupland interview, were sending Jessie letters and asking her to listen to their own troubled stories, as well as encouraging her in her healing journey.

A poke in his ribs drew his attention back to Jessie.

"Josh? Rafael is asking if you are having your own coffeecake or are you just planning to snipe off my plate?" She was grinning wryly at him, eyes twinkling.

"Uh, I'll share with you if you don't mind, Jess. I just want a bite. Gotta watch my waist, you know." Something in his eyes bothered Jessie but she knew that her friends didn't have the same level of comfort she did on the Downtown Eastside. She shrugged and summed it up to nerves, especially after their recent few months in the tranquil sanctuary of P.E.I.

She held up one finger. "One coffeecake, Rafael, please," she said, and then to her husband, "what do you want to drink? Drip coffee? Raf says they've got a good AA Kenyan on today." Her eyes narrowed. Josh was closely watching something at the back of the little café. Or someone, perhaps. Jessie wheeled around to look.

It took her a moment to adjust her vision to the liquid warmth of the dimly lit space. When she did, she stared wholeheartedly, not even trying to disguise her curiosity about the pair who seemed to be reacting to her presence. Jessie was used to stares but, like Josh, she detected that somehow she meant more to the obviously distraught woman than usual run-of-the-mill curiosity.

"Huh," she said, squinting to see better, wondering why these two felt so...familiar.

As the comforting security of Josh's strong arm urged her to move away from the cash down the bar where they could watch the always interesting preparation of Josh's vacuum pressed Kenyan coffee, Jessie turned her eyes towards the espresso machine and her ears to the coffee grinder. But Revolver was a deep, narrow café; the distraught woman could not get past Jessie to exit without brushing by her, without touching her. She seemed frozen—the man now had both arms gripping the woman's biceps, her head was down, she seemed in shock. Jessie was about to go to her to see if she could be of any assistance when the woman looked up and met her eyes. Jessie had turned her head back at the same time and, when their eyes met, she felt her knees give way. The woman's face was a hazy, murky memory, her sharp green eyes a vision from many nights of foggy amorphous dreams. Somehow in Jessie's consciousness it hit her that she once knew this woman well and, when she looked up at the sorrowful face of the man, she realized she knew him too. But they were Downtown Eastside ghosts, these two. They were a smartly dressed couple who didn't fit the homeless vibe, yet they lived here, Jessie knew that without a doubt. She also realized that she once knew them intimately, but she could not remember how or why. The when was clear, though. Their acquaintance was made during Jessie's time living on the Downtown Eastside, before Charlie and Jack Deacon, before *Drifters*, before Josh, before Arnie, even.

Josh felt Jessie's shock without seeing her face. Instantly he was on guard, although the couple didn't appear to be a threat. He watched tensely as the woman steeled up her guard and turned her body towards Jessie.

"Hi, Jessie," she forced as she raised her head high, a frown edging her cherry red lipstick. She raised a hand tentatively in greeting, the umbrella sleeves of a faux fur white hip length coat drooping.

Jessie's eyes darted from the woman to the man and back again. Her face paled and she didn't react when the barista slid her iced mocha towards her on the bar.

"I know you," she said in a murmur, trying to pull the memories towards the front of her mind. Behind her, Josh frowned and his eyes narrowed towards the couple. Around them, the busy café buzzed and the grinder grated on his nerves. He was tired after their cross Canada trip and he was suddenly once again on high alert for Jessie. Her reaction to this curious couple was immediate and puzzling. He didn't want more drama, not here, not now, when they were finally together.

The woman's eyes softened as she realized that Jessie couldn't quite piece together the puzzle parts of her past life as a runaway on the Downtown Eastside.

Tentatively she reached out a soft manicured finger and took Jessie's hand in hers. Astounded, Josh watched as she gazed at Jessie with a mixture of deep concern, fear, and—was that love?

"My name is Caryn," she said. "With a—with a C at the beginning and a y near the end. We knew each other a long time ago. This is," she twisted a little and pointed at the tall man near her side, who was watching both Josh and Jessie closely, "Eric. He's my husband."

"I'm s-sorry," Jessie stammered. She took a deep, questioning breath, narrowed her eyes and focused on Caryn. "I know that I know you, I just…" She seemed to be reaching for the memories but they apparently wouldn't—or couldn't—make their way to the surface. Her shoulders deflated. "I don't remember you. Vaguely, that's all. I don't remember much of living here." She was taut, defensive, her head held high, shoulders rigid, and eyes narrowed into slits.

Intuitively Josh felt she was, on some level, lying. He could bounce thoughts across to her and sometimes could read hers as well. And she was tense. She was holding back. Caryn and Eric seemed to sense that as well. Caryn swallowed, somewhat disappointed, and nodded at her. She couldn't take her eyes off Jessie and she appeared about ready to break into tears, but she was stronger than she appeared. Something firm crossed her expression then, her eyes flickered as she accessed some deep reserve of strength.

"Well, you look wonderful," she managed. "You've done well, Jessie. I'm glad."

Josh looked down. The woman was still holding Jessie's hand and Jessie seemed powerless to let go. They stood and searched each other's eyes as Jessie swallowed nervously and reached for deep reserves of strength of her own.

Then, Eric nudged Caryn, but she was reluctant to let go. She sighed deeply and her shoulders drooped, as if she hated to let Jessie go.

"We have Pilates, Caryn," Eric said, and gently pushed her forward.

Surprising all of them, Caryn slipped her hands up Jessie's arms and pulled her close. To Jessie she smelled familiar, of lavender and hope and comfort and love.

"Why?" Jessie whispered to her back when Caryn finally let go and walked ahead of her husband out of Revolver and into the late afternoon crisp Vancouver sunshine. "Why now?"

Eric paused and turned to Jessie before following. He searched her face. He seemed uncertain, unsure. Then, "I'm glad you got out," he said to her. "Really glad, Jessie. You were always too good for us. For this neighborhood." He glanced towards Josh and patted him on the shoulder as he turned sideways in the narrow café and brushed by him. "Take care of her, man. She's one of the good ones."

Josh and Jessie were silent after the couple's exit. They took their coffees and their coffeecake to metal chairs at the front bar by the window but Jessie ate only a few bites, leaving the rest for Josh, who was hungrier than he originally thought. They gazed at the interesting characters running back and forth traversing their busy lives on Cambie Street in front of them; neither spoke, but Jessie felt sick as she nursed her iced mocha, not because of Revolver's memories as she once feared, but because of the hazy remembrance of a tall couple named Caryn and Eric.

Her eyebrows knitted together in concentration as she bent over her mocha, elbows resting on the wooden bar facing Revolver's large window overlooking Cambie. She swung around and faced Josh, who was patiently savoring his vacuum pressed Kenyan roast while pondering Jessie's sudden thoughtfulness. Jessie studied the things she loved about him—his strong hands, the way his plaid vintage shirts with the pearl buttons always fell open over his hands, the way his lips were now curving down just slightly as he waited patiently for her to illuminate the mysterious couple's identity and role in her life.

Jessie took a deep breath and laid a hand over his on his coffee mug. He took his hand away and she drew the mug towards her own lips, tasted it, then set it down and licked her lips. "Ummm," she said, savoring it, before bending back over her iced mocha. "A hint of citrus in there, I think. Orange, maybe."

"With a chocolate aftertaste," Josh replied, smiling as he nodded towards Jessie's mocha, which she was now sipping on through a straw.

"Dweeb," she said, grinning as she laid a hand on his thigh and shifted her body weight towards him. Watching as a white BMW like Deirdre's teetered back and forth as the driver tried unsuccessfully to parallel park in front of them on Cambie, Jessie felt a twinge in her heart. As the driver in front of them gave up and pulled out of the small space, she spoke quietly to Josh.

"The thing is, Josh, those two—Caryn and Eric," she was surprised at how easily their names slid off her tongue, as their familiarity haunted her, "they were part of my old life. One of my old lives..." She glanced up at Josh. "I don't want to resurrect those days. Any part of them. I don't want to talk about that time in my life, after Charleston. When I first got here, to Van. I feel like...like going there would be like going to a place where no one would be proud of me. Not you, not Dee, not...me."

Josh laid his warm hand on hers and rubbed it as he considered how to respond in a way that would satisfy his curiosity without pushing Jessie further than she may be willing to go.

"You remember them."

She looked up at him, hesitant, unsure.

He added, "You told them you didn't. Remember them, I mean."

She wilted further into his space, leaning more heavily on the arm on his lap so that Jessie was almost falling off her own chair and landing on his. "I half remember them," she said softly. "If you can count how I find myself feeling about them."

He raised his eyebrows and forked up a portion of the coffeecake, which he offered to Jessie. She shook her head no.

"I knew them well. I know that. I really cared about them at one time... I worked for them for a while but..." She shook her head. "There are things I don't understand about them. I think they hurt me, somehow, but I don't know...it's not like I was afraid to see them, like with Deuce or anything. I think they are good people, Josh, I just..."

She turned her body sideways and, at her serious countenance, Josh set the fork down by the remainder of their late afternoon treat. He frowned.

"Josh, I think we should have a rule where we don't have to share everything about the past. We both went through some crappy times but we've moved on. Let's just let bygones be bygones."

"No more secrets, Jess," he said quietly, a tiny alarm bell ringing somewhere in the back of his mind. His eyes deepened, narrowed as he implored her to stop running from her past. "Besides, you're being hypocritical. You want to explore your past, in terms of that lovely legacy George left you in a white box back on the east coast."

"Yes, but..."

"No buts. We swore, Jessie. No more secrets." He didn't want to push her but Josh could sense that this unexpected meeting with the tall couple was already working some insidious dark magic inside Jessie's heart and mind. He could sense that she was reaching for the memories and that already, they troubled her. Josh lifted his arm and wrapped it around her shoulders so that Jessie by now was snuggled into him. She adjusted her position and laid her left arm around his back and her right around his belly so that her face was half buried under his arm. She closed her eyes and felt his concerned sigh as it echoed throughout her body. Brushing her hair off her cheek with his right hand, Josh spoke again.

"Jessie, what's that thing they say about rainbows? They show up in the midst of storms, or something like that. You're my rainbow. I hope I'm yours."

A tiny whisper floated up to him. "You know you are."

"Then let's just trust each other, okay? If those two people caused you pain or came from a troubled time in your life, then so be it. But don't try to hide them from me. Cause that would be like hiding a part of who you are, and I've got news for you, little one. I want all of you. All. The good, and what you might consider the bad."

"I know, Josh, it's just...well, after the Deuce thing, and the journal..." Her shoulders sagged. The mocha now sat untouched in front of her. She chided herself for ignoring it because she knew once she went back to it the ice would have melted and taken over the drink so it would taste watery and thin. "It's just that I feel like I've exorcised some demons this summer, you know. So all of a sudden I'm a little pissed that suddenly there seem to be some new ones. I can't help but wonder if there's going to be a limit to how much you can take."

Josh had to tilt his head towards her to hear Jessie's last admission. A chill prickled him as it edged stealthily up his spine. What the hell else had his girl endured in her lifetime that she felt was a potential threat to them as a couple? He almost groaned out loud.

"Look, I know life hasn't been roses and butterflies for you, Jessie. You lived on the Downtown Eastside for, what, two years?"

"Yeah. About that." She still couldn't raise her head to look at him. Suddenly her brain was on fire—a slide show featuring Caryn and Eric was shuttling through her mind, and Jessie didn't like what she was seeing. Her breathing increased and she started to tremble. She closed her eyes and forced herself to count—*1, 2, 3, 4, 5…*

Josh placed a finger under her chin and tilted her head upwards. He forced Jessie to open her eyes and meet his trusting gaze, but frowned when he spied a new terror in her eyes. "Look," he said, trying to quell a suddenly rising panic. "When you're ready, just know that you can tell me, okay? I'm here for you. Just…no more secrets. Deal?"

Her voice was small when she answered him. "Not sure what's happened in the past counts as secrets."

Josh sighed. "Jessie, meeting this couple has freaked the hell out of you. If it's in the past and done and gone, then why all of a sudden are you so worried?"

A thought struck him and he froze. Jessie knew the instant he figured it out. His face fell and shock replaced the earnestness of his plea for simple truths. "Oh Jesus, Jessie. Did you say worked for them? Just what kind of business do those two run?"

"Don't hate me," was the tiny response as tears formed in Jessie's eyes. Then a flicker of self-loathing crossed her face and she removed herself from Josh's comforting embrace. She fixed an icy stare on Josh's somber brown eyes. He would have shivered, if he didn't know already that his new wife was in fact sweet, loving and kind. But Trudy had warned him—the old mask would come up when she needed it. And now it was clearly evident that whatever memories seeing Caryn and Eric had conjured, Jessie needed her mask.

She folded her hands squarely in her lap and raised her shoulders high, proudly. "It was a legitimate business, Josh. Legal."

He watched her as she turned her head away and finally leaned forward to take a sip of the iced mocha. On Cambie in front of them a girl walked by wearing a skirt so short that Josh averted his eyes when she bent over to pat a passing dog. He glanced at Jessie and her mask dissipated as suddenly as it had crossed her face as she realized what he was probably thinking—that the girl on the sidewalk across from them likely made a living through prostitution. And…well, when Josh turned his head away and finished off his coffee without responding to her comment about Caryn's business, Jessie felt the old demons creep up her body.

"I had my guitar," she whispered. "But I wasn't in any shape to play it at first."

"You clearly remember, then. Who they are and where you fit in their lives." He said it without looking at Jessie as, across the street, the hooker sidled off down the slight hill that was Cambie. Childlike, she seemed to be whistling, her skirt riding so high that it barely covered her buttocks.

"Where are the films?" Josh queried Jessie absently, his eyes glassy, but she couldn't hear him over the low growl of the coffee grinder behind them. He had to turn his head back towards her and ask her a second time, louder. Jessie's fearful expression belied the fact that she felt, more than heard, his demand.

"Damnit, Josh!"

"Where are the films, Jessie? The movies? Who has the originals?" *Jesus,* he thought. *Imagine if those things get loose.*

"Josh, just let it go, okay? Please. It was a lifetime ago."

Nodding, Josh stood and his chair scraped on the old wooden floor as he backed it up. "Let's go to North Van. Charles and Dee are waiting." His words were biting, sharp.

Miserable, Jessie didn't move. Josh pulled her left hand out from under her right. She was digging her nails into it again, so deeply that she left small cuts that were leaking pinpoints of blood. He yanked a little harder so that Jessie had no choice but to rise and follow him.

Behind him her small voice trailed along as they stepped down towards the sidewalk. "This is not something Charles and Dee need to hear about, Josh. Ever."

He turned to face her, hands on his hips. His face was white. He caught himself wondering if he would ever know and understand all there was to know and understand about Jessie Wheeler. She was staring at him with a mixture of fear and naïve innocence. She was biting her bottom lip as she implored him to let Caryn and Eric slip eternally out of his mind. Jessie held her breath as she waited for Josh to speak.

"How many films, Jessie?"

"I don't know."

"Bullshit."

"I don't. I just know there were some. Not many, I don't think." She swallowed nervously.

"You're wrong about Charles and Dee. They need to be prepared."

She shrugged. "It hasn't come up yet. Why should it now?"

Josh grasped Jessie's hand and led her down the hill towards the King Ranch. He was silent but Jessie knew this wouldn't be the last she would hear of Caryn and Eric. In Josh's mind, though, the next time he would be dealing with the Downtown Eastside couple, he would be doing it alone.

But for now, the Keatings awaited. Carlotta, with Dee's help, and maybe even Charles to peel the vegetables, was whipping them up a belated celebratory Thanksgiving meal of roast turkey, sweet potatoes, turnip, squash and other harvest veggies. Charlie and Jane were invited, and Jonathon and Giselle. There was lots to celebrate—a wedding, new relationships, family and friends.

When they pulled into the gracious curved driveway of La Casa, the sun's rays were dwindling, their butter-ginger hue alighting the windows of the Spanish Villa so that it looked as if it were aglow just for their homecoming. Inside, family and friends awaited the couple that fought so hard for love.

Josh removed the keys from the ignition and leaned back in the saddle leather seat. His eyes were aching, sorrowful, in a way Jessie did not expect to see again anytime soon. She swallowed and frowned, then sighed as she met his gaze. This time when she drove her nails into the back of her hand Josh didn't notice.

"Jessie," he said sadly. "I hate that you felt you had to do that. Back then."

She stared at him blankly. Then, after a moment, came her response.

"It doesn't matter, Josh, how much therapy I do or how hard Trudy tries to convince me to love myself. I'm always going to be someone less than I want to be. Aren't I? Because that's who I am."

"We've been over this, Jessie," he answered honestly. "Both of us have to get past ourselves. But this most recent revelation of yours may someday have to be managed. That's all."

"Please please please don't tell Dee...Josh, please!"

"I won't," he said. "But you will."

"Not tonight."

"No, not tonight. But soon."

"She likely already knows, anyway. Or senses."

"Good, then it will be that much easier." He sat still, making no attempt to exit the truck. Jessie met his gaze and, although she knew she could trust him, and his love for her, in her heart the same old truths were rushing back to gnaw at her. She was nuts to think any new/old family in Ontario would want anything to do with her, a homeless whore. She was nuts to think she hadn't sunk in Josh's esteem by virtue of her admission at Revolver. So much for going to the trendy cafe to try to find a new start, new beginnings, to get over old fears.

Sickened, she turned to leave the truck, hoping she and her new husband could pull off some semblance of normalcy in front of their friends and family, that no one would question why there was suddenly a new chunk of bitter fear clutching at their bellies.

Josh grabbed her arm before she could open the door. She whipped around to face him, steeling her nerves and trying valiantly without success to swallow the new fears as they chased up her arms, legs, and filled the hollow cavities inside her quaking body.

Josh was crying, which scared her. His body was shaking and tears were leaving tiny glistening trails on his cheeks. The images of Jessie—after the unequalled horror of Charleston, a scared, wounded young woman suffering from such serious post-traumatic stress that she hardly spoke for two years—making a living on the Downtown Eastside in a seedy black box studio, afraid and alone, was breaking his heart anew. How many men...? The thought was unthinkable. He pushed it away.

"I can't stand it," he whispered to her as he pulled her close and kissed her forehead, her eyes, her cheeks, her pink lips. "I can't stand it."

Jessie didn't respond. The bliss from their recent union was gone, it had floated away on the invisible wings of the late summer fairies upon which it was born. The sun was setting and the cabin of the King Ranch pick-up was darkening. Outside, shadows were lengthening and a cool mist was settling over their mountain-hugged city.

Suddenly, Jessie was sobbing too, and her own body was trembling in mimicry of Josh's newfound pain. These memories were new to her, they were erupting fast and furious now, and her long-buried time living on the Downtown Eastside was falling into place. Was it Vancouver? Would there always be a darkness hanging over her here in the west coast hippie city? Prince Edward Island and its lovely expansive patchwork farmland, its laid back mantra and its quaint lady slippers and fragrant lily-of-the-valley and pretty purple and pink lupins flitted across her heart.

When their tears were spent, Josh placed his palms flat against Jessie's cheeks and implored her to climb inside his own sad eyes. He kissed her again, his furtive lips pressing against hers as he struggled to make sense of how Jessie was handling this new wave that had just today come crashing over them, threatening to pull their feet out from underneath their hard-earned foothold in the ever-shifting sand. Judging by her pained expression, she was not handling it well. But Josh knew her, he could read her thoughts, they could bounce their pain back and forth on an invisible wire. Like iCloud, they could tap into each other. He knew she was screaming from the inside out, he knew she was once again terrified she would lose him. So he did what he did best when it came to Jessie Wheeler.

He loved her.

His smile started in his heart and worked its way up his chest where it warmed his throat and then formed on his lips. And, as Josh Sawyer gazed into the diaphanous eyes of his beloved new wife, Jessie *Sawyer,* he told her what he believed, and what she needed to hear.

"Jessie," he started, and she was melting in his arms before he even got the words out. For suddenly his expression said it all—the chocolate eyes were lit from within now, as if some hidden power had set happily buzzing fireflies free within his soul. "Always and forever, little one," he reminded her. "Always and forever. Your new family, my two dads, my past, your past, our clumsy attempts at trying to figure this thing called life out...we're doing it together. Remember? Together. You and me."

"I'm—starting—to remember—more," she gulped, in between each word a gasp for air that frightened Josh. "I can't take this anymore!"

"You can, and you will. And I'll be there alongside you every step of the way. You're not alone anymore, Jessie. You're not alone. Inside that gorgeous home are people who love you, who love us. We've got everything we need, and if someday it all disappears inside some ubiquitous bubble that keeps haunting us, then at the very least we'll have each other. Right? Am I not right?"

Her sobs quieted and Josh fought the urge to ask her what she had seen behind those lovely blue eyes that had the power to sink him. A hint of hope tinged her voice as Jessie found it in herself to respond. Her own little hard-fought fireflies started to flit in her belly as she told herself *one day at a time.* One hour at a time. One sweet simple breath at a time. One beloved hug at a time.

She leaned in to Josh and rested her head against his chest as her answer came and quieted them both in its simplicity.

"You are everything, Josh. Everything. And more. I can't do this without you."

"Well," he whispered with a smile. "That makes two of us."

He used his thumbs to wipe away the trails of tears on her rose-petal cheeks, and Jessie did the same for him.

She laughed then, a small laugh but a valiant attempt at lightening the dark mood that had snuck in and taken them hostage. "Aren't we the happy couple?" Sarcasm dotted the edges of her voice.

Josh stared deeply into the windows of her soul. With unfailing belief in her, he wiped away the pain and fear of a lost—and then remembered—life.

"Yeah," he said softly. "Damn straight we are, Jessie."

"Luv you, Sawyer," she whispered softly, brushing the backs of her fingers against his stubbly cheek.

He grinned, took her hand, and kissed it, sorry that his kisses could not completely eradicate the pinpricks of blood her nails left as testimony to a new knowing neither of them wanted to consider. "Luv you too, Sawyer," he said, and winked.

A voice hollered at them from the welcoming curved entry as the Keatings' mahogany door flew open. "Jesus, you two! Some of us are hungry!"

As Jessie dropped out of the passenger side and then circled the back of the truck, she laughed heartily at Charlie, who was walking towards her with a wide-eyed grin that almost split his face in two. Jane was under his arm, one hand on her belly comforting the baby growing within. Josh, keys dangling from his hands, met them behind the pick-up as Jessie wrapped her arms around Charlie.

The two old lovers held tightly to each other, their eyes closed as they rejoiced in the simple company of family and friends, and an evening that promised to be a celebration of new beginnings.

But, as Charlie relaxed his grip on Jessie and he slowly let her go, his sparkling eyes met Josh's. Jessie moved to hug Jane then, tentatively touching her belly first, wide-eyed with wonder. Her back to the boys, she didn't notice a solemn silence pass between Josh and Charlie that, to Charlie, was significantly more pronounced when Josh couldn't hold his glance, and ducked his eyes away. Curious, sobered for a reason he had yet to understand, Charlie cocked his head and placed his hands on his hips.

Frowning then, because there was a certain comfort now in Charlie's presence, Josh pawed at the ground with the toe of his boot.

"What?" Charlie demanded. "What, Josh?"

The girls were on their way in to the brightly lit house now, and Dee was at the door throwing her arms around her girl, welcoming her home. Jessie threw one last look over her shoulder at Josh, and her heart sank when she saw Charlie suddenly turn back to her, curious now, and maybe even a little afraid. She noticed Josh shrug but she couldn't hear what he said to Charlie then, when the boys were once again facing each other, which was, "What do you expect, Charlie? It's Jessie. That's all. Jessie."

"If by that you mean that she's impulsive, flighty, stubborn, independent, unmanageable, unreachable, and sometimes even incorrigible, then yeah, I hear ya, Sawyer."

There was more, and Charlie knew it. But for tonight there was the heavenly scent of sage and roast turkey wafting out the door towards them, and Dee was hollering, "Come on boys, you're letting the penguins in," so Charlie clapped a hand on Josh's back and nudged him inside the lofty home.

Josh had brought Jessie back to them, and for that Charlie was glad. And despite the dried mascara trails Charlie noticed on Jessie's cheeks, and the faint red tinge cutting into the back of her left hand, what Charlie saw before him that night was a couple who touched each other all evening. One always had a hand in the back pocket of the other, or a hand wrapped around a finger. Often, there were gentle kisses, and soft knowing whispers. But underneath all was a new current, an insidious current that frightened Charlie, and mystified him.

Josh avoided his eyes for the rest of the evening, and Charlie noticed that he avoided Dee's eyes as well when he could get away with it. But he didn't avoid Jessie's opaque baby blues and, instead, he seemed buried in them, in some deep dark level that held him relentlessly and heartlessly captive.

At dinner in the magnificent dining room with its gauzy curtains standing sentinel, wafting waves of affection and love over the gathered friends and family, Dee toasted the newlyweds. "To Jessie and Josh, may your love always be a light in your lives that keeps you close and brings forth years of peace and happiness."

"And grandbabies," tossed in Jonathon as Charles laughed heartily.

They drank to life and love and, as Josh sipped on a ginger ale and gazed adoringly at Jessie, Charlie framed them in the everlasting memory of his mind. Something was up, but tonight was a night of reunion and celebration. Everything they had all been through over the past few years was enough to sink a lot of ships; enough to bury entire flotillas, for that matter. But they were survivors, this group and, whatever it was that etched a new sorrow on Josh's face, it would not be insurmountable. They would face it head on, and they would persevere.

Jessie turned her head then to meet Josh's eyes. Charlie wasn't sure, but he thought he spied a small nod pass between them, a look of recognition and acceptance. It was as if they were telling each other to be strong, to fortify themselves for the journey. A Mona Lisa smile eclipsed Jessie's lips then, and she leaned in to Josh for a sacred kiss to seal the deal.

Charlie let them have their moment, and he looked away, for he felt as if he was spying. He placed a hand on Jane's widening belly and prayed that their child would live a life of only love and wonder and butterflies.

Across from him, Josh was whispering to Jessie. "Okay?"

"Okay," she smiled softly in response.

Fingers entwined around each other, Jessie and Josh leaned in so that their foreheads rested against each other. They closed their eyes, whispered silent *I love yous* and, for a few brief moments in the comforting presence of trusted family and friends, they let life fall away, and simply disappeared.

The End.

*Hello!*

Thank you for reading *Riptide*—I truly hope you are enjoying the Drifters series! I wonder if I can ask you a small favor—writers like myself rely on ratings and reviews to help other readers discover our books. If you could take a moment to go to Amazon (Kindle), Goodreads and/or Smashwords and rate and/or review any of my books, I will remain humbly grateful forevermore.

Thank you so much!
Happy reading!

*Susan*

**www.susanrodgersauthor.com**

Facebook: search **Susan Rodgers, Writer**

Twitter: **@srbluemountain**

**www.bublish.com**

email: **fatcat@pei.sympatico.ca**

# About the Author

Susan Rodgers' first novel *A Certain Kind of Freedom* was a Finalist in the Writers' Federation of Nova Scotia Atlantic Writing Awards for unpublished manuscripts. Her short story from the novel of the same name, published in two anthologies, has received rave reviews, as have the Drifters novels, Susan's all-time favourite books to write.

Owner/Operator of Bluemountain Entertainment, Susan is a 'Diploma With Honours' graduate of Vancouver Film School. She produces mostly documentary style client films and short dramas with plans to one day shoot a Feature Drama based on the novel Atlantic Blue.

Formerly a Museum Curator, in winter Susan lives with her partner Steve and her striped cat Oliver (Lucy Maud Montgomery once said the only good cat is a striped cat) in Summerside, Prince Edward Island, Canada. In summer, she hides in a small trailer in Darnley, P.E.I., where she writes novels, paddles kayaks, and crafts sandcastles on the beach. She makes frequent trips to Vancouver to visit her son Christopher, where she enjoys life in the hippie city while listening to great music and sipping on good espresso.

# *Books by Susan Rodgers*

Drifters series:

*A Song For Josh*

*Promises*

*No Greater Love*

*Riptide*

*Whispers of Home*

*And Then There Was Silence*

*Let the Music Cry*

*If I Could Sing You Home*

Other:

*A Certain Kind of Freedom*

*Seasmoke*

*Atlantic Blue*

Feature Screenplays:

*The Story of Jack & Emma*

*Atlantic Blue*

*Beautiful Jane*

*They Were Dreamers (adapted)*

Short Stories:

S12

A Certain Kind of Freedom

A Gentle Peace

www.ingramcontent.com/pod-product-compliance
Lightning Source LLC
Chambersburg PA
CBHW060604030726
47498CB00005B/1531

* 9 7 8 0 9 8 6 9 5 0 2 8 5 *